RIDDLES
OF THE
ANCESTORS

Also by Ayn Cates Sullivan, Ph.D.

Legends of the Grail Series

Nimue: Freeing Merlin
Heroines of Avalon & Other Tales
Legends of the Grail: Stories of Celtic Goddesses

Cards

Celtic Elemental Tarot
Fair Folk Oracle

Poetry & Nonfiction

Mythic Adventures
Three Days in the Light
The Windhorse: Poems of Illumination
Tracking the Deer: Early Poetry
Consider This: Recovering Harmony & Balance Naturally

Fables & Fairytales

Whisper Angel
Eala: Mother Swan / La Madre Cisne
A Story of Becoming
Sparkle & The Gift
Sparkle & The Light
Kachina's Rose
Ella's Magic
Undina's Spell

Anthologies

*Thresholds: 75 Stories of How Changing Your Perspective
    Can Change Your Life*
Quitless: The Power of Persistence in Business and Life
High Profit Secrets

LEGENDS OF THE GRAIL SERIES

RIDDLES OF THE ANCESTORS

AYN CATES SULLIVAN, Ph.D.

Infinite Light Publishing & Media LLC
Free Union, Virginia, USA

Infinite Light Publishing & Media LLC
Free Union, Virginia, USA
www.infinitelightpublishing.com

First Edition
Riddles of the Ancestors
Legends of the Grail Series

ISBN Hardcover: 978-1-947925-72-4
ISBN Paperback: 978-1-947925-66-3
ISBN eBook: 978-1-947925-74-8

Young Merlin and his sister Ganieda discover a Round Table that holds secret star codes that can activate a template for the New Epoch. Before Gaea (Mother Earth) can be reborn, several riddles must be solved in different timelines that involve the druids of Mona, the Olympians, and King Arthur's court. A group of demi-gods must gather in 21st century London for the shift in ages to occur, but there is always resistance. *Riddles of the Ancestors* is the fourth book and second novel in the Legends of the Grail Series, which can be read in any order.

Lead Editor: Robin Quinn
Interior Design: Ghislain Viau
Cover Design: Lucinda Rae Kinch

This novel is dedicated to my husband,
John Patrick Sullivan,
Who keeps the fires of Celtic romance alive.

May the blessings of the Otherworlds
always be with you!

Contents

Note to Reader: There is an extensive glossary at the end of the book, which is useful when learning new Celtic names and places.

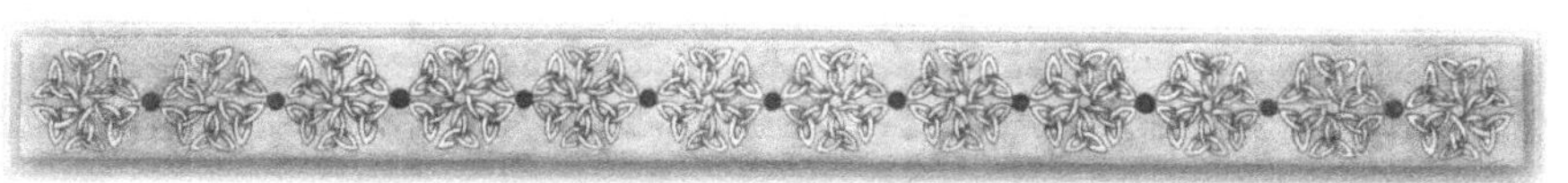

Chapter 1

Young Merlin
& Ganieda
Foretime

Two children ran through a meadow filled with tall grasses and wildflowers that perfumed the air. Ancient trees encircled them like wise and protective friends, silver branches bending low. The children's laughter was as delightful as the colorful illumination of the afternoon sun. The boy's curly dark hair, the color of raven feathers, framed and elongated his slender face. After calling to his sister, Ganieda, he put out his right hand and, in his palm, created a flame that sparkled with golden light. He smiled broadly, proud of his magical feat.

Ganieda had hair as blonde as summer grains. The light of the sun danced across her fair cheeks and her eyes twinkled playfully. Suddenly she rushed toward her brother and swatted his flame out. He howled with disapproval, but then she motioned for him to watch her. Within seconds, she produced a silver flame from her own palm that hovered up into the air gently and took the shape of a butterfly. The boy snatched the alchemical creature from the air and ran away. The protesting girl followed closely on his heels.

A tall and slender woman with flame-red hair walked toward them holding a large silver platter shaped like a crescent moon. On it were cakes and cups of warm herbal tea that Adhan had prepared for her children. The gentle breeze blew tree blossoms into her hair. Adhan smiled at her son, who grinned back, and then she noticed her daughter's frown.

The girl explained what her brother had taken.

"Merlin!" Mother Adhan scolded. "Give your sister back what is rightfully hers. You two must learn to work together."

The boy turned and handed the crumpled silver butterfly to his sister. Ganieda looked at it with some disdain. Her eyes filled with tears.

"You ruined it," the girl said. She was crying and one of the tears fell like a dewdrop onto her dress.

Merlin lifted the bead of moisture up carefully on his fingertip. After closely examining it, he lit a new flame in his other palm, and this time it was violet. Deliberately he dropped the tear into the fire on his hand while humming. At once there was a loud pop! Merlin jumped back, and then they both looked at an object glowing in the grass.

"Why it's a crystal heart!" Ganieda exclaimed. "How beautiful!"

They examined the multiple facets that glimmered with rainbow colors.

"It's a diamond imbued with love from my heart." Merlin disclosed.

Ganieda picked up the multifaceted diamond that glimmered as if happy to receive her touch.

"I made it for you, so you always have a piece of my heart," Merlin replied, referring to diamond. "Made from your tear and the healing of celestial songs, this diamond will protect you. I now name it *Kardia*, which means heart. If you wear it, no one will ever hurt you and it may also heal others."

Merlin pointed to the butterfly that was flapping pitifully in her other hand. Ganieda held the butterfly and the glimmering diamond heart in her palms for a moment. Brother and sister watched as the magical creature metamorphosed back into a healthy butterfly. This time, the magical creature had a hint of gold on its thin, silver wings.

"My little heart *Kardia* healed him. Why that's true magic, Merlin," Ganieda said smiling at her brother, who blushed. "Creative magic is the best kind."

The radiant butterfly flew north toward the forest. The children giggled with delight as they watched it disappear into the dappled light. Ganieda started to put *Kardia* in her pocket for safekeeping. Merlin stopped his sister and asked to hold the diamond heart for a moment while he created a silver chain. Ganieda smiled and put *Kardia* around her neck as a pendant.

Adhan had been watching them and admired the beautiful heart pendant.

"My twins, you are equally magnificent," Adhan declared. "Love each other. Defy the forces within you that wish to fight and conquer. You two were born to unify humanity."

Ganieda gave her brother a hug and then they smiled at each other with genuine affection.

"People may know of Merlin in the days to come. But without you, Ganieda…" Adhan did not finish her words but clicked her tongue and shook her head, as if chasing away shades and shadows. "One day people may remember the importance of sisters."

"I can't imagine life without Ganieda," Merlin noted. "Without her, I would feel broken."

Merlin let out a joyous roar and sprinted toward the forest, seeking the great Oaks that still lived and grew, long before man thought to cut away what was magical from its roots.

Following her brother through the meadow, Ganieda suddenly stopped and shouted at Merlin. "I have something for you too!"

Ganieda made a sharp turn to the left, then trotted along an almost unseen deer path, before disappearing into a cave. Merlin was out of breath moments later as he drew up alongside her inside the hallow. Drawing back an old, dusty tapestry, they could see a shiny stone table. It was large and a bit taller than usual, about four feet in height. Circular in shape, the black table looked as though it could fit a dozen or so people around it. There were numerous pockmarks and holes, which seemed to be a sign of its age.

"This is for you, Merlin!" Ganieda said. "I know the table is seeking you."

"I wonder how long this has been here?" Merlin touched the table respectfully. "It seems to be alive."

"Let's awaken it with love," said Ganieda. "I heard it say it fell from the stars."

"The table speaks?" asked Merlin, observing the many indentations.

"There's a little triangle that pops up and shows images," Ganieda replied.

"Show me!"

"The fellow that speaks says his name is Morfessa," Ganieda affirmed. "Wisdom of kings."

Merlin paused, listening, but did not hear a murmur.

They walked around the round table sunwise three times to bless it, then Merlin waved a golden flame across the table to cleanse it. Ganieda placed crystals and flowers that she conjured on top. A variety of songbirds entered the cave and dropped seeds onto the table, as if to add to the display.

All afternoon the two children pranced around the table inside the cave, often breaking out in song. By evening, the old stone table had become an altar to the natural world. The silver and gold butterfly entered the cave, circled the table, and then alit in the middle. Merlin and Ganieda watched with fascination as a triangular pyramid emerged from the center of the table. They walked around observing the novelty, noticing that the tetrahedron had three side faces that could be observed.

"Mother, come look!" Ganieda shouted out the opening of the hollow. "I think the table is going to talk."

Adhan, who had earlier set down the moon-shaped platter nearby, was busy collecting a variety of wild herbs. Hearing her daughter calling, she picked up the platter and entered the cave. The cakes and tea were unexpectedly still warm, but she knew the Moon Dish was charmed. She offered nourishment to Merlin and Ganieda, but the two were so distracted that they only nibbled. Adhan looked at the curious black triangle that had arisen in the center of the table.

"A tetrahedron is a foundational shape, stable, and quite masculine," Merlin remarked, continuing to walk around the table observing the triangular pyramid.

"I think the table has a scrying screen," said Adhan. "I haven't seen one like it since I last saw your father. Does one of the screen faces show images?"

As she examined the tetrahedron, colorful lights began to flash.

"The table wants to speak," said Ganieda. "But it doesn't seem to have a full signal."

"See what happens when you put *Kardia* on the table," said Merlin.

Very carefully, Ganieda took off her heart pendant and set it on the edge of the round table. At first nothing happened, and then the meteorite table began to groan and shudder. All three of them leapt back when the heavy table lifted into the air, as light as the silver and gold butterfly. Just before the table levitated beyond her reach, Ganieda snatched back her glittering *Kardia* and the table landed heavily on the ground, groaning like an old man. All three visible sides of the triangular pyramid flashed several times, then a person's face appeared on one of the triangles, then disappeared.

Merlin gasped.

"It *is* a scrying screen!" exclaimed Adhan with glee.

The black pyramid acted as a galactic FaceTime. Colors swirled inside the tetrahedron, then an image became sharply focused. At last, they could see the visage of a very old man.

"Good day, Adhan, Merlin and Ganieda. I have long awaited this moment."

They were enchanted by the scrying screen, but even more astonished to meet a star traveler. They bowed their heads with respect to welcome the figure who spoke. His long silver hair was filled with the light of stars.

"I am Grandfather Morfessa, the creator of the Round Table," he told them. "I am from the city of Falias, far to the north."

Morfessa's grey eyes were as bright as the planets, Jupiter and Venus. The second screen showed the constellation of the Northern Cross.

"Look," said Merlin pointing to the second screen. "It's Cygnus, the Swan!"

"Cosmic," Ganieda whispered. "Cygnus is very far north."

Adhan was gazing at the first screen. "I knew the wizard Morfessa, but he had another magical name," Adhan tested him.

"Mórfís," said the flickering image.

Adhan gasped and then a tear ran down her right cheek.

"Where is my husband?" asked Adhan. "Where is Madog Morfryn?"

"My son is also here in the scrying screen," Grandfather Morfessa stated.

Curious, Ahdan and the two children walked past the second screen still showing the constellation of Cygnus and circled around the table to the third screen. The triangle flickered off then back on again.

"Dear ones!" A man wearing a grey cape trimmed in silver and black looked at them affectionately. A wooden staff with hissing snakes and a crystal ball was held in his right hand. His beard and eyes were grey, and there was an air of mystery surrounding him.

"Morfryn!" Adhan exclaimed reaching to touch the third screen.

Madog Morfryn smiled at Adhan and the twins, then added, "I have missed all of you."

Both children gasped and looked carefully at the flickering screen. Adhan's knees gave way, and she slumped down beside the table, trying to steady her breath.

Ganieda helped her mother find a stone to rest upon.

"Are you really our father?" asked Merlin with curiosity.

"Yes, Merlin," said the man on the screen. "I hope to visit with you soon."

"What has kept you away?" asked Adhan, now resting on a stone. "There are those who say my children are fatherless, or worse."

Morfryn frowned, then stroked the hairs on his grey beard.

"The Niente drove me underground," Morfryn explained. "I have to live in a parallel Inner Earth with the Sidhe."

"Take us with you," said Adhan. "Take me to Mag Mell where it is always spring."

"Not yet, dear one," said Morfryn. "Be brave. There is work that must be done, but one day I will collect you in my ship and we will sail away."

"Father, how can we help you?" asked Ganieda.

"You must act as protectors of the magical children and the guardians of the Round Table."

"The Round Table," whispered Ganieda, lovingly running her fingers over the rough table. "That is your name."

"The Round Table with magic from Falias," Merlin added placing his fingers on the image of a crab holding the sliver of a moon.

"Learn the star map," Morfryn told them. "And you will learn the secrets of the ages."

"Start in the west and look carefully," Grandfather Morfessa instructed. "You will see the zodiac that surrounds the table."

They walked around the table once more, and this time they noticed the ram's horns of Aries etched in white stones into the table. Moving counterclockwise they then perceived the circular face of the bull with horns for Taurus. The next image was of the faces of twins looking at each other, then the crab with the moon. Ganieda recognized the face of a lion etched into the meteorite.

"It's the lion of the constellation Leo," Adhan clarified.

They walked around the table noticing all twelve constellations with their accompanying image.

"The letter "M" is for Virgo's maiden," Merlin professed.

"The whole zodiac is here," Adhan informed the twins.

"The Round Table is a map of the Golden Age," Grandfather Morfessa explained, the stars in his hair glittering. "In the fifth century BC, the Athenians of Greece will understand the map and this flowing wisdom from the stars will activate the flourishing of culture, philosophy, art, literature, and science. The enlightenment will influence Western civilization for centuries."

"If the secret of the Round Table is kept," Morfryn added. "There is the possibility that another Golden Age will arise in the twenty-first century."

"Find the Olympians after which is the constellations are named," Grandfather Morfessa encouraged. "A New Time will come when the unicorn appears."

"The Greeks called Morfessa 'Hermes,' the *magos*," Morfryn said. "Hermes always carried a serpent staff known as the Caduceus."

The screens flashed intensely.

"You have activated a consciousness, which is as old as the star Deneb," Morfryn remarked. "Access to the mysteries is yours now, if you choose to study."

The table shuddered and inside the flickering tetrahedron the image of their father took on a warm rose-colored glow. The next screen also showed Morfessa, who was smiling.

"The butterfly and diamond heart you created, which both rested on the table, have animated the wisdom of the ancient ones," Morfessa imparted.

Adhan and the twins stared at the three screens in wonderment.

"Ganieda, keep the healing heart safe," Morfryn directed. "The Niente cannot create magic and will be jealous of you. Be very careful. They will try to steal Kardia and destroy you too. Even now they can feel us speaking. We must be brief, and then we must break contact until the next epoch."

"Why so long?" Adhan asked. "I miss you."

"It is best if they think you are a widow," said Morfryn sadly.

"But we miss you too!" Ganieda protested.

Morfryn smiled at his daughter and then his son.

The second screen with Morfessa began to flicker, and they turned their gaze to their grandfather. His eyes were dazzling, so light grey they were almost silver.

"You have all three been given a very important assignment," Morfessa stated looking serious. "In the time to come you will have the opportunity to birth an entirely new era. There are several riddles that must be solved, and the magical people must come together again from different realm. There is also a thirteenth secret. There will be many centuries that will seem dark but never lose heart. That is why you must always wear Kardia, for you, Ganieda, are linked to the heart of Mother Earth.

Ganieda bowed her head, and Merlin also gave a nod of understanding.

"We will meet again when the sun is shining brightly, and we will feast and tell happy stories," Morfryn said. "But for now no one must know how to find me."

Merlin looked at his sister with tears in his eyes but did not complain.

"I will leave you with a gift," said Morfryn.

All three screens flickered. As they watched, golden light took many forms, from gods and goddesses, to children and angels. As the images slowed, Ganieda noticed a silver hand-mirror on the table and grabbed it. Merlin tried to wrestle it from her.

"The mirror is for my daughter," said Morfryn sternly. "The Round Table is for your keeping, Merlin."

Merlin pouted but let Ganieda go, and she held the hand-mirror close to her chest. Adhan stood slowly and then joined her children, who pressed their bodies into the table getting as close as they could to the screens.

"Merlin, you must know something," Grandfather Morfessa said.

Merlin stood erect, his full focus on the starry wizard's flickering face.

"The Round Table template is known as Logres and will be utilized briefly by a utopian kingdom that will flourish in Britain and influence many generations. You must protect the table with your life."

"Yes, Grandfather," said Merlin, who then noticed a staff lying on the table. It was made of intertwined black and silver snakes that seemed to writhe.

"The Caduceus will act as an extension of you and strengthen your magical powers. The crystal at the tip is known as the Star Spirit. The Serpent Staff has a life of its own and it may take you a while to befriend it."

Merlin noticed that his grandfather in the screen was no longer holding a staff but had sent it through time and space to him.

"Never forget that your power comes from the Sun, which is always benevolent and life-affirming. And remember that Ganieda is as much a wizard as the rest of us."

Ganieda's ears turned pink, but she smiled and squeezed her mother's hand.

Merlin carefully picked up the staff and admired the way the light shone from the Star Spirit. Suddenly a flash of light burnt Merlin's hand, and he dropped the staff on the table.

"It may take you a while to learn the ways of the Serpent Staff," Grandfather Morfessa stated. "The Caduceus is meant to be used for diplomacy, peace and healing."

Merlin was eyeing the staff with curiosity as it inched away from him.

"The next time you place the staff upon the Round Table—many years from now—it will awaken the promised age, an era of harmony and peace amongst human beings. Known as the Fifth Epoch, a change will occur on the living Earth in which all who live on the planet will make a shift in consciousness. At that time, Gaea will transform in a way you cannot yet imagine."

Merlin snatched the Caduceus up again and the two snakes hissed. Frightened, he threw the staff on the ground and jumped back as they tried to bite him.

"Perhaps ask them if they will work with you," Morfessa added with a chuckle.

"That's some serious magic," said Ganieda. "What about my mirror?"

"Little Albion has old magic from the starry realms," Morfessa explained. "The mirror will shatter if anyone tells a lie and mend itself when the truth is spoken. Use it to protect the magical children. The mirror knows who they are."

Ganieda apprehensively examined the mirror and then looked at her image.

"Remember, when the Planetary Earth Star opens, I will return," Morfryn promised.

"When will that be?" Ganieda asked her father.

"When the celestials decide it is so," he answered.

Merlin was still struggling with the staff and snakes, trying not to get bitten.

"We will need to sign off now," said Grandfather Morfessa. "Make sure you eat the food from the Moon Dish, for it is the sister of the ancient *Undry* made by the wizard Semias in the city of Murias."

"As long as you have the Moon Dish, you will never go hungry," Morfryn revealed. "And Adhan," he added, "I love you."

All three screens flickered out and then the tetrahedron went dark. A breeze blew into the cave and through the holes of the meteorite table, making, at first, a whistling sound and then music. They listened as a great melody of life celebrated them. When it stopped, the cave, once again, became still and dank like any moist earthen place.

Adhan looked at the dish she had set down earlier in the cave, noting that it was still brimming over with warm food and herbal tea. All three attempted to be brave and not cry.

"Who would have thought the Moon Dish was so special?" said Adhan, noticing a new loaf of warm bread had appeared on the platter with some scones and honey cakes.

The children abandoned their new treasures temporarily, circling around their mother and the platter, looking at the lovely delicacies. Adhan handed each child a piece of bread and tore off one for herself. They all enjoyed the gratifying taste, and the food filled them with the life-affirming warmth of the Otherworld.

Merlin offered the silver snake a piece of bread and then the black snake a piece of honey cake, and they seemed to doze off after eating. After he carefully picked up the staff, it magically reduced in size to match his small stature.

Mother and children walked back out into the ebbing sunlight. They carefully covered the entrance of the cave with vines, then made their way back toward their home. Adhan had a happy spring in her step.

"I have a feeling that finding the Round Table was no accident and that it will be a part of our lives for a long time," said Adhan.

"Magic," said Ganieda, inspecting the silver mirror.

"Magic," said Merlin, clutching his staff with the sleeping serpents.

Chapter 2

Tea in Hampstead
London, 21st Century

The morning sun shone through the red curtains, and along with the hum of cars, she could hear birds chirping. Nina yawned, stretched and realized she was happy. It felt good to be alive. Her bedroom was on the top floor of what used to be a grand house; the building had been turned into three flats. They were living in the upper flat, which had the most stairs but also the best view of Hampstead Heath.

It was April, and there was still a chill in the air. After tossing a woolen green shawl across her shoulders, Nina tottered sleepily to the kitchen. Switching on the electric kettle, she nodded to her mother, Diana, who was quietly writing in her journal at the table.

"Would you like a cup of tea?" she asked Diana, who nodded but remained focused on her journal. "Daphne?"

Aunt Daphne was entering the room to join them for tea and breakfast. Under her light-grey robe, Daphne wore a flimsy green gown with depictions of laurel leaves. She was slender, and her long fair hair spilled over the back of her robe like a waterfall.

"Yes to black tea," said Daphne.

Nina waited patiently for the water to boil, then poured it carefully into a teapot containing loose Earl Grey tea leaves.

"Daphne," called a male voice, "could I have a cup of tea too?"

"Blaise is going to Oxford today to teach a class on the mythological logos of the major civilizations," Daphne explained.

"I'll take the tea to him," said Nina, reaching into the cabinet to get another cup. Diana was still focused on her journal, scribbling insights that were meaningful to her. Nina thought it best to let her mother write.

While waiting for the tea to steep, she lightly etched the images of the ceramic butterflies on the pot with her fingers which warmed her hands. After pouring Blaise's tea, she took the cup to his office.

Nina could hear her uncle shuffling through papers and then he received her with a smile. His office was wall-to-ceiling books and double books in some places. She noticed some pictures from Arthurian legend on the wall, and action figure toys on the bookshelves. The room smelled delightfully musty.

"I would love to talk to you about Grail legend one day," Nina said.

Standing by his desk, Blaise looked over at her through his horn-rimmed glasses and paused momentarily. His bushy white hair seemed luminous in the sunlight.

"It's a long conversation," he said. "But one well worth having."

He was distracted and continued to shuffle through papers on his desk.

"I brought you the cup of tea." Nina made some room for it on his desk. "Were Camelot and the Round Table real, or is it all just a myth?"

"Legends are based in reality," he replied.

Blaise gulped down some tea, spilling a splash of it on his blue shirt. He grunted and wiped the liquid away, ignoring the stain.

Nina thought most of the male professors at King's College London would probably have tea stains on their shirts.

"The table is linked to Logres," he added.

"Logres?" Nina asked.

"Some say Logres is a place, even Britain; others say it is a mystical template," Blaise expounded. "I suspect the latter, for Logres has a spiritual significance, perhaps instructions given by the divine. It may be a star map. Camelot was built around the magical table, and each knight had to swear to act honorably, to be just, and to protect those in need. If they did not, they lost their seat, and the respect of Arthur."

"Is there any reason to seek the Round Table again?" Nina inquired.

"Some say the table is infused with a starry template upon which an ideal world can be built," Blaise proposed. "So yes, if you treasure honesty, virtue and community, the map of Logres is to be cherished."

"Can the Round Table be found?" Nina asked.

Blaise stopped shuffling papers and took a moment to sip his tea before responding. "Some say it is only Merlin who knows how to find the Round Table for it disappeared after the fall of Camelot."

"I would like to find a template upon which an ideal world can be built."

Blaise paused, walked toward Nina, and then sat down on the chair beside his niece. He could sense that her impulse was genuine.

"When a nation is haunted, the soul of its civilization must be rediscovered," he said. "Sometimes Camelot is found in the very soil you stand upon."

Nina looked at her uncle and thought for a moment that he was over-lit by a golden other-worldly light.

"Now I must be off to work!" Blaise stood and started collecting his things.

Moments later, Nina returned to the kitchen carrying the empty teacup. Uncle Blaise was close behind her.

"I'll be back tomorrow!" he shouted as he went out the kitchen door, which closed behind him. The sound of his footsteps could be heard, as Blaise rushed down staircase shared by all three flats in the building. But he paused by the front entrance, and they heard him charge back up the stairs.

The door cracked open, Blaise stuck his head inside and added: "Nina, there is a landscape Round Table or Zodiac in Somerset. Some say there is a gateway to Camelot not far from there. But, of course, all things of the goddess begin at the Chalice Well."

Nina suddenly felt flooded with enthusiasm.

"Can we go?" she asked Daphne. "Now?"

"A visit to the stronghold of the goddess," Daphne echoed. "I love the idea."

"I believe the Landscape Round Table surrounds Glastonbury," Blaise told them. "But I have not located it myself yet. Why don't you go to the Chalice Well Trust and do some research?"

Diana, still dreamy from her writing, looked up and became more focused.

"I love Glastonbury and haven't been in ages," Diana reflected. "Maybe we should go. There's nothing like the present moment."

Blaise raised his bushy eyebrows.

"You never know what might happen on the Tor! You might have a run-in with Gwyn Ap Nudd, or another of the horned ones!"

Daphne noticed a twinkle in his eyes and laughed. "I'll try not to get into trouble, even if Pan and a multitude of nymphs show up!" she exclaimed, then rushed out of the room to get her things.

"Let's spend the night," Diana yelled to her. "It's a long trip."

"Beware of the faeries," joked Blaise with a chuckle. "I must be off!"

Nina could hear Uncle Blaise thump down the staircase, and she listened for the front door to slam shut and lock.

A few moments later, Daphne returned carrying a small suitcase, a backpack and an umbrella, looking ready for the outing.

"There are some boots here somewhere." Daphne started rummaging around in the kitchen closet.

"I'll grab my overnight bag," said Nina, then she went to her bedroom.

"I'll get dressed," said Diana before heading to her bedroom. Thinking about past adventures, Diana suddenly missed her husband. *Just get through one day at a time,* she told herself. *That's all we can do when our beloved has gone to the Otherworld without us.*

Nina felt a flush of excitement as she returned to the kitchen dressed in her jeans, warm shirt, red socks and sensible walking boots. She pranced across the room and took her raincoat off the coat rack.

Diana joined the other two women, dressed and ready for the day.

Daphne was standing by the door jingling the flat keys with her left hand.

"Let's go to the Chalice Well first," urged Nina with excitement. "I have never been! Do you think the Holy Grail was really hidden there?"

"Maybe," said Daphne. "Or maybe the Holy Grail was a woman."

They all looked at each other and then smiled.

"It's a wonderful secret," Daphne added. "I'm sure Blaise will have plenty to say about the Chalice later."

"I can book Little St. Michael's Retreat House," said Diana. "It's inside the Chalice Well Trust. Only companions of the trust can stay. Felix and I used to go and spend time in the gardens early in the mornings when it was quiet and meditate in the prayer rooms late at night when the spirits of the place are active. Miracles have happened in those rooms."

Diana sighed and her eyes looked misty as she thought of her times there with Felix.

"I am still a member of the Chalice Well Trust," Diana added. "I'll call them now and make sure there are rooms for us."

Nina and Daphne looked excited, then gathered some drinks and snacks into a picnic basket.

"We are all booked in!" Diana shouted moments later.

"I'll pull the car around," Daphne told them, then danced down the stairs.

Soon they were packed into the blue Mini Cooper. Nina thought it remarkable that the three of them could fit into such a compact car with all they brought. Daphne drove with precision south past Regent's Park and then picked up the motorway heading west. Once they were beyond the M25, the traffic became less dense, and they could focus on their adventure.

The women enjoyed sharing stories, and the three-hour trip seemed like it was passing by quickly. They all let out a delighted whoop as they passed Stonehenge. Then they turned their full focus on the topic of the living landscape of Somerset, and tales of King Arthur, Camelot and Avalon.

Nina enjoyed the high-spirited conversation as they traveled toward Glastonbury, one of the oldest pilgrimage sites in the United Kingdom, and a Goddess stronghold. The most ancient Welsh name was *Ynys Wydrin,* meaning the Island of Glass. Nina had the feeling that they were being guided, and that Somerset was full of magic.

Chapter 3

The Magic of Glastonbury

Glastonbury, Somerset, 21st Century

Daphne dropped her passengers off in front of the Chalice Well Trust. Because there was no parking, she went to find a place along Glastonbury High Street. Diana and Nina took their luggage into Little Michael's Retreat House. The bedrooms were small with sparce furnishings and shared bathrooms, but the space was clean, and the energy felt spiritually uplifting.

Daphne joined them, and they walked out to the Chalice Well Trust to enjoy the English faery-filled gardens. Foxgloves, snapdragons, roses and an entire array of blossoming flowers were a visual delight. Walking past the apple and hawthorn trees, Nina felt in harmony with nature.

"This is the Vale of Avalon," Diana told Nina. "The Chalice Well is known as a sanctuary of peace and tranquility, and some say the Holy Grail, or Chalice, was hidden here by Joseph of Arimathea in 1 AD."

Nina and Diana felt called to meditate beside the Wellhead. Nina intuitively circled sunwise, asking that the Lady of Avalon come and

23

guide her on this adventure. Diana sat on a cold stone step, peering into the mossy well that was covered by a black metal grate. After circling, Nina settled on a nearby step. With her eyes closed, Nina did feel a presence.

Nimue listen, the voice said.

Nina opened her eyes and looked around the garden. The only other person there was Diana, who was enjoying her own contemplation. The young woman closed her eyes again and heard the voice once more.

Remember Merlin.

Nina looked up into the sky and thought for a moment that she could see a dragon in the clouds above. She blinked, and the image faded. Nina could hear light footsteps and, without looking, knew Daphne was joining them.

After a little more reflective time, the three women stood up and meandered down the path to sip from the Red Spring. The water cascaded from a wall, making a fountain out of a stone lion's fierce mouth, before falling onto a stone dais and then flowing down a waterfall into the brick-lined healing pool known as King Arthur's Court. They followed the path of the water to the pool.

Nina felt increasingly introspective, as she pulled off her shoes and walked barefoot in the iron-rich waters. Daphne and Diana joined her. They both let out a yelp as the icy waters encircled their ankles, then did their best to refrain from laughter.

Nina could only stand the cold water for a few minutes, and soon all three sat on a bench beside the water. They allowed the gentle breezes to dry their feet, before putting their socks and boots back on. Nina thought the small waterfall on her left looked rather like a landscape witch. She wondered if it was just her imagination, but little lights seemed to flit amongst the water and the garden.

"I think there are faeries here," Nina whispered to Daphne.

"And tree-spirits," Daphne added.

Then the three women all wandered toward the top of the garden. There was a gnarled apple tree that had fallen but was still determined to grow. Sitting on the ground by it, Nina put her back up against the old trunk. Diana sat on the fallen tree and looked toward the distance, then closed her eyes.

"I can sense the apple trees of Avalon."

Standing nearby, Daphne also closed her eyes and took in a deep breath.

Nina felt called to return to the well and she told the other two, who followed her contemplative stroll. Nina followed her inner prompting, stopping to look at the colorful flowers and ripening apples.

They wandered down to the circular stones that surrounded the well.

Gazing at the black metal cover with the two overlapping circles, Diana whispered, "The symbol is called the *Vesica Piscis*. Some say it means union, or the point where heaven and earth meet. Early Christians called it the womb of the universe."

Nina peered down into the black well. Even though a grate blocked the entrance, looking past the mossy edges, she could sense the water far below. She thought it could indeed be a portal to the goddess. It seemed auspicious to her that they were visiting a place where the Otherworlds were close.

Daphne looked down into the well and then up to the hill behind them.

"The Chalice Well is the feminine, but the Glastonbury Tor which is high on a hill is the masculine," Daphne whispered. "We need both for life to flourish. You can't cut out the feminine and expect life to go on."

"The goddess is life," said Diane, looking into the well. "I can sense a powerful feminine energy here."

They all three closed their eyes and felt the nurturing presence of the Lady of Avalon. Some other travelers waited patiently for them to finish their reverie. Daphne stood up and the other two followed her out to the back of the Chalice Well Trust where the Tor could be seen.

"Apparently *Annwn,* the Celtic Underworld, is located below the Tor," Daphne said. "And did you know the sister of Gwyn Ap Nudd, the ruler of *Annwn,* has a twin sister named Gwenabwy?"

"You sound like Uncle Blaise," said Nina with a giggle. "I think you are trying to scare me."

Daphne and Diana exchanged looks but did not say anything for a few moments.

"Gwenabwy is also known as the White Goddess," Diana continued. "But I've never met her."

"Let's walk up to the summit and take in the panorama of Somerset," Daphne continued. "And see what other mysteries we might find there."

"Glastonbury Tor is a place that calls you back again and again," said Diana. "As if we can only handle opening to other realms and realities in stages."

Nina, Diana and Daphne paused at the gift shop, then exited the Chalice Well Trust. Walking out of the gates, they all moved counterclockwise around the outside of the garden walls to the White Spring where they took a sip from the zinc-rich water. Then the women turned and looked upwards, taking in the increasingly magnificent site of the Tor. Now it was time to walk up the steep steps that curved up the hill to the 14th century ruins of St. Michael's Tower.

The three women arrived at the top of the Tor somewhat winded, but excited to see the views. A druid in white drummed respectfully inside the Tower. Nina was aware of the Christian and Pagan overlap of beliefs and could sense the even more ancient elementals and faery-folk. For a moment, she thought of her father and Pan and imagined them playing music on the side of the hill.

Nina sat down on the stones with her back against the ruins of the church. Her whole body seemed to buzz with energy.

Daphne came and sat down next to her. "How are you?" she whispered.

"I feel fully alive," said Nina. "But it is also as though I've forgotten something I need to remember."

They looked across the hill at Diana who was gazing off in the distance.

"I hope she find another man," said Daphne. "Romance can be a healer."

Just before the sun set, they walked down the steep steps back toward the Chalice Well. They returned to Little Michael's Retreat House for a cup of tea and a rest before heading to town for a warm dinner.

That evening, the three women went into the prayer rooms at the top of the Retreat House and enjoyed the silence.

"When three gather, magic happens," Daphne whispered.

Chapter 4

The Sky Temple

Elysium (Gaea's Sky Temple)
In-Between Time

ady Gaea, a tall and imposing figure, stood inside an airy temple with tall white pillars and an open roof. The walls were made of mist, and a lawn covered in an array of colorful flowers encircled them. The Lady watched as a flock of doves flew inside the temple and landed on a circular black table. They began to peck at the seeds that were encased along with gemstones in the stone surface.

"I am not ready to activate the template of Logres yet," she said, waving the birds away with a sweep of her hands. They encircled her and some landed in her hair. "Logres is as old as the star Deneb of Cygnus, but planet Earth is not quite ready for that amount of light. Only the Faery understand the life-affirming potency of the star map."

Lady Gaea wrapped her long blue cape around her body, then sat in a plush green velvet chair beside the Round Table. She was motionless, yet the auburn hair cascading down her back was teeming with tiny chirping birds and blossoming morning glories.

29

"As soon as I start to activate the template, the Niente will come in like a ferocious storm to stop me," she added. "It happened in Greece, Rome, Britain, and now the same dark forces threaten the magical ones of the twenty-first century."

A horse-sized dragon lay curled beside the table.

"I'm here for you," the dragon said sleepily without moving. "Not much gets past me."

"Thank you, Delphyne," Lady Gaea said. "The dangerous Niente and others like them are why we are in a parallel dimension."

The Lady casually stroked the dragon's green and gold scales, then moved her fingers thoughtfully across the black stone tabletop. The inset gemstones glistened in the shape of stars and constellations. Her finger stopped on a large white star, and she drummed her fingers on it thoughtfully.

"Has the star activated?" the dragon asked without looking up.

"Not yet. You can rest for a while longer."

Lady Gaea patted the dragon. Gemstones that were starting to flash on the Round Table caught her attention.

"Actually, I think the Earth Star is beginning to stir," Gaea added. "I'll check the scrying screen."

Taking off a necklace, she placed a crystal in the shape of a thirteen-pointed star at the center of the table. It activated a black pyramid that rose up at that spot. At once, a tetrahedron with three screens began to show a variety of scenes. She focused on the images that appeared in the first triangle.

The scene was of Diana, Nina and Daphne sitting on the summit of the Glastonbury Tor taking in the scenery of Somerset. But then the second screen activated, and the Lady walked around the table to see Gwyn Ap Nudd and his twin sister Gwenabwy conversing in the Underworld.

Gwyn sat on his birch throne surrounded by his white dogs with pink ears. His radiant sister stood beside him.

"We must prepare for the wild hunt," said Gwenabwy. "Diana and Nimue have returned to Avalon and the dark forces are gathering."

Gwyn gazed at his sister, then noticed several faery women assembling around him looking concerned.

Back in the Sky Temple, the third screen on the black tetrahedron activated showing the dark magicians of the Niente gathering in the city of London. At first, they seemed like businessmen in grey suits, but as Lady Gaea watched she noticed that they looked like robots. She knew the Niente were programmed to enslave and kill.

Lady Gaea observed the second screen once again showing Annwn.

"The Niente want to kill the magical people so the Planetary Earth Star cannot activate," said Gwenabwy. "They want to prevent the Golden Age."

"Can the New Time be stopped?" asked Gwyn Ap Nudd. "Or is destiny fixed?"

As if in response, his hounds began to whine and snap. Gwenabwy looked at her brother with sad eyes.

"Destiny is a choice, brother."

"We have to find Merlin and Ganieda," said Gwyn Ap Nudd. "They have held the knowledge of the Round Table and how it activates Logres since Morfessa gave it to them in the Foretime."

"I have seen Ganieda roaming the planet," Gwenabwy stated. "She goes about as a healer in London, and no one knows the wiser."

Turning to one of the faery women, he said, "Saddle up my stallion, Carngrwn. Tonight… we ride out!"

A cheer went up amongst the Fey.

Chapter 5

Abigail's Healing Garden

London, 21ˢᵗ Century

bigail Sibley liked hosting the healing group that met weekly in the back garden at her home in Hampstead, a leafy suburb in North London. She enjoyed the comradery of women, the laughter, and the simple practice of running energy with others for a higher purpose.

Abigail had always thought of herself as a very normal human being, until Max became ill. Her husband's cancer diagnosis had changed everything abruptly. To help Max when he was in pain, she had placed her hands on him gently. One night as Abigail was praying, she realized that light would come out of her palms to soothe him. Soon afterwards, Abigail had started a healing group and found several other gifted women to join her too.

This weekly gathering had helped her face life, and death. Over time, she realized that experiencing the healing light was not so unusual for her; she had just not recognized it before. A similar vital force moved through her when she was gardening, an energy she secretly

33

called her green fire. Often the fire burned so intensely within her that she had to sleep outside.

After Max's passing, Abigail had begun spending long hours in her walled garden and loved it deeply. During the spring and summer months, the attractive mulched beds were filled with flowers. The vibrant colors brought upliftment to all who came to visit. Abigail particularly loved Delphiniums, and she thought it strange that flowers so beautiful to behold could simultaneously be so poisonous. She also liked growing the old garden favorite, the *Antirrhinum Majus*, also known as Snapdragons.

When her children were young, she told them that a dragon and several faeries lived in the garden, and they believed her. Sometimes when the Moon was full, she wondered if her claim were true. Abigail missed her children who were now scattered around the globe off on their own adventures. She also missed her husband Max, who had been gone for more than three years. His illness had been a long one, and so in some ways, Abigail was relieved that she no longer had to watch him suffer.

She thought wistfully of the time when they were young but knew that it was important to focus on her life now. The healing light in her hands had made the entire process tolerable. Focusing on the present moment, Abigail was in love with her garden. Although still attractive in her mid-sixties, she did not expect to find a partner again, so her floral friends and the healing group were more important to her than ever. Sometimes she felt the flowers wanted to speak through her, but she laughed the idea away.

I am becoming a mad old lady, she thought.

Abigail loved the days when Ganieda would make an appearance in her garden. There was something mysterious about the woman. Ganieda was elusive, moving around Britain to different sacred sites, healing groups and spiritual centers. The woman never seemed to age but would appear and disappear just at the right time. She also loved Ganieda's knowledge of the magical Celtic traditions. Interesting events always seemed to happen when Ganieda joined in. Not in the least shy, Ganieda always wore light-colored clothing, and her long fair hair spilled in ringlets down her back. She was wonderfully eccentric, often weaving swan feathers into her clothing. Sometimes she threw a silver scarf over her shoulders that would sparkle in the Sun.

Ganieda was unique and happy to be authentically herself. During the healing group, she would bring out a crystal heart pendant she always wore, and it seemed as though a violet healing light would radiate from it. She wondered if anyone else had noticed the necklace. Abigail watched now as this wizardly woman walked amongst the flowerbeds speaking to the blossoms and possibly sensing the faeries that might be flitting back and forth.

There was another healer in the garden that summer afternoon. She observed Nina showing up and exchanging greetings with Ganieda. The young woman had recently arrived from New York City. After the death of her father, Nina had followed her British mother, Diana, to London. Occasionally, Diana would also join the group but often, like today, she simply stayed home working on her novels, which featured Greek and Roman deities.

Abigail had heard stories of time travel to other realms, and she wondered if such things were possible. Observing Ganieda and Nina, she felt that in some way they were two primeval beings living in the modern era. Nina's long dark hair seemed in direct contrast to Ganieda's blonde locks.

Deep in conversation, the two healers walked slowly around the garden together admiring the flowers as if they were free from the cares of the world. Abigail suspected that they would also be discussing some of the medicinal herbs that were growing and their uses. She noticed that Ganieda's light-colored clothing was also in direct contrast to Nina's dark garb.

After smiling at Abigail, Ganieda and Nina walked to the center of the garden and began to place chairs in a circle. Ganieda called to her using the nickname, Abae, and motioned for Abigail to join them.

People were slowly arriving for the healing group. Nina finished arranging the circle of seating by putting one chair in the middle, which they referred to as the "hot seat." She invited the first client to sit. The woman said she had an issue with digestion. Ganieda stood behind the woman and Nina sat in the grass front of her. They both held up their hands, sending healing energy toward the woman. Now seated in the circle, Abigail felt spiritual warmth fill the garden and, closing her eyes, absorbed the vitality and unconditional love. She noticed a flash of violet from Ganieda's necklace.

"Raise your hands and join us in directing the healing energy," said Ganieda to Abigail. "Let sunlight pour through you."

Abigail smiled and raised her hands. Then all three healers were sending positive energy to the person in the center "hot seat." The woman closed her eyes and enjoyed the energy.

"What is troubling you?" asked Nina.

"If I eat grains, my stomach bloats, and I can be sick for days," the woman told her.

"Apples will help, Amira," said Ganieda, who pulled a red apple from her medicine bag and handed it to the woman.

"How do you know my name?" The woman looked slightly shocked but took the apple. "Are you a witch?"

"Bite into the fruit," directed Ganieda. "I'm just who I am."

"Strange for sure," Amira said.

When Ganieda made no response, the woman cautiously took a bite of the apple. Amira soon chewed it with enjoyment while the healing women sent light to her belly.

"There is power in intention," Ganieda told those gathered. "When three or more people focus on the same outcome, miracles can happen." She smiled and added, "And apples keep the doctor away!"

The three healers all chuckled in a good-natured way. It felt good to laugh, to be surrounded by flowers, and to feel the love shared in that special garden. Abigail placed her fingertips on her ruby necklace and felt the orb in the shape of a red apple tingle. Ganieda had given the necklace to her and told Abigail the gemstone would help her connect to Avalon, the mystical isle of women. It did not worry Abigail whether the place was real, because just the thought of Avalon made her happy and that was all that mattered.

Abigail had left the garden gate open, and more people were arriving. With some discomfort, she realized Sue had come with her daughter. A shy teenager, Elen always wore a dark green floppy hat. Her mother, Sue, constantly spewed negative energy that was difficult to clear. At the last healing group, Abigail had thought about asking Sue not to come back, and she observed the misshapen, middle-aged woman with some contempt. Sue had short, cropped grey hair, a pale complexion and generally wore a frown. Abigail thought it odd that the woman always wore army fatigues, which made her seem more like a grumpy WWII veteran than a mother.

Maybe Sue suffers from PTSD?

Waving Amira out of the spot, Sue claimed her place in the healing "hot seat" stating that she felt dizzy. The healers turned their focus onto her. Abigail felt agitated almost immediately. She wasn't sure exactly how, but she sensed a violent energy in the etheric field of the woman. Abigail withdrew her hands and stood as if to leave the group.

Ganieda glanced at Abigail, who blushed realizing the healer could read her thoughts. Then Ganieda winked at Abigail and indicated that she should continue to send healing energy. Abigail reluctantly agreed, but it went against her intuition. Nina observed this interaction within the group with fascination. Energetically, much was taking place in the garden.

Sue always tried to compete with Ganieda. It was absurd since the healer had no interest in competition. The point of the healing garden was to create circles of friends and to open a pathway to love and unity consciousness. The focus was on the intelligence of life. Ganieda hoped that Sue would relax and realize they were all there to support each other. Still, she knew intuitively that today would be difficult. Sue and drama always seemed to accompany each other. Everywhere Sue went, battle would ensue.

During the previous gathering, Abigail had asked Ganieda if they should be more selective with the people who came. The wise woman had simply shrugged and said, "Moths and butterflies both come to the light."

"What about people who are just simply mean?" Abigail had asked.

"They need healing the most," Ganieda had answered. "And don't forget the power of three or more healers!"

As usual, Elen wore her floppy green hat in a way that almost hid her eyes and fawn-brown hair. Elen rarely smiled, but when Ganieda looked at her, the girl beamed. Beneath her hat, shy Elen was quite pretty, in a child-like way.

"Would you like a private healing consultation today, Elen?" Ganieda asked.

Elen grinned and nodded in the affirmative.

"You know what to do," Ganieda said to the other two healers. "Carry on. Abigail, you lead. And Nina, you guard the group."

With her inner power, Ganieda drew a magical circle around the group to keep them all safe until she returned.

Sue's eyes followed Elen as her daughter headed to the bungalow with Ganieda.

Still standing, Abigail moved to take Ganieda's position. Nina sat in the grass by Sue's feet, so that the person in the healing chair would be positioned between the two healers. Feeling honored to lead the group, Abigail decided to overcome her issues with Sue and just focus on the healing light. Sensing the powerful support of Nina, she observed the energy flowing from the woman's hands. Nina looked up and smiled. Her dark hair waved in the breeze. Abigail had an inner vision of apple blossoms drifting in Nina's direction.

Nina has some serious magic too, thought Abigail. *She's one of the Avalonian women for sure.*

After leaving the client chair, Sue settled down and seemed to doze off. Abigail and Nina sent energy to several other women who took the hot seat, none of which were difficult to work with.

Birds were singing in response to a perfect summer day. The hollyhocks that grew along the back wall were in full blossom and already had reached a great height. The tall flowers also hid the compost pile. Yet roses were Abigail's deepest love. She felt that the fragrance and the hardiness of the roses were most like herself. She was resilient and could live anywhere, at least as long as there was a garden. She also grew medicinal herbs such as vervain, drying the leaves to make tea.

Abigail stepped over to Nina after the last client had left the chair, and she whispered, "I'll serve soup and tea to the group when Ganieda and Elen return."

Suddenly, an image came to Nina of an antlered woman. Her neck was bleeding, and her big brown eyes seemed to beg for help. Nina shook her head, willing the image away, and she forced herself to focus on sending rays of healing light to the whole group. For some time, the healers and other women simply enjoyed the chirping of birds and the happiness of being together.

About half an hour after they had left, the healer and Elen returned to the group. The young woman sat down quietly in a chair and looked very contemplative. Sue opened her eyes and glared. Nina looked at Elen, and once again, the vision of an ancient antlered woman flashed before her.

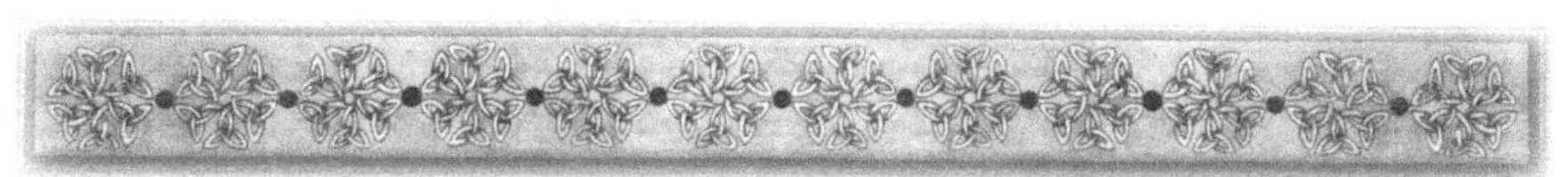

Chapter 6

Lady Gaea
& the Dragon

Elysium (Gaea's Sky Temple)
In-Between Time

*other Cosmos is ready to make a shift," Lady Gaea said. "I have the feeling that many demi-gods are going to come to see me soon."*

The dragon stretched and raised her body up to observe the black pyramid. They both watched with curiosity as the first scrying screen showed a comet plummeting across the sky.

"Is Earth going to be hit by a comet?" Delphyne asked.

"I believe so."

"When?"

"When the thirteenth constellation, Ophiuchus, calls for Asclepius, the serpent bearer."

"So, we don't know exactly," said Delphyne.

"But Merlin and Ganieda know," Lady Gaea noted. "So does Rasalhague."

"Rasalhague, the ancient star?"

Lady Gaea nodded. "He's sentient."

41

The second scrying screen flashed, and they walked around the table to observe Ganieda in twenty-first century London in a home garden. Ganieda looked as though she was in her mid-thirties, but they knew the magician had been on the planet since the Foretime.

"Why does the twenty-first century matter so much?" Delphyne asked.

"It's when the shift of the ages is scheduled to happen, and the gods can return."

"Oh, the dawn of a new era," said the dragon. "Can we arrive in a spaceship and terrify people?"

"There's always a drama when the ages change," Gaea added with a chuckle.

The third screen focused on Abigail working in her garden. They noticed that small faeries emanating rose-pink rays of light were following her as she tended her flowers.

"That's lovely," Lady Gaea stated, continuing to observe the work of the nature spirits. "That scene makes me miss living on the planet."

She closed her eyes and enjoyed the moment while the dragon purred.

"Lady Gaea," the dragon said with a husky voice, "I am sorry that you have been exiled from Earth for so long. You are Mother Earth after all. All living beings need you!"

The Lady, with her eyes still closed, ran her fingers across the codes of the meteorite table. The M of the maiden of Virgo glimmered under her touch. Then a star map flashed, showing the rest of the images of the zodiac. The scales of Libra flowed into the tail of the Scorpion, then the archer of Sagittarius set off his arrow into the cosmos. Glyphs of the Sun, Moon and Venus appeared in silver. At the same time, silver stars appeared in Lady Gaea's thick hair, which was full of sparkles.

"We had to protect the Round Table from the dark magicians and the Niente," she said, opening her eyes. "During the dark ages, Merlin

asked me to hide the template of Logres where no one thought to look. Like Latona, I knew I also needed to hide in a misty in-between place. My temple is rarely noticed by mortals. Most just think it is a lenticular cloud and so I travel unnoticed. Thanks to the scrying screens, I can still observe all places and periods of time."

"The perfect place for a goddess and an oracle," Delphyne noted.

They focused on the second screen which was fixated on Ganieda.

"I think the Round Table loves Ganieda," the Lady mused.

"We live in a starship with intergalactic viewing," the dragon snorted. "I like being able to relax and just monitor the scenes the tetrahedron decides to exhibit, even if the main stories tend to center around Ganieda and Merlin."

"Star beings have been coming and going on the planet for over 25,000 years, most undetected."

Deep in contemplative thought, Lady Gaea pensively gazed out at the cosmos.

"Do you think Uranus will return to you?" the dragon asked.

"Perhaps," said Lady Gaea.

Chapter 7
Foxes in Hampstead
London, 21st Century

After the healing group dispersed, Nina took a stroll to the Hampstead Ponds, then as the sun set, she walked toward the village along Willoughby Road. It was dusk, and the streets were dimly lit. As she strolled past the buildings, she glanced through the warmly lit windows of the well-tended flats. She thought it odd that people did not mind being observed as they made dinner and went about their ordinary lives. Nina wondered if she were looking at a hologram that generated a multitude of images, none of which were real.

Off in the distance, she could hear horses trotting along the road. She thought it was odd and wondered who would be riding at night. The tale of Gwyn Ap Nudd and the Wild Hunt came to mind, but she shook her head questioning why that tale felt relevant. Still, she felt a chill in the air and quickened her pace. Nina heard the neigh of a horse, then was startled by a movement in the shadows. She thought she saw a gargoyle scowling at her. Suddenly a cat cried out, then darted across the street. Her heart was beating quickly, and she felt she should make her way home.

She crossed the road in haste, then saw a figure standing beneath a streetlamp. The woman revealed a black boot, then Nina saw the flourish of an emerald cloak.

"Morgen, is that you?"

A statuesque woman wearing an emerald-green dress and matching cape stepped into the lamplight.

"It has been some time, Nimue," the woman said.

"I am Nina."

"But I am seeking Nimue, the interdimensional time traveler. Merlin's true love."

Nina started to turn and walk away, but Morgen grasped her by the shoulder and spun her around. Startled, Nina looked into Morgen's astonishing violet eyes and knew that an ancient time was calling her once again. The memory that had tried to reveal itself to her while she stood on the Glastonbury Tor was resurfacing now with increasing strength.

"Nimue," she whispered. "That was once my name."

"Wake up, Lady of the Lake," said Morgen. "The world is in danger, and we need to find Merlin. Gwyn Ap Nudd rides out tonight to gather the souls of the dead. He will protect us for a little while."

Morgen placed her long pale hand on Nina's forehead. The young woman tried to pull back but suddenly a vision swept over her. She was Nimue, and the magician Merlin was close to her, as though he was going to kiss her. His hair was dark, and his eyes were indigo and seemed to glisten with starlight. A towering silver tree loomed over them, and then he was gone. Nina gasped.

"The White Deva released him," said Morgen, sharply taking her hand off Nina. "Merlin is close by."

Even though it was summer, Nina felt cold. She shivered, and it seemed as though eyes were looking at her from the shadows.

"I remember," said Nina. "What do I need to do?"

"Find the Round Table."

Nina laughed, but then realized Morgen was serious.

"And help activate the Planetary Earth Star," Morgen continued.

"I have no idea what you are talking about," said Nina, trying to walk past the woman in green.

Morgen became enraged. Grabbing Nina's arm, she turned her around with a jerk, then tapped her sharply on the forehead. Nina gasped, but suddenly her life in Avalon came flooding back.

"Morfryn, son of Morfessa, gave Merlin the job to guard the Round Table," stated a man stepping out of the shadows. He was wearing sunglasses, even in the dark, and Nina knew immediately who accompanied Morgen.

"Good evening, Accolon," Nina said, her past life memory now intact. "I have no idea where Merlin is."

"He's looking for you," said Morgen to Nina.

Tall, muscular, yet lanky Accolon stood beside Morgen and looked down at Nina, who felt small compared to the supernatural couple. There was a commotion in the shadows; a cat hissed. Then they were all distracted by the chattering of foxes. One ran swiftly to Nina, who thought it odd that the little red fox wasn't frightened of her.

"Scat!" Accolon shouted, waving his arms.

Morgen chuckled and bent down to pet the fox.

"Don't you recognize him?"

The fox had a rusty-colored coat, black legs and a white-tipped tail. He seemed shy but friendly and gazed again at Nina. Suddenly she recognized the dark indigo eyes.

"Merlin?" Nina asked.

The fox stood upright, stretched and transformed into a man.

"We must be quick," Merlin said, putting a gentle hand on Nina's cheek. "I had forgotten how beautiful you are."

Nina gazed into Merlin's dark eyes and a deep love began to reawaken in her.

"I wish there was more time," Merlin said. He was close, looking at her lips as if he wished to kiss her. Then he whispered in her ear, "Ask Ganieda to bring *Kardia*. Time is of the essence."

Nina had so many questions for Merlin, but he had already begun to step away.

"We need to know where the Round Table is now," said Morgen.

"Ask Lady Gaea," replied Merlin. "She knows where the meteorite table from the city of Falias resides."

They heard an eerie howl.

"The Niente are about," said Merlin. "The dark magicians know their time is ending, but still want to destroy all of us while they can."

Statues in the shape of gargoyles seemed to stare at them from the shadows. Nina shivered. She could hear the horses of the wild hunt neigh again.

"It is likely that the Inner and Outer Earth will split apart, one light planet and the other, a dark place. It will happen close by," Merlin noted, and then he added quickly, "I must go. We are all in danger."

A streetlamp flickered off and on, then off and on again. Merlin transformed back into a fox and disappeared into the night.

"Who are you talking to, love?"

The question had come from a man in a black overcoat, who was leaning against a gate, staring at Nina. A dark cap blocked the eyes of the person, and she felt a chill in the air.

"Lots of ghosts are out tonight," he added.

Nina knew he was one of the Niente but ignored him. Merlin, Morgen and Accolon had already shape-shifted and made their escape. Nina hurried toward Hampstead High Street where there were lights and people. She could sense the man in the overcoat drifting near her, and knew his shoes made no sound. Nina had to remind herself that the man wasn't real, just a ghoul.

After going quickly inside a Tesco grocery, Nina bought some popcorn and grapes. Taking her time checking out at a self-service counter, she reminded herself that as Nimue she could shape-shift into a stag and outrun almost anyone. However, she felt it best to seem purely human, for that way she would not be of interest to the dark magicians who always wished to distort those with powers.

For a moment, Nina thought of Merlin, and how close his lips had been to hers. She wondered if there would be more to their love story.

When Nina stepped back outside, the night seemed ordinary. The man in the overcoat was nowhere to be seen, nor were the foxes. Nina made a dash for Uncle Blaise's flat and hoped her mother would be home.

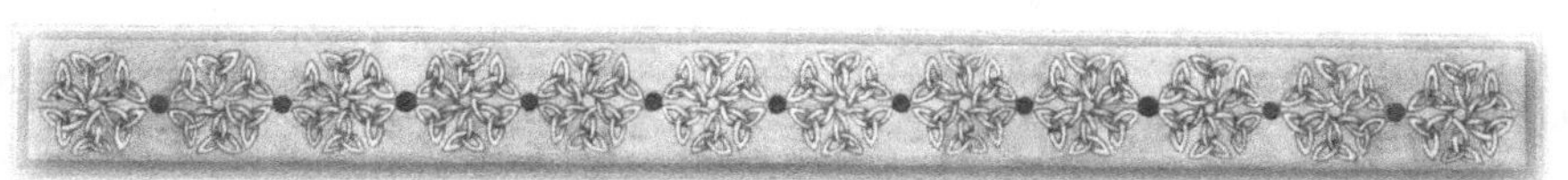

Chapter 8

Morgen &
Accolon in Elysium

Elysium (Sky Temple)
In-Between Time

A green dragon swooped down and gently caught two foxes in her sharp claws, then flew across Hampstead Heath into a veil of mist. Delphyne set the creatures on the floor of Gaea's Sky Temple. The foxes sat on their haunches before shifting into standing humanoid forms. Morgen's gaze rested on Lady Gaea, then the dragon, after which she breathed a sigh of relief. She took Accolon's hand, then they bowed their heads respectfully to the Lady.

"Morgen, goddess of the seas. I hope you are well." Lady Gaea turned her attention toward Accolon, noticing the man's red-dragon tattoo on his right forearm.

"Welcome to you as well Sir Accolon," the Lady said.

Morgen and Accolon looked around the Sky Temple with curiosity.

"Delphyne collected you two before the Niente had a chance," said Lady Gaea. "I believe Gwyn Ap Nudd and his riders protected you, and Merlin and Nimue got away."

"It was a dark night," Accolon affirmed.

"Lady Gaea, and Delphyne," Morgen said focusing on the Sky Temple. "It has been many Moons since we last met."

"Your place is like a silver-star dance hall with a dragon. I like it," commented Accolon, flipping his long dark hair behind him and giving his hips a playful shake. He removed his sunglasses, did a little jig, then spun in a circle. Morgen winked at him.

"Located between time and space, this is a Sky Temple," Lady Gaea explained. "The ancients refer to this realm as Elysium."

"The Blessed Realm of Elysium," noted Accolon, with an approving nod. After a final glance at the Temple, he put his sunglasses back on.

"Realms overlap here," said Lady Gaea. "The world is not what it seems."

Morgen's emerald dress and cape shimmered as if in response to the ancient magic. Her long dark hair snaked past her waist.

"Elysium is intriguing. But why has an ancient Greek Mother Goddess called a dragon to collect us?" Morgen asked.

"You asked Merlin about the Round Table," answered Lady Gaea. "And we could use your assistance. Those who are called are starting to gather for the activation of the Planetary Earth Star."

Gazing around the temple, Morgen noticed that the roof and walls were made of clouds. The gentle breeze on her skin was soothing, and it reminded her of Avalon. She thought of riding ocean waves, and her memory took her back even further. Then her eyes rested upon the Round Table.

"You have the template of Logres!"

"The Niente cannot see the Sky Temple," the Lady pointed out. "To everyone on the surface of the planet, it is just a lenticular cloud."

Morgen placed her pale hands on the Round Table and rubbed the surface gently watching closely as the black tetrahedron arose. The table began to moan, and the three scrying screens glimmered. The first scrying screen focused on Morgen in Avalon standing in a currach, an ancient boat. The priestess raised her hands and then disappeared into the mist.

"You are a practiced time traveler," Lady Gaea observed. "You know how to rend the veils between worlds. Your services will be needed soon."

"The cities of light will arise one day," declared Morgen, as though she were calling the Spirit from within Logres. "Albion, my love. The sweeter older England, with the scent of Daffodils blowing in the breeze, still lives within you."

"Don't forget the Delphiniums," the dragon offered.

"And the Apple trees," Morgen replied wistfully.

"There has been a battle for the soul of the land for a long time," said Lady Gaea. "And now the Niente are desperate to stop what is coming."

The Lady rested her hands on the Round Table. "Logres, please show us the future."

The second screen flashed, and the face of an old man emerged. Morgen looked shocked and took a step back.

"Madog Morfryn," said Morgen, with a bow of her head. "I did not know that you were still amongst us."

"It is best that way," said Morfryn. "Until the turning of the ages, no one must see me, or my wife and children will be in danger. Many centuries ago, I entrusted magical treasures to my family that will aid the opening of the Planetary Earth Star when the alignment takes place."

"Your secret is safe with me," Morgen replied.

"However, there are several riddles that must be solved before the Planetary Earth Star can open. The zodiac must be remembered in an unexpected way."

The specter of Morfryn faded, and the second screen activated, showing Ganieda walking amongst flowers. Then a steady stream of images appeared in all three screens of people in a garden in twenty-first century Hampstead.

Morgen let out a sigh.

"I believe you know Ganieda and Nimue," Lady Gaea stated.

"Yes," said Morgen. "And Abae, the serpent woman of Delphi."

The dragon turned around with a fiery snort. "Once we worked together, but she does not remember now."

"The oracles were eventually silenced," Lady Gaea reminded them.

"Then the Niente became violent," said Delphyne with a shudder. "They started killing dragons."

"Abae was one of the most powerful of the oracles," recalled Lady Gaea.

"Once she was stunningly beautiful," Delphyne added. "The words of Apollo flowed through her lips like ambrosia. As an oracle, she served as a channel for his prophecies."

"Are you familiar with Elen and Sue?" the Lady asked Morgen.

The third scrying screen responded by showing images of the mother and daughter.

"I don't recognize them," said Morgen after a pause. "But Sue has a dark shadow around her, and Elen seems to be controlled by it."

"Ganieda is unraveling the Welsh riddle," the dragon disclosed.

"Both of you need to rescue the children so the ancient magic will live on," Lady Gaea said. "It all begins with Elen."

Chapter 9

The Songs of Stars

London, 21ˢᵗ Century

As the sun set over the western wall, Abigail served warm nettle soup in small ceramic bowls to those who had gathered. She knew that, once cooked down, the mineral-rich stinging nettles she had grown and gathered served as an anti-inflammatory ingredient. The soup would detoxify and help with circulation, but she never mentioned this to the group. Abigail just hoped they would feel better. She loved to cook, and this was simply another way she had of sharing her medicinal gifts.

Leisurely, the participants of the group placed their bowls in her outdoor garden sink and then departed, still smiling and chatting. With dusk, the garden became silent once again. Abigail, Nina and Ganieda sat on the grass, looking up at the night sky as the stars appeared. They had a mutual fascination with the stars that formed the Northern Cross.

"If you look closely"—Ganieda pointed toward the sky—"you can see that the Northern Cross has wings. It is known to the ancient ones as the Great Swan, or the constellation Cygnus."

Abigail imagined flying through the universe, weaving the songs of the stars with the souls of the lost and bringing the world back into harmony.

"A dream keeps visiting me," Nina told the other two women. "In it, I see Mother Gaea and a green dragon inside a misty temple. I feel they are trying to convey messages that I do not quite understand."

The night air was getting cool.

"Let's go have some tea," Ganieda said, standing up. As she walked toward the house, the healer remembered that she had also been receiving a similar dream.

Abigail joined the other two in the kitchen and boiled water in the electric kettle. She put hot water and some dried vervain leaves into a porcelain teapot, then placed a cozy in the shape of a swan over it so the tea could steep.

"It will need exactly three minutes," said Abigail. "The number of the Empress in the tarot."

The three women settled into seats around Abigail's round, wooden kitchen table. The room was small, and the radiators kept it cozy.

"I've been learning tarot," shared Nina. "I had no idea how powerful the cards can be in the right hands."

"They're a useful art if you use them well," Ganieda agreed. "Magic can be used for good or ill, and the same is true for divination."

Ganieda paused thoughtfully, then continued. "The magical arts take practice and skill, as well as inner knowing. There are many ways of tuning into the field of wisdom if we hold the right intent. Abae's herbalism is an ancient art also."

"Three witches by a cauldron." Nina chuckled.

Abigail's face grew pale. "I prefer healer." She stood up to check on the tea.

"We have been called many things," said Ganieda. "The world needs healers and light workers, even though we are often disregarded."

"I prefer to be undetected," Nina shared softly. "But I was followed home last week."

Ganieda glanced up at Nina, nodded, and then put a finger to her lips. She did not want to scare Abigail. Nina understood that some things needed to be secret. Standing now by the counter, Abigail was focused on preparing the tray for the herb tea, and she had not heard Nina's news.

"There are forces gathering," Ganieda whispered. "But let's not speak of them here. Abigail has not yet remembered her role, but you have. Isn't that true, Nimue?"

Nina stared at Ganieda for a moment, then sighed.

"I really do try to be normal," Nina said.

Ganieda chuckled, and then Nina also laughed.

"Let's see if the tarot cards can awaken a glimmer of memory," Ganieda suggested.

After carrying the tray to the table, Abigail placed a large ceramic teapot, and three teacups and saucers on the placemats. Placing a floral cozy over the teapot, they waited for the herbs to steep in the hot water. Abae sat down again with the other two women.

Nina pulled a deck of tarot cards out of her purse. Then she fanned the deck open and offered them to Ganieda, who closed her eyes and drew a card. She had picked the "I Magician" card. They all laughed with delight.

"Of course, you would pull the Magician card!" said Abigail.

"Magic," observed Nina, who then selected a card for herself. Her eyes grew wide, and she turned the card around to show Abigail and Ganieda the "0 Fool" card, which can indicate new beginnings.

"I guess I'd better just trust what is to happen next," Nina supposed.

Abigail closed her eyes and then pulled a card. "Eight of Wands, the travel card," she said, placing it on the table. "I wonder if I'll be taking a trip?"

"Maybe a journey down memory lane," Nina suggested.

Ganieda put the medicine bag that she had been wearing across her left shoulder on the empty chair beside her. Nina noticed that the feathers on the bag had fluttered gently as Ganieda set the medicine bag down on the chair.

"It's called a Crane Bag," Ganieda told them. "I carry my magical tools with me."

Opening the bag, she took out a small black purse and set it on the center of the table.

"If you are ready, I will present my silver mirror that I call my Little Albion," she told them.

Nina nodded with curiosity, but Abigail looked concerned at first. Somewhat reluctantly, she then also nodded with approval.

Ganieda untied the strings of the black purse and brought forth a silver hand-mirror. The object was nearly flat, quite reflective and circular, with a handle that curved like a willow branch. She carefully placed it on the table. Nina felt drawn to it but held herself back. Abigail had the sense that she wanted to flee the room. Ganieda noticed her response.

"Let's have some tea," Ganieda said. "It will relax us. Then we can look into the depths."

"It's a tisane," Abigail corrected her. "An herbal infusion."

Nina poured them all some of the still-warm infusion from the teapot.

Ganieda dropped a few leaves into each of their teacups.

"What is this herb?" asked Abigail.

"It's from the Foretime," said Ganieda. "It enhances creative seeing."

Nina sniffed the cup, and recognized the scent as from Apple blossoms.

"It's just flowers," Nina said encouragingly to Abigail. She took a sip. "Oh! It tastes like honey!"

Abigail looked at her cup, took a sniff and tasted the hot liquid.

"Oh gosh!" she exclaimed. "It's Otherworldly!"

"Tarot can help open the intuition, but eventually you only need a cup of tea," said Ganieda. "And one day you just see all the time."

"Is that overwhelming?" asked Abigail.

"Only if there is any fear left in you," Ganieda replied. "Why not see what's real?"

Nina felt drawn to the mirror. It seemed to sing to her, and she bent her head forward. Ganieda observed her closely.

"So, Nina," said Ganieda, "tell me what you see."

Nina shifted her focus so that she moved into a state of awareness, and gazed into the blackness. The crystalline surface seemed to open up as a dazzling gateway to another world, then pictures began to move like on a television screen. Almost immediately an image of a woman in emerald green appeared.

"Not Morgen," Nina groaned. "My nemesis."

"Morgen is a healer," said Ganieda. "The best."

Nina did not seem convinced, but she sat back and sniffed her tisane thoughtfully. "It's as though you can see the whole world through Little Albion."

"So, you are a seer," remarked Ganieda with a smile.

Nina settled back into her chair, but pushed the teacup away.

"Abae, you have a look," Ganieda prompted.

Abigail was reluctant to peer into the mirror.

"Do I have to?"

"Aren't you curious?" asked Ganieda.

Abigail sighed, then peered into the mirror. At first it all seemed black, then an image appeared. Looking puzzled, she leaned back against her seat.

"I saw two women, a man and a dragon peering at me," she told them. "So odd. The dragon seemed familiar."

"The veils are becoming thin," Nina concluded.

Abigail gave Ganieda a puzzled expression.

"I feel like I can almost remember something, but it's just beyond a thick veil."

"That's accurate," Ganieda told her. "But the veil can be removed."

Abigail rubbed the rim of her teacup nervously.

"Why are we being shown these figures?" Abigail asked. "What do they want from us?"

Nina looked at Ganieda for permission to speak and the healer nodded slowly.

"There's a spiritual battle going on," said Nina. "We can't just let the Niente win."

"Who?" asked Abigail, becoming pale.

"The Niente are ancient soulless forces who have worked against the magical people since the fall of Atlantis," Nina explained.

Ganieda slipped the silver mirror into the black purse and placed it back in her medicine bag.

"The Niente?" Abigail asked. "Are they real?"

"They are responsible for slavery, division, and the fall of civilizations," Ganieda explained. "They work against life, and they seek to destroy the magical people who work towards the health, well-being and liberation of the people."

"What do they do?"

"They enslave us if they can, or kill us," said Ganieda. "And try to steal our souls."

Nina shivered, and Abigail looked nervous.

Ganieda pulled an old scroll from her medicine sack and set it unopened on the table. Nina eyed it with curiosity.

"For a long time, we lived in harmony with the planet and each other. Our motherland Mu, and Atlantis are real. I will show you, but once you see this map your memory will return, and you may long for Elysium again."

"Elysium? Isn't that a place in Greek mythology?" asked Abigail. "A place where the souls of heroes reside inside the earth?"

"A parallel realm," Ganieda explained. "It's very beautiful and serene, more like a floating sky temple."

"Reality can be very strange," Nina reflected.

"We are currently in a similar pivotal time as when Atlantis fell in the Foretime," said Ganieda. "We are soon approaching the shifting of the ages. We have a choice. Either we will be destroyed by the power and greed of the dark magicians and all history will be erased, or we will choose to begin again and work with the changes that are coming."

Ganieda looked at Nina and Abigail who both nodded for her to continue. Uncoiling a leather string, Ganieda spread a map out in front of them. They all looked very carefully at a series of nine realms that seemed to be moving like floating islands.

"Many gods, goddesses and devas have been erased from history," said Ganieda. "Yet they remain close, in parallel dimensions."

Nina was drawn to the realm of Avalon. A silver wave of mist seemed to be flowing over it. In her aware state, her focus shifted to a floating island called Delos. Putting her finger on the location, her eyes filled with tears.

"I must visit this place."

Abigail looked at the map, her eyes growing wider.

"I feel sick," she said. "Like my skin is burning up."

"We will be tested now to discover for ourselves what is real," Ganieda told them. "We must let the traumas of the past remain in history where they belong."

Abigail was drawn to a realm called Delphi which was encircled by a green dragon. When she stood and put her finger on Delphi, the dragon arose from the map and stared at her. Abigail let out a shriek and backed up against a seated Ganieda.

"What is that?"

"Stay with it," urged Ganieda gently. "You are meeting the Python, also known as Dracaena Delphyna."

"Will she hurt me?" Abigail asked with some desperation.

"The dragon protects Lady Gaea and her oracles, and prefers to be called Delphyne."

As if in response to being acknowledged, the dragon flattened herself against the map and became part of the drawing once again. Abruptly, Abigail turned, rummaged in a cabinet, grabbed a bag of cookies and set them on the table. Sighing, she dug around in another drawer and produced a few chocolate bars.

"I need grounding," she said, snapping off a piece of chocolate.

"Let's go back outside and look at the Moon," proposed Nina. "It always helps me to know that the cosmos is assisting us."

Ganieda nodded and rolled up the map, putting it back into her Crane Bag.

Abigail hastily took three wool blankets off a bench by the door. She was trembling and the warm wool helped her relax.

"We must tune in to the higher forces and stay aligned with the proper timing of events," said Ganieda. "We will know when it is time to act."

She added, "Go ahead outside…. I'll join you in a little while."

Abigail and Nina each chose a blanket, and Nina also picked up the extra one. She then followed Abae out the door.

Ganieda had a reason for staying inside. She had a burning question that could not wait. After watching the two women leave, she took out her silver hand-mirror once again and peered into the depths.

Little Albion, show me, she said to the mirror.

Colors swirled, and Ganieda could make out a man riding a black horse. He wore a black sheepskin across his shoulders, and his clothing was also black. A long blade was fastened to the left of his ornate saddle. Its scabbard bore sacred symbols. Sensing that someone was observing him, he grabbed the hilt and partly withdrew the blade. The sword glimmered with blue light, then went still.

"Guiomar," Ganieda whispered between time and space.

The young man looked up and could see Apple blossoms falling around him like snow. Ganieda longed to join him but knew this was not the right time.

"Soon you will need to protect us," she told him between worlds.

Guiomar heard her and placed his hand on the sword that rested peacefully in his scabbard on his left side.

"I hear you, Lady Ganieda," he said. "I will come to your aid."

Guiomar's horse suddenly shied and reared. Ganieda quickly disconnected from him and the mirror went blank. The lights in the kitchen flashed on and off, then on again. Power surges were common when Otherwordly communications occurred. Ganieda quietly observed the room for a few moments to see if she had also attracted the attention of the Niente.

The kitchen was undisturbed, so she slipped Little Albion back into the black purse and placed the mirror in the medicine bag. Ganieda sighed, sensing that it was only a matter of time before the dark magicians located her. She wished to avoid another battle with the Niente.

It's better to be unseen, she thought.

The night was inviting, and Ganieda wandered out beneath the stars to join Nina and Abae. The two women were standing and gazing up at the bejeweled sky. Taking the extra blanket from Nina, Ganieda asked Abae how she felt.

"I feel scared," admitted a trembling Abigail, as she stared up at the Northern Cross. Ganieda took her by the hand, and soon Abae's shaking stopped.

"Let's just enjoy the moment," said Nina.

All three women lay down in the grass, covering themselves with their blankets. Ganieda wondered how she could help Abae remember her original self. Under the stars, she asked three times for help.

Chapter 10

Ganieda's Request

Elysium (The Sky Temple)
In-Between Time

Lady Gaea, Morgen, Accolon and the dragon Delphyne had gathered in the Sky Temple and were observing the triple scrying screens on the black pyramid. In the first screen, they witnessed Ganieda holding her silver mirror and her conversation with Guiomar. In the second screen, they watched the Guiomar, Lord of Avalon, riding his black steed through the sacred forests.

"Ganieda always did have a fondness for that chap, Guiomar," Accolon noted.

"It's unrequited love," Morgen added, "the sort that tugs at your heart the most."

Accolon looked at Morgen and gave her a loving smile.

"Ganieda asked for help three times," noted the dragon, interrupting the intimacy.

"Three is the magic number," said Lady Gaea. "Let's bring Ganieda to Elysium."

Morgen poured herself a cup of tea, and offered a cup to Accolon who declined.

Lady Gaea sipped Rose Tea thoughtfully.

"I'll go collect Ganieda," Accolon said. "She knows me."

Accolon walked to the edge of the temple grounds, then gazed down through sky at the moat-like sea far below. His long dark hair flew madly around his head in the wind. Grabbing long strands of hair, he made a man bun. Looking down, he was hesitant to move. He took off his glasses, then glanced at Morgen for guidance. His pale blue eyes sparkled like the sea, and Morgen found him once again to be enticingly beautiful.

"Best to walk to Ganieda in the dream time," Lady Gaea offered.

"The mist is the easiest way to time travel," snorted the dragon. "May I? I'd be happy to help."

They all nodded with approval. Accolon re-joined Morgen and pulled out a plush crimson chair from beside the Round Table for himself, and then chose a yellow chair for Ganieda. He then patted to the rose-colored chair beside him, encouraging Morgen to join him.

She raised an eyebrow before seating herself. "I didn't know you were so fond of Ganieda," remarked Morgen.

"She's my cousin," Accolon explained. "Mother's side."

The conversation was interrupted by Delphyne who had stood up on her haunches and was growing larger by the moment. The dragon was able to change her size at will. Her usual horse-size expanded to a terrifying magical height of thirteen feet, which did not include her long barbed tail, that whipped around like a snake. Delphyne began breathing a fiery mist. Golden flames and silver stars magically flickered across the stone surface of the Round Table. Soon the entirety of the Sky Temple was engulfed in white.

As the steam cleared, Ganieda could be seen sitting in the yellow chair and blinking. Noticing that she was beside the Round Table, Ganieda bent down and kissed the surface of the template of Logres.

"I've missed you," she said, stroking the table.

The Round Table shuddered and sent out rose-pink rays of light. Ganieda looked at the magical team that had gathered beside her.

"Lady Gaea," said Ganieda with a respectful bow of her head. "It has been a long time since I have seen you." She nodded respectfully toward the dragon and Morgen, and then offered Accolon a large grin.

"Hello, cousin. It's been a while." She stood up and gave him a peck on both cheeks. "I haven't seen you since Camelot!"

Accolon blushed and Morgen watched them closely, wondering if she should feel envy.

After looking around Gaea's Sky Temple with curiosity, Ganieda turned her attention back to the Round Table. She observed the stone surface with fondness, marveling at the stars and seeds. She could see the claw mark where one large pearl had been inserted.

"My tear," said Delphyne. "When I cry, I make pearls and the table likes them."

Morgen pushed a cup and saucer in Ganieda's direction, and the newcomer noticed that the roses on the cup seemed to be perpetually blossoming.

"I was trying to get some guidance about Abae," Ganieda said, changing the subject. She took a sip of the infusion, which confirmed her suspicions. "By the way, I prefer Apple Blossom tisane to Rose Tea."

Morgen snapped her fingers, sniffed the teacup, and handed the Apple Blossom variety to Ganieda, who took it with a respectful nod.

"Apple Blossom Tea makes me miss Avalon," said Morgen.

"I'll second that," Accolon agreed.

The dragon chuckled, sending up a puff of smoke.

"Why am I sitting at the Round Table with my good Companions?" Ganieda asked.

"Companions, indeed," purred the dragon. "It's a good term."

"Earth is still an invisible battleground between the Niente and the Companions," said Lady Gaea.

"The Niente are the ones who agree to oppose us so we can have a good drama," explained the dragon, raising her large head and peering over the table at Ganieda.

"They are definitely entertaining in a dark sort of way," Morgen concurred.

"We will need Abae to help activate the Planetary Earth Star," said Lady Gaea.

"Abae is in the healing garden," Ganieda told them. "In Hampstead with Nina."

"Ganieda," said Lady Gaea with a serious tone. "Abae will only fully remember her next role when she meets Taliesin. Only then can they both fulfill their twenty-first century destiny."

"Why the poet?"

"It's time to make peace with the past and turn toward a brighter future," Lady Gaea explained. "Sometimes we need to upgrade our archetype. She plays a pivotal role in the New Time. Please help her remember."

"I will do my best," Ganieda promised. "What's her new archetype?"

The dragon began to breathe mist again and soon, like a cloud blown by a gentle breeze, Ganieda was back in Hampstead.

Chapter 11
Abigail's Far Memory
London, 21st Century

When Ganieda opened her eyes, she was lying in the healing garden beside Abigail and Nina who were discussing the nighttime sky. Although she had visited Elysium, which was as close and far away as a dream, it was as if no time had passed. No one else had glimpsed Gaea's Sky Temple. Ganieda pondered the oddities of interdimensional time travel between parallel realms of existence.

Beyond the garden walls, an ambulance passed by on the way to the Royal Free Hospital, its siren blaring. The three healers sent loving light to whoever was in the vehicle. As the sound disappeared into the hum of the city, Nina stood up and began folding her blanket.

"I promised Blaise and Daphne I'd be back in time for dinner," she said. "Blaise suggested that he had something special to share with me, perhaps about the magical history of the Round Table."

Ganieda opened her mouth but then decided not to speak about the Round Table yet. She knew the wisdom of Logres had a way of revealing itself when the moment was right.

Nina looked at Abigail, who gazed back at her with soulful dark eyes. She wondered if it were time to reveal her ancient identity as Nimue, or to mention the challenges that awaited them, but decided to allow the peace of the night to linger.

Life will bring the awareness soon enough, Nina thought.

Ganieda caught Nina's gaze. "You are safe tonight but go straight home."

Nina nodded to Ganieda, then gave Abigail a peck on the cheek. The other two women watched her walk out of the gate and into the shadows. The waxing crescent Moon rested like a smile in the sky.

"Nina is a true mystery," said Abigail.

"She's more magical than you know," noted Ganieda. "And good to have on our team. Let's go to the healing room."

Ganieda did not want to retraumatize Abigail and knew she had to be gentle while she awakened the far memories. She motioned for Abigail to follow her inside. They walked through the garden, ducked under the ivy covered archway, and went into the bungalow.

Abigail blinked as she readjusted to the lights in the healing room. Ganieda pointed to a bench in front of the color potion shelf. Abigail sat down with Ganieda standing behind her. Staring at the color potions, Abigail felt they must hold some ancient secret that was awaiting her acknowledgment.

"Do you know that the British Isles have been a place where people around the globe have come to learn about magic for thousands of years?" asked Ganieda.

"It certainly feels that way," responded Abigail, closing her eyes and enjoying the warmth that ran through Ganieda's hands and down her spine.

"Even the Greek and Roman oracles would come to strengthen their skills here."

"I have heard people say London once had a Star Temple," said Abigail. "A place people came to remember their life purpose and mission."

"The Planetary Earth Star is still here and will soon be fully active again," Ganieda revealed. "The northern tip of the star is in Hampstead Heath, which is where the new star is awakening. Walking there can help seekers find their place in the world and remind them of their human mission. I also know that the Niente would like to block this awareness."

"The dark forces can be strong."

"Ultimately, Earth will not allow the Niente to win," said Ganieda. "Have you been recording your dreams?"

Abigail smiled and produced a journal, showing Ganieda that she had indeed been creating colorful drawings and writing poetic fragments, as well as notes of her dreams of the faerie folk. Ganieda noticed that she had drawn flames around the edges of most of the pages.

"Have you heard of Elysium?" Ganieda asked as she flipped through the intricately drawn images of the fey.

"Of course, I have. It's the Greek Otherworld," replied Abigail. "It's the land of eternal youth where heroes go."

Abigail took the journal from Ganieda and scanned through a few sketches until she found an image of green fields, pomegranate trees with ripe red fruit, and a blue sky with a radiant sun above. Sapphire blue sky surrounded an open circular temple supported by white pillars that stood high up on a mountain peak. She showed Ganieda, who smiled and nodded with approval.

"Are you ready to look more deeply into who you were in the past?" asked Ganieda, taking the seat beside Abigail.

She took the silver mirror out of her Crane Bag.

Abigail hesitated but accepted the shimmering mirror into her trembling hands.

"I feel so hot," said Abae, looking at the crystalline reflective surface of Little Albion. At first, all she saw were refracted lights, and then images began to appear. She gasped and dropped the mirror.

Ganieda grabbed the object from where it had landed on a soft area rug.

Abae's eyes were closed, and she was shaking.

"What did you see?" asked Ganieda, studying Abigail's demeanor. She paused, then suggested, "You might want to lay on the floor and look again."

Abae nodded and found a yoga mat to curl up on. Ganieda put a blanket over the woman, then placed a pillow under her head. Ganieda sat on the floor beside Abae's left shoulder and handed her the mirror.

I must be by her most clairaudient ear, thought Ganieda.

"I am in a cave that is full of white steam," said Abigail.

Ganieda noticed that the mirror did not shatter and so the truth was being observed.

"It is an ancient temple, the pillars are carved with symbols, and there are hanging baskets overflowing with medicinal herbs. When people are there to see me, I come out. In the distance, beyond the people, I see the sapphire sea, with ripples of dark blues and greens flowing with the multiple currents. As I watch, the sea becomes lighter and clearer, almost transparent. The land is desert with a few cypresses and other small trees. I believe this is ancient Greece."

"What else do you see?" asked Ganieda.

"I am wearing a light-colored dress and people are coming to hear me speak. Steam rises up from below me. I am standing on large rocks that cover a misty cave. The scent is intoxicating, almost overwhelming. I can smell herbs and incense. A dragon sleeps at my feet. Oh...."

"What is it?"

"I am an Oracle of Delphi," said Abigail. "I am attuned to Apollo."

"What is your name?"

"The Oracle Abae," she remembered and laughed. "You have always called me Abae."

"And what is your purpose now?" asked Ganieda.

Abigail paused, listening to the push and suck of the waves of the Aegean Sea. It seemed that a man's voice was also speaking through the wind. Apollo seized Abae's body, took over her voice, and spoke through her.

"Solve the riddles so Gaea can reincarnate," Apollo uttered.

Abae was quiet, listening to the various voices that spoke to her psyche. Apollo flew out of her body and back to Olympus. She observed men coming to tear down the temples and statues.

No! Abae cried, but no sound came from her lips.

"Step outside of the Oracle Abae's body and view the lifetime from here," Ganieda explained gently. "Come back to the present time."

Abae started to shake. "I have snakes on my arms..."

"Stretch and yawn," Ganieda instructed, as she took the mirror. "You are in the twenty-first century and all is well here."

Abigail opened her eyes. She looked startled but also fully alive.

"I want to see what happened next," Abae stated.

Abigail received the mirror from Ganieda and gazed into it. She could see the Oracle Abae's body burning inside a Temple.

"I was burned alive," she stated flatly. "I want to see where my soul went next. I am relieved that we keep going to another time."

Abae was not focused on her body but on another island. Ganieda could see that Abae had reincarnated as a druidess.

"The veil has been removed," Ganieda related. "You became a seer of Mona, a Banduri of the Druid Isle."

Abae sat up and rested her body against Ganieda's solid form. She pushed the silver mirror away. "That's enough for now."

"*Ynys Môn* is the ancient name of Mona," Ganieda persisted, not wanting to lose the potency of the moment. "It's the poetic name, the one most linked to the bard Taliesin. Have you heard of him?"

"No," replied Abigail. "All I know is that I thought I would be safe amongst the Druids. But I sense something dreadful happened in Mona…. in *Ynys Môn*… I have refused to see visions since that lifetime. I know that without scrying."

"Look into the mirror one more time."

Abigail grimaced but looked into the mirror again, then gasped and put it on the floor.

"A man was trying to kill me," she shared, panting. "A man with cropped curly hair. He wore what seemed to be silver armor with an eagle on his breastplate. He seemed Roman. It was so real!"

Abigail stared at Ganieda. Her hands were trembling.

"There were men with torches," Abae continued. "They saw me…."

"See it, then let it go."

Ganieda pulled Abigail into her arms.

"Come back to the present moment," directed Ganieda. "You are here with me now and safe."

"It has something to do with Elen!" Abigail exclaimed. "And enchantment."

"Yes," Ganieda agreed. "It seems that it is time to solve one of the oldest puzzles of the British Isles."

"It's about the destruction of *Ynys Môn,*" said Abigail, as this sunk into her awareness. "The site of the Druids, and probably the last that was seen of the Oracles."

"The first century was the time of the dismembering of the spiritual people," Ganieda told her. "It's been too dangerous for us to gather for a very long time, at least on surface Earth."

"Somehow Elen kept the magic alive in Welsh forests," Abigail added, as this knowledge came through to her. "She stayed hidden, until... oh... That is enough."

Abigail put her face on Ganieda's shoulder and allowed herself to cry with loud, even fierce sobs.

"They cut off her antlers."

Ganieda pulled a red apple from her Crane Bag, which was resting beside them on the floor, and she handed it to Abae.

"It's a healing apple from Avalon," said Ganieda. "The magic lives on, and so does Elen. It will be your role to ensure that she does survive."

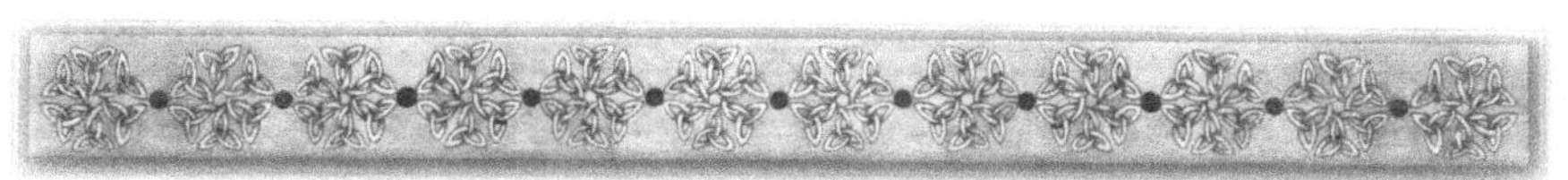

Chapter 12

Riddles Of the Ancestors

Elysium (The Sky Temple)
In-Between Time

"I'm finding the destruction of the temples to be really upsetting," said Delphyne with a snort. "And I never liked being called your son, Python. What idiots."

"Now, now," Lady Gaea said, soothing the dragon.

"Why do we need to see all of this anyway?" the dragon asked, circling the table and then lying down with a thudding crash.

"There are ancestral riddles that need to be solved," said Lady Gaea. "So we can all step into the New Time."

"What is the first riddle?" asked Morgen.

"How is the soul of a nation broken?"

Morgen looked at the Lady, then at the black pyramid. In response, all three screens began to flash. On the first screen she saw the Pythia muttering her prophecies., and the priests standing around her trying to comprehend her words. She looked over at the dragon, who appeared to

77

have fallen asleep. She had heard tales of Apollo murdering the Python, but the image did not appear on the scrying screens.

She walked around the table sunwise and Accolon joined her. On the second screen, they saw the Temple of Delphi burning and knew it marked the end of an era. The third screen flashed, and they watched as a new village was built over the ruins.

The first screen changed focus, exhibiting scenes of the Roman Empire's impact on Britainnia. They were well organized. Roads were being built, and towns emerged. They functioned under new laws. She contemplated the Roman Empire's impact on Celtic women. The second screen flickered with images of beloved Mona burning, the cries as the Druid order died and the soul of the land broke into pieces. Accolon took Morgen's hand and gave it a comforting squeeze. The third screen displayed scenes of Boudica, Queen of the Iceni tribe, who revolted against the Roman Armies.

"Boudica's revolt never ended," the Lady said, also witnessing the scrying screens. "She just took her fury, and her daughters, underground."

"Go back further," the dragon said without lifting her head. "It gets better eventually."

In response the scrying screens exhibited images from ancient Egypt, Mesopotamia, then the fabled city of Atlantis with its concentric rings.

The first scrying screen showed scenes from the Sky Temple looking down, and they could see an island in the Atlantic Ocean between Ireland and America. The second screen zoomed in, revealing a Golden Temple that stood on a mount radiating golden light. A path made of glittering gemstones led to the temple. On either side, waterfalls flowed with luminous sapphire water. There were moats with concentric circles that protected the temple.

"The Atlantean Temple looks like your Sky Temple," Morgen said.

"Elysium lives on even now," the Lady acknowledged, "in a lenticular cloud that only mystics can find."

The images on the black pyramid ceased and the screens went dark. Morgen considered all she had seen.

"To break the spirit of the land," Morgen reflected, "you kill its spiritual people."

"Not my favorite answer," Accolon said, "but true."

"Second riddle—how do you then heal the soul of the land?" asked Lady Gaea.

"No one knows," said Morgen.

"Perhaps some do," countered Lady Gaea.

Delphyne opened her eyes and gazed at the Lady.

"The dragons know how," Delphyne claimed. "To heal the land, you find the spiritual people and bring them home."

"We have been trying to accomplish that since the fall of Rome when the soldiers finally left Britain," Accolon said. "That's when Camelot arose."

"For a while," said the dragon. "Celtic tribes like to fight."

Accolon seemed to become infuriated, and he stomped out the back of the Sky Temple down some steps into a meadow filled with blooming flowers. Morgen started to follow him, but Lady Gaea put her hand out and stopped her.

"He must learn to forgive the foibles of humankind."

"It's not easy," the dragon vented.

"Third riddle," Lady Gaea stated. "How do you heal the spiritual people if they have become a broken people?"

Morgen looked out at Accolon, who was pacing amongst the flowers.

"Help them find love and community again," Morgen replied.

"And purpose," Delphyne added.

Chapter 13

Elen's Trackways

London, 21st Century

Abigail's healing group reconvened the following Wednesday as usual. It was a sunny day; the birds were singing, and the garden's multi-colored Dahlia blooms were still vibrant. Fragrant Star Jasmine perfumed the air, and the climbing Hydrangeas that ascended the side of the house produced a spray of white flowers. When Sue and Elen arrived, they took their seats in the group. Ganieda stood in the middle of the garden with Abigail and Nina on either side.

"Take a moment to fully experience the exquisiteness of this garden that Abae so carefully tends," Ganieda said to the group. "Our role is to care for life."

Collectively they breathed in the splendor of the day, which seemed to lighten the mood of everyone present.

Smiling, Elen walked over to Abigail and handed her a sketchbook.

"Your flowers are magnificent," Elen said. "I have drawn a few from memory."

Abigail looked at the wildly creative flowers Elen had drawn. Each blossom had a Sylph sitting beside it.

"These are beautiful," Abigail replied. She observed Elen carefully and realized that she felt innately protective of the girl.

"I have been keeping all my dreams and visions in here." Elen opened her journal to another page. She showed the images to Ganieda, who noticed that although Elen's face was shadowed by her floppy green hat, her eyes were sparkling with happiness.

Ganieda scanned through the sketches, and she could see that Elen had drawn a series of pictures of forest scenes with deer as well as women wearing antlers.

Noticing that the healing group had formed, Ganieda used her *Kardia* pendant to cast a magical healing circle around them. The work had begun. Little did most of the participants know that light was now flowing to them from the Foretime. Ganieda nodded to Abigail and Nina to carry on with the light work.

Ganieda knew it was time to heal individual souls. She motioned for Elen to follow her inside the house.

Once they were in the potions room, Ganieda asked Elen to select a color bottle. Elen picked a sky blue and light green bottle.

"How can it be two colors?" Elen asked.

"There is oil infused with herbs over colored water."

"What does it mean?" Elen turned toward the healer while holding the bottle upright in one hand.

Ganieda was swaying. A vision had come over her. She saw Elen in full horned headdress standing beside a hide tent. There were other young women around her, and they were all involved in ritual work. Ganieda knew that the woman she stood beside was none other than Elen of the Ways, a very ancient and magical deity. She paused for a moment wondering how Elen had lost her magic over the centuries. Images flooded her consciousness related to the many slayings of the deer woman Elen had once been. A terrible vision flowed through her mind of broken antlers and a decimated body. Elen of the Ways and the health of magical Wales were intertwined.

"Elen," she said. "Would you like to remember who you were a long time ago? When you were very magical and powerful?"

"But I'm nothing, definitely not magical," Elen responded. "My mother tells me that all the time."

"I give you permission to be magical again. You have been all along."

Ganieda was overcome by another vision. She saw the girl as an ancient shamanic deity of the land. The healer blinked, wondering at the power and beauty of the ancient Elen, an antlered deity who was surrounded by shimmering starry trackways.

"What do you see?" asked Elen, blinking her large doe eyes.

"That you and your mother have some karma to work out. Sometimes old enemies incarnate into the same family to solve ancestral riddles."

Elen was gazing at the sky blue and light green potion. She held it up to the light, then placed it against her heart.

"It's the color combination for Lady Gaea," Ganieda told her. "We are all gathering in honor of Mother Earth. It is time to heal the land and feel at home again."

"The colors make me feel so happy," Elen shared. "I want to feel this way always."

"There is more to this world than most people understand," said Ganieda. "It's holographic. We live in multiple dimensions."

"I understand," responded Elen. "I see that when I draw."

"We should go and join the others."

Ganieda walked toward the door, then turned back toward the girl. "Wait, I want you to see something."

Ganieda took Little Albion out of her Crane Bag and offered it to Elen. The girl looked carefully at the silver mirror but did not immediately accept the scrying tool.

"This mirror will show you who you truly are," said Ganieda. "Take your cap off and ask her to show you the image of your most ancient self. Little Albion does not lie."

Elen nodded, then carefully grasped the silver mirror. As she gazed at her reflection, her eyes filled with tears.

"I have antlers," Elen said. "And I'm beautiful."

"You were a guide for kings and queens, for heroes and heroines," revealed Ganieda. "A magical way shower for nature and the human soul since the Stone Age. You were called Elen of the Ways."

"I'm remembering," said Elen, gazing into the distance. "I hear drumming. I sense a deer running in the mist. Maybe I don't even know when I guide souls. I see shimmering trackways."

"Let's take Little Albion to your mother and let her look," Ganieda told her slipping the mirror into the girl's handbag. "And there is no reason to wear that cap anymore. You are beautiful as you are."

Elen and Ganieda walked quietly back to the circle of chairs in the garden. The scrying mirror in the black cloth was still in Elen's possession. Sue was sitting between the two healers, and she looked slightly nauseated. Abigail looked up and gazed with curiosity at the pair of women reentering the circle. She recognized the twinkle in Elen's eyes.

"Thank you, Sue, for receiving the healing," said Ganieda, motioning for the woman to rise. "It is now Elen's turn for some group healing so she can integrate."

Sue moved reluctantly so that Elen could take the "hot seat" and the healers could pass their warm hands over the girl.

"You stupid girl, you took your hat off," Sue snapped.

Elen ignored her mother and sat down on the healing chair. When she looked up, her eyes were full of tears. Abigail was furious but held her tongue.

"I'm not sure I want to be the center of attention just now," Elen told them, a tear rolling down her left cheek.

Sue was glaring at Ganieda and Abigail scowled at Sue.

Oh dear, Nina thought as she prepared for spiritual warfare. She glanced at Abigail, who frowned. They continued to send healing light to Elen.

"How dare you fill my daughter's head with your nonsense," Sue hissed to Ganieda.

Sue tried to grab Elen's hand and drag her from the hot seat. Abigail stepped forward to assist the girl, but Ganieda held up her hand demanding peace.

"You have no idea what you're doing," accused the angry mom. "She is damaged enough without your wild fantasies messing her up even more. What have you been telling her?"

"Maybe things that you forgot to," said Ganieda. "Like who she truly is."

Sue tried again to pull her daughter out of the healing chair. Elen resisted the tug of her mother, and instead sat firmly. Rooted to the earth, she successfully slid her hand from her mother's grip.

However, Sue bumped Elen's handbag, and it fell to the ground. Little Albion slipped out, uncovered as planned. Seeing the silver mirror, Sue grabbed it. Elen let out a shriek of protest, but Ganieda chuckled.

"Why don't you gaze into the mirror, Sue, and discover your true face?"

Sue hesitated, then faced the hand glass. She seemed mesmerized and then horrified. "I'm no bloody Roman general," she shouted. There was the sound of a crack, then a sob as Elen realized Little Albion had shattered.

"The only thing that heals the mirror is truth," said Ganieda calmly. "Sue, why not say, 'I am a Roman general,' and just see what happens?"

Sue laughed. "So, you know how to mend shattered glass? Okay then… I am a Roman general."

Sue's smile vanished as the silver mirror healed in front of her.

"Why not say, 'I once was Gaius Suetonius Paulinus'?"

Sue stared at the mirror, enchanted and yet horrified.

"I once was Gaius Suetonius Paulinus," she said, and then remembering a history lesson added, "the one who massacred the druids of Anglesey."

From a side angle, Ganieda glimpsed the image in the mirror and could see a tough-looking Roman general with a closely cropped beard wearing a galea, a metal helmet.

Sue blinked, then threw the mirror to the ground. It did not shatter.

"The whole lot of you are insane and should be incarcerated!" Sue shouted. "I am tired of your magic tricks!"

Ganieda observed Sue and Elen carefully. Elen's eyes were shut but Sue's words and energy were cutting. What was Elen supposed to do with the dark energy coming at her? Abigail's face began to turn red with fury, and she felt like tossing Sue out of the group. She looked at Nina, who merely shrugged.

"So what if I was a Roman commander?" Sue barked. "That doesn't help me now."

"You could ask for forgiveness for the murders," said Ganieda. "You could ask for forgiveness for breaking the soul of a nation."

"What hogwash! You make stuff up. Nothing that you tell me to do ever works," Sue told Ganieda vindictively. "My suffering never ends!"

Nothing. The words resounded in Ganieda's ears. Sue was somehow linked to the Niente, but how?

"And I thought you were so special," Sue finished with a snort. "And you two are even worse," she added, glaring first at Abigail, then at Nina. "Three rotten witches. I should have you all arrested for practicing medicine without a license."

Elen let out a gasp. "Mother, don't be so horrible."

Sue tugged at her daughter's hand again, but Elen remained rooted to the chair—as if by magic.

"And put your hat on so people don't stare at your hair or the weird nubs that mark you."

"Mother, you are soulless," snapped Elen.

Ganieda felt protective but refused to be emotionally triggered. Little Albion had revealed Sue's past. Sue was trying to block Elen from living an ancient mission. The healer summoned her inner power, and then she cast a glamor to knock the negative words and thoughts out of her energy field, and also out of the healing circle. She called healing green rays from the earth up into her body and additional violet ones down from the sky. This was indiscernible to all without inner sight, but the entire healing group sensed the electricity in the air. At Ganieda's command, two invisible shields came together above the group forming the *vesica piscis*. The central almond shape of the mandorla locked into her auric field and around the group. With this ancient healing magic, no dark lords could stay.

Sue began to squirm and back away.

"Rotten witch, vile creature of the shadows," Sue hissed.

"Sue, you may leave the group now," Ganieda instructed. "This is a place for positive support."

The other two healers seemed shocked but continued to send healing light to Elen. The young woman ignored her mother and unrelentingly sat with her eyes closed absorbing the healing energy.

After a while, Ganieda picked up the silver mirror from the ground where Sue had tossed it.

"The work of Little Albion is done," Ganieda voiced, putting the mirror into her Crane Bag. "I reclaim her."

Sue had backed away from the circle but continued to glare at Ganieda, who smiled in return. Nina started humming to calm the dynamic tension. Abigail sent light.

She's definitely a moth, Ganieda thought to herself. *And one of the Niente, a soul destroyer. But not this time... I won't let her.*

"You call yourself a healer," Sue hissed. "You just make everything worse."

"Abigail and Nina, take over for a bit," Ganieda directed. "I must tune in to see what is going on. I feel some foul play at work. Don't let Elen leave yet."

"I'll do my best," said Nina, looking doubtfully at Sue who was marching around the garden like an angry solider.

Ganieda walked under some blossoming Wisteria and then back inside the bungalow. Once in the color healing room, Ganieda sat down on the bench by the potions. She took out her silver mirror and gazed into it until Lady Gaea's face became clear.

"I need the help of Elysium," Ganieda stated.

At once, the dragon mist surrounded her and Ganieda moved through space and time to the Sky Temple.

Chapter 14
Merlin's Serpent Staff
Elysium (The Sky Temple)
In-Between Time

The sleeves of Lady Gaea's blue and green cloak draped across the Round Table. Her fingers scanned the gemstones as if searching for an answer. Astrological symbols were starting to emerge on the Round Table, forming a celestial wheel. This time she noticed Capricorn, the goatfish, the shape Pan can take when escaping monsters. The scythe shaped glyph of Saturn was in the realm of the eighth house glowing bright and then fading. She thought it symbolic of the change she was experiencing.

Morgen noticed the placement of Saturn.

"Change is upon us," Lady Gaea told her. "Ganieda is traveling through the mist and will join us now."

Ganieda sat beside Accolon blinking. The dragon diminished its size and rested.

"Have a chocolate. We observed the healing circle today," said Morgen, sliding a box of chocolate-covered truffles in Ganieda's direction.

Ganieda selected a white chocolate truffle.

"One thing I like about slipping between worlds is that I can take the weight off," Morgen shared. "Then again, maybe that's the magic of the chocolates working."

Ganieda picked up the truffle and nibbled at it. "Delicious." She smiled at Morgen as she continued to chew.

"We have been observing Abae's healing circle for a while," said Lady Gaea. "Good work is being done there. Now, of course, the Niente are trying to infiltrate and cause discord. Good work with the mandorla."

"Sue has not changed much over the ages," noted Morgen with a grimace. "She is one of the Niente assigned to keep Elen imprisoned in confusion. It's a favorite spell of the dark magicians."

"I had that feeling," Ganieda agreed.

"Many of the Niente are still unknown," Lady Gaea told them. "They hide, often in political, educational, military or religious groups, places where they know they can abuse power and bend people's minds toward chaos and destruction. Some are parents."

"I'm starting to think that being called a rotten witch is a good thing," Ganieda said with a giggle.

Morgen let out an owl-like hoot, and they all laughed.

"I would like to know how to break this spell that is upon Elen," Ganieda declared.

"It's time to call upon the ancient ones for guidance," Lady Gaea articulated.

Ganieda took off her pendant and placed Kardia on the center of the Round Table, which shook violently. A moment earlier, the table had just looked like an old, pockmarked slab of meteorite. Once her star touched the Round Table, the ancient seeds and gemstones remembered her. A strong breeze blew across the room and the air was filled with sparkles. Ganieda gasped when she saw her old friend, the silver and gold butterfly.

"*Elen is the Way,*" *said the butterfly.* "*She has been flying between worlds since the Stone Age.*"

"*Merlin?*" *asked Ganieda.*

The little butterfly twitched and then Merlin stood in the Sky Temple.

"*Brother!*" *Ganieda stood and gave him a loving embrace.*

Merlin looked around the room, giving each deity a nod of recognition, and then his eyes rested on the Round Table.

"*The template of Logres has been well hidden by Lady Gaea.*" *He bowed respectfully in her direction.*

"*We will need your Serpent Staff soon, and Adhan's Moon Dish,*" *the Lady told Merlin.* "*Meanwhile, Elen, our little sun ray, needs assistance. Elen is an elemental spirit of the old trackways. She has been under attack since the fall of the Llewellyn dynasty. Before that*

The tetrahedron emerged from the table and the first screen revealed the image of a Welsh fortress.

Morgen pushed some popcorn in Merlin's direction.

"*This is becoming quite intriguing,*" *said Morgen.* "*Do you think folks can put aside their differences and gather for the New Time?*"

Merlin took a fistful of popcorn and chewed thoughtfully.

"*I need to find the Serpent Staff.*"

"*I will reveal the location of the Caduceus when the time is right,*" *Ganieda whispered.*

They all observed Elen transforming from young woman, to doe, to an antlered deity. The second screen showed a scene from the 13th century, the moment that Elen's heart broke and she lost her way.

Chapter 15
Llywelyn the Last
Dolwyddelan Castle, Wales, 1282

"Llywelyn ap Gruffudd, you're in great danger," Elen said, looking across the Snowdonia mountains from the roof of the fortress of Dolwyddelan.

Llywelyn gazed at the antlered deity, sensing the protective magic she had woven around him and his lineage for centuries.

"If anything happens to me, you must protect my daughter," Llywelyn replied.

He also peered across the mountains, but did not sense the dark clouds gathering.

"Gwenllian is only a baby," Elen pointed out. "Her mother has died, and she cannot thrive without you."

"Nothing will harm us," Llywelyn insisted. "We have your magic."

He touched her antlers, then her cheek. She blushed.

"Magic can only protect you when you're living in full alignment as our prince and leader."

Llywelyn leaned forward and kissed her on the mouth. Elen paused, then licked her lips and finally backed away from him. Gazing into his eyes, she felt such a rush of love that she moved forward and kissed him in return. Their fawn-colored hair mingled in the breeze.

"I bestow kingship on you," Elen proclaimed.

She leaned forward and placed her left antler on his forehead.

Off in the distance, there was the bleating of sheep. For a long moment, Elen and Llywelyn looked from the top of Dolwyddelan Castle at the cold stream that ran down the mountain slopes and at the sheep that grazed by the stones that stood like dragons in the green landscape.

"If you lose your way, I'll wait for you always," she promised.

Elen watched as Llywelyn walked away from her down the stone steps, then past the ramparts that kept them safe. He mounted his chestnut stallion and gave Elen a wave, then turned and galloped down the steep slope and out of view. She knew he would not return.

Baby Gwenllian let out a cry, but Elen did not respond to the child. She knew the child's nurse would come soon. Instead, she wept, shape-shifted into a deer, then ran down the slope following Llewellyn. But she had been seen. Six men grabbed her and pinned her to the forest floor. A dark magician approached and began to chant.

London, 21st Century

Ganieda opened her eyes. She knew the spell, also how to counter it. With gratitude, she returned to the healing group. Nina and Abigail chatted casually but kept an eye on Sue, who stood nearby, still grimacing.

"I'm going to call the police when I get home," Sue threatened, but they ignored her.

Elen was blinking her bright eyes at Ganieda, awaiting some wisdom.

"There is unfinished business," Ganieda whispered to Elen. "I must do a soul retrieval to free you. I need your permission. Do I have it?"

"Yes, of course." Elen blinked again.

"I'll break the spell on your behalf," said Ganieda. "I'll explain more later. It will benefit all of us."

"Thank you."

"And Sue," Ganieda said turning to Elen's mother. "I love the Hampstead police. Go ahead and invite them over."

The sun set as the healing group concluded, casting golden light over the women. Ganieda watched Sue snatch Elen's arm, but the girl pulled away from her mother and walked of her own volition.

"We have an issue," Ganieda told Nina, after walking up to her in the garden.

"What is it now?" Nina asked.

"Elen is an ancient deity who has lost her way because of a spell cast on her by the dark magicians," Ganieda revealed. "I watched her shape-shift several times. She loved Llywelyn ap Gruffudd, and when he died, she was overwhelmed. Her head and antlers probably still grace some old castle."

"She loved Llywelyn ap Gruffudd, the last native prince of Wales?" asked Nina.

"We had great hopes for him," Ganieda remembered. "And then Edward betrayed him…." Her words trailed off as though she did not want to recount the horrors of history.

"That was centuries ago," said Nina.

"Elen was Llywelyn's guardian," Ganieda pointed out. "And when he died, so did the soul of Wales."

"His soul feels at peace," noted Nina, after tuning in.

"Yes," said Ganieda. "I sense that he has moved on to happier hunting grounds. But Elen's soul still waits for him, even if she does not remember. As I said, there is unfinished business. Elen also promised to guard Gwenllian, his baby daughter, but she could not. I sense Gwenllian was abandoned by her tribe and remains imprisoned in the astral plane."

Nina groaned and Ganieda looked even more pale than usual.

"Should you take Elen to the fortress?" Nina asked.

"She's not ready," Ganieda stated. "Elen is just starting to remember who she is." "And Sue is doing everything she can to block it," Nina added.

"I can't understand why human beings are so cruel." Ganieda shook her head, pink fury raising up in her cheeks. "We must go to the fortress of Dolwyddelan and call back her soul. To break the spell, it is imperative that we stand in the place where the magic was stolen from the Welsh people."

Nina shuddered, the asked, "What happened to the child?"

"Gwenllian died as a middle aged woman after spending her life in a convent. However, the promise to protect her was made at Dolwyddelan Castle. If we are going break the spell placed upon Elen, we must stand in the place where the words were uttered. It's time to make a trip to Betws-y-Coed. Dolwyddelan is not far from there, although now it is only a ruin."

"I love the Snowdonia mountains," said Nina, but a chill ran up her spine.

"We also need to find Elen's antlered crown and reinstate her as Elen of the Ways so that her magic returns. This soul retrieval will require an actual visit to the fortress and perhaps an encounter with the Ninete."

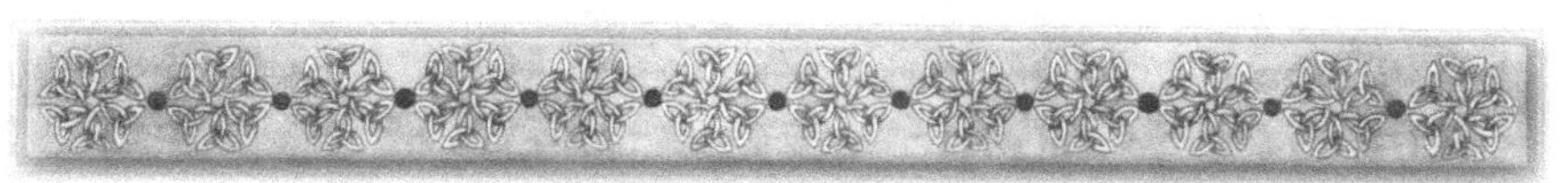

Chapter 16

Finding Gwenllian

Wales, 21ˢᵗ Century

he next morning, Ganieda and Nina were able to catch a fast train from Euston Station to Llandudno Junction. After disembarking, they rented a car, and it took just over half an hour to drive to the fortress of Dolwyddelan. At first, they could not see it, but soon the mist cleared, and the tower appeared.

They parked in a farmyard and then walked the long row of damp, moss-covered stone steps up a muddy hillside to a road that led past a flock of sheep to the ruins of the fortress. Ganieda had hardly said a word throughout the entire journey, and Nina had simply held space for the wizardess to work her magic. A final set of crooked rocky steps led directly to the fortress. They were even more slippery and steep, but soon the two women stood by the castle where Elen and Llywelyn ap Gruffudd had once kissed.

Entering the ruins of the fortress, Ganieda began to hum and circle sunwise. Suddenly a doe appeared, blinking at them as if in wonder. Then the deer made a great leap and scampered down the rocky steps.

"That is what Elen did," said Ganieda. "That was her last act of magic."

Nina could feel the presence of the ancestors gathering. She stood inside a ruined doorway shielding Ganieda as she began to call to the spirit of Llywelyn ap Gruffudd. The skies opened, and rain drenched them, but still Ganieda called out. Then Nina could feel the spirit of the fortress change, and the ghost of Llywelyn ap Gruffudd stood before Ganieda. His fawn-colored hair held droplets of mist from the Otherworld.

"You forgot your daughter," she told him sternly. "You forgot Gwenllian."

Llywelyn ap Gruffudd looked at her and then laughed. "You called me from Annwn for a girl?"

Ganieda's face turned pink with rage.

"A woman brought you into the world and a man took you out with his sword," said Ganieda. "Which was the more powerful act?"

Llywelyn ap Gruffudd stared at the wizardess for a moment, then recognized her. "Forgive me, Ganieda." He bowed his royal head. "My wife, Eleanor de Montfort, died giving birth to the child. I know little of the mysteries of women."

"You are not forgiven," Ganieda replied haughtily. "While Eleanor may have returned to the celestial realms, Gwenllian remains locked in a Christian convent, which is not the home for those of her lineage. She has not been allowed to return to Annwn, Brocéliande, or any Otherworld. Your child drifts as a ghost, a wandering fragment. The Lord of the Underworld, Arawn, is still seeking her, as she seeks him."

Nina observed the proud Prince of Gwynedd and how he responded to Ganieda the wizard. He seemed angry but he was also listening.

"And what castle holds the head of the deer Elen? Perhaps we should remove that from the wall so the deer deity can stop waiting through lifetimes for your return and live her life too."

Llywelyn ap Gruffudd suddenly looked anguished. Then he put his face in his hands and wept. After a moment, he looked up at Ganieda and told her, "Elen promised she would look after my daughter."

"Elen never had a chance," said Ganieda harshly. "She was seized before you lost your life. Did you ever think of them?"

Llywelyn wiped his wet face with the back of his hairy hand. "I have not seen either of them in a long time."

"Gwenllian and Elen remain locked in promises, riddles that that have become curses," Ganieda declared.

"What must I do?" asked Llywelyn.

"Call your daughter to you," said Ganieda. "Then, henceforth, remember that your children are your responsibility, in life and in death. Did you ever wonder why your child wasn't with you? Did you look for her in the convent?"

"No," admitted Gruffudd. "I thought of her, of course. But she was so young then and in Annwn there are distractions. Soon one forgets this world."

"Her spirit is in the Gilbertine Priory at Sempringham, trapped like a caged bird. Your lack of awareness brought ruin upon your people! It is your role as King to heal the soul of your nation!"

"I am a cursed man." Llywelyn ap Gruffudd looked at her sadly.

"Or a native hero," said Ganieda haughtily. "Depending on who you speak to."

Ganieda gazed at him thoughtfully for a moment and then added, "The way you begin to restore a nation is by honoring the spirit of the land. That includes the women who bear your children and the legacy you leave behind. I will call Gwenllian forth from the Priory, and together we will set the princess free."

Then Ganieda began to sing. The rain cleared and a rainbow began to shine above them. *Y Ddraig Goch*, the red dragon of the Welsh people, circled the skies. It landed beside them, with a young and very pale girl riding its back. The girl looked at Llywelyn ap Gruffudd, leapt off the dragon, and then ran to her father, her arms outstretched. He took her up unto his great arms and held her gently.

"Oh Gwenllian, how I've missed you," he said.

"I knew you would come and get me as soon as you could!" Gwenllian exclaimed.

Llywelyn ap Gruffudd caught Ganieda's direct gaze.

"Yes, yes, my dear," Llywelyn said to his daughter. "I apologize for my delay."

"But at least you are here!" Gwenllian said with joy.

They could hear hoof steps clattering up the stones. A radiant unicorn stepped into view wearing a crown of antlers around his slender neck.

"A unicorn!" Gwenllian exclaimed.

A ray shone from the horn of the beast's head. He pawed the ground, and the fortress shook. Then he lowered his head, and the crown of antlers slid to the earth.

"Due to your care, the spell is broken," the unicorn told Ganieda. "The Niente have fled, and the souls of the magical ones are now free."

Mist filled the fortress, and the magical creature was gone.

Holding his daughter gently, Llywelyn picked up the antler crown and then brought it reverently to Ganieda.

"May the magic of Wales be restored," said Llywelyn with a bow. "May Britain find peace and protection."

Ganieda held the crown thoughtfully. Now in third dimensional reality it was heavy.

"Elen served our family well for generations," Llywelyn declared. "She did not deserve her capture."

"Neither did you," said Ganieda. "I wish it would have been otherwise."

"I believe you will know what to do with these antlers now," Llywelyn declared.

Gwenllian tugged on her father's hair, and he gave her a loving smile. As the sun came out, the forms of Llywelyn ap Gruffudd and his daughter faded. Ganieda looked relieved and knew her work was now complete. The King, his daughter and the land had been restored, and she had Elen's crown.

Ganieda gave Nina a nod. Then without another word, they walked to the carpark taking turns with carrying the heavy crown of antlers. Nina listened to a rushing stream as they hiked past gnarled trees covered in green moss. Off in the distance, she could see a deer observing them.

"Why did you bring me with you?" Nina asked once they were in the rental car.

"Because we are at the turning of the ages," replied Ganieda. "And we need to solve the riddles of the magical ones we can so that Lady Gaea can bring in the New Time. Besides, someone has to help me carry the crown of antlers."

Nina watched the flow of the River Conwy as the sun set over the mountains of Snowdonia. She looked up at the final, colorful show of sundown. Nina wondered if it might be her imagination, but it seemed as though the red dragon was following them behind the clouds.

"You have a riddle of your own that needs to be solved next," Ganieda told her. "It's not a realm I am allowed to enter, so only you can do it."

Nina was surprised to hear that there were places the wizard could not enter.

"It's your riddle to solve," Ganieda noted.

The stars were out as they returned the rental car and then waited for the train at Llandudno Junction. Ganieda looked up as if reading the messages they held for the day.

"What are the stars saying?" inquired Nina, knowing Ganieda's ways.

"In the Western hemisphere, we know the constellations as Roman deities. The feminine tends to hide in the parallel realms even still."

"There's the Moon, Venus and Jupiter," said Nina, pointing.

"We know of Jupiter, but what of his wife?"

"Juno?" asked Nina. "I believe she is read sometimes in astrology charts as a goddess asteroid."

"Yes, the wife is included, but the mistresses tend to be largely overlooked in astrology," said Ganieda. "Although sometimes their offspring are well known."

"What does this have to do with me?"

"It's Nimue," Ganieda told her, "your Avalonian self that must right an old wrong. Your grandmother, Latona, was the mistress of Jupiter and was hated by his wife, Juno. Latona was exiled from Olympus and forced to wander the world. Eventually, she found an in-between place to give birth to Diana and Apollo. Often, to be free, we must solve the riddles of the ancestors."

Nina stared at the planet Venus and then at Jupiter as the train back to London roared into view.

"Why should we care about our ancestors?" asked Nina.

"Because without the love of the ancestors, the heavens stop moving."

Chapter 17
Nina's Riddle
London, 21st Century

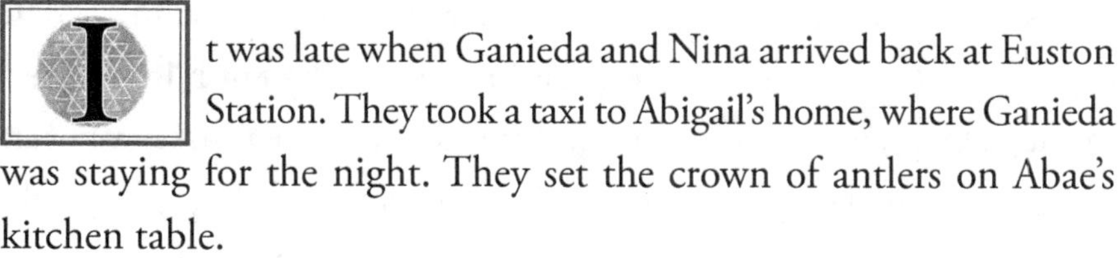

It was late when Ganieda and Nina arrived back at Euston Station. They took a taxi to Abigail's home, where Ganieda was staying for the night. They set the crown of antlers on Abae's kitchen table.

"You get some rest," Ganieda told her. "I know how to guide Elen from here."

Nina decided to clear her head and walk to Uncle Blaise and Aunt Daphne's spacious upper-story flat at the top of what was once a grand house. She and her mother Diana were currently living there. The walk gave Nina time to think about the events that had taken place in Wales, and in the realms in-between. She did feel connected to ancient magic.

Hampstead Village was generally quiet, but tonight she saw a tabby cat rush past in the road ahead of her. The cat looked at her with eyes that seemed familiar, then it disappeared into the shadows. The streetlamps flickered as Nina walked beneath them. Nina shook her head, ignoring the shadows. Instead, she decided to focus on the stars twinkling above her. In her imagination, she even felt the sweep of the feathers of the great swan, Cygnus. Nina had been on healing adventures with Ganieda before, and they were always full of intrigue. The wizardess had refused to say more about Latona but the subject weighed on Nina's mind.

Her mother, Diana, had left the entrance lights on for her, and Nina could see lilac roses blooming by the front door. She took the black dirk she always carried and cut a few blossoms with the dagger, flowers perfect for the vase that stood on her nightstand. Nina took a deep breath, while holding one of the roses by her nose, and enjoyed its natural perfume.

Nina opened the front door and entered the interior staircase that connected the three flats in the building. For a moment Nina paused in the hallway, wondering what the grand old house must have been like before it had been divided into flats. A friendly feeling of a family busy with their lives strummed through her heart. Nina wondered if the family still lived in the house as specters, never quite meeting the families that lived with them in the twenty-first century.

"Mom, Daphne, I'm home!" Nina yelled after reaching the top of the stairs and going into their foyer.

"How was Wales?" asked Aunt Daphne from the kitchen.

"Full of mysteries," said Nina. "I'm exhausted. I'll tell you more tomorrow."

"Don't forget our trip to Glastonbury this weekend."

"How could I?"

She went to her bedroom, switched on the light, and put the lilac roses in the vase. There was a pitcher of water, and she used part of it for the flowers.

Sitting on her bed, Nina observed that the white walls were the perfect background for her colorful floral bedspread. She felt as if she could almost smell the wildflowers in some otherworldly meadow. The curtains looked burgundy in the low light, and she decided to draw them closed against the darkness of the night. Exhausted from the adventure, she lay down in the bed and was soon asleep.

Elysium

"Should we call Nina in yet?" asked Delphyne, huffing out a puff of smoke.

"Let her rest," replied Lady Gaea.

"Maybe she will hear us in her dreams," the dragon mused, blowing sparkles through time and space.

"Since they are going to Glastonbury, we could lay out a plan that takes Nina to Cadbury Castle," noted the Lady.

"That seems to be her destiny," Delphyne murmured. *"She seems forever linked to the knights that sleep there."*

Chapter 18
Glastonbury Calls
England, 21st Century

This time they were prepared for the trip to Glastonbury. They had booked Gaea's Rose Cottage for the weekend and their bags were packed and by the door. All they had to do was load everything into the blue Mini Cooper and then head southwest.

"Did you dream?" Nina asked her mother as she turned the electric kettle on for morning tea.

"Yes," Diana said, looking pensive. "The dream was so real."

"Tell me about it. I love your imagination."

"I was in a round Roman Temple. The sky was filled with stars, and many animals were gathering around a table. I felt Apollo was close by, and another man who seemed familiar. It all felt so real I decided to write it down."

Diana glanced up at her daughter but seemed distracted. "And you?" she asked.

"I also had a dream visit me," Nina shared. "I was in Glastonbury by the Chalice Well. Someone was waiting for me. I could see a light flashing and then I woke up."

Diana nodded and continued to write. "I also have this sense that destiny is calling us on a quest."

After allowing the tea to steep, Nina poured her mother a cup and then one for herself. As she added milk to her own cup, it reminded Nina of the mist that encircled the well in her dream, as though it was surrounded by a secret veil.

"What about you, Daphne?" Nina asked, after her aunt had joined them. "Did you dream too?"

"Yes, I was being chased by Apollo, and Gaea saved me by turning me into a Laurel tree," Daphne replied.

"That's straight out of Greek mythology," noted Diana, tapping a pen on her journal. "Why are we all having mythological dreams?"

"I need tea before I can go that deep," responded Daphne with a yawn.

With Diana's face bent down toward her journal, Nina noticed that her mother's hair now had streaks of silver.

Glastonbury, Somerset, 21st Century

The three-hour drive went quickly, and soon they were walking along the paths of the Chalice Well Trust. The late summer gardens were filled with Marigolds in full bloom and a variety of Rosemaries. There were so many flowers, including Evening Primroses, Feverfew and Scarlet Pimpernels. Daphne and Diana decided to continue their stroll and enjoy the blossoms.

Nina made her way to the well alone, where she found a step to settle on and planned on a long meditation.

After a while, something glittery caught Nina's attention and, for a moment, she wondered if it were a Chalice. When she looked up, Nina was surprised to see her friend Owen standing by the wellhead. The silver image of the Gundestrup Cauldron flashed in the fading light.

"Owen Pelleas!" she exclaimed.

Owen was tall, lanky and yet fit. He had splashed his face in the red spring and his dark brown curls had water droplets in them, and his hair seemed to shimmer. His gaze turned toward Nina, and when he saw her, his cheeks became ruddy. Nina admired his strong jawline. Owen gave her one of his half-smiles; his parted lips and beaming grin revealed the slight gap between his front teeth. Nina thought that perhaps even the white knight Lancelot wasn't as handsome as Owen.

Nina had known Owen since the 10th grade. They both had attended a Rudolf Steiner based school in New York City. Owen was interested in ancient artifacts, especially grails and cauldrons. She had been smitten with the boy, but Owen said he could not commit to a relationship because he had important work to do. He had been searching for the Holy Grail in its many forms. The story didn't stop there. When Owen mysteriously disappeared, Nina discovered him with Morgen, who claimed the boy was a knight of the Round Table. After a wild adventure to the Otherworld, they had returned to London. Neither of them had ever told their parents exactly what had taken place.

"Nina!" he said, bending down to embrace her. "I'm so happy to see you!"

"Three years have come and gone, Sir Yvain," Nina cryptically remarked.

"Well, yes," acknowledged Owen, clearing his throat. "The Grail Quest takes time. I'm studying now at Oxford."

"That's great," replied Nina. "I'm at Kings College London."

"I can't believe we haven't kept in touch." He shook his head. "I'm sorry."

"Much has happened," said Nina. "And it's good to see you now."

Diana cleared her throat, and Nina stood up from the step where she had been sitting. She noticed that Diana and Daphne had joined her at the well on a nearby bench at some point during her meditation.

"We're going to go check into the cottage," said Daphne, giving Nina a wink.

"Feel free to spend some more time here," added Diana.

Nina nodded and smiled at Daphne and her mother.

Taking her arm, Owen walked with Nina up to the Apple Orchard, both bending down to look at the symbols etched into the stones that lined the footpath. Soon Owen and Nina were discussing the insights they had each been having involving the ancient world and the secrets it held for humanity's emerging new earth.

He said, "I've been reading about the history of the Isle of Anglesey, known as *Ynys Môn* in Welsh."

"Mona?" Nina asked, going slightly weak at the knees. She was afraid for a moment that a far memory might overwhelm her senses.

"Apparently, Mona is where the Druids taught their students," Owen told her.

"It was invaded by Romans," Nina added. "The Druids were destroyed, and with them, the soul of Britannia. The magical ones went into hiding, awaiting the alignment of the New Time."

"Yes," Owen said. "I've done some research. In 60 or 61 CE, the Roman General Gaius Suetonius Paulinus invaded the island and subdued the Druids, and then later Gnaeus Julius Agricola finished them off."

"Why have you been researching this?" Nina inquired, wondering why the spiritual people of the world had been so ill-treated, misunderstood and abused. It made no sense to her.

"It's a rather long story," Owen said. "But let's put it this way, I believe it involves both of us."

No doubt, Nina thought. *The two of us and it probably involves many other magical people too.*

Nina sat down in the grass. Owen plucked an apple, then lay down beside her. Nina put her head on his chest and gazed up at the sky. She could hear Owen's steady heartbeat. He put an arm around her, and they just rested there enjoying each other's company. Nina noticed a Lenticular cloud hovering above them. She wondered if someone were observing them, and if so, why.

"That cloud looks like a spaceship," observed Owen.

"Perhaps the ancestral guardians of the planet are hiding in there," said Nina.

"I hope so," Owen replied. "We need them. The world has gone mad."

A wren landed on a branch of a tree near the couple and jumped excitedly.

Any messages, dear Merlin? Nina silently asked the bird.

Look to your heart for answers, the wren responded, or at least Nina thought it said so.

Owen turned to look into Nina's eyes. It was not the first time that she had felt she could disappear into his sky-blue gaze.

"I feel there is something important for us to do together," he said, picking up her hand and kissing her fingers lightly.

Nina felt excited but the feeling was accompanied by a sense of dread. From earlier conversations, she knew Owen was unable to commit. She wondered what truly blocked their relationship. She felt intuitively that there was another woman in his life.

"You're a good knight," Nina granted, withdrawing her hand and patting him gently on the cheek. "You may walk me to Gaea's Rose Cottage."

Owen smiled, and they walked hand in hand out of the Chalice Well Trust.

The two continued down Glastonbury High Street, past the George & Pilgrim Hotel, and onward to the tiny entrance of the cottage.

Owen paused by the door.

"Do you want to come in?" she asked. "My mother and Daphne are inside."

Owen hesitated and Nina wondered if he might kiss her, but he suddenly seemed to grow restless and distracted.

"There's something I must attend to first," he told her. "I'll come back later if I can."

Then Owen sprinted down the street and was soon out of sight.

Chapter 19

Gaea's Rose Cottage
Glastonbury, 21st Century

Nina was glad she was staying with her mother and Daphne at the bed and breakfast. Gaea's Rose Cottage felt like a home away from home. The rooms in the two-story cottage were small but warm and cozy. The kitchen was so tiny that it almost fit under the staircase. The front living room was large enough to hold four people.

Settling on the living room's love seat, Nina listened to her mother and Daphne chat about their day in town. Then she thought of Owen dashing down the street and wondered what he needed to do. She wasn't sure what she really felt about Owen. He was certainly a friend, but once he had meant more to her. Nina sipped her cup of hot chamomile tea and then pulled a linen throw across her legs. It was nice to simply sit together with her family. She dozed off.

There was a sudden rap on the door, which awakened her. Nina noticed the quickening of her heart as Diana opened the door. Owen Pelleas entered. He had brought a bouquet of flowers for Diana, who was delighted.

"These are for you, Goddess Diana," Owen said with a small bow.

"That's so kind, Owen," replied Diana, blushing slightly.

Nina watched as Diana put the flowers in a vase, and she wondered how long it had been since any man had given her mother flowers. Nina thought about her father, Felix Liber. It had been several years since his death, and there was still a void that would never be filled. Even so, she admired her mother for getting on with her life. After all, that's what Felix would have wanted.

Diana poured some mint tea for Owen and offered him a digestive biscuit, which he gratefully accepted. When Nina picked up her own teacup, her hands were shaking. Daphne winked at her.

Get it together, woman, Nina told herself silently, as she willed her nerves to calm. After sipping her tea, she grinned at Owen and gestured for him to take the place next to her on the love seat. His dark hair curled in ringlets around his face, and Owen smiled as he sat there. Nina returned the smile.

"I bought this for you," he said to Nina, after pulling a package from his backpack.

Nina quickly unwrapped it. The writing journal had a colorful cover showing the magician Merlin riding on the back of a red dragon. Merlin's cape was flying in the wind.

"I love flying on dragons," Nina responded in a low voice, admiring his gift.

"I remember seeing that happen," he whispered to her.

She winked at him, and he chuckled. Their adventures in the Otherworld would always remain a secret between them, or so she thought.

"How's the Grail quest going?" Daphne asked Owen, remembering that he had been studying Grail literature with Blaise.

"I have not yet located the sacred cup," said Owen. "Although now I am beginning to think the hallow appears as a platter or cauldron and it has some relationship with the Round Table."

"Perhaps it's a platter," said Daphne. "Like the *Undry*, with endless food that can truly nourish."

"I've heard it called a Moon Dish," said Diana.

"Of course, a goddess of the moon would see it this way," Owen said, giving Nina's mother a beaming smile.

Nina observed Owen with interest.

"Is this cauldron one of Britain's hallows?"

"I don't know," he replied. "But I would like to find out."

Nina stared into his blue eyes again, and she felt as if she might drop into a lake of her own making. Owen looked away.

"I picked up this book at The Speaking Tree bookshop," said Diana, handing him a copy of *A Legacy of Druids*. "It's conversations with modern-day Druids. The Druid spiritual leaders of the British Isles were almost wiped out when Roman general Suetonius Paulinus took his legions to Anglesey years ago. It's a gift for you."

Owen flicked through the pages, then handed Nina the book to take a look herself.

"I'll read every page," he promised, then flashed Diana another brilliant smile.

"The attack on the Druids sounds like a woeful time," noted Nina.

"Let's be in this glorious moment," proposed Daphne. "There is nothing like now."

Diana opened some gift bags and showed off the crystals she had purchased on the High Street.

"This one is for you, Daphne." Diana handed her an oval black obsidian scrying stone.

Daphne took the crystal lovingly into her hands and then peered at the dark reflection. For a moment, Daphne thought she glimpsed a gentle goddess with antlers, and let out a gasp. The next moment she was simply holding a black stone.

"Magic!" she said, rising and giving Diana a kiss on the cheek. Daphne looked in her own shopping bags.

"And this one is for you." She handed Diana a piece of orange citrine that seemed to radiate light. Diane smiled and held the stone close to her heart.

"It feels like mother-love energy," Diana said. "Speaking of which, I have a gift for you, Nina. Close your eyes."

She placed a stone into her daughter's hands.

Mother and daughter often played the healing crystal game, guessing the colors and usages without looking. Nina opened her eyes and was fascinated by the piece of black and white Merlinite that seemed to vibrate healing into her hands.

Diana and Daphne had also chosen several essential oils at a shop called Star Child.

"Elemi essential oil," Daphne called out, passing around the small open vial. "It is for initiations and new beginnings."

Owen took a sniff. "It makes me think of nature spirits," he shared.

"It is also meant to be used during rites of passage," Diana added.

"My father asked me to give you this." Owen handed Diana a small cloth bag. "He keeps texting to remind me to give it to you. It must be important."

Diana received the present, and then looked at the silver pouch carefully. It was covered in sequins and tied shut by a red ribbon.

"My goodness," she exclaimed. "Why did Lance Pelleas send this?"

Diana opened the pouch and pulled out a golden necklace with a charm in the shape of a harp.

"It's the golden harp from Bala Lake," said Owen with a smile. "Dad has been obsessed with *Llyn Tegid*. It's the largest natural lake in Wales."

"Tell me more," Diana urged, blushing slightly.

"Bala is historically a center of nonconformist religions, and the town is tolerant of folklore. Some say that the giant Tegid Foel and his wife Ceridwen live there, and that it was the birthplace of the great poet Taliesin."

"It's enchanting," Diana responded, looking at the harp charm. "I will call your father soon and thank him."

"Let me help you put it on," said Daphne. "It looks expensive."

Once she was wearing the necklace, Diana admired the charm using a hand-mirror.

"It's beautiful," she said. "And so sweet of Lance."

Nina wondered if there was something going on between her mother and Lance that she didn't know about. She decided not to ask.

They chatted for a while longer, and then Owen turned toward Nina. They sat on the love seat staring at one another, and this time he did not turn his gaze away. Diana and Daphne took the intimate scrutiny as a sign that it was time to say good night. They started up the stairs to their bedrooms, glancing back with a smile.

Nina had been pleased that Owen decided to join them at the cottage, but she now felt uneasy. They had not been alone together for several months. The two of them sat on the love seat awkwardly, looking at the essential oils.

"Which other oil do you like?" Nina asked.

"Rose," he replied, moving closer. "And Opoponax Essential Oil," he added. "Because it helps a confused soul find his true path."

Owen was looking right into Nina's eyes with admiration. Even in the dimly lit room, his blue eyes seemed full of sunlight.

"Your eyes are the color of blue sapphires," Nina observed, becoming increasingly mesmerized. They reminded her of something, but she couldn't remember exactly what.

Owen's thigh was resting against hers and she noticed that he was trembling, like she was. How long had Nina thought about this moment, and how it might play out?

Putting the Merlinite into his hands, Nina reached for the Rose Essential Oil and then shook a few drops into her palms. Very gently, she passed her hands through his aura, and then hovered over his heart. The movement calmed her, and then he reached out his right hand and placed the Merlinite on her heart.

Nina could feel her breasts moving up and down as her breath quickened. Owen's breath seemed more rapid too, and then following a passionate inner impulse, he leaned forward and kissed her. Nina's body responded with an inner harmonic that pulsed and then she allowed herself to move fully into his arms.

The embrace was loving, and then the fire of passion washed over them. Suddenly they were fumbling with sweaters and feeling the warmth of each other's bodies. Intimacy came easily to them, and they made the melody as old as time. It seemed to Nina that the Goddess had smiled upon them.

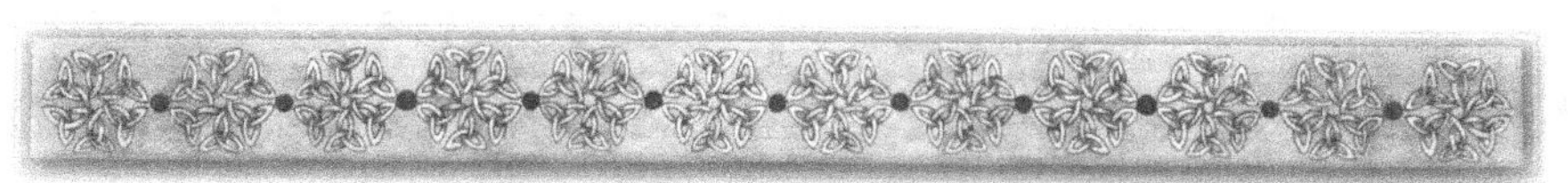

Chapter 20
Seeking Camelot
Somerset, 21st Century

Nina, Diana, Daphne and Owen all chatted happily as they took turns making breakfast in the tiny kitchen with a table for two. That morning Nina was enjoying the crush of company. Then Owen and Nina decided to eat at the coffee table in the living room for a little privacy. When they sat down to butter their toast, Owen sat close to Nina. She could feel pulsations of excitement running up her spine. Owen was quiet with a slightly pink complexion.

What's happening? Nina asked herself, looking at the young man.

A short time later, Diana entered the living room with Daphne, and she announced that she felt they should have an outing. They discussed going to Glastonbury Abbey. But since they all had a fascination with King Arthur and the Holy Grail, they decided to pick another destination.

"Let's see if we can find Camelot now," said Daphne. "Shall we visit South Cadbury Castle?"

"Great idea," replied Owen. "Dad always told me not to go there for some reason, but actually I've always wanted to explore the hillfort."

"When a nation is haunted, the soul of its civilization must be rediscovered," said Nina. "Sometimes Camelot is found in the very soil you stand upon."

Daphne stared at her and then Nina laughed.

"The words came from Blaise."

Daphne pulled the blue Mini Cooper in front of the cottage. It looked as though it was going to rain, and they were happy to climb into the vehicle. Their raincoats had been stashed in the backseat.

"Dad asked that you give him a call," said Owen from the back seat. "I'm not sure why."

"Oh," responded Diana from the front passenger's seat. She placed a finger on her necklace and blushed slightly. "I'll call Lance when we get back to the cottage. I need to thank him."

Owen flashed Nina a dazzling smile. Sitting beside him in the back, she took his hand.

Daphne continued to drive. Along the way, Diana chatted about magical Somerset. The old roads were sunken in places, the dense network of gnarled roots forming banks that were lined with trees. Under the heavy summer foliage, it seemed that they drove through tunnels. Nina sat quietly in the back seat with Owen, her hand entwined in his, admiring the ethereal beauty of the landscape.

"Some historians, including Blaise, claim Cadbury Castle was the location of Camelot, home of King Arthur and his knights," noted Nina.

"Do you believe that King Arthur was a real person or that he is a mythical figure?" asked Owen.

"According to Blaise, he is a bit of both," answered Daphne. "He's an archetypal hero who appears in some way in each age."

"Interesting," said Owen. "Some say he was a Roman soldier, but he does seem to appear in many different centuries."

"Arthur is not actually a person, but a title given to a leader who can bring unity to the people," Diana asserted.

Daphne had to stop along the side of the single-track road to allow a car to pass. The side-mirror scraped the branches of the thick hedgerow.

"Darn," exclaimed Daphne. "These roads are so narrow!"

"I have heard Blaise say that Camelot is a code of goodness that humanity can aim toward, a template upon which an ideal world can be built," Nina added.

"Let's see what we find," said Diana.

As they approached the hillfort site, there were dark clouds above, and it was drizzling lightly. Daphne parked the Mini Cooper in a small parking area. Everyone put their raincoats on and hoods up, and then they began making their way up the steep tree-lined incline.

"The weather in this area never ceases to amaze me," said Diana.

"Perhaps the spirits have something to say," suggested Owen. "Water can act as a conduit."

Large ferns glistened with raindrops and the branches of the trees seemed to bend toward them as they walked. As they reached the top of the path, Owen opened the wooden gate for the women, then carefully closed it to keep the cattle in the field.

Daphne seemed to brim with excitement. She told them, "There are storytellers who say that Arthur and his Knights sleep in these hills awaiting the time of their return. Blaise often speaks about this mystery."

Owen shivered in the light rain and noticed that the storm clouds seemed increasingly menacing. He wondered if it was smart to be on the hill.

"Where did you and Blaise meet?" Nina asked Daphne.

"It was beside a laurel tree," she shared with a smile. "I love to make garlands."

Chapter 21

The Riddle Of Cadbury Hill

Elysium (The Sky Temple)
In-Between Time

Lady Gaea, Morgen, Accolon and Delphyne had gathered at the Round Table to speak about the remaining unsolved riddles, when all three screens on the black pyramid activated. The first scrying screen began to flash with images catching their attention. They observed a scene of Owen and three women walking up a hill in the rain. The second screen focused on Nina, and the third showed the view of Cadbury Hill. The intelligence behind the tetrahedron seemed alarmed.

"Owen is NOT going to Cadbury Hill," remarked Morgen, her eyes widening with concern.

"He's climbing it right now," Lady Gaea noted, shaking her head.

"My son has unfinished business with Laudine de Landuc," Morgen declared. "He seeks a Grail he will not find until he is reconciled with her. Nor can he be with Nina in the future until this is healed."

"I think Nina and Owen made out already," said Accolon.

Morgen glared at him.

125

"I know Yvain was my son with Uriens," Morgen snapped. "Owen or Yvain, he's still my son."

"That was a past life," said Accolon. "Uriens is now Lance Pelleas."

"I get tired of time loops," Morgen snarled. "We all seem to repeat the same old patterns until the issues are resolved. It's such a slow process. And who needs ex-husbands?"

Accolon shrugged.

They all stared at the scrying screen as Owen walked up the tree-lined path with the group of women. He was laughing and flirting with Nina.

"At least he looks happy," Delphyne observed.

"We could land the Sky Temple and collect him," Lady Gaea suggested. "Plenty of mortals are abducted in clouds or mist."

"It would be easier if I swoop down and pick him up," said Delphyne with a fiery snort.

"He's forgotten Laudine de Landuc," Morgen added with apprehension. "But he swore to protect her lands. Now he's trapped by an ancient promise."

"A curse," Accolon remarked.

"Maybe it's more of a riddle," Delphyne suggested. "The riddle of Cadbury Hill."

"Sir Yvain was a faithless knight," said Accolon. "Actions have repercussions."

They continued to observe Owen on the scrying screen. He was walking up the hill easily, taking in the scenery and enjoying the day.

"I know it was a different lifetime," said Accolon, observing the scene closely. "But Lady Laudine still resides in the forest of Broceliande. Even though she told him not to come home, she still waits for him."

"Lady Laudine tried to force Yvain to remain with her," Morgen explained. "She told him that if he returned to Camelot, he would be struck by lightning."

"But she didn't say when," Accolon added with concern. "And he did leave her and returned to Camelot. I was there with Yvain, the Knight of the Lion. He deserted his wife when she was pregnant."

"Cad," said Delphyne with a snort.

They watched as Owen walked closer toward the summit. The young man was imagining what Camelot might have looked like in its days of glory, not yet remembering he had been there as Sir Yvain.

"My son has to correct a wrong, before he can love again," Morgen reiterated. "I suppose there is no time like the present."

"Where's his lion now?" asked the dragon.

"He might need the lion," Gaea noted.

They watched the first screen in silent horror as Owen arrived at the top of the hillfort. Ominous clouds had rolled in. They could hear the rumbling of thunder, and, off in the distance, they could see flashes of lightning.

"This is getting serious," Morgen gasped.

"Let's keep him alive," Lady Gaea declared.

"I'll think of something," said Accolon, who then made a hasty departure.

"We might need Merlin too," Morgen added.

Chapter 22

Knight of the Lion

Cadbury Castle, Somerset, 21ˢᵗ Century

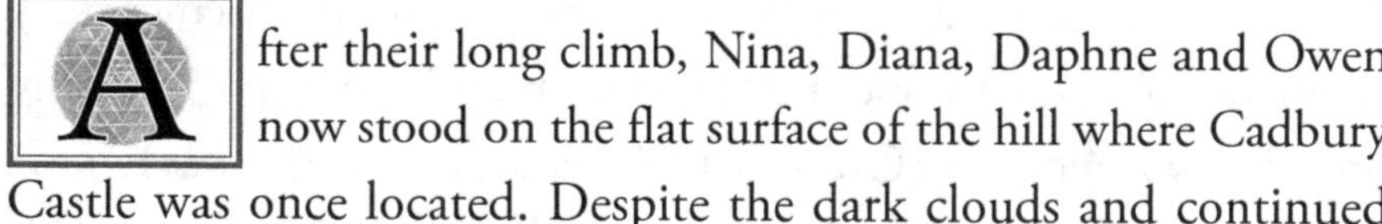

fter their long climb, Nina, Diana, Daphne and Owen now stood on the flat surface of the hill where Cadbury Castle was once located. Despite the dark clouds and continued rain, they took a moment to look at the view around them. Below, the freshly mown fields, lined with darker green hedgerows, were beginning to turn golden. Blackbirds sang, but the other birds had sought shelter and were now silent.

Daphne was slightly out of breath as she surveyed the surrounding landscape.

"Why are you so fit?" Daphne asked Diana, who seemed to be ready to race into the forest.

Diana just laughed, and she pretended to shoot a bow into the sky. Daphne decided to do a tree pose.

"I read that the fortress dates back to at least the fifth century BC," Owen shared, gazing into the distance. "Archeologists report that a Romano-Celtic temple once stood here."

"Perhaps we are standing inside the grounds of Camelot," said Daphne dreamily.

"The seat of perfect harmony," Diana added.

"The flowering promise of Logres," noted Owen.

They all stood imagining how Camelot must have looked. They discussed whether or not the entrance had large wooden gates, and whether they were plain or covered in gemstones. They also pondered whether Camelot was more of a mysterious portal or stargate than a castle.

They paused where a sign stated the timber halls of a fortress once stood. The group imagined knights in shining armor walking or riding fine horses beneath a dragon banner. Gazing off in the distance, they could just make out the mound of Glastonbury Tor over the low-lying mist that was encircling Cadbury Hill. Perhaps because it was raining and a light mist had formed, it seemed that the veils between worlds had become thin. Magic and mystery appeared to crackle in the air.

"Local folklorists say that King Arthur's hunting track or causeway is used by many spirits who ride at night on the wild hunt gathering the souls of the dead," Owen told them.

"Extraordinary," Diana replied with a shiver.

"I've always wanted to meet Gwyn Ap Nudd and his twin sister, Gwenabwy, the White Goddess," Owen added.

The wind shifted, and they noticed that a greater storm was beginning to brew. They walked on bravely, determined to face the tempest.

"Who can name the knights of the Round Table?" asked Daphne, changing the subject as she pulled her raincoat more tightly around her.

The gauntlet was laid down, and they all had to think of the tales they had heard and the movies they had watched.

"Only three achieved the Grail," said Diana. "Galahad, Bors and Percival."

"There is also Percival's sister, Dindraine, who achieved the Grail, but she is generally left out," Nina added.

"Handsome Sir Lancelot, of course," said Daphne. "But he went mad in the forest due to his love for Guinevere."

"And didn't brave Gawain almost achieve the Grail?" Diana asked. "He did face the Green Knight in the beheading game."

"There were twelve main knights of the Round Table, I believe," Owen recalled. "Their names vary. In addition to the ones you mentioned, some well-known figures include Sir Lamorak, Sir Kay, Sir Gareth, Sir Lucan, Sir Palomedes and Sir Bedivere, who returned the sword Excalibur to the Lady of the Lake. That makes eleven."

"Who can forget Sir Tristan?" Diana asked with a girlish sigh.

"There was also Bleoberis de Gannes of the ill-fitting coat, and then others began to join such as the fearless Brunor le Noir," Daphne offered.

"So there were more than twelve," said Diana.

"And let's not forget Mordred, who caused Arthur's death," Owen tossed in. "Some tales recount up to one hundred and fifty knights."

"Oh, that's too many to count," Diana declared. "But we've done well."

"So let me get this right," said Nina. "Albion is the ancient immortal Spirit of Britain which has existed from the beginning of time. Logres is the civilized Arthurian template out of which Camelot can be rebirthed as a symbol of humanity's goodness."

"And the template of Logres has been magically hidden inside a Round Table, which is currently missing," Owen added.

"When Camelot appears, the land and the people flourish," Daphne offered.

"The stories of Camelot live on in our hearts and souls," Diana said wistfully. "The wish for unity, peace and harmony is always with humanity."

They looked across the summer landscape and, even in the rain, could see 360-degree views of Somerset. They watched as the mist began to gather around the hill making them feel as though they truly were in the land of myths and legends.

"I believe Owain was a knight of the Round Table too," shared Nina. "Or Yvain."

"Oh yes," Daphne said. "Yvain was the child of Morgan le Fay and King Uriens."

"Yvain or Owain means 'noble-born' in Welsh," Owen told them with a twinkle in his eyes.

Nina glanced at Owen. His cheeks were flushed, and she once again admired the slight gap in his front teeth. Nina could still feel his full lips on hers from the previous night. Owen stared straight ahead as if trying to recall something lost in memory.

"Yvain became a ferocious warrior," Daphne continued. "Legend tells us that he made his way to France, to the forest of Broceliande where he fought and defeated the Black Knight."

Nina glanced at her and said, "You make quite a bard."

Daphne pretended to play a harp and then let out a playful giggle. She kicked her heels up like a deer and pranced across the meadow.

"And, if I remember correctly, Yvain went mad for a while," Diana added. "It's the way of the Celts. They seem to need a period of madness in the forest."

"That seems like a useful tradition," Owen teased, taking Nina's hand. He looked at her and smiled, and his radiance penetrated all the way to her heart.

Nina wondered if this was the man who would win her, or if he already belonged to another. Nina was curious to know more about the history of Yvain, the Knight of the Lion.

Is there something I should know about Owen before I fully give him my heart? Nina asked herself.

She noticed that a mist seemed to be encircling the summit of Cadbury Hill like a cloud-dragon. Nina could sense that the dragon was speaking to her, warning of some cataclysm. She wanted to have fun with Owen, so refused to focus on the whispers, no matter how insistent.

They were the only people at the top of Cadbury Hill when the sky decided to replace the drizzle with a downpour. With no place to go, they simply kept their raincoat hoods up, added umbrellas and stood in the rain. With the side winds, the umbrellas soon proved useless and were abandoned.

"I'm soaked through!" Daphne shouted, while dancing in the deluge.

Diana joined Daphne with her own moves, and they frolicked like children.

Somehow it rained even harder, water penetrating their coats. Shrieking and giggling, the four eventually scampered over the steep bank onto the tree-lined path that led down the grassy hillside. They could hear a cow mooing off in the distance. The storm became increasingly ferocious. Thunder boomed loudly overhead, and lightning lit up the sky.

Nina began to feel nervous and wondered if they really were disturbing the spirits of the place. Out of the corner of her eye, she could sense the mist dragon encircling them. It was increasingly hard to see the landscape because of the deepening haze. Nina stumbled and let go of Owen's hand.

"Is that the Grail?" Owen asked. Something was flashing in the grass, and he made a dash for it.

The energy around them was oppressive. Seemingly unaware of the dark ambiance, Owen picked up the cup and turned to face Nina with a puzzled look.

Suddenly there was a flash of lightning, a scream, and then Owen fell and lay still in the grass. Nina ran to his body. Owen was pale and seemed lifeless, from being hit by the lightning. Ignoring the rain pelleting down on her coat that was now soaked through, Nina stood over Owen attempting to shield his body from the elements. She knew this was no ordinary lightning bolt. Nina, Diana and Daphne hovered around Owen's ashen, limp body. His eyes were closed, and he didn't seem to be breathing. The cup he had been fascinated by had disappeared.

"Let me help!" called a stranger.

They hadn't seen the tall man approach. But then he lifted Owen up as though he were a kitten and started down the hill with the body. He was wearing sunglasses, and Nina recognized him as Morgen's man, Accolon.

"Where are you taking him?" Nina demanded, but it was too late. She tried to keep up with Accolon's pace, but he moved quickly even though he appeared to walk.

You can never keep pace with faery folk, Nina could hear Morgen say. She thought she could see Morgen's spirit, but it shape-shifted into a crow, and then multiplied into three crows.

Looking for someone? the voice of the bird-woman specter asked.

Breathlessly, Nina watched as Accolon carried Owen into the forest, and then the two disappeared from sight. Nina thought she could hear a car start up and drive away.

Damn it, Morgen, she muttered under her breath. *Can't I just have a romance like an ordinary girl?*

"I don't know if he will survive that lightning bolt," said Diana, looking shaken. "What should we tell Lance?"

They heard a screech, and then another. Three crows flew overhead, then dove straight at them. Scattering, the three women managed to avoid the sharp beaks and talons.

"Run!" Nina yelled to her mother and to Daphne. "Morgen does not want us here!"

The three women ran as quickly as they could down the hill toward the trees, holding their arms over their faces for protection. Once there, Daphne and Diana sprinted into the woods in the direction of the carpark, but Nina stumbled and fell on her knees on the hillside. When she raised herself up, Morgen was standing in front of her. Nina recognized the pristine shimmering green dress.

Nina was out of breath and furious. "Where is Owen?" she demanded.

The rain cleared for a moment, and she could see Diana and Daphne still running down the path through the woods. Nina stood motionless, glaring into Morgen's violet eyes.

"Luckily, Owain's safe," Morgen answered with a smile.

"Why did you try to kill him with a lightning bolt?" Nina yelled, furious.

"It's amazing how much I get blamed for," Morgen said. "Maybe I saved him. Did you think of that?"

"No," replied Nina with a snarl. "Somehow that thought just slipped my mind."

"Well, it's time you called on some magic," suggested Morgen. "If you remember any. Ever heard of Laudine de Landuc?"

"Who?"

"The one who cursed him."

Morgen disappeared as quickly as she had appeared.

Nina could hear groaning in the landscape, as an earthquake hit. Large stones were falling over, and oaks crashed to the ground.

Chapter 23
Nimue's Flashback
Somerset, 21ˢᵗ Century

Nina stood on the side of Cadbury Hill soaked to her bones and wondering if she could summon the old magic. The old tales spoke of Morgen or Morgan le Fay, sister of Arthur, appearing either as his healer or nemesis. Since Morgen was in the area, it was likely Merlin would be also. Nina wondered if he might make an appearance too and thought wistfully of Owen again. Although she had loved Merlin earlier as Nimue, she had released him to Guendoloena's faery embrace long ago.

She remembered that in previous centuries the density of the earth plane was lighter. When Nina was Nimue, she had been a doe that had run beside Merlin. She had been able to breathe underwater with the Tylwyth Teg, the mermaids of the ancient world. She had visited the Underworld and been kissed by its ruler, Gwyn Ap Nudd, and lived to tell the tale.

But now I am Nina, not Nimue.

The rain was coming down hard again, and the land continued to shake and groan from the earthquake. Nina could hear her mother and Daphne shouting from below in the carpark. Not looking back, she fled down the hill as fast as her feet could carry her. She made it into the back of the car, just as mud began to slide across the road. The other two women had hopped in front. A large tree crashed down in front of the car, narrowly missing them. They all shrieked with alarm. To get around the tree, Daphne shifted the car into reverse and drove backward as fast as she could, before shifting gears and heading with alacrity down the road.

"I think you need to tell us quickly what's going on, Nina," Diana insisted.

Nina noticed that her mother's voice was calm, but there was a tone that she knew well. It was time for a confession.

"Why are the dark magicians trying to kill us?"

"I was Nimue in a previous life," Nina revealed. "A Lady of the Lake."

"Different timeline!" Daphne shouted, steering past mud and trees.

"The Niente have been trying to kill the magical people on the planet for centuries," Nina explained.

"I'm not sure they are just trying!" Daphne yelped, steering around more flowing mud.

"Did you know I was Nimue, Mother?"

"Of course, I am a Roman Moon goddess," Diana shared. "And I gave you to Priestess Anna in Avalon for safekeeping. Your father was Bacchus."

Another tree crashed onto the road, which caused them to swerve. The way the rays of sunlight were playing with the mist caused more specters to appear. Nina thought for a moment that a lion was running beside the car.

"Did Yvain have a lion?" she asked.

"Yes," Daphne said. "He saved it from a dragon."

"I think he's here."

The lion stood in front of them, blocking the road. Stopping momentarily, Daphne realized the image was a play of light.

"Someone is toying with us!" she shouted, shifting into first gear, then second, and the tires of the blue Mini Cooper squealed. Diana and Nina were speechless as their bodies leaned with the car's movements. Then Daphne shot the car forward down the road, narrowly avoiding rocks and mud.

"I was supposed to be a virgin, so I gave my love child away," continued Diana, glancing toward Nina in the back seat while holding onto her front passenger seat. "This lifetime I get to keep you."

They reached a stop sign, and Daphne hesitated momentarily.

"I was turned into a laurel tree to avoid the lust of Apollo," said Daphne, who then shifted gears again and sped down the narrow lane.

She swerved to avoid water in the road, and almost drove the car into a ditch.

"Whoa!" yelled Diana.

"Is Apollo now Uncle Blaise?" Nina asked incredulously.

"I guess he won in the end," Daphne laughed. "Yes."

"Why is it that an Arthurian enchantress, a Roman goddess, and a Greek tree nymph are in a car running from an earthquake?" asked Diana, who then looked out the window and gasped. "With a mythical lion running beside us?"

"Why is it that a boy was struck by lightning and driven away?" inquired Daphne. "It had to be a mythical abduction. Owen can't be dead."

"Maybe it has to do with the curse of Laudine de Landuc," Daphne pondered.

"Who is Laudine de Landuc?" Nina asked.

"She's from a twelfth-century Arthurian romance written by Chrétien de Troyes," Daphne added, sounding like Professor Blaise.

"What's myth and what's reality?" Diana asked, glancing out of the window again.

"Morgen has kidnapped Owen before," noted Nina. "She says he's her son, Yvain, and his father is King Uriens."

"Accolon is more likely Yvain's father," said Diana. "Morgen loves the guy."

Nina stared at her mother for a moment. Diana shrugged and added, "Only a mother knows the true father of a child."

Daphne giggled. Then she let out a yelp as water flooded into the road, almost overturning the car.

Nina knew that long ago, as Nimue, she could speak with the elements. She realized that she must remember how now. Closing her eyes, Nina tried to recall what Merlin had taught her about calming the weather. Just thinking of Merlin seemed to bring the mysteries closer. Nina stilled her mind, banished confusion through pure will, and asked for inner guidance.

At once, a memory arose out of the dark stillness of her unconscious. It came to her from some part of her soul that remembers how to think in multi-dimensional worlds. The ancient word for peace came tumbling onto her lips like warm butter. "*Síocháin,*" she said.

"What?" her mother asked.

"*Síocháin,*" Nina repeated. "The word means peace in Irish."

"*Síocháin,*" they all three chanted together. "*Síocháin, Síocháin, Síocháin…*"

In the Celtic world, a word said three times can produce a charm. It worked a miracle this time. The rains calmed, the ground stopped shaking, and they simply sped along in the car through the British countryside, wondering what would happen next. Even as they raced on, time slowed. Only a few raindrops splashed into the sunroof.

Out of the corner of her eye, Nina thought she saw the white cloud shape-shift into a red dragon, and then Merlin was riding the dragon laughing. Just as suddenly, the image faded. With her inner vision, Nina could see webs of light forming a pearlescent dome of protection around the Mini Cooper. The car looked like a great cocoon as they sped away from the devastation. Nina thought she could hear Merlin and found the entire experience confounding.

"Stay awake and aware," he warned her.

When the three women arrived back at Gaea's Rose Cottage, they did not know what to say. Diana made a pot of black tea, and then, in the living room, they sipped the hot brew in silence. Nina wondered where Accolon and Morgen had taken Owen and what their plans were with him. It was still raining, although lightly now. The stormy scenery matched what Nina felt inside. They all seemed to be in shock, not believing Owen had been kidnapped and was injured or worse. None of them knew what to think, or say, or do.

He's just in the Otherworld, Nina told herself. *Merlin knows where he is....*

She also knew that any quest was full of challenges. Every time a message came through on her iPhone, she glanced down quickly, but there was no message from Owen.

"I can't tell Lance about Owen's kidnapping over the phone," said Diana. "I need to go to Wales."

Nina and Daphne nodded.

"We'll take you to the train station," said Daphne. "Call Lance so he knows to collect you."

Diana went into another room to make the call, but Nina could still hear her mother speaking on the phone with Lance Pelleas.

"Lance," said Diana, her voice shaking, "I have something I must tell you in person…. Yes, yes, I'll come tonight. I'll let you know when I arrive at the Betws-y-Coed train station. Meet you at the Royal Oak Hotel?"

They dropped Diana off at the Castle Cary train station, and then Daphne drove toward London. She and Nina traveled in silence, not knowing what to say. They glanced at Stonehenge, but magic and mystery suddenly seemed dangerous to them. Several hours later, they arrived at the parking area behind Uncle Blaise's Hampstead flat.

"Don't tell Blaise about Owen," Daphne said, as she turned off the ignition. "He already thinks I'm crazy and would never let me go out again."

Nina nodded, then followed Daphne up the staircase to the flat. She collapsed into her bed from exhaustion but lay staring at the lilac roses in the vase on her nightstand, They seemed magically as fresh as the day she had picked them. Somehow, the flowers made her room seem normal and safe. They provided harmony in an otherwise chaotic world.

Nina needed to sleep, but images of Owen's pale body kept flashing through her mind. She didn't understand why it had happened, or why Accolon had appeared and taken him away. Nina supposed it was a faery kidnapping. But why? She was exhausted and her room began to whirl. She closed her eyes, asking for a dream to explain the mysterious events.

Merlin, I need you, Nina whispered as she fell asleep.

Dream World

As soon as Nina began to doze, she found herself in a dream in which the landscape was animated with many magical creatures. The bedroom walls moved apart, and Nina walked through a forest of talking trees. She saw a doorway in the trunk of an old Oak, slipped inside, and walked down the spiral stairs into a cave with glimmering crystals. Morgen appeared in front of her, wearing the shimmering green dress.

"I have no idea why you're so reluctant to use your skills and gifts," said Morgen, her left hand on her hip.

"How did you get here?" Nina asked, wondering if she were dreaming or awake in some in-between world.

"I think it's the ruby system," Morgen told her, looking at the red color on the door. "Are you coming?"

"No," Nina replied.

"If you want Owen back, there are some riddles you must solve."

"Riddles?" repeated Nina. "Like why you kidnapped Owen?"

"Before I can answer your question, you have to crack the curse of your grandmother Latona," Morgen informed her, then abruptly disappeared.

"Latona?" Nina said aloud. "Ganieda said the same thing."

Diana's mother, she could hear Morgen say. *The exile of Delos.*

Nina was not sure if she were dreaming now, or if she was simply walking between worlds. She did know that once the mystery called, there was not much she could do but respond. The gods of Mount

Olympus were summoning her, and she could also hear a Titan goddess, a granddaughter of Gaea.

"Grandmother Latona," called out Nina, "help me find you."

Elysium (The Sky Temple)
In-Between Time

Lady Gaea observed Nina's dream with approval, then sent a giant eagle to convey her to the holy island of Delos, the most sacred island of ancient Greece. Delos, like Avalon, was an in-between world. It was there that another ancestral riddle would be posed. The Lady knew that if the riddles were solved one by one, the Golden Age would draw closer.

"Lady Gaea," Nimue shouted from the back of the huge eagle. "Please tell my mother I've gone to Greece!"

Chapter 24
Latona in Delos
Delos, An Otherworld

Lightning flashed through the sky. Ocean waves tossed fretfully below, making crests like the manes of white horses. Across the surface of the water flashed a glint of silver light, followed by the shadow of the eagle, then a sudden expansion of gold as the sunlight made its way between realms. The eagle soared easily between time and space, flapped its great wings, and then it landed on the sand. Nina slid off its back and stepped boldly onto the white beach. She turned, and bowed to the eagle, then looked across the sandy dunes.

"Grandmother?" she called out. "It's me, Nina. I mean Nimue."

Latona would know Nina by her ancient name. *I must be Nimue now,* she thought.

Nimue gazed around the rocky island, and then at the surrounding azure water. The ocean was so blue that sea and sky seemed to blend into one aquatic world. She wondered if Delos had been intentionally split away from the abode of the gods in Olympus, creating a veil between worlds. The water around her ankles felt more like air than liquid. Off in the distance, she could see three conical mountains. It was then that Nimue heard weeping.

A short distance away, she could see a veiled woman facing a pool of muddy water held within a stone fountain. Nimue wondered why the lady would be focusing on a murky area when they were surrounded by such pristine sea and sky.

As she walked closer, Nimue could hear the woman speaking, even wailing to something in the water. The woman faced the opposite direction, but Nimue could make out these words: "I have had to wander the heavens, earth and sea, and still," she choked, "I have no home. My sister took pity on me and for this Juno turned her into an island. Why does no one pity the mother, the refugee? I had two children at my breast! It was not I who chose Jupiter's affections!"

It became clear to Nimue that she was indeed on Delos listening to the words of her grandmother, Latona.

"Here I am now, where the crystal-clear pool has been muddied," the older woman continued. "The Goddess Latona, beloved of Jupiter and cursed by his wife, Juno. Here I turned the people of Lycia into frogs through an enchantment. The simple folk would not let me drink. For shame, a mother with two children left to die of thirst, but the trick was on them. We can be thirsty, but we cannot die. Shame on the peasants, the silly people who must live forever in the slime of their pond."

The enchanted green frogs would sometimes stand as still as statues, and other times they would croak and jump. When Latona became upset, they froze; these half-human and half-frogs turned their faces skyward as if begging the gods of Mount Olympus for their freedom.

Latona wailed and then crumpled to her knees in front of the fountain. As she struck it with her fists, her white hands made the clouds rumble and it started to rain. She cupped her hands and then drank the rainwater. The water seemed to satisfy her, and she sat back on her heels. The rain stopped.

"Grandmother?" Nimue asked tentatively.

Latona turned around with fright, her eyes wide. She flung her arms out, and wind started to swirl. Nimue did not want to be engulfed in a tornado or turned into a frog.

"Grandmother," she said, attempting to calm the wrath, "you are known across the world as a protector of young children, the beauty of the night."

Latona laughed with bitterness, and it occurred to Nimue that even a kind Mother Goddess can only take but so much abuse.

"I mean *NO* harm!" Nimue added quickly. "I am your granddaughter."

Latona looked at her suspiciously. It was then that Nimue noticed her grandmother's incredible beauty. Her body was full, and her olive skin was youthful. Long thick brunette hair had been tossed by wind and sea, yet no tangled curl could take away from her exquisite form. Although she was the epitome of feminine loveliness, her large blue eyes looked bloodshot from weeping.

"My mother is Diana," Nina continued. "I am known by both Celts and Romans as Nimue."

"Nimue?" the older woman questioned. Latona paused for a moment, then said, "We always wondered what happened to you."

"You don't know?" Nimue asked, her eyes filling with tears.

"We knew that to survive my daughter, Diana, walked into the wild woods where she was worshipped by some," replied Latona, offering a radiant smile. "But she had to forget herself."

The wind responded to Latona's mood and calmed. The dark clouds vanished, the sunlight returned, and the sea sparkled blue again. A flying fish took a heroic leap beyond the waves.

"It isn't magic exactly, child," Latona said, reading her grand-daughter's thoughts. "It's that the elements do my bidding."

Nimue knew her grandmother was one of the great oracles who now lived in exile. There were many ladies of lakes, rivers and seas who had experienced similar fates. She wondered how many women lived as outcasts due to the love of one god or another. Latona stood and put a large warm hand on Nimue's shoulder, then paused as if reading her granddaughter's life, or perhaps her many lifetimes.

"Diana gave me to my foster mother, Anna," Nimue told her. "I do not know my family."

"Ah, my sweet grandchild," said Latona, taking her granddaughter into her great arms. "I loved my children, Diana and Apollo, and raised them as well as I could on Delos. Eventually they left me here, and although I was sad, I knew they had their own destiny."

Latona's breasts were full, she smelled like sweet milk, and her embrace was like that of a friendly wave tumbling to shore. Her power was immense. It had never occurred to Nimue that a Roman Goddess could be so enchanting.

"All goddesses have their charms," shared Latona. "Mine is motherhood. Jupiter couldn't resist me, whatever his wife, Juno, thought."

"I heard Juno was jealous," said Nimue.

"There was no end to it." Latona shook her head. "Juno sent her serpent, Python, to chase me and made Gaea promise there would be no place to give birth, no place to rest or drink or raise my babes."

"What did you do?"

"Neptune showed us this floating island that is neither of earth nor sea. It is a place in-between."

"Juno or Python couldn't find you here?"

"Juno has trouble seeing through granite," revealed Latona. "So Jupiter shielded me, then caused a storm and brought us here."

Latona took her granddaughter's hand, and they walked toward the beach. The terrain was unfamiliar to Nimue, yet she felt as though she had seen it before. The living landscape was made of white, blue and tan. She could not see any trees or buildings, just a wide expanse of water, earth and sky. There was no place to find shelter here beneath the hot sun.

"They worshipped Dionysus on Delos," she said. "The Romans called him Bacchus, and those who worshipped him would become possessed with the spirit of wine, women, and the lustier elementals." She paused and then looked at her granddaughter thoughtfully. "He was your father."

"Yes, I know," said Nina. "But though Diana told me that too, I have never met Bacchus."

"Oh, he drove Diana mad," Latona told her. "Later, people started tearing down her temples and she had to hide you away. The time of the goddess, of nature, and love… our ecstatic way of life ended abruptly."

"I'm sorry, Grandmother," consoled Nimue sadly.

"Fools." Latona looked angry, but then her expression softened. "Well, we all need shared life experiences."

Latona began to walk up the central mountain toward a series of abandoned columns. She was strong and moved quickly. Nimue struggled to keep up with her. Reaching a ledge, they stopped and gazed out across the cerulean sea.

"I imagine Diana felt the Priestesses of Avalon would tend to you well and allow you to become what you are meant to be." Latona looked at her granddaughter with affection.

"Perhaps she was right," Nimue responded. "Otherworldly Avalon is the place where I am called Nimue; a place Merlin knows well."

"Jupiter was well practiced at traveling through the Olympian Round Oak to the Blessed Isles," Latona shared. "And he learned how to shape-shift into an eagle, or walk through a lake, to see you. Your grandfather, Jupiter, has always loved you."

Nimue wondered in this landscape where a great Oak might be found. Delos seemed mostly tree-less although there were a few Palms with yellow-flowered iceplants and some daisies growing at their base, but perhaps there were Oaks in Olympus. As she walked behind Latona, Nimue pondered whether the giant eagle that had brought her to Delos might be Jupiter but did not feel it was the right time to ask.

"I was sent away from my family," Nimue pointed out. "And made an orphan."

Latona stopped and turned around. From high up on the island, they looked out again across the glistening water. Birds circled, then dived into the water looking for fish.

"I was also exiled from my home and to this place between sky and sea," said Latona. "I am comfortable enough in my solitude, but I have never grown used to it. The sun never sets, so there is eternal light."

The air was warm, and Nimue noticed again that it did not seem that Latona had aged in this in-between world. Nimue knew what it was like to feel you were an exile, a displaced person, to long for your home and true family. She wondered why women so often had to endure abandonment and loneliness. Even Latona's children had left her and had not returned, though she had given life to them. *We all have destinies that we must live into,* Nimue thought.

"Granddaughter of the god of sky and thunder, you were given to foster parents for safekeeping. You are semi-mortal with many gifts."

"I am between lives," Nimue explained. "I am known as a dark sorceress, the one who sealed Merlin in a tree. The one reviled by Camelot."

"And so, the prophecy is true." Latona looked thoughtful. "You were Merlin's lover.... And... Exiled like me...."

"I had no wish to harm Merlin," Nimue revealed. "Or to destroy Camelot."

"Love can be very strange," observed Latona. "Sometimes we cause devastation when there is no intention to cause harm at all." She sighed and continued walking up the steep incline.

Once they reached the first marble pillar, Latona placed a large warm hand on one of the statues carved to look like a white dog. Looking behind one of its paws, she located a long and narrow chest half-buried in the sand and picked it up. The chest, which was about three feet long, had carvings of running deer carved into the wood. Latona looked at it carefully and then dusted it off.

"Diana loved her bows and arrows. All she left me was an empty quiver; she said it would be important one day. I feel it is for you."

Latona opened the chest and took out the quiver, which Nimue accepted with gratitude. This was the first and probably the only physical gift she would ever receive from the Diana who was a revered Goddess and her Roman mother. Looking at the intricate patterns in the leather, she could see crescent moons, deer and hounds carved into the skin. It was only at this moment that Nimue realized she was not crazy at all but truly from a lineage of magical women. These were women who had been betrayed and exiled, but nevertheless they were mystics.

"Those are Diana's symbols," explained Latona, pointing to the quiver. "She said one day it would help someone important solve a riddle."

As Nimue touched each symbol, she felt that a part of her ancestral self was restored in her body and soul. The quiver was her true vessel, the deer her gentleness, the hounds her strength, and the crescent moon her wisdom. She was the daughter of Diana, goddess of the moon, wild animals, and nature, and linked to the even more ancient Greek goddess, Artemis. Looking at these symbols, Nimue felt she did not know her mother at all. As she studied each carving, it was as if something deep within her psyche activated; her ancestral roots grew, and Nimue understood she was also an Olympian.

"I do love Jupiter in a way…." Latona was saying as she gazed out at the ocean. Her sentence had trailed off, but now she turned to Nimue and resumed. "Many women love powerful men and most know they cannot keep them. Perhaps you were lucky that you could be Merlin's jailor."

For a moment they laughed together by the sparkling sea.

"Merlin was wrapped in the arms of the White Deva for a long time," Nimue told her. "But he is free now."

"Wise Merlin continues to live into his destiny," Latona revealed, as she sat down on a flat boulder. "He is older than the Olympians. I have seen his origin in the Foretime. He knows Neptune well but calls him Manannán. Like many of us, the old sea god is also a shape-shifter. That's what we must do at the turning of the ages, if we wish to survive into the New Time."

They sat together taking in the beautiful view, enjoying the nourishment that comes from the love between grandmother and granddaughter. Then the two continued their climb to the summit where the clear crystal pool acted as a mirror between worlds.

Chapter 25

Curse of The Crystal Pool

Delos, An Otherworld

Nimue sat on a stone beside her grandmother and peered into the crystal pool, looking at their reflection. For some reason, she felt very sad, as though the wound of her heart was attempting to reveal itself. Perhaps, like Latona, she also yearned to be touched, wanted and admired.

"I believe you are the one who can free me from the curse of the crystal pool," said Latona.

"It looks more like a mirror," Nimue observed.

The muddy pool at the base of the mountain seemed very different, disturbed somehow. But this pool appeared almost transcendent.

"The lower pool is like me," said Latona. "It's soiled and cursed. While the upper crystal pool is more like Juno, reflecting the clear sky of the Olympians."

"There's more life in a muddy pond than a stagnant reflecting pool," Nimue noted, gazing into the mirror-like water. An image began to blaze inside the pool, and Nimue bent over to take a deeper

153

look. For a moment she thought she saw a woman's face, but then the image shifted to a pure flame.

"How long have you been here?" Nimue asked.

Sadly Latona reported, "For centuries, I have been in the in-between world of Delos. I have left, but something always chases me back here to this veiled place. I am a refugee but generally safe here from Juno's wrath."

Nimue thought she could see eyes again in the crystal pool and wondered if Juno could observe her through the water. She was certain that the goddess would not be impressed to discover her there. After all, she was the semi-mortal daughter of Bacchus whose mother, Semele, had been consumed by fire. Hiding her unborn in his thigh, Jupiter was able to save the child who would one day be known as Bacchus.

"Jupiter created a cloud to hide our amorous actions from the judgments of others."

"What year is it?" Nina asked.

"There is no time here," Latona answered. "The sun is always in the same position."

It occurred to Nimue that spending centuries in a place without night must be very strange. On enchanted Delos, there was no movement between day and night, no moonlight to show her the way, no shadows where she could hide and rest.

"Is Juno still angry?" Nimue wondered. "It has been thousands of years."

"Time exists in spirals, and so you can say there is no such thing as linear time, or not here at least," Latona explained. "Juno's jealousy remains the same."

"Perhaps I could appeal to her?" Nimue suggested.

"That would be unwise," Latona warned her. "She might try to kill you."

Nimue shuddered, remembering the stories of Juno's wrath. She also remembered the heat of jealousy that arose within her when the White Deva wove her icy web around Merlin. Even though she would always miss him, Nimue had allowed Merlin to choose his own destiny. The old wizard was unbound, and so was she. There was only love in her heart now. For a moment, she thought of Owen, and what had passed between them at the cottage.

Peering into the mirror pool, she thought some more of Owen. An image emerged of a Faery woman with long fair hair sitting beside a flowing fountain. Owen sat with her and she noticed a strange dark ring on his finger.

"He's married to a Supernatural woman," she thought. *"Now it makes sense. He's not free but caught in an ancient promise."*

Latona leaned in and looked into the mirror pool.

"That's Laudine de Landuc," said Latona. "She's another woman who is bound to a fountain."

"Why?" asked Nimue. "And who is her husband?"

"Generally, the Black Knight," said Latona. "But the young lion, known as Yvain a knight of the Round Table, killed him and thus became bound to the land and to Laudine."

Nimue stared into the pool thinking that it is not only women who get stuck, but also men.

"Is there any way to liberate him?" she asked her grandmother.

Latona looked at her, and then patted her hand.

"Are you in love with him?"

"In a different timeline," she explained. "But I always felt he wasn't free."

"I believe they have a child," said Latona. "Not that children necessarily stop a deep love."

Nimue continued to look into the mirror pool, and she could see a little girl with blonde curls playing with the sparkles that flew out of the flowing fountain. They observed Yvain kiss Laudine.

"He's in love with her," said Nimue. "I'm glad to know his heart lies elsewhere."

It was at that moment that Merlin's face arose to the surface of the Crystal Pool.

Merlin, Nimue thought. *How do I help liberate Latona?*

End the curse, she heard in response.

The scene in the Crystal Pool shifted and Latona and Nimue could see silver dolphins, which made them both laugh with delight.

"We cannot be trapped by old jealousies," Nimue asserted.

Latona sighed.

Does Latona not believe it's possible? Nimue wondered.

They began to make the long trek back down to the base of the mountain. Nimue realized that this mountain encased by sea was Latona's eternal world. Even at her time imprisoned in St. Nectan's Glen, Nimue knew the incarceration would end. She thought of the despair that comes with perpetual confinement, no matter how beautiful the home or landscape. Nimue thought of Guinevere and the many queens who lived in solitary confinement within the walls of castles or priories. Meanwhile, other women slept unprotected in the wind and rain. She wondered where the fall of the feminine had occurred, and if it would be possible to heal it.

There is a flame within all matter, Nimue could hear someone whisper. Looking around, she wondered if it was Merlin.

"Grandmother," said Nimue, "I believe the exile is deeper than the personal wounds we carry. It's as though the Divine Feminine consciousness has been taken off the planet…. I believe Mother Gaea was intentionally removed by those who wish to control and dominate others."

Latona stopped in her tracks and turned around, staring at her granddaughter.

"The two pools must flow together again," said Nimue. "That's the way out of the banishment. Juno on Mount Olympus is as separated as we are, just confined in the sky with an unfaithful husband that she cannot control. Maybe she feels just as betrayed as we do. In some way, we are all exiles."

Latona blinked, registering what her granddaughter was saying.

"Yes. We need Mother Earth's dimension of love and natural justice to return to Earth," agreed Latona.

"To the Greeks, she was the first immortal, Gaea, the Mother of all Creation," Nimue continued. "She lived before heaven and earth were separated and remembers wholeness. In the future, she is known as Lady Gaea, because she is evolving into an eleventh-ray ascended master."

"This mountain has been erected to divide the starry feminine from the earthly mother," Latona explained. She hurled a rock into the sea with fury. "It's all so obvious. Jupiter fooled me. By Rhea, may all gods be damned."

They made their way back down to the lower pool in silence. Latona's curse of the gods lingered over her like a black cloud; even her countenance had darkened. Nimue attempted to ignore it, but she knew the face of the dark goddess also has wisdom.

Sitting beside the muddy fountain again, Nimue watched the enchanted green frogs as they leapt and played in the mud. They caught bugs with their tongues and caused more mud to slide into the pool. Even the flowers that lined the edges had become soiled.

Nimue struggled with her feelings. She looked up toward the sunlight and refused to be taken over by sorrow. Instead, she focused on what was around her in the present moment. She trusted the signs and symbols that were always around, unseen and ready for discovery. *Life is always trying to evolve,* she thought.

A frog jumped on her feet. Tickled by their movements, she giggled. As she watched the frogs jumping in and out of the water, Nimue realized that they must have been Latona's only source of entertainment for centuries.

"I suppose it could have been worse," Latona admitted. "It has just been a bit dull."

"You are needed again," Nimue insisted. "The Planetary Earth Star cannot open without you."

"I doubt I am important in the future of this world."

Latona's indifference and apathy irritated Nimue.

"Do you know how many sad displaced refugees there are right now on the planet because of changing climates, crime and violence?"

"I have seen world events in the Crystal Pool," Latona shared. "The twenty-first century is a difficult time for humanity and the planet."

"The planet can thrive again," Nimue stated. "But we must free ourselves so the new energies can flow in and around us."

The landscape around them was desert-like except for the flower-lined stream that ran to the muddy fountain and then meandered to the ocean. They were still sitting on large flat stones by the edge of the lower pool and dipping their toes into the muddy water. Nimue was slightly disgusted by the filth but also hot. One of the frogs jumped on her foot and looked at her with big bulging eyes, and then he glanced up toward the mountain top.

Poor thing, she thought. *You are also enslaved by an enchantment.*

The frog croaked and then jumped back into the muddy water.

Looking up, Nimue was certain there was once a waterfall that connected the higher and lower pools. *Perhaps that is what the frog was trying to tell me?*

"Why don't you release these people from their curse?" Nina asked, pointing to the frogs. "Perhaps they have learned their lesson by now. Next time they see a thirsty mother, they will probably offer her a drink!"

The green frogs started croaking in unison, as if agreeing with her.

Latona trailed her long fingers in the water, creating a figure of eight. Occasionally she snatched at a frog, but they jumped away.

"We need you and your elemental superpowers for more important tasks," Nimue noted.

Nimue noticed that Latona's eyes were as blue as the big sky that surrounded them. Off in the distance, a white veil flapped in the breeze like a bird. It approached them, and then suddenly a strong wind blew it onto a boulder. For a moment, the rock looked like a standing stone from Stonehenge wearing a shroud.

"Jupiter is announcing his arrival," said Latona, standing up.

There was a loud thunderclap and then a bolt of lightning that shook the ground so hard Nimue fell and tumbled by the edge of the pool.

When she stood up, there was a giant of a man standing in front of her. She knew at once that he was her grandfather Jupiter, although he wasn't what she had expected. He was wearing a business suit and carried a large briefcase with blue Thunderbolts etched into it along with an eagle. But his wild tawny hair and blazing eyes were unmistakably those of Jupiter. He exuded a power she had never known before, and Nimue automatically knelt. With his large right hand, he touched her right shoulder.

"Rise Granddaughter," he said. "Let me see you."

Nimue stood, trembling slightly. There was some sort of electric current that made her hair stand out. She tried to pat it down and Latona giggled.

Then, suddenly, Jupiter turned and swept Latona up into his arms and gave her a sensuous kiss.

"I've missed you, my love," he told her. "Maybe we should have another set of twins."

Latona brushed him off fondly and replied, "Not by a muddy pond, Jupiter. You have promised me more than this."

Jupiter turned back around to observe his granddaughter. She also watched him, noting the aura around this handsome man that glowed like a full moon.

"I generally like my children," he remarked. "How is Diana, my wild little huntress?"

"From what I hear, she is busy protecting the forests, and we need heroines in the woods these days," Latona responded. "All over the world animals are going extinct."

"I hear the humans are cutting the forests down for toilet paper and soon no one will have oxygen to breathe." Jupiter sighed. Then he added, "I've never understood human beings."

"Where have you been?" asked Latona, pointing to his briefcase.

"I've been in Manhattan trying to convince corporate executives to use a new technology I've developed for sustainable power and travel." He held up a lightning bolt and grinned. "They seemed to think humanity isn't ready yet. So I suggested the use of hemp and bamboo, which are much easier to grow than trees. They say it is easier to make new plastics and cut virgin forests than to recycle."

"Our civilization needs to make new choices," Nimue said. "Quickly."

"Or it will collapse like Rome, and then all of us will be relegated to an island in the sky," Jupiter predicted. "But Rome had to fall. It happens. And then Olympus ceased to exist also. The roles of the gods must change with the times."

"Why did Rome fall?" asked Nimue.

"Economic corruption, bribery, slaves, endless wars," Jupiter answered. "The German tribes took over in 476 AD. The most organized force generally wins."

Nimue looked at him for a moment, blinking.

"I've been walking through corporate offices reminding them of the inherent rights of all people, the separation of powers, the importance of liberty and order."

"Do you believe the Western world will fall in the twenty-first century?" Nimue asked.

"When there is too much division, debt, inequality and economic ruin, even the greatest countries collapse," said Jupiter. "But I do believe in the West though, particularly America. The ancient principles must adapt to the times. Long may freedom reign!"

Nimue looked at her grandfather and thought about the symbol of the eagle.

"*Demokratis* does mean rule of the people," Latona remarked.

"Athena understood democracy and justice for all," said Jupiter.

"So why does this very erect mountain divide my two pools?"

Knowing he had been caught in a deception, Jupiter blushed, and then shrugged. "I made one for you and one for Juno."

There was a long silence as Latona stared at Jupiter, comprehending her millenniums of imprisonment.

"So it was all based on secrets and lies," she said sadly. "The division of powers also justifies the division of wife and lover?"

Jupiter looked at Latona, then back to Nimue.

"I wanted to be with you, my love," he said to Latona. "But the gods and their protocols. I have also been forced to play a role not of my choosing."

Nimue stared at Jupiter, and it occurred to her that the gods were also bound by laws they did not choose. She wondered if it would be that way in the future.

"Shall we hold an election?" Jupiter asked. "Gods change over time. I believe in fair process and social cohesion."

"No, we don't need a vote. I think you know it's time to come clean," said Latona. "Just tear down what divides the pools. Let's get back to one clear conscience."

"I'm not even sure where to begin," Jupiter said looking at the pools.

Just as at his arrival, a white veil flew past them. They could hear a high-pitched whistling, and then an eagle flew across the wide sea. The women watched him until he was only a speck in the sky, and Jupiter was gone.

Chapter 26

Freedom Begins With You

Delos, An Otherworld

"This prison sentence will never end!" Latona burst into tears. "He just leaves."

Feeling helpless, Nimue sat on a rock listening to the sobs coming from her grandmother. She looked up at the mountain that remained as exalted and solid as ever. An enchanted green frog jumped on her foot, then another frog. All around her, the frogs gathered croaking madly.

"Maybe freedom needs to begin with you, Grandmother," said Nimue, pointing to the frogs.

"They always make noise and drive me crazy," replied Latona with a frown.

"But their slavery is also yours," Nimue told her. "You share the same exile, the same destiny."

Latona looked at the green frogs suspiciously. Their ribbiting ceased and they looked at her with bulging eyes.

"They should be who they were meant to be," said Nimue. "Just people living their lives."

163

The frogs croaked jubilantly.

"But they were so ignorant!" Latona recalled angrily. "The stupid peasants deserve their punishment."

The frogs turned to look at Nimue.

"And as long as they suffer, so will you."

Latona stared at the frogs who stared back.

"They were peasants, not gods!" Latona exclaimed.

Nimue sighed, lost for words.

Latona put her finger into the muddy pool and drew circles that made small whirlpools. The frogs stared up at her silently, wondering if they should fear her.

"We need to adapt to the times we live in," said Nimue. "Maybe you are the one that has built the division between the two pools as much as Jupiter and Juno. It might be your hatred of the frogs that created the mountain. What if you invited Juno over for lunch?"

Latona thought Nimue's ideas were funny and started to laugh. She kicked her feet in the pool, causing water to fly and the frogs to scatter.

"This entire drama began when they refused to quench your thirst."

The frogs surrounded Nimue and started croaking wildly. Jumping up and down, they created a deafening roar.

"They just made a mistake," Nimue pointed out. "Don't we all?"

"They just dirty my pool," said Latona, picking up some slime and tossing it onto the barren land. "They are disgusting."

Latona took her great feet and attempted to stomp on a few frogs.

"Stop!" Nimue shouted. "Domination over isn't the answer."

"We all need to be in our rightful place," said Latona, then she burst into sobs again.

Nimue stood up and started to pace. She knew in the Celtic tradition that when you need magic to happen, you circle a place three times sunwise. She thought that the elementals of Delos would probably respond in much the same way. So she began to recall the magic words Merlin had taught her. Many moons ago, he had told her that the sounds came from the Foretime, when all of life was harmonious, before the fall of Atlantis. Walking sunwise around the pool, she began to chant the Irish word for peace: "*Síocháin, Síocháin, Síocháin…*"

Latona watched her granddaughter walk. The frogs began to follow Nimue, which made Latona curious.

"Do you think they know what you are doing?"

"Yes," said Nimue. "All sentient beings have their own wisdom. Priestess Anna used to tell me that frogs help us cleanse and heal."

Latona stood up and began to walk and chant with Nimue: "*Síocháin, Síocháin, Síocháin…*"

As they finished making the third circle, Latona began to cry again. This time her tears seemed different.

"I don't want to hurt them," said Latona.

"Let the people go, Grandmother," insisted Nimue. "I think next time they will let you drink, maybe even offer you wine."

Latona laughed, then said, "I know the curse but not how to undo it."

"Simply forgive them for their error," Nimue suggested.

"What?" asked Latona, growing furious again. "Those cretins wouldn't allow me to drink when I was thirsty. I had two babies at my breasts!"

"They regret it," Nimue assured her.

Latona frowned and decided to take another tact. "We could fry them and have them for dinner."

"That's still domination over another life form," said Nimue. "It's a huge error."

Latona sighed. "I think Juno sees me as a frog."

"Maybe," replied Nimue. "Relationships tend to be complicated."

"If I released them, I'd have to live amongst peasants," said Latona. "They would probably exclude me, take away my water, poison my air."

"For communities to thrive, we do need rules that both sides agree to," Nimue pointed out. "I believe in a world in which all can thrive."

"That's rather utopian," said Latona. "Idealism lands you into trouble."

"I give up!" screamed Nimue, who then marched off. She decided to walk back up to the mountain top to see if perhaps the crystal pool could offer some other type of advice.

Surrender, she heard her inner voice command.

"Don't go," cried Latona. "I know I'm being horrible. I love you, and Apollo and Diana, and even Jupiter."

"Can you love the frogs?" asked Nimue. "If you can summon compassion in your heart and forgive them, the love will set you and the frogs free from the curse."

Latona stomped on the ground with real fury, then let out a yell that shook many realms. "I hope you hear this, Juno!" she shouted.

Pacing back and forth, Latona began to flap her arms like a bird. Then she began to laugh and whirl.

"Oh, all right," Latona finally conceded. "I forgive the Lycian people who would not let me drink. I let them go. I release them from their curse."

"And Juno?" Nimue asked.

"Oh, I don't blame the incorruptible Juno," Latona told her. "I even forgive the other lovers and all the snakes. By Jove, I'm letting it all go. *Síocháin, Síocháin, Síocháin…*"

With those words, the terrain rumbled, and the frogs began to grow and bulge. They became round-bellied people who continued to jump and play.

"We're free at last!" they shouted in union.

Then one frog added, "We have learned that when someone is thirsty, then they should drink!"

"Hear, hear!" agreed the other frogs.

"Hurrah!" shouted Latona.

The metamorphosis was instant. The entire holy island of Delos shook in response to their joy. They could hear a rushing sound, and soon a waterfall began to rain down onto the muddy pool, which was instantly purified.

"This is absolutely wonderful, Latona!" Nimue cried. "I am so proud of you!" She threw her arms around her grandmother's neck. "Now you are free, and so are your children. This is a happy day."

Chapter 27
Jupiter's Three Gifts
Delos, An Otherworld

A white veil flew past the waterfall, and an eagle landed beside Nimue. There was the sound of whistling, and then Jupiter stood before his granddaughter. He quietly observed the flowing water between the two pools.

"Good work," Jupiter said. "I am inspired when reality flows."

Even with all that she knew, Nimue was charmed by this charismatic man who was her grandfather. Though Jupiter was thousands of years old, he was muscular and exuded sensuousness. Latona could hardly take her eyes off him.

"So you've discovered your sky roots." He smiled so brightly that Nimue had to close her eyes.

"Where did you go after Olympus fell?"

"People abandoned our pantheon," Jupiter replied. "So we moved on to other planes of existence that are more aligned with who we are. I like gentle climates and peaceful beings. You know we never die. I once was Zeus, and now I'm Joe the businessman. I like to be generous, but corporations can be tricky."

"Yes," Nimue muttered.

She really wanted to travel through the great Oak with Jupiter to *Ynis Witrin* and watch the expression on the faces of Naradek, Anna and Adhan and the other priestesses of Avalon as she introduced her grandfather.

"At least a planet is named after me." He laughed in a good-humored way.

"Jolly Jupiter," Latona nicknamed him, enjoying his positive vibe.

"I have business calls to make all over the universe," Jupiter shared. "I bring good luck."

He picked up his briefcase.

Nimue was sad that Jupiter was leaving so soon.

He looked at his granddaughter with soulful eyes. "It is your turn to care for Gaea. I wish you luck."

Opening his briefcase, he pulled out a golden arrow that buzzed and crackled with electricity.

"You might need this," he declared. "It's one of Diana's arrows."

Nimue accepted the arrow, which snapped and sizzled in her hands, although she remained unharmed.

"You have the gift of fire," Jupiter said with delight. "Aim well."

Nimue placed the arrow in the quiver and felt warmth along her spine.

"Use it for the greater good," he added. "The Olympian arrow wields powerful magic and will return to you after being fired."

Jupiter started to leave.

"Wait," she called out. "Where is my father?"

"Bacchus always seems to be at a party," he noted.

Latona giggled again. "Those ecstatic woodland parties can distract the best of us."

Nimue noticed a light in her grandmother's eyes as though she had memories of those orgiastic unions.

"Bacchus returns in each age," explained Jupiter. "Most of us do. Bacchus, Dionysus, Liber or Felix, whatever you want to call him. Haven't you noticed how well the wine industry is doing?"

"Can I see him?" Nimue asked tentatively.

"He's still alive in the spiral of time," Jupiter told her.

"We all seek the ones we love," said Latona.

Jupiter offered out a hand to Latona, and she walked toward him, then put her arms around him. Gazing lovingly at Latona, he pulled her into a tight embrace and gave her a kiss on the mouth.

"We are free to skywalk tonight," he told her. "Let's head to the Upper Worlds."

"But Juno!" Latona protested. "Your wife!"

"Juno has a new god," Jupiter shared. "And that's fine with me. Even the gods and goddesses can choose again. We broke up and I'm free to dance."

Jupiter turned toward Nimue one final time.

"You might need this," he said, handing her a giant eagle feather. "It will help you fly."

Nimue touched the feather and felt her body begin to levitate. She was not ready to go yet, so put it in her quiver.

"Thank you for the gifts, Grandfather," she said with a reverent bow of her head.

"I do not know when we will meet again, Granddaughter, but I am pleased to have seen you and know that you continue the ways of the ancient magic. One day you might outshine Apollo, but don't tell him I said so." He laughed in an amiable way.

"I should leave you with another gift so people know you are my granddaughter!"

A blue light shot out of his right hand. The Lightning Bolt sizzled with pure electricity and writhed like a sea serpent. Nimue was afraid it would kill her, or wound another, but accepted it into her hands, which remained as cool as a river stream.

"You are immortal," he reminded Nimue. "Never forget your roots."

Nimue realized he had granted her the ultimate boon of immortality. She wondered for a moment if her body would always stay youthful while others aged.

Suddenly the Lightning Bolt fully activated. Thunder shook Delos.

Jupiter smiled, then added, "Good things come in threes."

Then a bolt of lightning struck her. Nimue was flying through space and time. Everything was white, and for a moment she thought she saw an island in the sky. She wondered if she was catching a glimpse of Mount Olympus and if her family would be there, arguing and dancing. She also felt drawn to the older Olympus of the Ancient Greeks.

"Gaea?" she whispered. "Zeus?"

Suddenly a giant eagle grabbed Nimue in its talons. A storm began to rage. Continual flashes of lightning blazed through the sky, but did not seem to bother the bird. Off in the distance, she could see a large lenticular cloud.

Chapter 28

The Golden Harp

Elysium (The Sky Temple)
In-Between Time

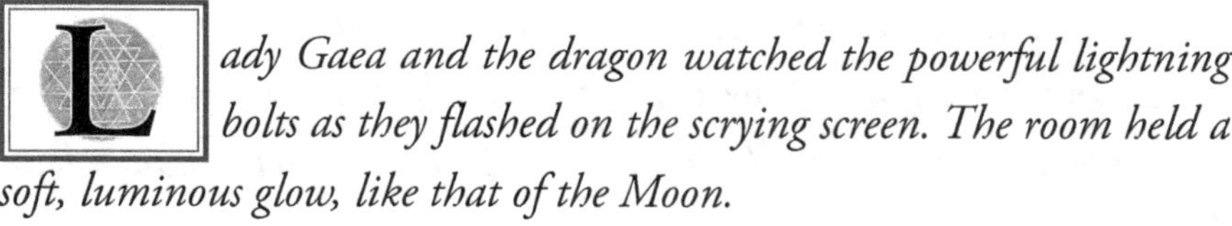

Lady Gaea and the dragon watched the powerful lightning bolts as they flashed on the scrying screen. The room held a soft, luminous glow, like that of the Moon.

"I am relieved that Latona is finally free," Lady Gaea said. "It has troubled me for centuries that she could not settle. It looks as though Diana's challenge comes next."

"Goddess Diana has always been well loved," Delphyne snorted, whisps of smoke rising in rings above her. "And the more ancient Artemis."

"Actually, Diana's temples were torn down," Lady Gaea countered. "She had to disappear and give her child away."

"That's sad," Delphyne replied, turning blue.

The scrying screen flashed, capturing their attention, and they watched a life scene of the creation of the Temple of Diana in Ephesus, which was lovingly created over centuries. The artisans used the purest white marble to construct one of the wonders of the world. Images of a goddess with many breasts flashed above the workers, indicating how well-loved she had

173

been. As time passed, Diana was shown with shining auburn hair and pale skin, a lunar disk crowning her head. As she pulled a golden arrow from her archer's quiver, a doe leapt beside her. Diana ran protectively beside the creature.

"I forgot how beautiful Diana was," remarked the dragon.

"She loved to dash through the forest with the wild animals," recalled Lady Gaea. "I've always had a deep love for her and her service to the natural world."

They watched as Diana ran, her lithe body shape-shifting into a deer. Her divine breath brought life to the forest and other animals scampered beside her. She arrived by a lake and settled into her own form. Bending down, she peered into the still water. It acted as a mirror and her eyes widened. Reaching into the lake, she pulled out a golden harp.

Diana stood up and the image faded. Then a modern version of Diana began to flicker on the screen. This Diana also had auburn hair, but she was sitting at a desk writing in a journal.

"Diana lives in the twenty-first century too," Lady Gaea pointed out. "Although she is less revered today."

"Maybe Diana is happier now that she doesn't have to stand on a pedestal wondering when she will be knocked down," the dragon speculated. "Amazing how the gods and goddesses always return. It gives me hope."

"I sense she is lonely, although she still loves her brother Apollo, or Blaise."

The images stopped flashing on the scrying screen.

"Diana is a goddess who survived better than others. She learned how to shape-shift with the times. Sometimes pretending to be ordinary is a good survival tactic."

"I can become a worm," said Delphyne. "Very hard to find and extremely mundane."

"*You can become anything you dream up,*" *Lady Gaea noted.* "*It's a useful ability. Besides, there's a spark of light in every being.*"

"*What is Diana's challenge?*" *the dragon asked.* "*And how can I serve her?*"

"*She's trying to meet with Lance Pelleas,*" *Lady Gaea replied.*

"*Is that so very difficult? She did marry Felix Liber, the wild old Bacchian shape-shifter.*"

"*Well, she might be ready for a new type of relationship, one that's a bit more stable and focused on her.*"

"*Dragons are less complicated,*" *Delphyne observed.* "*We just wrap around each other and create new dragons when we feel like it.*"

"*It can be hard to love again,*" *Lady Gaea shared.* "*It's time for her to remember the gift of the golden harp.*"

"*I can't wait to see what happens.*" *Delphyne let out a fiery chortle.*

Chapter 29

Remember The Ancient Tracks

21ˢᵗ Century Britain

Train Journey to Wales

Diana knew it would be a long train journey, but that gave her time to think and integrate all that had happened. She wondered how she was going to tell Owen's father, Lance Pelleas, that his son had been struck by lightning and then taken into a mythical realm.

Diana touched the necklace Lance had sent her. Running her fingers over the golden harp charm, she wondered if it would inspire her with a hopeful story. Diana knew Lance was a retired barrister currently living in Wales and learning about his Llewellyn lineage and Welsh folklore. However, it was one thing to be well versed in the *Mabinogion* and Grail legend, but another to lose a son to the Otherworld.

Worrying about Owen, she wondered if you ever did become sane again after an experience with the Otherworld. From time to time, Diana thought she could hear her mother Latona calling her name. Life looked different once you knew that there was more to reality than just the linear world. Diana had known since birth that reality was holographic, but she rarely spoke about what she saw. It was not something most people experienced, and she wanted to be ordinary. She longed to be a woman with a partner again in this time period—a woman who knew love.

What's the difference between ancestry and a myth? she wondered. The question remained with her as an unanswered riddle. She often had dreams of the Temple of Ephesus by the sea, its beauty once surpassing all buildings.

Humankind so often destroys what is beautiful, she thought sadly. *We do need to remember the golden templates of Gaea so what is good can resurface from the in-between realms. Maybe Delphi and the sacred groves and cities of light will also rise again, and with them the restored wisdom-keepers.*

She had telephoned Lance Pelleas before leaving the cottage. He had told her he was in his country home just outside of the town of Betws-y-Coed. She said that she needed to speak to him about a pressing matter involving his son, but Lance had seemed unconcerned. If anything, he had sounded distracted. Yet he was acting friendly too, and even appeared excited to be seeing her soon.

"Yes, come see me," he said with eagerness. "I would love to take you out to dinner. I have been reading the poetry of Taliesin and I've been contemplating the power of shape-shifting at will."

Diana thought his reading might prove useful but had not commented on it.

Lance then had asked her if she would like to go on an outing with him to walk beside the mystical Bala Lake. He was insistent that he had something important to tell her also.

Diana touched her necklace with the golden harp again and blushed slightly. She was being invited to yet another place where King Arthur and his knights had ventured on the Quest for the Grail, Excalibur, and the other magical Hallows of Britain. She wondered why she was being invited into new territory. Diana knew that Romans and Celts had danced and fought with each other for centuries, but perhaps something new was being called for now. After all, people had been coming to the British Isles for centuries to learn about magic.

Lance had invited her for dinner at the Royal Oak Hotel. Diana wondered why she was not being welcomed at his house. However, she decided that just meeting him in a neutral place might be better. She was traveling first to Llandudno Junction, where she would then change trains for a short journey to Betws-y-Coed, a town nestled in the Gwydir Forest with a view of Snowdonia National Park.

Blaise claimed that the Welsh tribe is one of the oldest in the world. Diana thought of the many centuries that people had lived and worshipped in this sacred country of Wales. It is the home of Arthurian legend, and for some reason, the spirits of Camelot were calling to her. Something had been left unfinished, and perhaps that was connected to Owen's disappearance. She hoped the young man had somehow miraculously survived. Looking out of the train window at the vista of mountains covered in snow, she became fascinated by the patterns on the ground.

The people would certainly have been protected here by these great mountain peaks, Diana thought to herself as she looked out at the dramatic landscape. The colossal mountains and the deep silver lakes made her think of the tales of Dinas Affaron, the Palace of Illusion, where the healers and wise people lived. The ones known as the Pheryllt resided nearby in a world between worlds.

The gentle sway of the train on the tracks was making her drowsy. Diana's head nodded as she fell into a light slumber.

Dream

There was a shadow on the white snow. As Diana looked more closely, she could see a face. In her dream, she was walking along one of the ancient trackways of Wales, Sarn Helen.

"It is time that we speak," a creature said.

Diana realized that she was speaking to one of the most ancient landscape goddesses.

"Elen," Diana replied with a bow. "Shakti of the British Isles, how lovely to see you."

"Goddess Diana." Elen of the Ways bowed her antlered head with mutual respect.

Diana realized that Elen's energy was intense, even fierce. The ancient deity, Elen, shape-shifted from a lovely young woman with fawn-colored hair, pale green eyes, and a long pale face to a reindeer with gentle dark eyes. Elen seemed to have interesting and contradictory powers: tenderness, sensual energy, and the force of liberation that made her seem both appealing and dangerous.

"I once ran with the deer people," Diana told her. "In a different lifetime."

"A true man is untamed," Elen noted. "He knows his own heart and follows it above and beyond all things. You need to remember that you are still a goddess."

In her dream, Diana returned to the train and Elen followed, then sat down in humanoid form on the seat beside her. She was so large that Diana needed to look up to meet her gaze. Elen's antlers were crowned with leaves and flowers. Her scent was of mountain meadows and fir trees. Elen's eyes were green and mesmerizing, and then they gently shifted to the eyes of a doe. Diana felt mysterious sparkling energies transfer into her body. She was also feeling powerful, dangerous, magical, and seriously appealing.

"To be your man, Lance must remember his fire," said Elen. "But that's only the beginning of rebuilding Camelot. Then you must find Cymru, the old Wales where the magic still lingers. It waits for you. Remember the ancient tracks."

Deer woman Elen then leapt out of the train as graceful as any doe and disappeared into the landscape.

Betws-y-Coed, Wales

"This is Betws-y-Coed," a passenger said to Diana, giving her a nudge.

Diana opened her eyes and realized she had been asleep and dreaming. *Or was it a dream?*

After putting on her backpack and grabbing her luggage in a hurry, Diana rushed out of the train before the doors closed. She had a short walk to the Royal Oak Hotel, where she would be spending the night after meeting with Lance Pelleas. It was late afternoon, so she had time to check in and rest before meeting him.

Betws-y-Coed was a beautiful little village with handsome stone and grey slate buildings surrounded by forests. Diana could hear the click of her boots as she walked on the road that ran beside the Llugwy River toward the Royal Oak Hotel. She remembered Daphne telling her that the hotel had once been a Victorian coaching inn, and later the residence of an Artists' Colony. The mountain air enveloped her like an embrace, and she felt that the magic of Snowdonia was welcoming her.

Chapter 30

Diana's Riddle

Snowdonia National Park, Wales, 21st Century

Diana awoke with a start. Her alarm was buzzing, and she looked at the time. She meant to have a quick nap at the hotel. Now it was 7 pm, and she had promised to meet Lance Pelleas in fifteen minutes. She threw a dress on quickly, rummaged around until she found her hairbrush and toothbrush, used both, and then quickly added some lipstick.

She ran down the narrow flight of stairs and onward to the dining room. Diana looked around for Lance, but he was nowhere to be seen. Checking her phone, she wondered if he was late and had tried to call. She had no cell service, but a reservation had been made for a table for two by the window. Diana sat down and looked at the single candle that burned beside a rose in a small clear vase. The flickering light made a pattern of deer antlers on the table that reminded her of the dream during her train ride.

After twenty minutes, Lance Pelleas had still not arrived, so Diana decided to order a starter. Once an hour had passed, Diana knew something was wrong. She connected her phone to the hotel wi-fi,

183

but there were no voice or text messages, nor did the front desk have any news for her. Eventually, she was able to put through a call to his house using a hotel landline, but the phone just rang with no answer.

After walking back to her table, she decided to have leek and potato soup. As she sipped the warm broth, the charm on the necklace Lance had given her bumped against the spoon. Diana sat bolt upright and touched the golden harp. Owen Pelleas had told her it was fashioned after the harp from Bala Lake. *It's a sign!*

Diana paid her bill, and then went to the front desk to ask if someone could tell her the legend of Bala Lake. The concierge, a very thin and pale girl, looked at her with a sparkle in her eyes and said that she did indeed know the tale. The girl introduced herself as Keri, and she walked with Diana to a private area where they could speak.

"The folks in this area say that there once was a palace in Bala where a giant lived," said Keri. "It's just folklore, of course."

"I love tales, especially ones related to golden harps," replied Diana, touching her necklace.

"The giant's name was Tegid Foel and he had a bad reputation, as really wicked. He was selfish and never helped the poor people of the area. Though warned by the gods to change, Tegid never did. One night during a feast, a harpist played but was warned to leave by a bird, and in his haste, he forgot the harp. By the next morning, the giant's palace had disappeared into the lake. The harp floated to the surface of the water, but the palace and the giant were never seen again."

"It sounds like the harp knows how to walk between worlds," said Diana.

"Or how to survive," Keri suggested.

Diana thanked the young woman and gave her a tip, which Keri gratefully received. Keri gave her a map with directions to the lake.

"Watch out for Teggie, the lake monster," the concierge said with a mischievous glint.

There was no word from Lance that night.

The next morning Diana rented a car, and as soon as she was able, she sped off along the narrow roads toward Bala Lake. After parking the car, she walked along the promenade. Looking at a sign, she could see the walk around the lake was fourteen miles. She breathed in the fresh air and gazed across the largest freshwater lake in Wales. She could see a pier that seemed to disappear into the mist and walked toward it. She thought of the giant, Teggie. The idea gave her a chill. She hoped Lance Pelleas had simply forgotten their meeting. She seemed to have come to a dead end.

She walked for a few miles, but eventually decided to turn around. Knowing that there are times when you simply must await the guidance of the guardians, she drove back to the hotel. Whatever was happening, Diana knew she would be shown the way when the time was right.

She telephoned Daphne from the hotel and spoke to her briefly. Daphne also thought it odd that Lance had missed their dinner and wondered if Morgen had anything to do with his absence. After she hung up the phone, Diana took out a notebook and began journaling. She needed to put all the pieces together. Feeling tired, she stretched on the bed and fell asleep.

Elysium (The Sky Temple)
In-Between Time

"It's time for Diana to visit us," said Lady Gaea. "She needs to remember her gifts."

"I haven't seen her in person for a long time," Delphyne replied. She snorted, sending white steam throughout the temple. "I'll go collect her."

"Just her dream body."

"Oh good," responded Delphyne. "Light bodies are easier to fly with."

The dragon dove off the side of the temple into the sky below.

Lady Gaea closed her eyes. One thing she had always loved to do was nap. She drifted off.

"Gaea… Gaea," the dragon said, awakening the Lady, "you have a visitor."

Diana sat in the yellow chair by the Round Table blinking.

"Where am I?" Diana asked, dreamily.

"Elysium," Gaea told her. "It's in-between worlds."

"The Elysium Fields, how wonderful."

Diana stared at the Round Table and then looked around the Sky Temple.

"I must be dreaming," said Diana, standing up and putting a hand on the Round Table.

"It is rather like a dream," Delphyne agreed. "We are in an alternate reality."

Diana ran her fingers over the crystals embedded in the Round Table, then looked intently at Lady Gaea.

"The pattern in the table is that of the Temple of Light," said Diana.

"Yes, the template was also called Logres by the ancient ones in the Foretime."

Diana touched the Round Table with reverence. It responded by glowing. An image of the Milky Way flashed across the table. "You must remember when the world was young and it was still a garden, an Eden," she said to the table.

"You are seeing the gold print of what is to come," Lady Gaea explained. "The divine blueprint of the Golden Age."

"An enormous change is about to take place on Earth," the dragon shared. "And the light workers are being called to assist in the rebuilding of the landscape zodiac."

"There is the promise of a Renaissance," Lady Gaea added. "A beautiful future for humanity."

"Do you remember your temples?" Delphyne asked Diana.

She blinked.

"Yes, several temples," Diana replied, after a pause. "Several zodiacs also, both on land and in the sky." She glanced around the Sky Temple and added, "They are not so different from your temple, Lady Gaea." Diana gazed up at the sky. "The temples of Mount Olympus are dazzling."

The other two also looked up and could see the constellations, as well as planets shining like radiant stars.

"There is a riddle for you to solve," Gaea revealed.

"And what is it?" asked Diana.

"How do a goddess and a knight meet?"

"By the design of destiny," Diana answered.

"Correct... second riddle," said Delphyne. "What is their purpose?"

"Whatever the gods choose," said Diana. "It's written in the stars."

Delphyne quietly observed Diana, who was now studying the patterns of stars and constellations on the Round Table. The double zodiac represented by the table reminded her of something from long before. She looked up at her companions.

"What if we are the gods?" Diana asked, her eyes wide.

Lady Gaea smiled.

"You are a goddess," said the dragon. "You solved the second riddle."

Diana's smile faded as thoughts of Owen and Lance returned to her.

"Who are you looking for?" asked Gaea. "You seem distracted."

"I'm trying to find Lance Pelleas," Diana responded. "And his son, Owen. They have both disappeared."

"Look into the scrying screens," Gaea suggested. "They show many timelines. All you must do is focus on who or what you wish to see. Sometimes our loved ones will find us; then again, we can get surprises."

The three-dimensional tetrahedron arose from the Round Table and three screens flickered. The first scrying screen opened to reveal the scene of a dinner party. Lance, Owen, Morgen, Accolon, Lady Laudine and a small child were seated at a long table enjoying a meal.

"Now that's unexpected!" Diana exclaimed. "I thought maybe he had been abducted!"

"Families can gather between worlds for dinners," Lady Gaea explained. "Especially when there is important business to attend to."

"In the twenty-first century, Morgen is Lance's ex-wife and Owen's mother," Delphyne shared. "It's karma from the lifetime when Lance was King Uriens, and Owen was Yvain."

"Actually," said Diana, observing the scene with great interest. "It's all starting to make sense now."

"Third riddle." Gaea gazed at Diana. "What is the mystical union?"

"It's the transformation from a non-believer into a believer," Diana answered. "The divine channel is open in one person, and then opens for another."

"The riddles are too easy for you," said the dragon. "It sounds like it's time for love. All you have to do is wait for the right time to meet Lance for dinner."

Chapter 31

Dark Magic
London, 21ˢᵗ Century

Now back in London, Daphne's guidance was prompting her to travel to Wales. She felt the trip was urgent. Diana had called to say that not only had Lance Pelleas missed their dinner, he now seemed to be missing, in addition to his son. Blaise was away at an academic conference. She sent him a text, but thought he would never check his phone; so she also wrote a note saying she would be back in a few days and to telephone her.

Daphne's phone rang, and she was glad to see it was Abigail who was calling.

"No one came to the healing gathering today," Abigail said, sounding disturbed. "Ganieda is not here. And neither Sue nor Elen showed up. Nina is also missing. Something is going on."

"Diana said something about Nina going to the Island of Delos to visit her grandmother," Daphne told her.

"Greece?"

"I believe so," said Daphne. "As we know, Diana and Nina have some Greco-Romano ancestry."

"Gosh," Abigail replied thoughtfully. "I'd love to go to Mount Parnassus and visit the Phaedriades Rocks. I would have gone with her if I'd known."

"From what I heard, the visit was rather sudden," Daphne explained. "Meanwhile, I'm packing to go to Wales. I'm going to join Diana in Betws-y-Coed. Do you want to go with me?"

"Betws-y-Coed," repeated Abigail. "I went there with Max years ago. It means 'prayer house in the woods' and it's like heaven there. The gateway to Snowdonia is a good place to start. Yes, I'm ready for an adventure."

"I'll pick you up in half an hour."

"I'll be waiting."

Daphne packed her bags in a rush, got the blue Mini Cooper out of the garage, and drove the few streets to Abigail's home. Abigail hurried out, carrying a heavy suitcase.

"Sorry, I wasn't sure what I might need."

Together they threw Abigail's suitcase onto the back seat, and then Daphne began the drive through the narrow and crowded streets of North London. Abigail looked out the window as they hurried past Hampstead Heath, then headed west. Soon they passed Brent Cross Shopping Centre, which was useful for necessary household items but too large and modern for Abigail's taste. Looking at the graffiti sprayed on several buildings, she wondered when London had become so filthy.

As their trip continued, Abae had the feeling that they were escaping a heavy fist that seemed to hover over London like a threat.

There are too many people, too many rules now. The traffic bottlenecked, and they had to slow to a crawl.

Although the sky was only slightly overcast, Abae sensed a darkness over them. She thought of the storm in Glastonbury and wondered if the dark magicians were following her movements.

"Hello love."

Abigail turned to see the driver of a large van in the next lane observing her from the open window of his vehicle. His eyes looked vacant and she looked away quickly.

"I think someone might be following us," she told Daphne with concern.

Suddenly the van swerved into their lane and Abigail shrieked, but Daphne deftly avoided a collision.

"You'd better take a back street."

Daphne turned off at the next junction, and the van exited too.

"Creepy," commented Abigail.

They exchanged a glance and knew they needed some magic to escape.

"Where's Nina when you need her?" said Daphne.

"Or Ganieda," Abae added.

"What's the Irish word for peace?"

"*Síocháin, Síocháin, Síocháin…*" they chanted.

A white mist surrounded the car, and soon the van was nowhere to be seen.

"I think we lost him," Daphne said.

"The Niente don't care for peace, do they?"

"Apparently not," Daphne responded. "And it looks like they are on our trail."

Soon they were on the M1 driving toward Birmingham.

"It will take about four hours to get to Betws-y-Coed, or a bit longer with traffic," Abigail told her, looking at the map.

"I have good night vision just in case we arrive after sunset, so don't worry," Daphne assured her. But her thoughts were on the dark magicians, and whether they were more powerful at night.

They continued in silence. The two women were both lost in thought, with many questions about the odd events that were happening.

"I suppose Diana did not say anything about Owen?" Abigail asked.

"No," Daphne confirmed.

"There is some sort of mystery going on. All of this doesn't make sense," Abigail noted.

"A riddle of the ancestors," said Daphne.

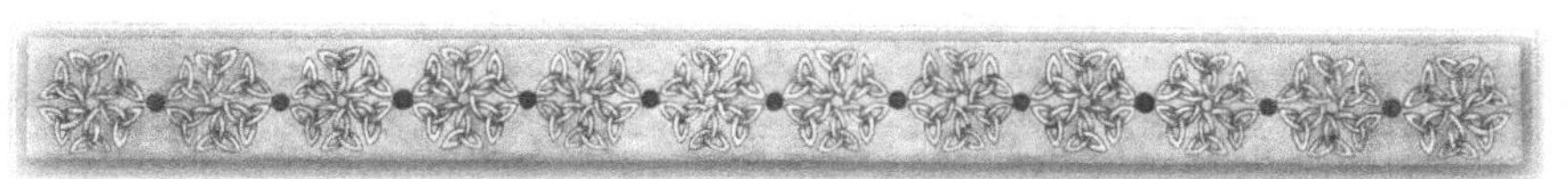

Chapter 32

A Welsh Faery Tale

Snowdonia National Park, Wales, 21st Century

Daphne and Abigail arrived at the Royal Oak late in the afternoon. They called Diana using the courtesy phones in the lobby, and she invited them up to her room. Upon opening her door, Diana was overjoyed to see them. The friends decided to sit in Diana's room for a while and catch up.

"I've been waiting since last night to meet Lance," said Diana. "I believe you already know but I think it's odd because a dinner reservation was made, and I never heard a thing from him."

Diana wondered if she was just on a wild goose chase. "Maybe Lance didn't really want to meet me, and I've been stood up?"

"With that beautiful harp necklace as a gift?" Daphne responded doubtfully.

"Do you think he's with Owen?" asked Abigail. "Maybe he was abducted too!"

"The thought crossed my mind, then I had a very peculiar dream," Diana told them. "I was in a Sky Temple looking at a viewing screen that showed a scene of Lance, Morgen, Accolon and Owen, with a lady and child having dinner."

Daphne's eyes widened with surprise.

"Maybe it wasn't a dream," Abigail suggested.

Diana knew that the quest they were on was not about planning, but instead required following synchronicity.

"Three of us are together now," Daphne pointed out. "I know our next steps will be guided."

Having had no word from Lance, Diana agreed to join them for dinner. The three women wandered down to the lobby of the Royal Oak Hotel and gazed out into the darkness. They could sense the gateway of the Snowdonia mountains, which off in the distance shimmered under a full moon. After the two new guests had checked in, the trio had time for dinner in the Grill Room.

As they waited for a table, the patterned carpet made Daphne feel dizzy, and she wondered at the variety of designs that somehow made a colorful and inviting restaurant. She also noticed a painting of a large black bull with distinctive black horns. The animal seemed to be staring at them.

"The cattle are called Welsh Blacks," said Abigail, when she saw Daphne studying the image of the bull. "The faery cattle some say the Druids used in their sacrifices."

A waitress motioned for them to sit in a large leather-lined booth with an Oak wood table.

"Did the Druids really sacrifice animals?" Daphne asked, as she scooted into the far corner which offered some colorful pillows.

Diana slipped in beside her and Abigail sat opposite them with her back to the river.

"Some say sacrifice was part of temple life," Diana told them. "I'm glad humanity evolved past that."

They all savored their warm leek and potato soup noiselessly while thinking of the history of the Druids.

"There is no evidence that the Druids ever committed human sacrifice," Daphne noted. "The Romans just had to weave a tale wild and terrible enough to make their legions assault unarmed men, women and children."

Haunting images of raiding boats, swimming horses and screaming people passed through Abigail's mind. She stretched and looked around the room, trying to think of something more cheerful to focus on.

"Do you know the Welsh tale of the mystical cow?" Abigail asked. "My grandmother, who was also named Abae, told it to me years ago and said the story might mean something to me one day."

"No," Daphne replied, then sipped some hot chocolate. "But I would like to hear it."

She leaned up against some pillows and settled in for the Welsh faerie tale.

"It's a legend about how the shaggy Welsh Cattle came into being. They are cultural icons," Abigail began. "Some say they arose from the Celtic underworld of *Annwn* through a lake. As local myth has it, elfin ladies used to haunt *Llyn Barfog*, the Bearded Lake, in the hills behind Aberdovey. In the early morning, when the mists ran down off the hills, ladies wearing green would appear with white hounds and white cows. One of the white cows fell in love with a bull that lived there in a field, and the old farmer was in luck one fateful day when he discovered a white faerie cow amongst his herd of black cattle.

"The white faerie cow had many white calves. Her milk was sweet, and the butter the old farmer churned with it and the cheese he made were the greatest known in Wales at the time. The faerie cow always had plenty of milk, and no one ever went hungry. It is said that many people who drank the milk of the white faery cows were healed of illness, even fools were said to grow wise, and depressed people became happy.

"Many years went by, and the farmer grew rich with his herd of cows. One day he decided that the faerie cow had become old, and so he prepared to kill her. The white cow gazed at him with large loving eyes. Unmoved, he swung the bludgeon only to find her shape-shifting back into a faerie woman. She shrieked as he spun backward onto the ground with his weapon still in his hand. Then she ran, and the herd of white faery cows followed her, all jumping into the air and over the clouds. Then they dove back into the lake and returned to the Otherworld. Only one white cow remained behind, and as the farmer watched, she turned black and shaggy. This magic cow is known as the mother of the Welsh Black Cattle."

"Well, that is quite a tale," Diana said.

"You just never know how a faery might disguise herself," pointed out Daphne with a smile. "Or any other goddess, nymph or oracle."

All three laughed with delight.

"I like the story," Daphne told them. "It reminds me that the faerie folk are real."

"And don't forget it," teased Abigail with a twinkle in her eyes.

Betws-y-Coed, Wales

In the morning, they decided to take a day to explore the area and wait for synchronicities to arise to guide them. The three women stopped at a pub for lunch. As they got back onto the road, Abigail realized she had left her sweater behind, so they retraced their steps.

Walking back into the pub, they were greeted as friends.

"You forgot your jumper," called out the middle-aged waitress. She handed the sweater to Abigail. "Where are you going today?"

"Trying to decide," Daphne answered casually.

"You must go visit *Bryn Celli Ddu* in Anglesey," the waitress insisted. "Some say the female Druids were initiated there." She gave them directions to the Isle of Anglesey.

"If Lance doesn't show up by tomorrow, I'm coming with you to Anglesey," said Diana. "I'll take this as a sign."

Daphne drove into the countryside to explore the nearby area, and she smiled, knowing they were being guided with their plans for the next day. The energy had shifted and there was magic in the air.

"The old ones are with us," said Daphne. "Can you sense them?"

In the passenger seat, Abigail nodded. Then she admitted, "I'm really sorry but I have to pee."

Daphne laughed and replied, "Don't worry. We can take a break. Plus, we're just going with what we're led to today."

Seeing a sign for a park, she turned off onto the next street. Then they rode across a rickety bridge to a carpark near a path leading into the woods.

"This will do," Abigail told her.

She got out of the car and disappeared behind some bushes.

The other two women climbed out of the Mini Cooper and stepped toward the hiking path to take a look.

Sensing a presence, Daphne began to hum near the forest path. The trees seemed young but one great Oak had branches that spread wide in a welcoming way, and it seemed to be inviting them into the forest.

Abigail returned. "There's still plenty of daylight. Let's explore the woodland," she suggested.

Laughing to herself as this matched her impulse, Daphne sensed it was the right choice. They ambled down the path and eventually reached a meadow. Noticing a lightly worn sidetrack that led to a dense grove of trees, Daphne decided to explore it and motioned to her friends. The route led them to a stream, where they stepped over some stones to the opposite bank.

Once the three women reached the grove, the sunlight on the path turned dappled, and as they went farther into the woods, the light almost disappeared into darkness. They heard something rustling in the trees. They stopped, wondering whether to be frightened. Then a doe appeared. She looked at the trio with wild eyes, and then bounded off.

"That's Elen of the Wild Ways," Daphne whispered. "An auspicious sign!"

"Helen, the wife of Maximus?" Abigail asked. "I saw a sign indicating that we are standing on Sarn Helen, the Roman road she had built."

"Elen is much older than that incarnation, although their soul is one and the same," Daphne clarified. "She is the Shakti, the lifeforce of the British Isles. The Romans would have called her Venus, the goddess of love. The deer is a good sign because Elen protects travelers."

"May the good deer woman continue to lead, guide and direct us," Diana affirmed.

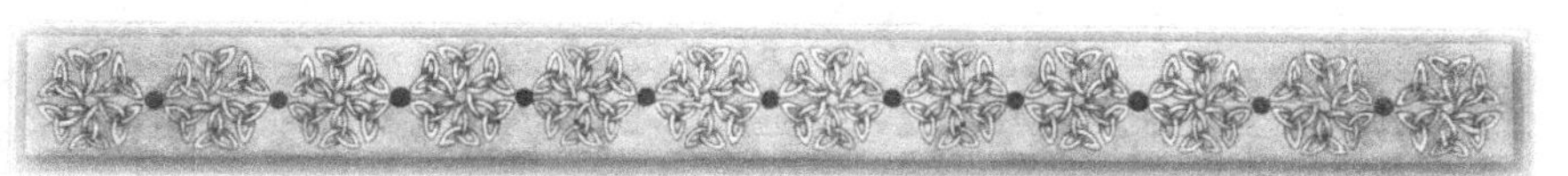

Chapter 33

Three Mystical Women

Wales, 21ˢᵗ Century

The next morning, they checked out of the Royal Oak Hotel, and the concierge produced a map to help them find their way through the mountains of Snowdonia to Anglesey. There was no guarantee that they would have a cellphone signal. Daphne repacked her blue Mini Cooper to make room for a third person, as Abigail and Diana took a walk along Holyhead Road to view the river as it flowed under a stone bridge. Strolling in the heart of the Conway Valley, they took in the sights and sounds of the quaint town of Betws-y-Coed, made magnificent by the Gwydir Forest. A sign by the bridge read that it was here that three tributaries flowing from the West joined the River Conway: the Afon Llugwy, the Afon Lledr and the Afon Machno.

Daphne met up with them and they listened to the flowing water together.

"A place where three rivers meet is magical," Abigail said.

"What happens when three mystical women meet by a place where three rivers converge?" asked Daphne. "Double magic, right? Has to be."

"What will it take to bring Owen and Lance back?" Diana muttered, then sighed. "I feel that I should be frightened and yet, really, I'm just confused. Why am I standing in the middle of a place that's thought to be the origin of Arthurian legend looking for a knight? How does it all connect?"

"The Kingdom of Gwynedd was one of King Arthur's strongholds," Abigail pointed out, while leaning down to regard the river. "And this area was part of it. Can you sense the energy?"

A young couple walked past speaking Welsh.

"I love the language," said Daphne. "It's so ancient."

Diana nodded. She had heard that for many centuries the Welsh language had been banned. In that moment, she was glad to hear people speaking the old tongue. Some nearby children were singing songs that seemed to arise straight out of Arthurian legend. Off in the distance, Diana could see the shimmer of a partial rainbow.

"What are we meant to be remembering?" Daphne asked the water.

"Jump in the river and find out," joked Abigail, giving her friend a bump with her hip.

"I think I'll take the car today instead," Daphne replied with a laugh.

Somewhat reluctantly they climbed into the Mini and set off west toward Anglesey. The sun was shining, and they took their time driving through the unspoiled scenery. The rock-strewn mountains and dense forests were lined with silvery blue lakes.

"As in the tale of the mystical cow, the lakes here are sometimes called the gateways to *Annwn*," Abigail told them. "Gwyn Ap Nudd, Lord of the Underworld, lives there."

"Do you think he's hot?" asked Daphne.

"Sacrilege!" Abigail exclaimed.

"I'll bet he is," said Diana.

"I wonder why the Underworld beings did not rise up and stop Suetonius Paulinus and his Roman legions as he passed this way to Mona?" Abigail asked.

The question was left unanswered.

A shimmering silver lake with a wide carpark seemed to be a good place to stop and stretch. A main path went along the water, but they decided to take an unbeaten one. As the three women walked around the corner, there was an enormous Oak. Its branches reached skyward, and they witnessed its majesty with complete awe.

"It is powerful to meditate beside a great Oak," said Daphne.

Bowing to the tree, they approached respectfully, and then Daphne, who was attuned with tree spirits, performed a ritual to gain access to the inner worlds.

"Here, take these," she told Diana and Abigail, giving them small stones with tiny spirals etched into them. "And hold space for me."

The two friends held the stones reverently, as Daphne continued her ritual.

Promptly a doorway opened within the trunk of the Oak, and Daphne was able to walk through. Diana and Abigail stood patiently, waiting for her return.

After a few moments, Daphne stepped back out of the tree.

"We need to go to *Oriel Ynys Môn*," Daphne told them. "From there we will be guided."

"Where?" Diana and Abigail asked in unison.

"It's a museum on Anglesey."

As they climbed back into the car, Abigail thought about the stories she had heard of the blood-drenched altars of the Druids of Mona. As the women had discussed, no evidence had ever arisen to support those claims.

"It's very easy to destroy the reputation of a person or a people," Abigail pointed out. "I feel the Druids are still upset."

Behind the wheel, Daphne was quiet and focused, paying close attention to the narrow road. The traffic moved quickly past the rugged scenery.

"All you have to do is call us crazy and our power is completely undermined," Abigail continued with a grimace. "I think one of the most harmful things you can do to someone is mirror them incorrectly."

"And tear down their temples," Diana added.

As Daphne gazed out of the front window, she could see herself reflected in the glass. Behind her face was the vast expanse of dark mountains. She smiled at herself, and her mirror image smiled back.

"Why don't we teach children from the beginning the truth of who we are?" Daphne asked with a sigh. "It would be a different world. What if children were taught how to work with the elements, how to find their hallows and sacred tools from the beginning, how to open to their direct knowing?"

Abigail sighed. "The Merlins of this world do hold space for the young ones to retain the memory of their essence. The Druids knew that the teacher was found within the inner heart. You know that when you tap into source, you find the inner teacher, the inner tuition, your intuition."

Daphne could sense a wave of energy passing over her body/mind, and she turned her focus toward her heart. Even as they zipped along the A5, she could feel the sanctuary of her one heart, her inner refuge. It did not matter if they were traveling quickly along a road or sitting in meditation in the forest. Peace was always as close as the body, emotions, her own heart.

"Those who want to conquer us seek to divide us," Abigail remarked, intuiting Daphne's inner process. "A divided person can be easily ruled, and so can a divided people. If you disconnect children's bodies, minds and souls, then you have slaves."

"Why did the Druids let it happen?" Daphne asked with agitation. "Surely they knew they were going to be slaughtered."

The memories came rushing back in, and with her inner vision, Abigail saw the horrifying scene of the Roman soldier with the sword. *Not again,* Abae muttered to herself. For a moment she thought of Ganieda and wondered when they would meet again.

"The Spirit of the Oak said there was something you need to remember," Daphne told Abigail. "When I pull over, you can tap into that lifetime again. I sense Elen of the Ways will guide you."

Chapter 34

Daphne & the Spirit Of the Oak

Wales, 21ˢᵗ Century

aphne drove the car into the next carpark, then turned to face Abigail.

"Are you ready? The Spirit of the Oak said you will soon meet one of the ancient fair folk, and there is something to know first."

"I am ready," Abae said. "Let's stay in the car so we will be undisturbed."

"I'll hold space," Diana told them from the back seat.

"Let the memory surface," Daphne instructed.

Abigail rested her head on the passenger-side car seat and closed her eyes.

"Remember that you are in the twenty-first century—and then look backward. You are here and everything is okay, and so you can be there."

Abigail nodded, asking her inner guidance what it was that she needed to know. Daphne put her hand on Abigail's forehead, activating a type of nature magic that only the forest spirits, the dryads, know.

205

Abigail traveled back in time through trees, roots and land. Suddenly, a Roman General's eyes looked right into Abae's. Their eyes locked, and Abigail let out a small yell and doubled over in pain.

"Come back here now," called out Daphne.

Tears streamed down Abae's cheeks. She still held her belly and felt as if she were vomiting blood.

"It's just a memory," said Daphne. "Stretch and yawn. You're in the twenty-first century and everything is fine."

"Why did I need to remember that I was run through by a sword?" asked Abae.

"There was a force that wanted to destroy the magical ones," Daphne replied. "It still does, following us even now."

"One race was never meant to dominate another," Abae commented. "There is a flow to reality in which all can thrive."

"That's correct," said Daphne. "And now I want to offer you a little dryad magic to heal the sword wound."

Abae stared at her friend, tears still streaming down her cheeks.

"I just don't understand murder and hatred," mumbled Abigail, holding her belly. "I really don't get mean men."

Daphne reached into the back seat and fiddled around until she found what she was looking for. She handed Abae a wand made from a living branch. Abae peered at it with curiosity.

"Watch," said Daphne, who blew on the wood. Immediately a blossom arose from the end.

"A blossoming staff," noted Abae, looking carefully at the budding flowers.

"Place the wand on your belly."

Abae placed it on her belly and felt as though a gentle breeze embraced her. At once, her belly stopped hurting.

"That's how we heal," said Daphne. "Even if we see very sad things in Anglesey, our job is to reinstate the flow of life."

Abae nodded. "I am ready for the next step now."

"Let's find the museum," said Daphne.

Daphne started up the car and they drove onto the main road. It wasn't long before they could see a large steel bridge that crossed the Menai Strait. It would take them onto the Isle of Anglesey, once known as Mona. Abigail felt a flurry of both excitement and dread rise within her.

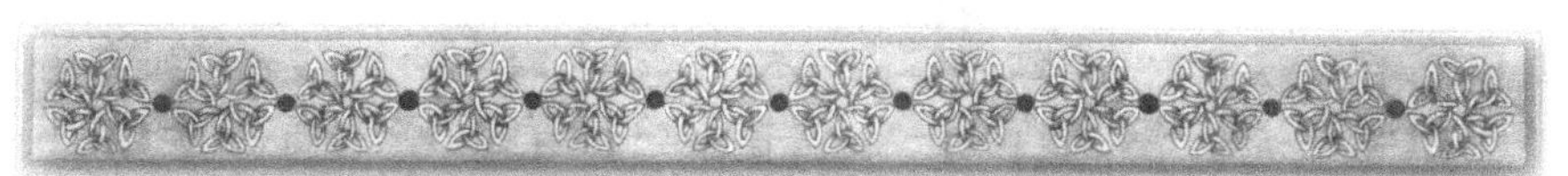

Chapter 35

The Museum

Isle of Anglesey, 21st Century Britain

They drove in silence to *Oriel Ynys Môn*, a museum and art gallery located in Llangefni. Few people were there, although they observed one man wandering around seemingly adrift in the parking lot. Daphne wondered how many souls were still lost, even now suffering from the systematic destruction of the soul of Mona.

The museum had a respectful ambiance. Daphne had the sense that whoever the Druids truly had been, they still represented mystical powers, and the innate desire to connect both to the land and to our ancestors. Reports revealed that, between 100 BC and 60 AD, Mona had been the stronghold of the Druids and a learning center for all of Europe. They were like Dalai Lamas in training as children, schooled for twenty years in the mysteries. Eventually, they would earn the green, then white robes, and become the wise leaders of their communities. The lake *Llyn Cerrig Bach* by the Royal Airforce base was listed as one of their most important sites of worship. There was little else to remind the Welsh people of their ancient traditions, for the Druids had passed their knowledge by oral tradition to keep it pure. With a flash of insight,

209

Daphne felt that in the landscape shrouded in mist, she would still be able to find the codes of the ancestors awaiting their return.

The only written account of the attack on Mona had come from the Roman historian Tacitus. He hadn't been there but described the Druids standing on the edge of the island. The image was haunting. He spoke of black-robed women with wild tousled hair holding torches beside the male Druids, all of them screaming curses.

After walking through several rooms at the museum filled with ancient Welsh artifacts, the three women decided to watch a short film. The documentary was a reimagining of the Druids who had tried to hold Mona against the Roman legions. It was clear that Druid magic was no match for iron swords. The Romans, who wanted to dominate and destroy the spirit of Mona, had their way. Times had changed, and those who wanted to dominate the feminine and nature had arrived. A time of spiritual darkness had come over the land. Meanwhile, the curses would live on in the hearts of men and women long after the massacre.

They did not need to watch the film to know that sacred wells, springs, trees and other sacred landscape features were no longer honored. The Celtic Church had been tolerant of the old ways, but the Roman Catholic Church, which was focused on converting the Pagans, had made it illegal to honor the wells and springs. While Christ was a known force for healing and good, the Niente and dark magicians infiltrated the most beautiful churches and holy sites causing division and confusion, especially amongst Celtic women who had once enjoyed equality. Christianity endured through the centuries, upholding the divine light and supporting the spiritual flames that still burned in people's hearts. But the unaware used religion to divide people from nature, and to control the masses. It was a time of confusion and darkness.

After the Protestant Reformation, there was a return to the natural world. However, those who did not believe in the authority of the Bible and Jesus Christ could be burned at the stake. In the 18th century, during the Enlightenment period, scientific inquiry separated itself from religious dogma. While science allowed freedom of thought, eventually humanity convinced itself that human beings were only a biological accident. Abigail wondered what life would have been like if human beings had been taught that light was both in the divine and in the natural world.

Is Earth just a classroom?

Abae thought about the healing circle and the children who remembered that the faeries, flowers and trees were alive. She felt her little gathering in the garden was, in fact, a great rebellion. Abae knew the illnesses that plagued humanity had long been orchestrated by the sinister Niente and the dark magicians who always lurked in the shadows causing discord and division. The light workers were constantly at odds with the dark magicians, who strived to achieve global domination through the enslavement of souls. Having become more subtle through the Ages, they now infected almost all institutions and corporations. Abae hoped that soon the vibration of the New Earth would spell the downfall and dissolution of the Niente and that a new era would spell the end of their reign of soullessness.

Daphne was also contemplative. She was thinking of how sacred wells were now filled with rubbish, and that trash blocked the passageways to the Otherworlds. Nature and her elements had been dishonored for far too long. She knew that over the centuries and especially since the industrial revolution, the soil, air and water had become increasingly toxic, and now fires burned on many continents. Trees that enriched and protected the soil had been cut down, largely to raise cattle (another gentle animal of the goddess), and there were floods and earthquakes, tornadoes and hurricanes.

All three women knew with certainty that humanity was walking toward doom—unless the wasteland could heal—both personally and collectively.

"It's time to go," said Diana. "We have work to do."

Daphne noticed that her friends' eyes were red and slightly swollen from crying.

They stood up and walked quietly back to the carpark, trembling slightly, yet the warrior within each of them had needed to remember the truth. They had to face what had devastated the spirit of the land, and the soul of the people. Still, the three of them now stood upon the soil of Cymru, so all was not lost.

"History can be terrible," Daphne remarked. "But we are resilient."

Abigail added: "When you have almost been destroyed, you have to reinvent yourself. You must dream yourself back into being."

"I suppose we do that all the time," Daphne replied. "Our forgetting and remembering."

"It's time to go to *Bryn Celli Ddu,* the mound in the dark grove, a place sacred to the Goddess," Diana told the others.

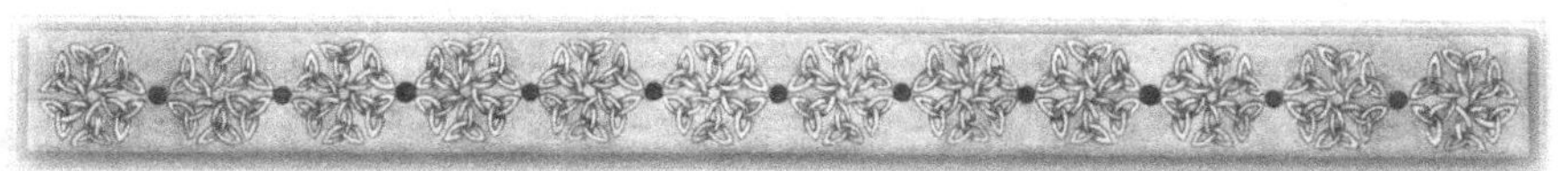

Chapter 36

Abigail & the Sidhe
Isle of Anglesey, 21st Century Britain

Abigail could feel buzzing in her ears, as they approached the five-thousand-year-old sacred site. It was as though the ancestors had something to say. In the apparent world, Daphne, Diana and Abigail were walking across a sheep field like any other in Anglesey. Only this one had a cairn, or burial mound, in the distance.

Abigail knew intuitively to open her sixth sense, so she could start reading the signs and begin connecting more deeply with the ancestors. There was a well-worn dirt path with a hedge that they followed to an open field. At last, they could see the *Bryn Celli Ddu* burial site up close.

They approached the sacred site with respect, and then Abigail placed a smudge stick, as an offering to the spirits of the place, at the base of a large standing stone that stood outside the chambered tomb. Pausing by the grass-covered mound, they noticed that the door looked like a stone vagina, an entrance to the Goddess. They walked clockwise around the structure following a ring of curbstones chanting *Awen*, an old Welsh word of enchantment and inspiration.

213

Then they stood by the entrance, hoping that the deities of the place would welcome them..

It was then that Abigail heard quite clearly: "Enter."

Abigail bowed her head in reverence, then climbed through the tight passageway into the womb of the structure. Daphne and Diana were close behind, but the voice said, "Not the tree nymph or the huntress."

Abigail turned, and she shook her head toward her friends.

Daphne and Diana stopped in their tracks and backed out, understanding that what was to happen was for Abigail alone.

The light was dim inside the cairn, but Abigail could see a tall figure with white skin, hair and clothing. He had long ears with pointed tips, and eyes that seemed yellow-gold, almost as if there were a fire inside of them. Abigail recognized him as one of the old root races, now known as the Sidhe.

"What do you want?" he asked. His voice demanded respect.

"I enter as a friend," Abigail responded gently.

"Humans always want something," he remarked tersely. "Speak."

"I want to heal from an old wrong done to the Druids," Abigail told him. "I sense I was one of them."

He eyed her curiously, and Abigail understood that he was reading her soul field.

"Hum," he said. "It seems so, Abigail. You speak the truth."

Abigail was startled that he knew her name.

"Back then, you had another name. It was Abae, the seer," he noted. "It does not matter now. Names only help us locate ourselves in space and time."

"Welcome, ovate of long life, renewal and health," he continued. "May the circle of the year finish happily, and may a feast be offered in your name."

"What is your name?" Abigail asked, feeling timid.

"You can call me Currach," he replied. "That is not my name."

"Currach," she repeated carefully, remembering that a currach is a type of sea vessel. "Can you help me?"

"Perhaps," he said. "But it does require a journey to Tír na nÓg, the realm of the Fair Folk and the Tuatha de Danann."

"Will I return?"

"Probably, it's a wormhole."

The floor gave way, and Abigail fell through a void. She did not panic, understanding that the wormhole had opened, and she was simply being shown a way into an Otherworld. As Abigail fell, she allowed herself to dissolve into the arms of the great mystery. She made no sound as her body vanished. Images of her childhood flashed before her, then the smile of her young husband, Max, at their wedding. It seemed that all the family members in the pews were smiling upon them. Next, she could see the funeral, his coffin being lowered into the ground. Weeping, she acknowledged that she still felt this loss.

The perception of movement slowed. Abigail wondered if Max had made a similar journey at his death. Sensing the love of the ancestors, Abigail then took on a new form in a different dimension. When Abigail opened her eyes, she was standing beside a pink ocean with silver sparkles. There were undercurrents of deep blue, but the surface was that of a blossoming rose. The lilac sky was lit with many stars and two suns.

A dock appeared in the water where a ship with white sails was waiting for her, and on it, she could see faerie women with long, flowing white dresses. Knowing she was being invited on an Otherworldly adventure, Abigail walked respectfully onto the ship. Then the vessel set sail across the magical sea to Tír na nÓg.

As the warm sea wind blew through her hair, Abigail realized the temperature was more like that of Greece or the Caribbean. It was balmy, and salty. Sea birds screamed overhead, and silver fish jumped in the wake.

And then off in the distance, she could see the land of Tír na nÓg.

The inhabitants of the island knew of her arrival. Abae noticed that the faery women did not disembark with her, but she had the sense they would wait for her return. She was greeted instead by Elfin-soldiers wearing black, white and red armor who stood in an orderly line. Abigail walked off the ship, bowing respectfully, and they nodded courteously in return. They were about her size, or smaller. As she walked onward, Abigail noticed that there was a large ring of much taller Fair Folk, probably a hundred or so in number. They all wore the same ceremonial armor. She could not recognize a gender.

As she stepped into the greater circle surrounded by large standing stones, Abigail heard the light clank and clack of their spears on their silver shields. She walked slowly, clockwise around the enclosure they had made. Each time Abigail nodded to one of the Elfin-folk, they would smack their spear against their personal armor. It made a loud clatter, which sent a jolt of alarm through her body, but she remained calm on the exterior. Although Abigail peered at them, they did not look her in the eye, but beyond her into a distant future or a far different past. She intuitively knew they did not wish to be touched. They stood in the open-air temple, beautiful beneath a lilac sky.

At last Abigail arrived beside the one who appeared to be a leader. She also looked like one of the Sidhe, tall but not as tall as Currach. Her skin was very pale. Her light blue eyes with golden specks were hauntingly attractive. Similar to the faery women, this Sidhe woman wore a white dress, only her clothing was finely woven with white pearls in the shape of tears. There was an elegant ruffle behind her head that looked like a soft blue and silver seashell, and it gave the sense that she was wearing a crown.

"Welcome," she said in greeting.

All the elves smacked their spears against their shields, and the sound was almost deafening.

"I come in peace," Abigail responded.

It was then she noticed that she did not seem to fit in with this elfin world. Abigail thought she must have seemed very plain to them. Her hair was loose and windswept. She had not been prepared for a meeting, especially not a celebration.

"My name is Abigail," she told the leader. "I need your assistance. I hope you may help me so that I might assist your people in turn."

The Sidhe-woman eyed Abigail curiously. Abigail knew she was reading her energetic field.

"Abigail," the Sidhe-woman repeated. "But we know you as your older name—Abae."

"Yes, I am also Abae." Abigail bowed to her, and the woman bowed in return.

"I am Una, Queen of the Sidhe," she said, snapping her fingers. "You need not hide amongst us. We have formed a ring to celebrate you. Here we shall call you Abae."

Abae was doing her best to be fully present and aware, when one of the elfin women handed her a white cloak, as fine as anything she had ever seen. Abae bowed and Una placed it around her shoulders. Then Una produced a silver cup lined with precious stones and urged Abae to sip from it.

Never drink from a cup offered by the faery folk or you might never return, Abae could imagine Ganieda saying.

"It will help you through the times of coming change," Una explained. "Sip the herbal-infused *Mulsum,* it will protect you."

Hopefully I'll return, Abigail thought, accepting the silver cup into her hands. Inside it, she could see what looked like a raspberry held in a shimmering elixir. Abae threw all caution to the winds—and she ate the raspberry, then drank the elixir. A raspberry seed was stuck in a groove between her teeth, but Abae thought it would be unattractive to pick it out. Instead, she placed her tongue against the dental fissure and looked at the elves surrounding her. Una observed her with a strange smile as if expecting something unique to occur.

"Healing happens in stages, as you know," Una said, her long ears protruding through her fine silver hair. "What we have helped you accomplish is the reconnection with the line of faerie that has been broken. Please return to your people and also help human beings remember that they are meant to be the bridge between the Fair Folk, who understand the wisdom of nature and the earth, and their sky guardians. The world does not revolve around human beings, although they would like to think so."

"Please forgive us," Abigail urged Una, closing her eyes and making a sign of prayer. "We have been living in darkness and ignorance."

"It is affecting all of us," the Queen said with a grimace. "People need to return to the sacred places in nature and become the stewards of the land once again."

"How do we start?" Abigail asked humbly.

"A time is coming now when humanity will be in such peril, that they will simply have to change their ways."

Abae opened her mouth to speak but Una raised her long white hand to stop her.

"Do not be too concerned, Lady Gaea has a plan in place."

Abae was fascinated by the vines that interwove between Una's faery fingers, creating rings of blossoming flowers.

Meanwhile, Una gazed at Abigail as though reading her destiny. The entire company of elves went silent. Then she swept her great hand lightly across Abae's face. All of her lifetimes flashed simultaneously.

"There is a thread that runs through each soul's lifetime," she said. "Can you see it?"

Abae could taste the raspberry seed between her teeth, which seemed to be activating in her mouth. She could sense warmth running down her spine, and cosmic roots growing from her body deep inside the soil. The magical raspberry seed was acting like a hallucinogen, and she surrendered to the vision. Silver threads surrounded her like an inner-earth web, and she observed the elementals at work creating forms. She witnessed how gnomes held seeds gently until the time of their ripening and birth. Then, ever so gently, the gnomes passed the seeds to the watery undines, who moistened them, and lifted them up so the heads of their little green shoots showed above the soil, and then the sylphs danced around them, joyous of their emergence. As the etheric imprint of the raspberry bush grew inside her, the sun spirits, called salamanders, kissed the buds and the blossoms opened, sending their sweet perfume across the land.

"I see how it works," Abae told her. "We need to live in harmony with the flow of life. And we will again. Humanity is changing."

"Yes." Una nodded in agreement.

The silver threads vanished, and the vision subsided. Abae felt purified and wholesome.

"I have one more question," Abae said, placing her hand on her heart. "How do we forgive those who have betrayed us, killed us, killed our people?"

Some of the Fair Folk let out a gasp and some murmured a light language. Una stomped her staff, and the tribe became silent.

"The cruel ones are ignorant," said Una, her eyes flashing with rage. "We are aligned with life and disengage with murderers."

"How can I align more fully with my highest destiny?" Abae asked, her eyes welling with tears.

Una walked around Abae, reading her energy field.

"You stay aligned with your role as a human being, the bridge between heaven and earth. You act as an example for others, in all lifetimes, even when others act out of ignorance. After all, your soul is eternal."

Abae could see an image in her mind of the raspberry bush losing its leaves in winter, the upper part of its body sleeping, as the energy sank deeply into the soil to dream with the land.

"All phases are sacred," Una pointed out.

"I understand, even times when we are cut down like a plant."

Abae had a vision of a raspberry bush being pruned, and although the plant registered shock, there was still strength in the roots. In the spring it would blossom again, with more vigor and strength than ever before.

"And so it is with the journey of the soul," Una continued. "We return to Source for our true healing."

"Yes," said Abae. "Do we each have an eternal soul?"

Una studied Abae, and then told her, "Touch my heart."

Abae could hear a surprised gasp amongst the Fair Folk, but she nodded and very gently placed her hand on Una's chest. The vibrations that came from the light elf were so high they almost knocked her out. Lights swirled before her, but Abae managed to keep her balance.

Abae felt a spark inside her mind, that was also moving down her spine. It glowed in her heart too.

"I can feel my soul spark," Abae murmured. Tears ran freely down her cheeks.

"We may join you at the turning of the ages," Queen Una said. "You are now ready to enter Mona, a place reserved for healers."

Abae could not only hear but also feel the clatter of spears on shields.

Abae found herself sitting against the cold central stone of the sacred mound all alone. She wondered how the faery women had spirited her home. Feeling the raspberry seed between her teeth, she decided to leave it there for now. Abae thought about trying to plant it in her garden and wondered if it would grow.

Abigail sat for a moment, integrating all she had seen. Whether it was an actual voyage into the Otherworld, or simply a vision, made no difference. The Sidhe and the Fair Folk had opened the Otherworld to her, and what mattered was that she had returned with wisdom… and with her soul spark.

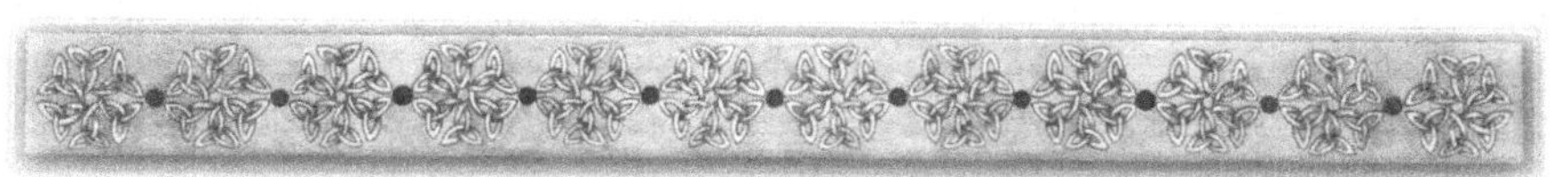

Chapter 37
Limousine & Bull Hide
Anglesey, Wales, 21st Century

Daphne was waiting for Abigail when she crawled outside *Bryn Celli Ddu*. She listened carefully to her friend as Abae described what had happened with Currach, Una and the Fair Folk. Then she explained that Diana had decided to go back to the Royal Oak Hotel to look for Lance.

"How long was I gone?"

"About an hour," Daphne replied.

"It seemed like weeks," Abae said. "The cairn acts as some sort of ancient time-traveling machine, maybe a Stargate. I visited Tír na nÓg in my body."

"I just saw old rocks and sat in cold damp grass."

"I wonder why it will direct some people and not others?"

"Do the Sidhe have a say in it?"

"I suppose so," Abae pondered. "There's an old magic associated with the place. It's as though it is full of tunnels."

"I have heard them called wormholes."

"I rather like the term Stargate," Abae shared. "It's less frightening."

"I do tend to like to know where I am going."

"I think the Stargate just takes you there and you have to trust its wisdom."

The two women walked back toward their vehicle in silence.

As they approached the carpark, Daphne could see a limousine and a man wearing sunglasses standing beside it. He stood quite casually, as if waiting for something. Abigail's pulse quickened and Daphne grabbed her arm.

"Morgen and Accolon have come for us," Daphne whispered, backing into a hedge. But it was too late to hide.

Suddenly Morgen stood on the path in front of them wearing her magical shimmering green dress.

"You two are never hard to find," said Morgen. "Come along then. There is work to do."

"I am not interested in going with you," Abigail replied defiantly, then turned on her heels and ran back toward the cairn.

Accolon looked at Morgen, who said, "Don't worry. She will meet us there."

"What have you done with Owen?" asked Daphne hotly. "And Lance Pelleas!"

Morgen looked intently at Daphne, who then fainted onto the path.

"Oh dear, she's a light weight," Morgen observed, clicking her teeth. "Accolon! The dryad has fainted!"

Her faithful driver was beside Morgen in an instant, picking up the listless form of Daphne.

As he draped Daphne's body across the back seat, she looked lifeless. But then Morgen heard a door open and shut, and they saw Daphne run after Abae.

"I was going to give them a lift," said Accolon.

"They can do it the hard way," Morgen replied haughtily to Accolon. "Just drive into the damn cairn!"

"What if I run over them?" Accolon had some panic in his voice.

"It's too late to care," Morgen declared. "The Niente have located us. If we don't get to Mona soon, we will all die."

Morgen's driver swung the car in reverse, and then, shifting into first gear, drove over the rock barrier and through the barbed wire fence. The wires snapped.

Accolon could hear the wire scraping the limousine.

"Keep driving!" Morgen shouted. "It's truly an emergency."

The limo sped through the field and the hedges and past the sheep. Accolon was driving at such breakneck speed that it was everything Morgen could do to keep herself from screaming. As they approached the sacred mound of Bryn Celli Ddu, their view began to spin as though they were inside a kaleidoscope. At the last moment, the mouth of the cairn opened like an enormous vagina and then they were engulfed in blackness.

1ˢᵗ Century Mona

When Abigail opened her eyes, she was sitting inside the cairn, and her back was up against the standing stone in the center. She started to stand up, then stopped. She was naked under an animal's skin.

Where am I?

She seemed to be wrapped in the hide of a cow or bull. There was still blood on the skin, which remained warm to the touch. She threw it off, then remembered that druids and vision poets, perhaps priestesses of Mona, would sleep inside the hide of a bull, the *tarbh*, for mystical prophecy. Abigail could see clay pots with dried herbs in them; some were still burning. Smoke drifted toward a small hole in the roof of the womb-like structure. Abigail had the sense of an ancient presence and could smell roses, and apple blossoms.

"Please show me what is taking place now," Abigail asked her inner oracle.

Immediately the oracle took possession of her, but only partly and she could hear herself speak.

"Beware of the Niente," the oracle warned. "The dark magicians always seek to break the soul of the nation. They also wish to steal your soul spark, and as many other souls as possible."

There was a snap, and she noticed a sparkle of light in one of the clay pots as the herbs burned out. Abigail crawled over to the pot and looked inside. She could see a crystal stone glimmering and picked it up. It seemed as bright as a tiny piece of sunlight and was delightfully warm to the touch. She carefully replaced the shimmering stone in the pot and noticed that it heated the room.

Crystal heating, Abae thought to herself. *How innovative.*

Chapter 38

Abae & Taliesin
In Mona

Mona, 1ˢᵗ Century AD

Abae breathed deeply, warming herself and taking in her surroundings. She saw a loose-fitting green dress and taupe mantle on a post near her and put the wool clothing on. Over the lighter clothes, she pulled on a black cloak, fastening it shut with a moon-shaped clip. She peeked outside and was overwhelmed by the size of the trees in the forest; some looked over a thousand years old. The amount of life force coming from the Sacred Grove made her feel invigorated and very alive.

Crawling out of the mouth of the cairn, she could see an open-sided, tent-like structure with five youths sitting outside it in a circle accompanied by their teacher. They all wore patchwork cloaks of many colors. Their teacher was telling them a story, and the students seemed fascinated.

Abae took one good look at the magical blonde teacher, and seeing her shimmering heart-shaped crystal necklace, *Kardia,* she knew at once that this was Ganieda.

227

The healer wore the Druid's white wool cape, and an additional longer necklace made with gemstone shards, leather pieces and fragments of deer antlers. Ganieda smiled knowingly at Abae. Ganieda was tending the children, who seemed to be about eight or nine years of age. A man assisted her, laughing and moving effortlessly between Ganieda and the children. Abae was mesmerized. He wore natural-colored clothing beneath the sky-blue tabard of the bard. A forest green cape, casually tossed across the bard's left shoulder, was fastened to his tunic with a Celtic spiral clasp made of silver.

A girl with beautiful fawn-colored hair turned and gazed at Abigail with mesmerizing green eyes.

"What is your name?" Abigail asked.

"Elen," the girl told her, then smiled radiantly.

Of course, Abae thought. *Ganieda has located the original Elen and will save her.*

The male assistant moved closer to Abae. He was holding a harp at his side, and she assumed he was a bard. She knew the man from somewhere but couldn't place him. Abae closed her eyes and, using her will, tried to align herself with that lifetime.

Elysium

"Taliesin is his name," Lady Gaea whispered from the Sky Temple. "He's a poet and seer."

"And a real beauty," the dragon added.

1st Century Mona

"I hear there is trouble brewing by the sea," Taliesin said.

Abae blinked at him, still locating herself. The 21st and 1st century lifetimes blurred. She stared at his forehead, which seemed to glow with a powerful radiant light as though a sun lived inside his mind. His red hair tumbled down his back in waves. She also thought he was beautiful.

Taliesin could feel the bard awakening within him. He pulled his small harp up into a position to play it. Abae noticed that the musical instrument was made of oak, and the frame was etched with Celtic symbols, twisting vines, unfurling leaves, and flowers adorned with precious pearls.

As he began to strum the strings, the wind accompanied him. Turning toward the children, Taliesin sang what came to his heart:

"There was a great battle, and it grew so dark,

That no one would come, not even a shark."

Taliesin pretended to be a shark swimming furiously in the water, trying to bite the students, and the five children roared with laughter.

"Magic came in the form of a woman so dear,

That I held my breath just so I could hear."

He put a hand to his left ear, and Abae realized that he was waiting for her response. The children watched with curiosity. After a pause and no reaction from her, he continued on with his impromptu tale:

"His wife sang a song as old as the hills,

Knowing he would do whatever she wills."

Taliesin raised his eyebrows and then laughed. He plucked the harp, and it seemed as if his fingers interwove the chorus of nature into the strings. Abae noticed that the harp had gold etched into the wood and thought of Diana and her necklace, now in another time.

What is the connection with the golden harp? she asked herself. *And with this bard?*

Taliesin gazed at Abae intently. His eyes were like blue sapphires, sparkling like the summer sea. His tangled, partly braided, thick red hair seemed to have a life of its own as it blew in the breeze.

Ganieda looked on with amusement.

The children all shouted, "Hurrah!"

"Come, let's have a meal," directed Ganieda, interrupting the music.

She showed the children to a pelt where coarse bread, apples and cheese had been provided in woven baskets. A cauldron filled with steaming herbal tea also sat on the hide, paired with drinking horns.

"You should go spend time with your husband," Ganieda said to Abae, who then glanced over at Taliesin. "There will be much work to do later."

Abae stared at Ganieda, who winked at her and shook her hips. "Have fun," she added, and then the teacher began to feed the children.

Abae was stunned into momentary silence. Turning to look at her "husband," she decided she liked the idea of being with him.

Why not? Abae thought. *It's been a while.*

"I know how much you love the forest," Taliesin told Abae. "Let's walk amongst the trees to our Oak."

Abae hesitated for a moment. She knew she had to pay attention and that soon their lives would be altered forever by the violence to come. *Unless we can change it,* she thought.

Taliesin of the radiant brow hummed as he walked into the woods, and she eagerly followed him. Still wearing the sky-blue-colored tabard of the bard, Taliesin held a torch aloft as daylight dwindled. He placed his other hand on Abae's shoulder, then fondly touched her cheek. She shivered, and he tossed his green cape over her shoulders.

They came to an opening and a hush came over the forest. Abae noticed they now stood inside a *Nemeton*, a circle of sacred trees.

Gazing around her at the Sacred Grove, she saw several enormous Ash, Hawthorn and Oak trees. Tall Pine trees surrounded them as if protecting the circle. There was a presence of deep enchantment, and the trees whispered among themselves.

Welcome, they said to Abae.

Taliesin gave her a puzzled look, then added, "The trees do love you."

Arriving at a great Oak, she stared upwards. The trunk must have been ten feet or more in diameter, and perhaps a hundred feet tall.

"Bless you, great one," Abae said, placing her hand on its trunk. She could feel the tree respond with a rush of strong life force, which she gratefully received.

"May you always be loved and protected," Taliesin added with a bow.

They walked on through the forest. In 21ˢᵗ-century Anglesey (once Mona), there were very few trees. She wondered what had happened to all these great beings. In the mist, Abae thought she saw eyes blinking at her.

"Let's go home for a while," Taliesin said, taking her hand.

Abae noticed a wattle and daub roundhouse with a thatched roof and followed the poet inside, passing by a hide that served as a door.

A thought of Max crossed her mind, but her husband was cold in the grave.

I'm in the first century, she told herself. *I'm an Oracle and a Druidess. And I'm free to choose who I wish to be with. And apparently, I am the wife of Taliesin.*

He took off his clothes, revealing a fit, muscular, yet slender body lined with fine reddish-golden hairs that made his entire being seem radiant. He motioned to her, and she bravely embraced him, touching his naked body as if she had known him for years. Holding her gently, he unclasped her cloak, which slid to the ground. He kissed her lightly on the lips. She shivered.

Abae felt that she did know Taliesin, yet was learning about him all over again. She enjoyed the warmth of his body. Many tales had been told of Taliesin, but she had never heard of his wife. She wondered what "wife" meant on Mona, or even if it mattered just now before a battle.

"Did you have a vision in the bull hide?" Taliesin asked, kissing her now bare shoulders. "Did you see what is to come?"

Abae put her hand on Taliesin's broad arm. "It is good to be with you now," she said, kissing him back and sliding under a woolen blanket. She could feel him growing hard against her. His radiant brow gleamed even in the shadows, which made her sense that he was attuned with a divine and wise energy.

"Have you had any visions?" he asked again.

"Unfortunately, yes," she muttered, pushing herself away from his body and looking directly into his startling blue eyes. "I saw an invasion of Roman soldiers and the Sacred Grove being destroyed. The forests will go up in flames, but the stones of the cairn will remain. We must defend the shores or Mona will be destroyed."

Taliesin looked at her, and his forehead flashed with light again. She noticed that his hair seemed mystically lit with small flames, and then he laughed. Abae thought it was an odd response to the serious conversation.

His teeth seemed very white and straight for the 1st century, almost as though he were a demi-god. Abae looked at him closely, wondering if this magical child of Ceridwen was, indeed, an immortal. She hoped it was the case because then he could not die, and they could go on loving each other throughout the centuries.

"The Romans will never get past us," he said. "They have no magic."

"They have swords. They have armor, horses and fire," Abae pointed out, her eyes filling with tears. "They can break the spirit of Mona and its people."

"Only temporarily," he said. "Brutes never win in the end."

Taliesin opened his palm, and a flame sprang up in his hand. Then he threw it at Abae, who responded without thinking, knocking it back to him, as though they were playing volleyball with a tiny sun. The flame went out.

"My lovely Abae," the poet said. "We know how to shape-shift. That's how we survive the centuries."

Abae stared at Taliesin, not quite sure that she understood the meaning of his words. *Is he also a time traveler?*

"It's best to share what you see with Ganieda," he told her. "We know Suetonius Paulinus and his Roman legions are coming. He thinks they can be quiet enough to surprise us. But we will be able to hear the footsteps of the men, the splashing of their boats and the swimming of the horses."

"Can we hide the magic of the Druids somewhere?" Abae asked. "Is there some sign or symbol that will keep Mona safe?"

Taliesin's gaze was unfaltering.

"I have come from the future to warn you that something awful is going to happen," revealed Abae. "I'm a walk-in. And I'm really sad because I'm completely in love with you."

Taliesin responded to Abae's words by sweeping her up into his arms and kissing her. He pulled himself back, looked at her warmly, and said, "I thought you seemed a little different. So, you are a time traveler who has arrived as my dear wife? I always wanted one."

Abae thought of Ganieda's wink, and then realized she was the one who had been fooled. Then she laughed. After all, she was enjoying this moment.

She gazed at the poet and murmured, "I hope we can continue to love each other somewhere, in some time."

"I was born of the cauldron. Magic does my bidding," he responded. "I'm also a walker between worlds."

"Then how can we keep the spirit of Mona from shattering into a thousand pieces and being lost for all time?"

Taliesin closed his eyes and called upon the field of wisdom, which was his gift.

Finally he told her, "On the surface it will look as though all is lost, but beneath the waves another story will be told. We must move into a different realm."

"All of us?"

"There will be a battle on the surface," he simply said, then looked out to the trees that stretched as far as she could see. "All the gods and nations fall eventually."

Taliesin turned to Abae and took her face in his hands. "I want you to look at me and remember me forever loving you."

"Yes," she declared. "Yes, Yes."

"And now there is work to be done," Taliesin acknowledged. "Thank you for coming from the Otherworld. I have been seeing you in my visions for some time."

Taliesin reached into a trunk made of woven branches and brought out two glistening objects. One was a wide silver belt and the second, a golden torc, which he placed around her neck.

"It's best to fit in, dear Abae."

She positioned the silver belt around her waist.

He stood back to admire the ornamentation on her, and added, "Be safe and look wealthy."

They were disrupted by a loud noise. Abae heard someone shouting.

"They are here!" she cried. "The destruction is upon us."

"I will take the spirit of Mona below the waves," Taliesin promised as he pulled on his clothes. "Mona will be in the dream world for mystics and poets in the times to come."

"I suppose nothing is ever fully lost," Abae said with some sadness. She was not happy about losing this husband, as well as Max.

"Go to the cairn and prepare the children to come to me," said Taliesin. "I will make a brew in the cauldron that will keep everyone safe. Tell one and all to bring a small branch and meet me in an hour."

Before she could protest, he was gone into the shadows of the forest.

Abae looked up to see lights dancing around her head, and she thought she could hear faerie bells. It occurred to her that perhaps she could alter the past. Abae wasn't sure how much she could change, but perhaps she could help the children get away before the Roman soldiers destroyed the Sacred Grove. After all, the children held the magic of Mona within them.

Chapter 39

Daphne in Mona
Mona, 1st Century AD

anieda whispered between worlds, "Daphne, we are waiting for you in Mona."

Although she had run after Abae, Daphne did not see her inside *Bryn Celli Ddu* and thought her friend must have used the Stargate to escape. Shivering with anxiety, Daphne put her back up against the stone pillar and asked the spirit of the place to rescue her. At first, she just felt the cold stone, then mist began to swirl around her, and the floor gave way. She felt herself spinning in time and space. Finally the Stargate spat her out.

Opening her eyes, Daphne took in her environment. She was still inside the cairn but the roof was made of reeds, instead of mud and grass. Looking down at her feet, she could see thin leather boots. Daphne noticed she was wearing a dark woolen dress. She marveled that time travelers often, but not always, arrived in appropriate clothing. She noticed a black cloak with a copper leaf clasp and put it on over her shoulders.

Stepping out into the sunlight, she blinked. Daphne peered at a grove of enormous Oaks, Ash and other trees. The air was delicious and alive with sparkling energy. Walking amongst these giant trees, she touched the mighty trunks. Some shuddered from her gentleness. A few dyads came close and gaped at her.

"Hello, dear friends," she whispered, knowing that each tree had its own dryad, the way each person has a soul.

A breeze blew and a few branches waved in a slow response.

Off in the distance, she could hear people talking in a friendly manner and walked toward them. A blonde woman wearing a necklace with a sparkling star caught her attention, and she followed a winding path through the forest and caught up with the healer, who seemed to be out for a stroll.

"Welcome, Daphne," said Ganieda, glancing at her. "You found your way."

Five youths had been following Ganieda as she meandered through the woodland paths showing them the various medicinal herbs and mushrooms that grew there.

"Daphne is a dryad," Ganieda explained to the children.

They stared at Daphne and blinked, waiting for her to share more. Daphne recognized the five children: Fedelma, Leodogran, Gwenhwyfar, Bodhmall and Elen. They were those who would bring magic with them into future times. Fedelma would be a *banfilli,* a visionary in Ireland for Queen Maeve. Bodhmall would also travel to Ireland and become a foster mother of the great hero Fionn. Gwenhwyfar's destiny as Guinevere was to bring her light to Arthur and Camelot, and her father, Leodogran (right now magically appearing as a boy), would ensure it. Elen of the shimmering ways was the most ancient of them all and would guarantee that the magic of Britain would live into the future.

"But where is your tree?" asked Leodogran, a stocky red-headed boy with freckles.

"I come from another island far to the south," Daphne explained. "Once every tree had a dryad or wood faerie, but over time we learned how to leave our tree and eventually also the forest as you will one day."

"Why would you leave the Sacred Grove?" the young nature priestess Bodhmall asked, her auburn hair braided with a variety of flowering herbs and seeds.

"I felt called to an adventure," Daphne answered. "Do you ever feel called to another land? Perhaps you will need to take the gifts of the forest with you?"

The children stared at her and blinked, as if the thought of leaving had never occurred to them.

"I like the water as well as the woods," Daphne continued. "My father, Peneus, was a river god. I liked to hunt with a goddess named Artemis, and Peneus thought it was wise that I also know how to shape-shift into a laurel tree."

"Oh, that's clever," Elen said. "Can you show us how?"

Daphne looked at Ganieda, for shape-shifting took energy and was not considered a game.

"Young Elen might need to know how one day," Ganieda explained. "Although I imagine she might prefer to be a deer woman."

Daphne placed her hand on a large Oak, and then said, "*Mayévmata!*" and disappeared.

Elen leapt up into the air with delight. The other children cheered also.

Daphne then stepped out of the Oak.

"Can I try?" asked Elen.

"Certainly," said Ganieda.

"*Mayévmata!*" Elen said, then promptly knocked her head on the Oak. "Ouch!"

The other children laughed.

"It's a gift of dryads," said Ganieda. "But I might teach you how to walk through a Stargate."

"What's a Stargate?" Fedelma asked, showing great curiosity.

"It's a portal used for time travel," Ganieda explained. "It can take a person or people across time, space and dimensions to another Stargate."

"Are there many Stargates?" Bodhmall asked.

"They appear and disappear as needed," Ganieda explained, glancing at Daphne.

The Roman soldiers are coming, Ganieda said in her mind to Daphne. *Go out, walk east and examine the shoreline. We will need to turn day into night and light torches. The tribes of Mona are gathering, and it will soon be time to appear frightening. The Banduri have taken madder roots to make red dye and painted it on the trunks of trees so they think we have smeared sacrificial blood on them. The Druids will start hissing to build a wall of sound to protect Mona soon. Once the Romans arrive, the enchantment will begin, and every rock and tree will appear to be a man. The sky will rain with fire, and then snow will fall.*

Daphne felt the chill of fear, then nodded. They both knew the children should not see this, for it would fill them with terror.

As Daphne walked toward shore, the island was completely silent as though all seen and unseen beings were preparing for something. She hoped the trees would survive, but feared for them, and their dryads. Little faces of the dryads peered out from the trunks of trees.

As she stepped by the Sacred Grove, Daphne knew she needed to warn the forest.

"Come with me," Daphne whispered to them. "You will need to come to the land beneath the waves."

"But our trees," the dryads of the Silver Birches wailed. A few began to follow Daphne, but other dryads lingered in the forest. The most stubborn were the Hawthorn and the more ancient Blackthorn dryads. The spirits of the Oaks stood stoically beside the grand trees, also refusing to leave.

Daphne whispered to the trees in her ancient tongue, *"Blathe de ni-grathen."* This translates as "You will burn soon."

The trees groaned and the wind stirred. Birds were frightened and flew up into the air. Daphne could sense that the ancient trees, heeding her call, were drawing their lifeforce deep into their roots. Oaks threw their acorns onto the path, and Beeches and Hazels tossed down nuts. Ash trees dropped their winged samaras, and then many trees began to drop their seeds.

"I promise to plant your children," she told the trees, gathering as many as possible into her cloak where she was glad to find large interior pockets. Birds and small animals also collected seeds and nuts before departing.

"Where do we go?" asked the dryads and nature spirits who were all frightened.

"We will go to Tír na nÓg. Be prepared."

Looking east toward the mainland, she could see torches and hear the movement of the army. Daphne was suddenly filled with terror and fled back toward the cairn. Stumbling, she caught herself on the trunk of a tree, then saw a large cauldron in the distance and walked toward it. A man with bushy white hair was placing dried branches of wood around it. He looked up and Daphne was amazed.

"Blaise?" she asked.

"You didn't think I would let you do this alone, did you?"

Chapter 40

The Silver Boughs

Mona, 1st Century AD

"I am gathering the children around the central pattern stone," Abae could hear Ganieda whisper to her. Following the flickering lights, Abae quickly made her way in the darkness to *Bryn Celli Ddu.* She glanced anxiously toward the east and wondered how far off the Romans were. Entering the cairn, Abae was relieved to see the children safely in the enclosure with Ganieda. The interior had been lit with torches and radiant crystals. One by one, the youngsters sat in a circle around the central pillar of stone with their teacher standing by them.

Ganieda approached Abae. "We are almost ready for the ritual," she said.

Leaning closer, she whispered, "Daphne and Blaise have joined us, and they are preparing the cauldron. Taliesin will join them soon. The time of our departure draws near."

The children sat happily on fur pelts and Abae noticed most of the food had been consumed.

They are well-fed now, she thought. *Ganieda has prepared them for the long journey we will make on this dark night.*

243

"Today we learned more about Tír Na nÓg," said Elen, her antlered crown tipped to one side. "It is the land of joy, where no one ages or ever dies."

"You have traveled from far away too," noted red-haired Leodogran, looking at Abae's dark dress.

"That's correct, Leodogran," responded Ganieda. "Abae is an oracle from Greece, like our Ovates."

Leodogran? Guinevere's father? Abae thought. The timeline made no sense, but looking at the boy she could perceive that one day he would be a magical and fierce warrior.

"Abae and I are going to show you how to walk to Tír na nÓg!" Ganieda told the children, with a bright smile. "The beautiful land of milk and honey."

"Yes," agreed Abae, taking the cue and praying that something great would occur to her and that the Land Under the Wave would somehow magically arise.

"I'll lead the way," said Ganieda. "Let's use our imaginations to see that we are all walking through a Sacred Grove to the sea."

They all closed their eyes, and the stone in the center of the cairn began to pulse. It was clear to Abae that they would all be leaving soon.

Suddenly, Abae felt she had to go outside the cairn and see the battle. Quietly, she left and then tiptoed through the forest toward the Sacred Grove. She could see Druids in white robes and the female Banduri wearing black. Each one was taking their place and looked fierce.

She found Taliesin stirring a large black cauldron that bubbled furiously over an open flame. Then Abae saw that Daphne and Blaise were busily attending the fire, and also helping to stir the cauldron too.

"Daphne!" she exclaimed. "Blaise!"

"Let's keep working," they said.

Abae looked at Taliesin with a puzzled expression.

"We are making magic," Taliesin said. "Bring Ganieda and the children. Have each one bring a stick to dunk inside the cauldron. Each person needs to make a Silver Bough. In Irish, it is called *An Craobh Airgid,* and it is this Silver Branch that is needed if you wish to find your way to Tír na nÓg."

Abae hurried back to Ganieda, and soon they all stood beside the large cauldron

that was magically bubbling. One after the other, the children walked up to it, and dipped a stick into the Faery Cauldron. Taliesin then blew on one stick at a time, and each one miraculously became an enchanted Silver Branch. Some wands had bells on them that tinkled merrily, others had silver pears or golden apples. The youngsters giggled with enthusiasm and wafted their wands through the air. Blowing on their wands, they tried to get them to glow like an ember or a piece of starlight.

Ganieda smiled and Abae seemed relieved. Taliesin was keeping the darkness at bay.

"You also need a Silver Bough!" he yelled to the adults, handing them slender branches.

"Put them in the cauldron," directed Taliesin.

Magically, each branch became *An Craobh Airgid,* a wand that glowed as brightly as Taliesin's forehead. Blaise also seemed luminous.

"Now all of you are radiant ones!" the poet exclaimed.

Taliesin's own Silver Bough sparkled in his hand like a firecracker.

Chapter 41

Gather the Children

Mona, 1st Century AD

Once all the wands were fully alight, in succession, each child stood and walked back toward the womb-like shelter of *Bryn Celli Ddu*. Taliesin, Abae and Ganieda followed them protectively. Blaise stayed behind to observe the movements of Suetonius Paulinus's assault on Mona.

"I have to witness history in the making," he whispered to Daphne, while encouraging her to go on with the group. "I must see the Roman legions."

Daphne nodded. "Be careful."

"I'll meet you in a few minutes."

Daphne made her way back to the group, a few dryads following along shyly. As she reached the cairn, Daphne heard the children speaking.

"Did you know that Venus forms a five-pointed star as she moves through the night sky?" Elen asked.

The children all looked up and saw that the sky was filled with fiery lights.

247

"It's raining fire," said Leodogran.

"Put your Silver Bough above your head," Taliesin shouted. "It will protect you."

"It will snow soon too," said young Bodhmall. "The weather is full of wildness tonight."

Abae felt anxious, but knew she must remain calm for the children, as though this night were the same as any other. This was the only way to change the destiny of Mona, for if they wove their magic intricately enough, the spirit of Mona would go under the wave tonight with the children and the seeds from the Sacred Grove.

"Venus is there in the sky, whether or not you can see her," Taliesin said to the children. "To know her magic, you must form a five-pointed star."

The five children almost miraculously crossed each other's wands and formed a star. Suddenly, there was a flash of light that was so bright they all had to look away. In the middle of the star they had formed, a little diamond lay on the ground. The young ones carefully laid their silver branches on the ground and gazed at the glittering stone that seemed to emit a golden circle of radiance.

"What is that?" asked Elen.

"That is the soul spark of Mona," said Taliesin. "We will call the diamond, Lady Mona. Ganieda, please hold her."

"I would be honored," said Ganieda, carefully picking up the shining diamond.

"This was the last thing we needed before going to Tír Na nÓg," said Taliesin. "Are you ready to go?"

The children all cheered and waved their wands.

"And one day, at the turning of the ages," he said, moving his focus to the adults, "an Earth Star will open, and the magical ones will return."

Taliesin observed them all closely, and then he looked at Abae, his eyes sparkling like a summer sea.

He loves her, thought Daphne, observing them closely. Off in the distance, she could see Blaise running toward them, motioning with his Silver Bough that it was time to depart.

"It's time to enter the Stargate," announced Ganieda, who opened the doorway to Bryn Celli Ddu.

The womb-like cairn was making a whirring sound.

"A black box is coming from the stars!" Fedelma shrieked.

There continued to be an odd whirring sound. Then, in the center of the cairn, the image of a stationary car flickered on and off. The children watched with curiosity as the magical car made itself fit in the space. There was a sound of screeching and clattering. Eventually, the enchanted interior of *Bryn Celli Ddu* became large enough for the entire group and the limousine, although the vehicle seemed to be lodged in the stones.

"Fantastic!" Ganieda exclaimed. "Morgen and Accolon have come for us!"

Morgen's limousine fully manifested with Accolon in the driver's seat. Morgen rolled down the passenger's side window, and the children gasped.

"It's an emergency," said Morgen. "Get in. I'll explain later!"

"No! She has come to steal the children!" Abae yelled.

"Don't be stupid," said Morgen. "Daphne, please don't faint again."

Accolon opened the doors to the limousine, and Ganieda scrambled inside along with the antlered deity Elen.

"Everyone in!" Ganieda shouted with authority. "We can explain later."

Bodhmall was the next child inside the vehicle, and she clutched Elen's hand. Blaise and Daphne got in the back seat holding Fedelma, prophetic wisdom still bubbling forth.

"The war horses are coming," Fedelma screamed, and then she fainted.

"Don't worry. You can rest now," said Accolon. "I've got you."

"Leodogran, come inside!" shouted Blaise and the boy responded with a leap.

Abae looked frantically around for Taliesin, and finally she spotted him nearby.

"Where is Gwenhwyfar?" Accolon asked. "The Stargate will close soon, and we must depart."

"Gwen! Gwen! Gwenhwyfar!" they shouted, but no response came.

"I'll go find her," said Taliesin. "And then I will find the rest of you in Tír na nÓg. Go if you must! I know the way!"

Taliesin ran off into the darkness, seeking the lost child. Abae refused to step into the limousine with the rest of the spiritual family and instead fled into the night toward the battle that was raging on Mona.

At once, there was a loud whirl and flash, and the vehicle disappeared into another time and space.

Taliesin had not seen Abae's rebellion. He was focused on finding Gwenhwyfar, the May Queen, and he knew he must stay focused on the task at hand. There was very little he could do for the Sacred Grove and the older Druids, who had agreed to fight, but he could save the child. He knew Gwen would be a prize for the Niente and the Roman soldiers. Using the magic taught to him by his mother, the goddess Ceridwen, he shape-shifted into a hare and disappeared into the thickest part of the forest.

"Sound the alarm!" Taliesin heard one of the Banduri shout. She blew a ram's horn, summoning the other Druids to come and stand along the shore to protect the island. There were hundreds, perhaps thousands, of men and women in light and dark cloaks running with torches, staffs, wands, and wooden shields. The sky was filled with fire and the shrieks of incantations.

Abae felt the oracle within her and knew something profound was getting ready to occur. It was at that moment that Abae saw the Roman soldiers approaching, and then the General, Suetonius Paulinus. His eyes were fixed on her and she stood transfixed as he walked toward her. He snatched the golden torc off her neck, which rolled to the ground. Then he struck her in the belly with his sword.

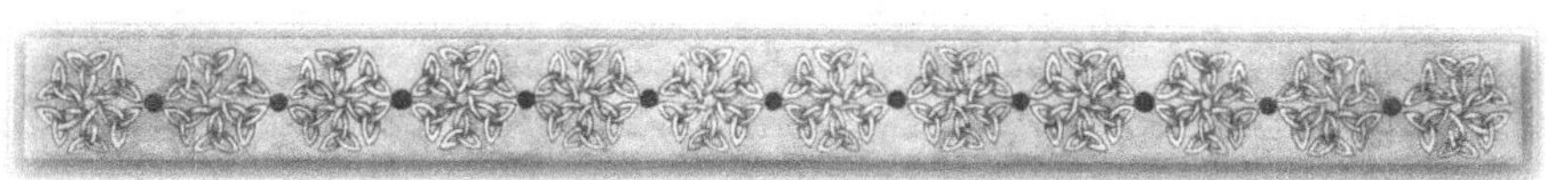

Chapter 42

Lance Pelleas Resurfaces

Wales, 21st Century

Diana woke up in a four-poster bed at the Royal Oak Hotel. Some mysterious person had booked the room anticipating her arrival. She blinked, thinking about the sacred mound where she had left Daphne and Abae, then her drive back to the hotel. She had simply felt compelled to continue her search for Lance Pelleas and his son. Looking up into the brown silk canopy above her, Diana shook her head side to side slowly.

What part of this is a dream? Diana asked herself.

She was wearing a soft linen nightgown and felt chilly. Even in the summer months, the Snowdonia Mountain air was cool. She stood up and walked over to close the window. Her suitcase was beside the radiator, and she put on a sweater. Drawing back the heavy curtains, Diana looked out at the view of the flowing Llugwy River. Just then, she heard her iPhone vibrate and checked to see who was trying to get in touch.

It was Lance Pelleas, who texted: "Please meet me downstairs for breakfast. Something very strange has happened. I'll explain."

Diana thought the message was curious, but she dressed quickly and hurried out of her hotel room.

Lance Pelleas was a handsome man with grey hair and the body of an athlete. He had always seemed like a king to her. He was well dressed, wearing a grey suit with a red day cravat. She reminded herself to stop staring at him, and to be concerned about his son Owen who, as far as she knew, was still missing.

"Lance!" Diana called out as she walked to him.

He stood up from the breakfast table and embraced her, holding Diana so close to his heart that she could feel his pulse. Lance smelled like a wild river during a storm. He literally took her breath away.

"It's so good to see you!" he exclaimed. "And I have some explaining to do."

"Three days late," Diana said coolly.

"What a cad I am!"

Lance bent and kissed her hand, then pulled out a chair so she could sit next to him. Wishing she had thrown a colorful shawl over her shoulders, Diana took her seat feeling underdressed in her jeans, green sweater and flat shoes.

"Let's order. I hope you are hungry," he said, settling back into his chair.

"Ravenous," Diana replied.

Soon Lance was looking up over the menu and giving her a seductive grin. The waitress interrupted the intimate gaze. With some input from the server, they placed their orders and then they continued with the conversation.

"Listen," said Diana. "I came to see you—some time ago—because I have been worried about Owen."

"Oh?" asked Lance. "How so?"

"Have you spoken to him?"

"Yes, he is the reason I have been away."

"Is he doing okay?"

"Yes, he is now. There was a bit of an emergency."

"I know!" Diana exclaimed. "I was with him when the lightning accident happened at Cadbury Hill. I wasn't sure he was going to make it. I wanted to tell you in person. I'm so relieved that he's still alive!"

Lance looked at her, as if wondering if he could trust her.

"What did you see?" he asked.

"A pale boy lying in the grass barely breathing, who was then whisked away in a limo by a man wearing sunglasses."

"That was Accolon," said Lance. "I know the man."

The waitress came with their coffees. Lance was silent for a moment as if trying to decide how to explain the situation to Diana in a way she would understand.

"Please tell me what happened. We have all been worried sick about the boy."

"It's a rather long story," said Lance.

"Well, I have all the time in the world," Diana told him. "But I do want to send a text to Nina and Abigail to let them know Owen is well."

"Certainly," said Lance.

Diana took out her phone and started texting.

"But he might not be around for a while," Lance added.

Diana glanced up at him and raised her eyebrows.

"I know Nina might be looking for him. There's something I should tell you about him that might trouble you."

Diana sent a short text to Nina and Abae that read: "Owen is fine. I'll tell you more soon." Then she set the phone down beside her coffee. "Just fill me in. I doubt you can shock me."

Lance cleared his throat, started to speak and then took a sip of coffee instead.

"Tell me how it is possible to lose three days?" she asked.

"Have you ever heard of time travel?" Lance asked.

Diana looked at him, then lowered her voice. "Of course."

"I had to go to Broceliande."

"The legendary forest in northwest Brittany?" Diana asked. "In France?"

"Merlin's place where legends are born, yes."

The waitress came with hot plates of food and set them on the table. Lance picked up his knife and fork and sliced into an over-easy egg. Diana took a bite of buttered toast and thought it tasted more delicious than usual.

"Before I forget, thank you for the gift of the room."

"Least I could do."

"How did you know I would be here?"

"Morgen told me that you would be here last night," he replied. "She is my ex-wife. She's with a lanky fellow called Accolon now and seems quite smitten by him."

"Morgen?" asked Diana.

"Yes, I generally call her Mo," said Lance. "She also told me Owen had been in an accident in which he had been struck by lightning! Of course I was frantic, so I drove at once to Imworth, to one of her houses. I wanted to see the boy, but he had been taken to Broceliande."

Diana seemed puzzled but slathered some blackcurrant jam on her buttered toast. Then she looked at him quizzically and asked directly, "To what century?"

"Fifth century, I believe," Lance answered, then chewed on his toast.

"That makes more sense," said Diana, as she cut herself a bite-sized piece of salmon and spinach omelet.

"Mo is an excellent healer, so she helped him. But it's all very odd."

"In what way?"

"My ex-wife is an impossible woman."

"Owen's mother?"

"Yes, but she was young and wasn't interested in raising him," Lance shared. "She found a younger man and disappeared out of our lives."

"I'm sorry for Owen," said Diana.

"Oh, not at all," Lance countered. "He was much better off without her. She's a bit mad."

"Did you see him?" asked Diana.

"Yes, in fact, he joined Mo, Accolon and me for dinner two nights ago," said Lance. "I planned on taking you, but Mo told me it was not a good idea."

"I wonder why?" Diana asked, feeling both curious and suspicious.

"Mo said it might disturb you. Owen told us about being picked up by Accolon who drove him in a limousine to Broceliande. There, Owen was unceremoniously delivered to his wife, Laudine, and daughter, little Lunette."

"Wife and child?" Diana choked.

"Yes," said Lance. "He married when he was very young. I know he also likes Nina, which is awkward. Laudine has a hold over him."

"It sounds like the lightning did not have a lasting impact," Diana noted. "Maybe it was more of a course correction?"

"Well, as of yesterday, Owen was alive and well, although angry with his mother for some reason," said Lance. "Laudine is a jealous woman, and not someone to mess with. Little Lunette is precious and a joy to have around."

"Owen should have told Nina that he was married," Diana pointed out. "He seemed like he was interested in her." She knew better than to relay any more information about what occurred at Gaea's Rose Cottage.

"Different timelines," said Lance. "Like I said, it is complicated."

"Has Mo ever said that you were once King Urien?"

"Yes, funny you ask. She told me some time ago that I had been King Urien of Gore," Lance said. "I have always been interested in Welsh myth and legend. Apparently, she believes she was my faithless wife then too." He chuckled.

Diana was dumbstruck.

"Listen, I have some business to attend to," Lance told her. "But I'd love to come back and meet you for an early tea and then take you to see my home. Would you like that?"

"Yes," replied Diana, who felt like she did need some time to metabolize all that she had just learned. "I would like that very much."

"There's a place known as the Ugly House Tearoom," Lance suggested. "It's charming and they have a wide tea selection."

"I'll see you there."

"Two o'clock sharp," said Lance. "And I promise to stay in this timeline."

<h1 style="text-align:center">Chapter 43
The Grand Tour</h1>

Wales, 21st Century
The Ugly House Tearoom

After Lance's departure, Diana went up to her room to get her boots for a day of hiking. The tearoom was within walking distance, and she thought the exercise would do her some good. Before going out, she decided to call Blaise to let him know where she was and what her plans were.

Blaise did not pick up the call, but she could imagine him asking, "Who dares to date my sister?"

"I'm visiting Lance Pelleas," Diana told Blaise in the voice message. "He's from an old and distinguished Welsh family. I'll let you know how it goes. And I just saw Daphne and Nina, who have traveled to the Isle of Anglesey."

She decided not to add, *And my daughter likes Lance's mysterious son, Owen, who is married and might actually be a knight of the Round Table in a different timeline.*

Diana had almost said more about Morgen but decided against it. She wondered if Blaise was also a time traveler. They had never discussed it.

How do I tell Lance that I am also a walker between worlds?

From what she remembered of Arthurian legend, Morgen or Morgan le Fey had married King Urien, but her heart was with his son, Accolon. She did not know the full story of her son Owen, or Yvain, not yet.

For a moment, she wondered if Nina would be furious with her for dating the father of a man who had essentially betrayed her.

Ah the webs we weave, Diana thought as she put on her hiking boots. *At least Owen is alive.*

At 2 pm exactly, Diana and Lance Pelleas met at the tearoom. The Ugly House, which she found charming, was constructed of stones and offered precisely one room. At the wall of teas and samples, the two looked over the selection with care. They placed an order for tea and biscuits and made their way to a table.

"I wanted to invite you to stay at my home, but I didn't think it was appropriate for an old single man to co-habituate with a young beauty like you."

"Well, I'm more of a mature widow, but I'll accept the compliment. We will see about sleeping arrangements."

"Widow?" Lance paused and thought about it. "Well, maybe we could get into some trouble together."

They both laughed.

"I've been meaning to thank you for my necklace. I haven't taken it off." She tapped on the golden harp pendant and smiled.

Lance peered at her neckline, and for a moment Diana thought he might kiss her. But then he dropped his gaze and looked at the pot of Oolong tea which was steeping for optimal taste.

"Let's have some tea and then I'd love to show you my home, and perhaps the Gwydir Forest after that?"

"Yes," responded Diana. "I have all the time in the world for you."

Lance peered at Diana, and his heart was skipping beats due to excitement.

Ever since Owen had described the beautiful Diana to him, Lance had wondered if perhaps a romance might spring up between them. During his last trip to Greece, he had found the necklace of Orpheus' enchanted golden harp, or lyre. He had made a wish then that the gods would bless him with a goddess.

Diana thought Lance was incredibly sexy, and his warm gaze made her blush. She hadn't felt this way since she met Felix Liber when she was only a girl.

"There's something special about Wales," Lance was saying. "An ancient magic lives here, as if we are surrounded by dragons."

A waitress poured tea for them and left a pitcher of cream. Putting a spoonful of honey in her tea, she thought it tasted as sweet as ambrosia, and also liked the smokey aftertaste.

The day was bright and sunny. The leaves gleamed in full green glory as Lance drove Diana to see his home. When she questioned him about Owen, Lance tutted, and said it was time for him to mature and accept the responsibility of being a man, husband and father. He did not seem like he wanted to share more, so she dropped the subject.

Lance lived in the outskirts of Betws-y-Coed in a home that looked rather like a fortress. Diana whistled to herself as he pulled his white Range Rover into the gravel drive that was surrounded by well-manicured landscaping. She almost expected a knight to come and greet her, but instead it was Lance who opened the car door. She loved his gentle brown eyes.

"Let me help you, my lady," he said, taking her hand.

Once inside his home, he gave her the grand tour. Diana stopped to admire several wall adornments, mostly framed, illustrated genealogies and the covers of books he had written on Grail Legend.

Once outside, Lance and Diana spent the rest of the afternoon walking in the forest, and then hiking the rough path down to a moody lake that was filled with waterlilies. Climbing back up the hill, the views were spectacular. The blue skies brought even more happiness to the day.

"Diana," he said, pulling her close, "you are a goddess to me."

When she moved into his embrace, she felt as though their bodies were made for each other.

Looking into his brown eyes, she replied, "Thank you for bringing me here."

Then he kissed her. It seemed to Diana that it was even more than a kiss because a fire ran through her body that she had almost forgotten she could feel.

When they reached his Range Rover, he kissed her again. Only this time, the weight of the embrace took them over the bonnet of the car. A passerby honked their horn at them, probably with approval.

"Come home with me," Lance urged. "I have asked my chef to make a proper Welsh dinner for you."

He certainly had, and they shared their first of many dinners together. Lance brought out some of his finest wines. She was reminded briefly of her first husband, Felix Liber, but she knew wherever he was in the Otherworld, he had moved on too. Felix was in the lineage of Bacchus after all. For a moment she wondered if Felix was, indeed, Bacchus, god of wine. Then she decided that the wine was going to her head and focused more intently on the handsome gentleman sitting in front of her.

After their meal, they moved into the library where a large fire blazed in the fireplace.

"That fireplace is large enough to ride a horse through!" she teased.

"Well, a pony," he said. "Owen had one named Llamrai, after King Arthur's mare."

Lance took Diana's hand and gazed into her green eyes.

"You look like a forest goddess." He drew her close.

She allowed him to draw her in, and for a moment they both felt the beating of their hearts. And then the two kissed with such passion, both of them had to pull back and catch their breath.

"Wow," Diana said.

"Yes, wow," Lance muttered, pulling her in for another kiss.

Diana drew back for a moment. "Should we talk about Nina and Owen? Should we worry about them?"

"They are grown now," replied Lance. "Trust the Grail to take the seeker exactly where they need to go."

"Even to timelines?" asked Diana. "Can we really trust that?"

"I believe so," said Lance, kissing her again. "But I am happy that you are right here right now with me."

"Are you a walker between worlds?" Diana asked tentatively, not wanting to disrupt the romantic intimacy.

"I think I am with Diana," replied Lance. "You are every bit the goddess and the one I have longed for throughout the ages."

He then lifted Diana and carried her up his wide, winding staircase, set her gently on his bed, and shut the bedroom door.

Chapter 44

Nimue's Task

Elysium (Sky Temple)
In-Between Time

*he great eagle set Nimue down through the cloud roof of the Sky Temple, and then flew off into the vast blue.*

"The curse has been broken!" Nimue declared. "The riddles of my ancestors have been solved."

"I am so glad to see Latona and Jupiter together at last," Lady Gaea remarked. "Wonderful work! I must have them over to the Sky Temple for tea."

"But there is another task in the first century," said Delphyne, wrapping her long tail around the Round Table. The black pyramid activated and the first scrying screen flashed with images. They watched with horror as, along the banks of Mona, men and women wearing black and white robes and shouting incantations were cut down by the Roman legion. She could see Abae being pursued by the Roman general, and let out a gasp.

"I believe you could go to Mona, open the Stargate, and let the rest of the magical souls walk through," the dragon told her. "After all, they were good at casting illusions, so maybe only shadows will be destroyed."

265

"That would be rewriting history," said Nimue.

"Would it?" asked Delphyne. "What is history if it is happening now?"

"Morgen and Accolon have already done some time altering," Lady Gaea noted. On the second scrying screen, they observed the limousine entering Bryn Celli Ddu and then departing with many but not all of the spiritual family.

"I need to save Abae, but how?" asked Nimue. "Is she dead?"

"Ask Gwyn Ap Nudd to make a tunnel through the underworld to Tír na nÓg," said Gaea. "Use your arrows to defend against the Niente, the soldiers and the dark magicians."

Nimue could feel the quiver buzzing on her back. The arrows wanted to release, but she wondered if she could take on Suetonius and the entire Roman legion.

"Save the druids of Mona, or as many as you can," Gaea urged. "Bring at least a dozen magical ones to me. Then I will open a Stargate and land the Sky Temple on Parliament Hill overlooking London. The Planetary Earth Star may open at any moment. And a new Earth will be birthed."

"I need to know the timing," said Nimue. "And I have no idea how to get them all there."

"Ask Morgen and Accolon," said Lady Gaea. "They seem pretty attuned."

The dragon added, "After all, we are speaking to the daughter of Diana and granddaughter a Jupiter. You are a demi-god who lives in the first, fifth, and twenty-first centuries simultaneously. Perhaps it is time for humanity to realize their potential and become gods too."

"How this will happen cannot be fully seen because the Niente would attempt to foil the plan," warned Gaea. "And this opportunity could be lost to time again for another twelve thousand years."

Nimue whistled.

"Where is Arthur now?" Nina asked. "He is supposed to rise again at the turning of the ages with his knights."

"Arthur sleeps in the planetary landscape of Avalon," said Gaea. "I know of his whereabouts, but it is not time to wake him until the New Earth rises. Besides, the new Camelot isn't ruled by Arthur, but by Guinevere."

Nimue looked at Gaea with wide eyes.

"There are eleven thousand temples hidden within the Earth," Gaea continued. "It is possible that when the Earth Star opens, they will all reactivate simultaneously."

"What happens to humanity?" asked Nimue.

"Each living person who is ready will receive the light to shift into the Fifth World."

"And if they are not prepared?" Nimue stared at the Lady.

Gaea was silent. The dragon blew puffs of smoke.

"We need your help, Nimue," said Gaea. "I am a mouthpiece for the planet, but you are the one who must act. We know that you can time travel, shape-shift, and you have your grandfather's gift with the weather. Plus, the Lords of the Underworld like you and one may need to be summoned."

And if I don't succeed in the quest?"

"Probably World War III will occur, as well as the destruction of humanity," said Gaea. "And every other sentient being on Earth."

Nimue took a deep breath. Her quiver was slung across her left shoulder and the arrows were buzzing with electricity.

"How do I find Gwyn Ap Nudd?" Nimue asked. "I have met him, but he generally does not like visitors."

Gaea and Delphyne looked toward the Stargate, spinning like a small tornado just outside the Sky Temple. Nimue could feel the wormhole calling *to her. She felt a shiver of fear, but knew she must trust the guidance. Nimue walked down the steps toward the swirling spiral.*

"Find Merlin and Ganieda's mother," Gaea called out. "Adhan holds the final key. Bring her back with you with her Moon Dish!"

"Oh, bloody hell," said Nimue, plucking up her courage and stepping into the Stargate.

"Well, here goes nothing!" Nina yelled, stepping into the void and feeling her body dissolve and reform itself in time and space.

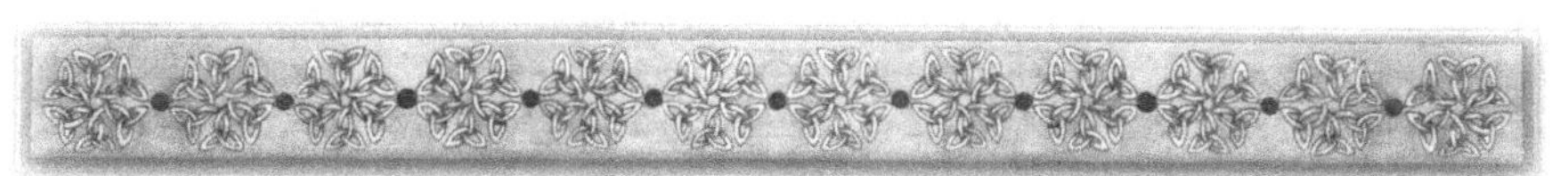

Chapter 45

The Fall of Mona

Wales, 1ˢᵗ Century Mona

Taliesin stood beside Abae's body, watching in horror as the war horses clambered to shore. Despite all their preparations, druids in robes were no match against soldiers with armor and swords. There was one man who moved without hesitation, slaughtering everything in his path. From his visions, Taliesin knew this must be Suetonius Paulinus, General of the Roman legion. Suetonius was more of a gliding shadow than a man, and his menacing presence was deeply depressing. The General seized a young fair-haired girl, who looked dazed.

"It's your time to fight for us, Gwenhwyfar," Suetonius shouted as he handed the girl a shield and sword. "Or would you rather fight against us?"

Gwenhwyfar! Taliesin felt pulled between the girl and Abae. He struggled to know how to act.

The light in Gwenhwyfar's eyes flickered with fury. Suetonius laughed, and he gave her a kick that sent her sprawling to the ground. She was quickly on her feet, ready to attack. The General ignored her.

Moving with his legions, he shouted: "Throw your javelins and watch as the savages crack under our strength. Knock them down with your shields and finish them with your swords. Do not listen to their cries. Victory will be ours today!"

Taliesin had seen the devastation in visions, but standing on Mona as the battle raged was beyond his worst nightmare. The poet knew that to survive he had to remember the goodness that existed in life, and he had to fight on as a spiritual warrior. The island was now filled with curses, screams and shouts. Looking down at Abae, he intuitively knew she was simply unconscious. The magical silver belt he had given her had changed the course of her destiny, or so he hoped.

That's why I am a time traveler.

Taliesin had been determined to save Mona. He told himself that Abae would be safe as he ran to defend Gwenhwyfar. He could shape-shift but regretted he had not yet learned to bi-locate. His mother, the goddess Ceridwen, had given him the wisdom of the ages. Now he must use his gifts, including some he did not know he possessed.

Merlin, you are needed, Taliesin thought, summoning his friend.

Most of the soldiers pursued the druids who lined the dramatic cliffs. Others were setting fire to the Sacred Grove. As the bard stepped beside Gwenhwyfar, the shadowy countenance of Suetonius focused on Taliesin. Suetonius let out a roar and swung his sword, making a gash in one of the revered Oaks that was covered in red dye. The imitation blood did not deter the wrath of the General. The forests would not be saved tonight. Taliesin had a deep love for the Sacred

Grove and watched with sadness as the dryads who had refused to leave with Daphne fled in terror.

Gwenhwyfar did not cry out, but stayed focused on the General.

Suetonius swung his sword at Gwenhwyfar.

"No!" Taliesin shouted, adding an elfin stun curse: *"Deeir naa-atch nom nom, icht nath fraith egharth."*

Suetonius's reaction to the words of enchantment was comprised of a sniff and a twitch, like an annoyed hound. Clearly, he did not like the magical verbiage. His gait slowed and then was temporarily paralyzed. Unable to move, Suetonius's sword and shield clattered to the ground. His body was rigid, but he could still turn his head.

"You can't run?" Gwenhwyfar shouted at Suetonius. "I guess you are dead."

Gwenhwyfar picked up his sword and shield and looked menacingly at the General. She knocked his helmet to the ground with the sword, and he grunted.

"How dare you hurt my people," Gwenhwyfar declared.

Suetonius turned and gazed at the fair-haired girl, then laughed. Taliesin noticed with revulsion that there was no light coming from the Niente's empty eye sockets.

"Fregeith naighth melka leymonte heira," Taliesin continued in elfin tongue, giving Gwenhwyfar energy.

He was determined to protect the elementals and what was left of the magic of Mona. Gwenhwyfar chanted with him, her royal elfin heritage shown in her brave face. But the immobility spell did not last long and soon the dark fury of Suetonius erupted. He leapt at them, and frightened, Gwenhwyfar dropped her weapon. Picking up his sword, Suetonius swung the iron at their heads.

An eagle screeched and swiped at Suetonius, who cried and stepped backwards. There was blood on his right cheek. Then Nimue appeared beside Taliesin wearing a black cloak. She motioned for Gwenhwyfar to stand beside her. There was a black stripe painted across Nimue's face. She looked terrifying. A white dog stood by her snarling, and Gwenhwyfar also bared her teeth. Gwyn Ap Nudd and other riders from the Underworld were flowing from stumps, caves and holes in the ground. A bright white orb flashed, and then Merlin joined them. With arms upraised, he caused the wind to howl.

"The tides will turn now!" Merlin shouted. "Magic is here!"

Nimue let out a roar as she threw a thunderbolt at Suetonius. "I am the granddaughter of Jupiter. I am Nimue. You have no power over me!"

The lightning bolt hit its mark, but Suetonius looked unfazed.

Nimue then drew back one of Diana's golden arrows and let it fly. The arrow found its mark but returned to her quiver. Suetonius laughed. When one arrow returned to her quiver, she let fly another. Once again, the arrow returned to the quiver.

A storm arose from the Underworld with enough gusting winds to terrify any mortal. Nimue ran at Suetonius, knocking his sword to the ground. Gwyn Ap Nudd took the form of a snarling beast and snapped at the betrayers of Mona.

"I am more than a general," Suetonius said, motioning for his cohorts to gather around him. The soldiers looked frightened, but he shouted, "Ignore these pitiful savages. They have already been beaten and deserve only our pity."

He pulled out a dagger and aimed it at Nimue's throat. Nimue thought of her dirk and struggled to pull it free from her cloak. One of the white hounds grabbed Suetonius's hand, and the man howled in pain. Nimue broke free, the hounds snarling and snapping, ready for the kill.

Suetonius's men were too fast for Taliesin. Several soldiers held him tightly.

Merlin looked back and forth at Suetonius, the wild sorceress Nimue and Gwenhwyfar, and then to Taliesin who was struggling to free himself.

"I am the one you are after," shouted Merlin. "I am the magic of Mona."

Ignoring Merlin, Suetonius placed his sword against Taliesin's neck. Weakened by the iron blade, the poet struggled to defend himself against the Niente who were draining his lifeforce. Taliesin hoped he would be able to regain himself in another timeline, and knew it was time to escape. Several soldiers had come to observe the scene.

"*Lichet de namora, preer de druir et lrean,*" said Taliesin, disappearing. At once there was no figure, only an empty cloak. Suetonius let out a roar of fury.

"Kill them, kill them all!" he shouted.

But the soldiers were scared. They trembled when they should be fighting.

Nimue glanced fretfully at Merlin, who pointed toward the Irish Sea. His white hair blew around him, making Merlin seem larger than life. The legions advanced toward him.

"More soldiers are coming!" Gwenhwyfar reported.

The white hounds snapped at the air, ready for battle.

"*Mynd,* go, depart," Merlin shouted to Nimue. "Take Gwenhwyfar and run!"

"Not without you!" Nimue yelled back above the crowd. "I've missed you."

Three soldiers grabbed Nimue and threw her to the ground. She could hear an eagle crying overhead. Lightning lit up the sky.

History cannot repeat itself, Merlin thought with growing fury. *Mona will not die tonight.* Then the old tongue was upon him, and the ancient words ushered out like a gale. *"Ek-lat brize, tor na borne!"* Merlin shouted.

The wind stirred, then blew wildly. Ice and fire flew through the air.

The Roman soldiers looked anxiously around as the oak branches began to sway violently from the wind Merlin was summoning. Dark clouds rolled in, and as the shadows fell, Nimue could feel the light of the Moon. It wasn't coming from outside, but from inside her body—like an enormous glowing pearl. The magic empowered her to endure.

"Frek na tooor, me kit so lore..." Merlin continued.

The trees were bending low now, protecting Nimue. The branches stirred, and Merlin called a wind so strong that it knocked the soldiers backward. Soon their heavy armor was pinning them to the ground, and they found it hard to rise.

Now freed, Nimue stood again and seized a new golden arrow in her left hand, and she held Jupiter's Lightning Bolt in her right as it sizzled and spat.

"Ek-lat brize, tor na borne!" Merlin shouted once again. *"Ek blte maken har!"*

Torrents of rain began to fall, and a mist arose that made it impossible to see. Then flames erupted in the sky. The white hounds of Annwn ran to Nimue, snapping their jaws, protecting her.

Surrounded by the dogs, Nimue and Gwenhwyfar ran until they reached the shore of the Irish Sea.

"Take Gwenhwyfar to her mother!" Merlin shouted.

There was one large boat waiting for them by the shore. It rocked back and forth on the ever-increasingly turbulent sea. They stepped quickly onto the curragh. Nimue continued to look for Merlin, her bow taunt, ready to fire an arrow or lightning bolt. Looking for oars, Nimue realized she had none, but she knew the magic that could carry them to the Otherworld.

Off in the distance, Merlin fought furiously along with many demi-gods and supernatural beings to cast out the invaders. Banduri in black cloaks shouted curses. Druids in white called upon the strength that they had always known.

"I'll get them," yelled a nearby voice.

With horror, Nimue saw a soldier, now climbing into another boat. His gaze was fixed on her. "Come now! I don't want to have to kill you," he taunted.

Nimue thought about diving into the water. As a Lady of the Lake, she knew she could disappear without a trace, and Merlin would survive somehow, but she did not know if Gwenhwyfar could swim. She briefly wondered where Abae was, and at once was shown a vision of her listless body lying on the ground. Nimue looked around frantically, trying to locate her on the shore.

Nimue knew how to divide herself in times of trouble. Just as she had done when Balin swung his sword at Nimue in a different lifetime, she pulled her light body out of her physical form. Now her magical double had the task of Gwenhwyfar to Annwn and safety. She hoped Gwyn Ap Nudd would understand Gwenhwyfar's plight and not claim her for the Underworld. She felt certain he would understand. The oarless boat moved with ease beyond the ninth wave, and out of harm's way. Then in her light body, Nimue dove into the strong currents of the Irish Sea. Calling on her strength as a Lady of the Lake, she asked the ocean's currents to carry her toward Abae.

When she surfaced on the east shore of Mona, Nimue could see the druids, torches in hand. They were battling on against the invasion. She could hear them whispering curses. Some were hissing, and others were shape-shifting into eels. At the same time, the Niente's emptiness was beginning to suffocate those in their collective web. The feeling of depression hung in the air like a dark vapor. Nimue feared few would escape this dark night, but she also knew that timelines can suddenly change. After all, she held the weapons of the gods.

Nimue pulled Jupiter's eagle feather from her quiver. Levitating, she floated over the battle scene. She scanned the burning island for her friend. Far below, she could see Abae's pale form. Nimue landed beside Abae and could hear her breathing. Then she knew, without a doubt, that to get her friend to safety she needed to call the Wild Riders of Annwn to her side.

Nimue let out a yelp that only the banshee and the lords of the Underworld would know, and soon the white hounds of Annwn had surrounded Abae. They sniffed her, and knowing she was not yet dead, encircled Abae but did not touch her. Gwyn Ap Nudd arrived, picked Abae up, and with his hounds, walked into the earth.

"To the Underworld," Nimue sang.

Chapter 46
Gwyn Ap Nudd
& the Underworld
1ˢᵗ Century Annwn, The Underworld

Abae blinked, her eyesight adjusting to the hazy world around her. The entire place seemed to be overcast with a silvery blue mist that blurred her vision. Little lights flashed on and off like stars. A winged faery walked forward holding a lantern, which Abae accepted gratefully.

"Thank you," she whispered.

A few dryads saw Abae and called to other nature spirits. Several faery women with insubstantial wings encircled Abae, dancing playfully. They seemed almost entirely made of light and wore diaphanous fabrics with hints of floral patterns.

A tall and slender white lady materialized, and the frolicking stopped abruptly.

"The White Goddess," one of the faery women whispered.

Then the fey withdrew respectfully behind a tall white oak with silver bark. Almost translucent, the White Goddess glowed with ethereal beauty, and the air about her was scented with roses.

"Where am I?" Abae asked.

"*Gwlad y Tylwyth Teg,*" the White Goddess answered. Noticing that Abae looked puzzled, she revealed that this was her home in a language she could understand. "You are amongst the Tylwyth Teg, also known as the Fair Folk."

Abae nodded, now placing herself in the Welsh Underworld of Annwn. She wondered if she was dead.

Nearby, a pale man with a black stripe across his face sat on a throne made of white birches. He stared at Abae as if reading her many lifetimes. He seemed a short distance away, but when Abae tried to walk toward him, he always seemed the same distance away. His white hounds encircled her, growling.

"You have met your death," said Gwyn Ap Nudd. "How do you plead?"

"I'm not ready to die," Abae stuttered.

"That's not an answer," he declared.

Abae recognized the command in Gwyn Ap Nudd's voice.

Abae blinked at the Lord of the Underworld. She felt dizzy, but lighter.

"General Suetonius ran me through with a sword," said Abae. "Maybe I am dead...."

"So easily swayed by the Niente?"

"Something sucked out my soul," Abae recalled. "I felt like I died."

Gwyn Ap Nudd stood and then walked through the circle of snarling dogs. Reaching Abae, he gazed into her eyes.

"Do you want me to knock death off you?" he asked. "Life or death?"

Abae looked at the items Gwyn held in his hands. She could see a black cup and a sickle.

"Which hallow calls you?"

Off in the distance, she could see Nimue and Gwenhwyfar. She wanted to go to them, but the white hounds stopped her.

"I wish to live," Abae avowed.

"Taliesin did not think you should die. He put his silver belt on you and saved you from the sword, changing your destiny," Gwyn Ap Nudd stated. "What do you say, Gwenabwy?"

Before answering, the White Goddess regarded Abae.

Then she said, "She's an oracle that will be needed at the shifting of the ages. Let her pass through to Tír na nÓg and return to surface Earth with the Others. Lady Gaea needs her."

Gwyn Ap Nudd turned back to look at Abae.

"I don't often allow visitors to return."

Abae looked at the sickle, knowing that with one swipe her life, perhaps all her lives, would be over. Then she looked at the cup, which seemed to glow.

"I would like to sip from the Faery Grail."

Gwyn held up his sickle, hesitating. "That means you are in the battle with the Fair Folk to the death, and perhaps beyond."

The White Goddess smiled, then nodded to Abae to show her approval. Abae knew she really had no choice; that she must accept the orders of Gwyn Ap Nudd and his twin sister, Gwenabwy.

"I choose life!" Abae declared.

Several faery women gathered around Abae, looking her over carefully. Gwyn Ap Nudd sighed, then sat down on his birch throne.

"The Underworld can be a friend to some," he said. "But others are meant to be inspired here with tales of the beautiful ones."

"Do not forget the poet, Taliesin, who awaits your return," said Gwenabwy to Abae. Then she turned toward Gwyn Ap Nudd. "Let her taste the Faery Grail and return with the Awen."

Gwyn nodded respectfully to his sister, then handed Abae the cup. Abae gazed at it. The liquid inside looked black but it sparkled with intensity, as though it was full of tiny stars. She sipped, then looked up at Gwyn Ap Nudd. There seemed to be a thousand lords of death staring at her.

"Go help with the arising New Earth," said Gwenabwy. "The White Goddess is with you."

The enchantment no longer necessary, Nimue's double faded. Gwenhwyfar walked toward Gwenabwy and took her hand.

"My name is also Gwen. Are you my mother?" the girl asked the White Goddess.

Gwenabwy looked startled but then smiled at the girl.

"Yes," the White Goddess answered. I am your mother."

Chapter 47

The Morrigan's Cry

1st Century, Mona

From the moment of invasion, the Morrigan had heard the cry from her brothers and sisters, and flew across the Irish Sea. Circling downwards, she observed the battle scene occurring in Mona. Storm clouds had been summoned by the druids. A light rain was falling but the weather was building in intensity. Soon there would be a downpour. The waves curled and rose with increasing ferocity, the tips of the waves looking like blue sea dragons.

Looking to the left, the Morrigan could see the black feathers that covered her arm. Her right arm was also that of a crow's wing. As she scanned the world below her, Morrigan Crow-Woman took in a turbulent ocean and then she noticed that the Sacred Grove was on fire. The ancient trees of Mona were burning. There was a great deal of fighting and tumult there, and she could also see more enemy boats. The Roman legion had now arrived on Mona in full force, and even more soldiers were coming.

Her three sisters, Badb, Macha and Nemain, having shape-shifted into crows, joined her mid-flight. Taliesin, in the form of a hawk, flew beside them.

281

"We need Guiomar," shrieked the Morrigan to her sisters. "Release the warrior from the Vale of No Return!"

Following her sister's command, Badb let out a sharp cry, turned and dove into the water. Macha and Nemain continued to battle on against the more invisible Niente. They plucked them off Mona like small bats, flinging them into oblivion. Taliesin focused on protecting the remaining druids.

More soldiers attempted to approach the island. The Morrigan screeched curses that turned into silver disks and then stuck to the side of the enemy's boats like spears. She dove at soldiers and clawed at their faces. The sky darkened. The wind blew, and a huge storm cloud approached, flaring with lightning.

In the middle of Mona, in a lake known as Llyn Cerrig Bach, the veil that divides the realm of faerie and the human realm opened. A black faerie horse galloped through. Its eyes were red, and steam poured from its nostrils. Guiomar, the Lord of Avalon, rode the horse without bridle or saddle, for he was at one with the beast. Behind him flew a stream of pale faerie women from the Isle of Avalon, white as ghosts and shrieking.

At first, the Roman legionaries pulled back, frightened of the specters. One of the Niente amongst the soldiers noticed the Morrigan and focused on her. An arrow hit her in the wing, pinning it to her side. She spun in the wind, unable to find her balance.   Macha saw her falling and called to her sister Nemain for assistance. The Morrigan Crow-Woman free-fell into the pounding waves. She was churning in the darkness, unable to breathe, unable to break the spell of the Niente.

"The Morrigan," someone shouted, and she could hear her name. And then her crow sisters were with her. But she was being dragged under by a force they did not seem to be able to stop. Pecking and clawing at a net now around her, the Morrigan began to lose consciousness. Then, when they had almost given up hope, Madog Morfryn, riding a gigantic sea dragon, lifted the Morrigan out of the water. Morfryn removed the net, pulled the arrow from her side, and healed her with a few incantations. She thanked him, and then he thrust her back up into the air.

Merlin saw his father join in the battle, and also that the Niente had noticed him. They attempted to form a net around Morfryn, so they could drown him. The sea dragon pulled the net away with its claws, and then flung it into the sea, where it sank with some of the Niente into the deep water. With one flip of the sea dragon's enormous tail, many of the enemy's vessels cracked in two and sank beneath the waves.

General Suetonius signaled to his men to retreat north. They ran, terrified and confused through the burning forest. The black magicians amongst the Niente conjured an enormous wave to hit from the south. It curled and rose up with demonic power. Taliesin, still in hawk form, cried out a warning to Merlin.

A wave of salty water hit Merlin in the mouth. The wave and accompanying tsunami covered the entire island of Mona. Merlin tumbled in the dark water. There was a scramble of bodies all fighting for their lives in the Irish Sea. Druids and Romans moved as if in slow motion.

The Morrigan and her three sisters circled over the island, observing the scene. They clawed the struggling soldiers, who yelped. The great head of Madog Morfryn's sea dragon arose. One by one the Niente disappeared into her great jaws. Then Taliesin watched as the dragon quietly sank beneath the waves.

Merlin grabbed a plank of wood and chanted to it until it became a living branch that floated with him on the water. There was a terrible silence as he listened for the chanting druids and banduri. All he could see was black water glistening with the reflection of stars and of light coming from the burning of the Sacred Grove and surrounding woodlands. Merlin was exhausted, and he sighed as the waves carried him out into the blackness of the Irish Sea. Mona gradually disappeared from his view.

Guiomar and the faery women of Avalon circled above Mona looking for any lost or struggling souls. A few of the faery healers swooped down for injured friends.

"And now Mona will disappear from surface Earth," Guiomar commanded. "The magic will no longer be available to anyone who seeks it, but only to those who respect the old ways. Lady Mona will live in Inner Earth until the New Time."

A golden circle appeared around the entirety of the island, and when it disappeared, all that was left was an island with smoldering fields. Not one trace of the ancient groves remained.

"To normal eyes, all they will see is a Wasteland," Guiomar noted.

Chapter 48

The Spirit of Mona

1st Century, Inner Earth

he children looked out of the limousine windows at the wormhole they were passing through.

"Is Mona broken now?" asked Leodogran.

"We are taking the Lady Mona to a place in the Inner Earth where she cannot be harmed," Ganieda told him, showing him a glimpse of the radiant diamond. "She is with me."

"We are the magic of Mona," said Bodhmall.

"Yes, we are," Ganieda responded. "That's why our journey is an important one."

Ganieda wondered what was taking so long. Generally, travel through stargates and wormholes was almost instantaneous.

"We are having trouble landing in Tír na nÓg," said Accolon. "There is interference."

"Try again," said Morgen.

"*Agored!*" Ganieda exclaimed. A light flickered, then sizzled out.

"Maybe we aren't supposed to go to Tír na nÓg," Fedelma offered.

285

"*Oscailte*," Ganieda said, trying another magical world, then she scratched her head. "*Fosgarra!*"

Ganieda was feeling exhausted from the incantational effort. She knew that she should be attuning to Inner Earth, not forcing her. She felt some anxiety about the children, which was interfering with her magic. She had no idea how long the limousine would be safe.

"Be opened—*Ephphatha!*" Elen exclaimed.

The Stargate shimmered with silver and the limo took a sudden left.

"Hurrah!" the children shouted. "Elen knows the way!"

A doorway opened, leading to a dark tunnel. The limousine soon stopped with a screech. The location was not what they were expecting. A silvery blue mist blurred their vision. Silver trees grew with emerald-colored leaves. Tiny faeries sat in the crooks of the branches.

Faery folk and nature spirits approached cautiously to welcome them. A few dryads flew out of the limousine to join their friends. Gwyn Ap Nudd's white hounds with pink ears encircled the vehicle. Off in the distance, they could see Gwyn Ap Nudd seated on his white birch throne, the White Goddess standing beside him. Their radiance lit up the Underworld like a full moon on a dark night.

"Why did you drive us to Annwn?" Morgen asked Accolon.

"This is where we were taken," Accolon answered.

"Did we die?" Elen asked.

"No," Ganieda answered straight away. "Gwyn Ap Nudd is protecting us."

Gwyn Ap Nudd stood and walked toward them, beholding the limo. His muscular form was covered in Celtic symbols and feathers hung from his hair. Although the Underworld seemed dark, a strange radiance shimmered off his skin. His white hounds continued to sniff the tires and peer at the children inside the vehicle. Blaise rolled down his window and stared at Gwyn Ap Nudd, as though he was absolutely thrilled to meet him.

"You can put me in one of your books later," Gwyn Ap Nudd told the professor. "Make sure it's fiction, though. If you tell anyone about this at King's College, they will think you've gone mad."

"Of course," Blaise stammered. "I know how to stay incognito."

"I know you better as Apollo," Gwenabwy added.

Blaise glanced sheepishly at Daphne, who was also still inside the limo. She looked surprised. Then Blaise smiled and kissed her hand.

"I always suspected that you were Apollo," Daphne laughed. "And these days I like your advances."

"I told you I would do anything in any world to be with you."

"You sly god," Daphne giggled, and then kissed him on the cheek.

The remainder of the frightened dryads, who had also come along in the limo, were delighted to be in the realm of Annwn and flew through the open windows of the limousine. They danced together before disappearing off with their faery friends in the silver oak forest, giggling with delight as they flew away. Daphne looked after them wistfully but stayed with her group.

"My friends!" Gwenhwyfar cried out.

"Gwenhwyfar!" One by one, the children climbed out of the limo and gave her a hug. "We were so worried about you!"

"Where is Abae?" asked Daphne.

"I am here," Abigail called out. Daphne opened the limo door and ran over to see her bruised but living friend.

"And Taliesin?" asked Blaise.

"With Merlin and Nimue," said Gwyn Ap Nudd. "They will find their way."

"Taliesin saved me with his silver belt," Abae said. "He changed my timeline."

"I'm so glad," said Daphne, giving her a kiss on the cheek and an even warmer embrace.

"I will miss Mona," said Bodhmall sadly.

"Me too," said Leodogran.

"Do not worry, children," Lady Gwenabwy said with tenderness. "The druids and banduri of Mona have been trained in how to cross beyond the veil. Most have already gathered in Gwynvid, and the others who have finished their reincarnation cycles have passed on to the spiritual realm of Ceugant."

"You are needed for the times to come," Ganieda told the young ones.

"We are the future?" Fedelma asked.

Gwyn Ap Nudd observed each of the travelers carefully, then nodded.

"Ganieda," he said at last, "the magic of Mona is in all five of the children. But there is also a special radiance you carry. I sense Lady Mona with you."

"She is…." Ganieda said with caution, secretly possessing the diamond.

"In order to pass to Tír na nÓg, you must give me Lady Mona as payment."

Ganieda hesitated. Now standing outside the vehicle, Morgen and Accolon stared at Gwyn to try to read his motives.

"They simply wish to open the stargate to Tír na nÓg," Accolon declared.

Gwyn Ap Nudd laughed. "So do they all."

The white hounds of Annwn sat quietly by his feet, observing the travelers.

"We must open the Stargate to Tír na nÓg on our own," said Leodogran bristling.

"Oh, little lion," said Lady Gwenabwy sweetly. "Lady Mona will be kept here where she belongs. She is part of the Welsh soul. The people need her."

Elen walked forward and touched Ganieda.

"She speaks the truth," the girl said. "They need Lady Mona here."

Ganieda offered Gwyn Ap Nudd the diamond they knew as Lady Mona.

"Please accept this precious gift as payment for our passage to Tír na nÓg," Ganieda said.

Without looking at the gemstone, Gwyn Ap Nudd handed it to his sister. The White Goddess placed the diamond in her left palm. Immediately, Lady Mona lit up the entirety of Annwn with the light of stars. The fair folk came out to witness the miracle. The ferns began to unfurl and flowers blossomed around them.

"Thank you for this gift," said the White Goddess. "Lady Mona will support the life of Inner Earth and all of us here in Annwn."

Gwenhwyfar walked close to her mother and gazed into the brilliant light.

"Go forth, my daughter, and bring life to the land," said Lady Gwenabwy.

Gwyn Ap Nudd observed his niece, Gwenhwyfar, and then he smiled. "You are worth saving, for you will bring in an entirely new time one day. One day you will be known as Queen Guinevere, although people will not understand you until later."

Morgen seemed annoyed with his flattery of the girl.

"They all just want the bright light of the Kingdom of Camelot," Morgen said with disgust. "There's more to it than that."

Gwyn Ap Nudd gazed at Morgen, then added, "Play your part, Morgan le Fay. All players have their role, and yours cannot be understated.

Morgen nodded, acquiescing.

Chapter 49
Sír Guiomar
Annwn, No Time

Morgen opened the door of the limousine and stepped into the passenger seat, then motioned to Accolon that she was ready to depart.

"I suppose a metal vehicle will not be allowed into Tír na nÓg," Accolon said. "But it got us all here."

"Yes, you are correct," the White Goddess responded. "Queen Una and the guardians of Tír na nÓg will not allow iron to enter."

Gwyn Ap Nudd's white hounds began to howl, for they know who goes where and when. Although Morgen was ready to leave, Accolon hesitated. He felt there would be further instructions.

"The hounds have announced that there are a few more of you who will not travel to Tír na nÓg, and I concur," Gwyn Ap Nudd said sternly. "Morgen and Accolon know the importance of their roles."

Morgen rolled her window down so she could listen.

"A dozen of you, or more, must gather in the twenty-first century on Hampstead Heath," said the White Goddess. "This will mark the start of the shift in ages."

"The exact place is in the meadow to the south of Boudicca's Mount in Hampstead Heath," Gwyn Ap Nudd clarified.

"This requires the Fey of Inner Earth to align with you standing on surface Earth at the right moment so the Cosmic forces can prompt the transformation of Gaea," the White Goddess told them.

"Gods, goddesses, humans and nature spirits must work together for the shift to occur," Gwyn Ap Nudd further explained.

"Blaise, Daphne and Abae, you will one day be welcomed into Elysium, the Fortune Isles beyond the pillars of Hercules. When it is time, Zeus will show you the way," the White Goddess said gently. "We all have our place in the Otherworlds."

Blaise felt like asking about his sister Diana but decided she would also be guided to Elysium. Abae, touching the silver belt around her waist, wondered what happened when an oracle and a bard fall in love but decided that the gods already knew.

"The dryads of Mona will remain here to help with the Inner Earth activation," Gwyn Ap Nudd said with authority. Then he added, "Ganieda will take the children to Tír na nÓg, for she has permission to enter."

Blaise, Daphne and Abae, who had been turned away from Tír na nÓg, looked at the limousine.

"Can we ride with you?" Blaise asked Morgen and Accolon.

"I promise not to faint," Daphne added.

Morgen gave a little laugh, and Accolon opened the door for Daphne and Abae, who climbed in the back, followed by Blaise.

"We tried to give you a luxury ride to Mona," said Accolon through the open doorway. "But we all arrive where we need to in the end." He shut the limo door.

"Send my regards to Lady Gaea," Gwyn Ap Nudd told Accolon, as the man stood by the driver's door.

"I will," Accolon affirmed, then he took his seat behind the wheel.

Morgen looked away, ready for the transition. Then, with a whirring sound, the vehicle promptly disappeared.

The White Goddess touched one of the larger white oaks, and a stargate opened. The children gazed at the spinning kaleidoscope.

"It is time to proceed on your journey," Gwyn Ap Nudd commanded. "I will summon the Lord of Avalon who has learned to rend the veils between the realms. He will act as a guide and protector, along with Ganieda."

A knight wearing mysterious black armor stepped out of the stargate. After looking around, he bowed to Gwyn Ap Nudd.

"I have been summoned," the knight said respectfully. "Who must I escort?"

"Guiomar?" repeated Ganieda, her heart missing a beat.

Guiomar's dark hair was cropped short, showing off a strong chiseled face. His green eyes were almost the color of peridot. Guiomar gazed at the group carefully, his eyes lingering on Ganieda.

"Ganieda and the children have been given safe passage to Tír na nÓg!" Gwyn Ap Nudd declared. "Please protect them."

With a flip of Gwyn's right hand, the stargate expanded, and they could hear ocean waves crashing.

"To Tír na nÓg!" Ganieda and Guiomar exclaimed.

"Hurrah!" they all shouted.

Gwenhwyfar looked back anxiously at her mother.

"We will see each other again," said the White Goddess. "Now ride to your destiny. My blessing is with you."

One after the other, the young ones stepped through the stargate, which acted as a doorway to narrow stone steps that led down steep cliffs to the sea.

Noting that the children had all entered the portal, the knight took Ganieda's hand just before she stepped through.

"I have missed you," he whispered.

"And I you."

Guiomar followed her, and the portal shut. He then led the way.

Eventually, he told them, "We must enter the Irish Sea and go out beyond the ninth wave."

One by one, they all boarded a large boat with white sails. Ganieda announced each of the children and Guiomar offered his approval.

"Bodhmall the druidess, Elen the way shower, Leodogran the warrior, Fedelma the seer, and Gwenhwyfar the shining, welcome onboard," he said.

Guiomar then shook the hand of each youth, and also touched Ganieda's hand.

"Now under my protection, I vow to find and protect you wherever you go," Guiomar told them.

Ganieda smiled at him, then turned to prepare the children for the sea voyage. The youngsters soon sat in a semi-circle around the bow of the ship, their eyes wide. Ganieda set herself down and joined them.

Once the others were all settled, Guiomar sat, put his arm around Ganieda, and said, "How good to be near you, my love."

The mystical travelers sailed out into the vast sea of the Inner Earth, an ocean which rippled with pink and lilac healing waves. Even though they were below the Irish Sea near Mona, stars shimmered in an indigo sky above them. They shared the good feeling that they were traveling to a place that could one day be their new home.

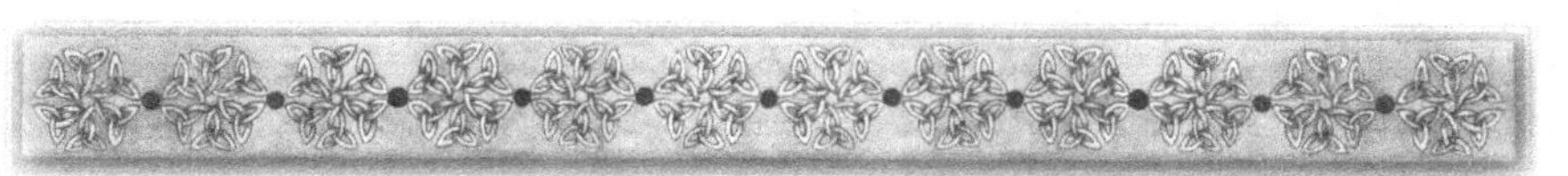

Chapter 50
Tír na nÓg
Land Under the Wave, No Time

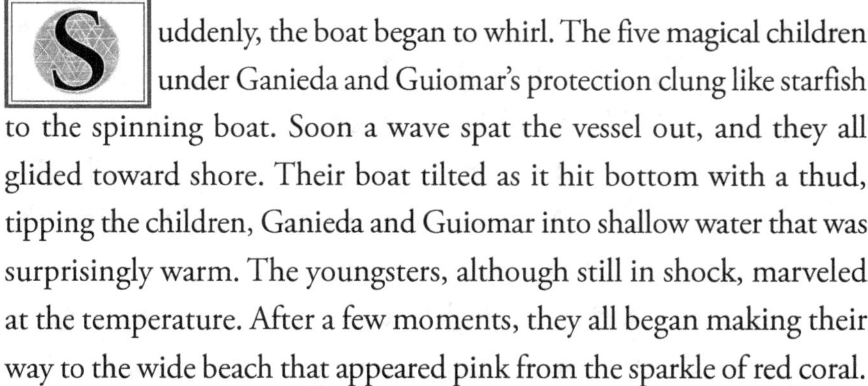

Suddenly, the boat began to whirl. The five magical children under Ganieda and Guiomar's protection clung like starfish to the spinning boat. Soon a wave spat the vessel out, and they all glided toward shore. Their boat tilted as it hit bottom with a thud, tipping the children, Ganieda and Guiomar into shallow water that was surprisingly warm. The youngsters, although still in shock, marveled at the temperature. After a few moments, they all began making their way to the wide beach that appeared pink from the sparkle of red coral.

A woman with flame-red hair was there to greet Ganieda as she waded ashore.

"Mother!" Ganieda exclaimed with warmth in her voice. "I have missed you."

"Greetings to my daughter!" said Adhan, who then kissed Ganieda and embraced her.

"Father?"

Madog Morfryn, a giant of a man, smiled at his daughter. Ganieda fell into his muscular arms and could feel the pulse of his great heart. He slipped off a pearl bracelet he had been wearing and slid it onto her left wrist, then kissed her on both cheeks. "A gift from Manannan, and from me."

Ganieda regarded the black pearl strand with gratitude. "Thank you. I promise to wear the pearls well. How wonderful to see you in person!"

Guiomar had taken the rear guard and now the rest of them were also reaching the shore. Wide-eyed and sputtering, the children had splashed through the waves and then walked cautiously onto land. Adhan, Ganieda and Madog Morfryn greeted them with open arms. Adhan touched each child with her long, white healing hands, which seemed to calm them. The scent of roses came from her pure essence and perfumed the air.

"I will bring the Moon Dish out soon and we will all feast together," Adhan said.

"Welcome Guiomar, Lord of Avalon." Morfryn gave the man a respectful nod. "Welcome to Tír na nÓg."

They could hear a shout and could see another person floating on a branch in the sea. Morfryn went to assist him, diving into the water and swimming with ease and power.

Adhan slipped her arm through Ganieda's and then led the children to a silver oak with a door that opened into an underground palace. Ever the protector, Guiomar followed behind. When they entered the main hall, the youngsters all gasped at the beauty of the place. Crystals, lit from some unknown source, glimmered in the walls like stars. Thorn trees with white blossoms grew in the four corners of the large room, and golden apple and pear trees grew taller, their branches hanging down with golden apples and silver pears.

Several smaller fey had made flower bouquets and wreaths for the newcomers. The children accepted the gifts, and they giggled with delight as the fair folk wove morning glory vines into their hair. The fey placed a wreath of bright yellow gorse flowers onto Ganieda's head.

Honored, she thanked the spirits of the place. They then placed a similar wreath on Guiomar's head.

"Welcome Ganieda and Guiomar," they said. "Welcome the magical children of Mona!"

"Children, you must be hungry," said Adhan, holding out a crescent-moon-shaped platter. "Whatever you imagine appears here in this dish."

The children eagerly leaned over the platter and, to their surprise and amazement, just the foods and drinks they wished for appeared. They clapped their hands, gathered up food, and then clambered away, showing each other their delicacies.

Madog Morfryn entered the fey palace with the bedraggled man. Guiomar went to help him, then found a bench for him to sit on.

"Merlin!" Adhan exclaimed, setting down the Moon Dish.

She dashed toward her son and, even though his clothes were soaked through, she lavished him with kisses.

"I will go get you some dry clothes," Adhan said, then rushed off down a corridor that opened through a thorn tree.

"What happened?" asked Ganieda, selecting a healing golden apple.

She then handed it to Merlin, who accepted it gratefully. Ganieda thought he looked exhausted.

"I left Mona and went out past the ninth wave and then dove, but the undertow was strong," Merlin said. "Luckily, I know a sea dragon who helped me locate a silver branch and a merrow who led me here."

Madog Morfryn could not take his eyes off his son.

"Thank you for the help!" Merlin told his father. After taking him in, he then added, "You look just like me!"

They both roared with laughter, then made flames in their palms.

"Have you seen Taliesin?" Ganieda asked Merlin with some concern.

"He was seized by the Niente, but disappeared leaving only a cloak," Merlin shared. "That bard is as slippery as a fish."

"And Nimue?"

"The last I saw of her, she had become a Lady of the Lake, or really a Lady of the Sea, and was helping the dragons find snacks."

Guiomar laughed.

Ganieda explained their journey to Gwyn Ap Nudd, and Merlin learned that many of their friends were driving by star portal to twenty-first-century Hampstead.

"The procession of the equinoxes is approaching," Merlin acknowledged. "We will need to make our way there soon."

Adhan returned with some fresh clothing for Merlin and offered him the Moon Dish. He looked relieved and plucked a delicious-looking scone off the platter. Elen ran over to give Merlin a hug, saw a scrumptious-looking seed cracker, and scooped it up.

Ganieda knew that once a person ate the food of the Otherworld, they would forget where they had traveled from, and hundreds of years would pass before they would think of Mona, or Wales, again. The other children had also taken food from the platter.

Relieved that the magical children had found their way to safety, Merlin looked at them with affection.

"Let me show you around the land of eternal youth, where it is forever warm," Merlin offered. "You always have your fill to eat here, there is no illness, and no one dies."

"It sounds magnificent," said young Gwenhwyfar, her hair now filled with flowers.

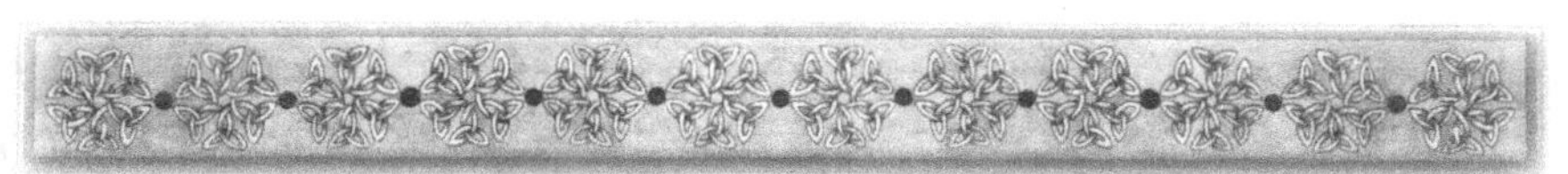

Chapter 51

Riddles of the Stars

Elysium (Sky Temple)
In-Between Time

Lady Gaea touched a few of the gemstones that had been carefully inlaid into the pockmarked Round Table, making the stones flash like stars. The dragon peered down at the glimmering table.

"It looks like a celestial sphere," said Delphyne. "Or a star map. Why is it flickering?"

"The Round Table has held the template of Logres since the Foretime. It's revealing the path of the gods," Lady Gaea told him. "I believe it's showing us that the shift is near."

The gemstones were no longer stationary stones, but tiny star tetrahedrons that moved through the density of the table.

"The golden topaz sphere representing the Sun is now a tiny Merkabah," Delphyne declared. "I can see the way the Sun traverses through Hera's Milky Way."

"A chariot of fire," Lady Gaea added.

She stood up and began to circle the table sunwise. The movement disturbed the birds that were weaving flowers into her hair, and they flew off and away out of the Sky Temple.

299

"It will soon be time for Elysium to land on the body of Earth," she noted.

"Where?" asked Delphyne.

"That part I do not know, but I suspect Morfessa comprehended the exact timing and place when he created the Lia Fáil or Stone of Destiny in the city of Fálias far to the north. Why else have I had to hold the Round Table in a secret temple all these centuries?"

A white crystal sphere gleamed at the northern part of the table.

"The northern star Deneb is flashing," Gaea observed. "It seems to be revealing that the origin of the map was from Cygnus, the Swan constellation."

"I like that Alpha Draconis is at the top of the map in the Draco constellation," said the dragon. "It puts the sky realms into perspective."

Lady Gaea continued walking sunwise around the table. She lingered over Alpha Draconis. "Ah, Alpha Draconis…. It was the northern pole star from the fourth to the second millennium BC. Draco was named after Ladon, the dragon with a hundred eyes that guarded the apples of the Hesperides. I gave the apples as a wedding gift to Hera when she married Zeus."

Lady Gaea stopped to trace the movement of the northern stars with her fingers. "Through the ages, the north star changes," she shared. The Lady observed the celestial sphere as a golden ring that had appeared on the table within which were held the shimmering stars of Alpha Draconis, Vega, Deneb and Polaris.

"Logres is fully on," said the dragon.

"Yes," Gaea replied thoughtfully. "Since Morfessa called the Round Table the template of Logres, the name places the map in Britain. But where?"

Lady Gaea circled the table counterclockwise for a different view.

"Morgen and Accolon have been time traveling to the twenty-first century observing Nimue, Diana and Abae in northern London," Delphyne added.

"Why would the Greco-Roman gods be gathering in London if it's not for this event?" the Lady said.

"And the Niente, who will try to stop you from landing," the dragon added with a snort. "Britain is a place of ancient magic, and the dark ones know it too."

"I'm trying to figure out the code. Can you see that the Earth is positioned inside the Astrological wheel?"

"Yes."

They moved their focus to the center of the table, where a large image of blue and green Earth gleamed. Encircling the Earth was an ever-changing Zodiac. Astrological glyphs flickered and moved.

"Earth looks like the center of the twelve-handed clock that Abae has on her kitchen wall in Hampstead," the dragon told her.

"That's a good point," Lady Gaea said.

"Can you read the design?"

"I am the embodiment of Earth, but I do not understand the movement of the celestials. I simply live amongst them."

"We need an astronomer," said the dragon. 'It's time to collect Merlin."

"How else will we understand the riddles of the stars?"

Chapter 52

Merlin the Wizard
Land Under the Wave, No Time

ild-haired Merlin walked along the blossoming gardens of Tír na nÓg with an equally wizardly-looking Ganieda. He took her hand and kissed it before proceeding under boughs of apple and pear trees.

"I've missed you, Sister," he said, pulling a silver apple off a branch and handing it to Ganieda who received it gratefully. She placed it in her Crane Bag, and then also selected a golden apple which she gave to Merlin.

"Our time here will be brief," Merlin continued. "I sense the call of Lady Gaea and the dragon. The template of Logres is activating, and there will be those who wish to stop it and destroy the Round Table."

"It is good that she kept the table safe all these years."

"Tír na nÓg is a fine place, but things are happening on surface Earth that need our attention now."

"I will align Inner Earth with the opening of the Planetary Earth star," said Ganieda. "I have discovered the location. If my guidance is correct, the event will occur in Hampstead Heath overlooking the city of London."

303

"London will be flooded with celestial light."

"It will be a sight to behold," Ganieda confirmed. "As though the Spiritual Sun has been reborn."

"That event will have many names," Merlin said thoughtfully.

They walked together in the garden, watching the sylphs and undines playing amongst the flowers.

"Can you imagine what happens on Earth when the garden returns?" asked Merlin with a grin. His tangled hair was still full of salt and seaweed.

"You look old, Brother," said Ganieda.

"It takes a lot of strength to swim beyond the ninth wave and not die."

"I have something for you."

Turning down a grassy path, Ganieda led her brother to an amethyst cave. A faery woman stood guard, but seeing Ganieda and Merlin she smiled and departed.

Pulling aside some morning glory vines, Ganieda opened a small door and withdrew a staff with two entwined serpents along the rod and a radiant crystal at the top.

Delighted, Merlin reached for the Serpent Staff, but the snakes hissed. He gave them each a piece of sunny golden apple, and Ganieda offered them both some lunar silver apple, and they quieted.

"You hid the Star Spirit well!" He tapped the crystal on the top of the staff.

The children ran past the cave, playing with their silver branches. Ganieda followed them with her eyes. Her focus remained on Merlin, who walked back out into the garden with his staff. He already seemed younger and more vibrant.

"I hear the call of Lady Gaea," Merlin stated. "Shall I transport the children?"

"Best to leave the children here for now," Ganieda noted. "Let a few centuries pass with them in the more refined energies found in this place."

They observed the children playing beneath the boughs of blossoming branches. Petals fell like snowflakes, and they giggled as they ran.

"They will each find their role soon enough," Merlin imparted.

"I have decided to stay here for a while too," said Ganieda. "I will reactivate the Heart of Inner Earth," she added, touching *Kardia*, the pendant Merlin had given her in the Foretime. "We will need to be strategic. You must stand on surface Earth."

She paused thoughtfully, then continued. "Then we will see how life unfolds. I have always been fond of Avalon, and Guiomar."

A knight wearing all black stopped to hand the children some silver bells. A black cape was thrown over his left shoulder, and Guiomar looked magnificent as he walked on the petal-strewn path. Eventually he reached Ganieda and stood beside her.

"Good day, Merlin," he said with a nod. Then Guiomar took Ganieda's hand in his, and smiled at her.

"Fair Avalonian Folk." Merlin chuckled. "You are lovely together."

Merlin held up his staff, causing a blue stargate to open. He nodded to the couple and then disappeared into another realm.

Ganieda and Guiomar walked on, enjoying the beauty and serenity of Tír na nÓg while knowing that they would soon need to depart.

"My grandfather Morfessa has relayed the exact location of the Planetary Earth Star and where it will open," Ganieda told him. "The

Star can only be spoken of right now in Inner Earth, and I do not yet know the exact timing."

"The Vale of Avalon resides half in this world and half in the Otherworld," Guiomar said, articulating what she already knew to be true.

"Gwenhwyfar and Leodogran are children of the Vale of Avalon," she told him. "Elen knows how to weave the Celtic hearts of the worlds together."

"What of Fedelma the seer, and Bodhmall the druidess?" he asked.

"They will have their roles to play," Ganieda explained. "There is a great Star-Temple that reflects the heavenly zodiac, and it is scaled to the map of Avalon." Then, with a new understanding arising, she added, "This map is written on the Round Table."

"Taliesin sang of the spoils of Annwn," said Guiomar. "But the secrets of the Glastonbury Zodiac are locked."

"Until the time of King Arthur's return."

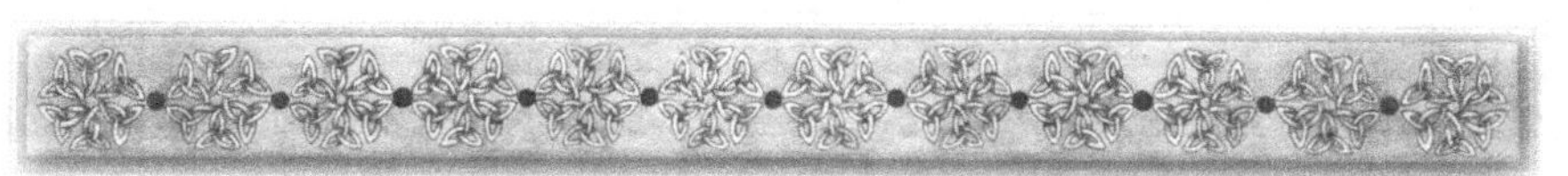

Chapter 53

Round Table Zodiac

Elysium (Sky Temple)
In-Between Time

When Merlin arrived in the Sky Temple, he noticed that the light was subdued and there were no longer any views of the external world. Lady Gaea and Delphyne were engaged in understanding the template of the Round Table so they would know how and when to land the ship. They were puzzling over how the event would create a Planetary Earth Star and create a rebirth but decided to trust the mystery.

"Welcome, Merlin," Lady Gaea said warmly, offering him a seat.

The Caduceus was buzzing with electricity in his right hand, and the serpents were active. Merlin nodded to her, but continued to stand, and then he joined her in a slow and deliberate circumnavigation of the Round Table.

"What do you know about star maps?" Delphyne asked.

"I have studied the Round Table since the Foretime when I became its guardian and protector." Merlin laid a hand tenderly on the surface of the table and it trembled ever so slightly. "The template of Logres has always been a mystery, but it is a blueprint that reveals how peace can be established on the planet so all sentient beings can thrive."

307

"The Round Table is happy to see you," Lady Gaea observed. "I'm happy we could assist in its care."

"This was the best place for the secrets to be hidden." Merlin observed that the table seemed to be undergoing some sort of transformation. In the Foretime it had been a dense and pockmarked meteorite. When it served as the Round Table for King Arthur and the knights of Camelot, it had become smooth and black. Now it was taking on an inner radiance and he noticed it was beginning to shimmer with light.

"The Round Table is responding to a new template, a gold print," Merlin explained. "What is dense will become increasingly light."

The Sky Temple was also continuing its transformation. They were encased in what appeared to be a milky white bubble with a silver shimmer.

"The Sky Temple is becoming a Mother Ship," Lady Gaea explained. "She is taking on the appearance of a lunar silver disk."

"And what of the Niente?" Delphyne asked. "Will they attack?"

"The energies of Saturn are waning. Soon there will be no place for them, unless perhaps they wish to visit Tartarus and live below Hades.

"I can't think of a better place for them," said the dragon. "Should we gather them up and deliver them?"

"No need," Merlin told him. "What is taking place has celestial origins. All we really need to do is work with the flow of reality."

"Hasn't that always been true?" asked Lady Gaea.

The snakes on Merlin's staff awakened once more and started hissing.

"They fight unless I placate them, rather like most human beings." Merlin gave them each a piece of apple. "I've never really understood war. Why not love?"

Merlin noticed that the serpents had turned their gaze upwards when he stood by the symbol of Capricorn's goatfish, which was also morphing into a unicorn. The Star Spirit on the top of the Serpent Staff began to glow.

"When you are ready, I can thrust the Caduceus into the Round Table through the constellation of Capricorn, which will subdue Saturn and the forces of darkness. Then the celestial secrets Morfessa placed there in the Foretime should be revealed," Merlin explained. "He did tell me the appearance of the unicorn would be significant."

"We are ready," said Lady Gaea, establishing herself in a chair.

Her birds flew back into her hair and began chirping. The dragon rose to her full height and peered down at the surface of the table.

Merlin made a motion to set his staff on the image of the unicorn, but it reared and pointed its horn west. The pitcher of the Aquarian water bearer flashed, and a hole appeared where the water flowed. Merlin understood what he must do next.

"With the Caduceus, I now activate the Template of Logres!" he declared as he thrust the Caduceus into the hole.

There was silence.

Then the Round Table activated. All three screens displayed maps of London's parks. The first screen locked onto Hampstead Heath, the second screen showed images focused closely on Parliament Hill, and the third screen fixated on Boudicca's Mount.

"I've been wandering around Hampstead Heath in the form of a fox, wondering when and where the Planetary Earth Star would open. The Niente almost caught onto me, but I'm sly." Merlin grinned. "When Morfessa arrived in the Foretime, he brought the knowledge from Fálias with him. One of the roles of wizards and druids is to watch the planets, asteroids and comets in our solar system orbit the Sun and understand the impact the stars have on humankind," Merlin noted. "It is more significant than most know."

All three stared down at the intricate designs on the shimmering table that were becoming increasingly visible to them.

"I'm glad you kept the vision of Earth high," the dragon told Lady Gaea, still peering at the star map on the Round Table.

"I love the melody of the skies," Lady Gaea shared, her birds continuing to chirp. "We are ruled by our destiny, unless we decide to choose a different direction and ask for the intercession of the gods."

"Certainly, there are times when great things can happen," said Merlin. "Otherwise, Morfessa would not have flown in his ship to grant us this gift from the stars. A grand precession of the equinoxes happens every twenty-six thousand years. It creates a wobble, also new possibilities, which is why I'm here staring at the Round Table with a goddess and a dragon."

Lady Gaea yawned and leaned back in her chair.

"I'm feeling so tired, so old."

Chapter 54
The Proposal
Hampstead Heath, London, 21st Century

Accolon stopped the limousine on Parliament Hill, overlooking London. Morgen was the first to step out and survey the scene to make certain it was safe to come out. She listened for a hum, but did not hear any sound.

"The opening of the Planetary Earth Star will happen near here," she proclaimed.

"When?" asked Accolon.

"Sea and sky are whispering to me," Morgen stated. "I will know soon."

Diana climbed out of the vehicle next, followed by Lance and then Abigail, Daphne and Blaise.

"I need to go find Nina," Diana said, beginning to walk down the slope toward Hampstead. Lance was soon close behind her.

"Let's walk home," Blaise said. "Come with us, Abigail."

"Yes, enjoy the afternoon, everyone," Daphne added, kicking her heels up and scampering toward their home with Blaise beside her. Abigail followed behind them, turning once to look at Morgen. She did not dare ask what had happened to Taliesin, but she could not forget the poet or the love she felt for him.

Morgen gave them a sour look, then got back inside the limousine and motioned for Accolon to drive on.

"They have no idea what's coming," Morgen muttered.

Diana and Lance watched as the limousine made its leisurely way down the grassy paths of Hampstead Heath, disappearing into the woods.

"I have a home here in Hampstead," Lance said. "Would you like to visit it?"

"That's rather wonderful, and convenient," Diana replied.

Lance took her hand. As they walked down the grassy paths past the Hampstead Ponds, he explained that for many generations, the Pelleas family had kept a home just off Hampstead Heath. Diana briefly thought of Nina, or Nimue, but intuitively felt she was well. She also knew that Jupiter would look after his granddaughter. She gave Lance's hand a squeeze and followed him to a tall stone wall that was covered in ivy.

Lance opened an almost imperceptible gate, and they followed a path that meandered through old trees which hid the property from the business of London and prying eyes. She felt safe inside the meticulously manicured walled garden. Looking up, Diana noticed what looked like a large lenticular cloud hovering over them.

"That looks like a spaceship," Diana remarked.

Lance also found the stationary cloud puzzling, and the two of them discussed the prospect of a gathering storm. There was very little wind, and the rest of the sky was blue. They shrugged and turned their focus back onto the Pelleas estate, and Lance offered to show Diana around the home.

The grove of old oak trees surrounding the property made the well-kept red brick house appear ageless. Ivy climbing over the garden walls made it seem even more mysterious. They followed an exterior stone stairway that wound up a hillock to the first floor and the main entrance of the home. Lance produced a key, and the large blue front door opened to an extensive and lavishly decorated hallway.

Lance showed Diana around the ground floor, before leading her up the interior stairway to the largest room of the house, a library that had extensive views of Hampstead Heath. Once again, they noticed the curious lenticular cloud, and Diana thought it looked as if a large spaceship were stationed over Parliament Hill.

Who is observing us? Diana wondered. *Sky gods?*

Lance led Diana out onto the library's balcony, which sported some outdoor furniture. Looking down at the garden below, they observed Oriental Maples and the other little trees and shrubs that grew there. Turning back toward the library, Diana could see her reflection in the sliding glass balcony door. For a moment, she glimpsed herself as a strong youth with a bow and quiver. Then Diana could see the mature athletic woman she had become.

She unfastened her ponytail and let her long hair cascade down her back. Since the death of Felix, life had not been easy for her. But Diana was innately courageous, and she had accepted each day as any spiritual warrior must. In the presence of Lance, she was feeling beautiful again.

"Are you happy?" asked Lance, taking Diana's hand.

"Yes," said Diana, giving his hand a warm squeeze.

The tall windows in the library were stunning and must have generally had a good view, except now they were white with mist.

They sat down together on a love seat. She suspected that all of North London would soon be covered in mist. The moment seemed potent, even dream-like. She thought she could hear humming.

"Do you see that silver disk in the sky?" Diana asked.

He did not respond.

When Diana turned to look at Lance, he was down on one knee holding out a ring. She gasped.

"Will you marry me?" asked Lance Pelleas.

Diana was stunned as she looked at the diamond that sparkled in the ring. She looked through the mist toward the silver disk that glimmered like a spaceship in the distance. Life seemed exciting, and Diana knew in her heart that a beautiful new time was coming. Felix Liber danced with the gods now in the Bacchanalia, and she was free to go on with life as she chose. An adventure with Lance seemed like the best of all possibilities.

"Yes," she said. "Yes! Yes!"

Lance stood up, pulled Diana into his arms, and kissed her long and hard. Then he slipped the ring onto her finger.

A sudden noise caused them to turn their gaze upwards.

"Do you think that silver disk is really a spaceship?" Lance asked, walking to the edge of the balcony. A mist had settled over the garden. The world seemed entirely white due to the haze. The silver disk hummed, then seemed to stop and hover, emitting a high-pitched chime like sound.

"It can't be a spaceship," replied Diana, who was focusing on the ring.

"How odd," Lance noted looking toward the silver disk. "I've never seen such thick fog in this area. And Morgen did say a gathering would happen soon."

"Walk into the Heath and see what's going on," said Diana. "And celebrate the beginning of our life together."

Diana took Lance's hand, and they walked beside the curiously quiet East Heath Street into Hampstead Heath. As they walked in the thick fog past the swimming ponds, they could still hear the hum and chiming of the silver disk. Diana was intuitively drawn up toward Well Walk and then along a forest path that led to Boudicca's Mount. The trees looked like ghostly giants, pale leaves like waving hands. As they wound their way to the grassy mound, Diana thought she saw white faery cattle.

"It's as though the veils between the worlds are thin," Lance commented.

When they arrived, an iron fence with padlocked gates blocked their entry, so they followed a hazy path in the direction of Parliament Hill. Looking back, Diana thought the tumulus looked as though the faery folk had opened a portal to Inner Earth. Off in the distance, she could hear the baying of hounds. The mist had cleared just enough so they could see people standing below an enormous silver disk that was about sixty feet in diameter. The hum stopped abruptly, and the chimes gained momentum. As the disk began to lower a dark circular object was beamed onto the ground. As the mist cleared, they could see people gathering around what appeared to be an old stone table.

As they walked closer, Lance stiffened.

"What is it?" asked Diana.

"It's the Round Table."

Chapter 55

Healing Tribes of The Western World

Elysium (Sky Temple)
In-Between Time

As guardian and protector, Merlin had studied the zodiac map of the Round Table closely since the Foretime. He had noticed that the template of Logres had changed over time, as if adjusting to each generation. What was once a blueprint now appeared to be a gold print.

"The constellations are not aligned like they were in the Foretime when the table was created," he told the dragon. "But this can be used to our advantage. The Niente will not have an accurate map, which will slow their assault."

"What is going to happen?" asked Delphyne, glancing at Lady Gaea who was asleep in her chair. Birds alit beside her, placing flower blossoms in her hair.

"The Round Table is deciding where to land," Merlin noted. "It seems it will be somewhere in North London, possibly Hampstead. There are those of the good magic who will feel an inner call to gather. Then perhaps humanity will begin to experience the sweetness of Elysium."

317

"Even a taste of that celestial happiness could change everything."

"For some," Merlin added.

They could feel the gravitational pull. Silver sails billowed out around the temple, so that it felt as if they were riding inside a sailing ship, or a great silver butterfly. The walls of the Mother Ship had become increasingly translucent yet shimmered with lunar light.

"We will be landing soon," said Lady Gaea, her eyes still shut. "And all things will change."

The ship continued its metamorphosis, its wings looking now like a silver disk. They could see out of what seemed like large windows, yet they did not feel the wind.

They could see London below them, the River Thames snaking through the city. An unknown force was guiding them north over Big Ben and the Houses of Parliament. They flew over Hyde Park, where people were having picnics and boating along the Serpentine Lake. They sailed on slightly northeast over the Inner Circle of Regent's Park, where the ship hesitated. Hovering over Queen Mary's Gardens, they could see the colorful display of the famous roses in full bloom. Then a strong breeze caught the sail, and they cruised on northwest over Primrose Hill, and Hampstead Village, and floated on across Hampstead Heath. Then a white mist surrounded them, and the entire area disappeared into a cloud-like fog. The silver ship halted. Humming changed to chimes, and a slow descent began.

"As we enter the Age of Aquarius, Uranus becomes the ruler," Merlin said to Lady Gaea. "Have you seen him?"

The dragon opened her eyes wide and gazed at Lady Gaea, who also opened her eyes momentarily.

"Time heals," Delphyne stated. "And even gods change."

"*Uranus is a gigantic star-spangled sky god," Gaea said wistfully. "I always liked his rebellious nature and groundbreaking ideas, even if he is a bit unpredictable."*

Their winged ship was increasingly enveloped in white mist. A strong breeze blew, causing disturbance and the Round Table began to thump.

"I think we are supposed to climb on top of the table," said Gaea, hiking up her skirts and stepping from a chair onto the middle of the table. "I'm going to sit on the shimmering image of Earth."

The birds flew from her hair and out into the Heath. Delphyne flew too, circling protectively around them. Merlin stood, his staff raised. Merlin leapt onto the table behind Lady Gaea and stood beside his Serpent Staff, which had sprouted wings. He felt compelled to lift the Caduceus. As he held the staff, a light surrounded them. A set of multicolored wings sprouted from within the Round Table then surrounded in a beam of light, the ship began to lower them to the ground.

"It's landing time!" shouted the dragon.

"The Star Spirit is aligning with Ganieda's Diamond Heart in Inner Earth and the Caduceus," Merlin yelled to Delphyne. "The Round Table will find the true alignment and Logres will activate."

Lady Gaea sat in the center of the winged table, looking dazed. The protection that had once encased them vanished, and she felt vulnerable. Her hair and cloak flew wildly about, and she laughed sweetly.

"The Moon orbits the Earth, and the Earth-Moon orbits the Sun," Merlin declared. "The Sun traverses through the center of the Milky Way…. And now it's time for the alignment of Sky, Earth and Sea."

Lady Gaea looked increasingly excited as the winged table found its place to land.

"In the Fifth Epoch, gods, humans and the fey will live together again," Merlin stated. "At least that's the prophecy."

"I love flying with you," said Delphine, encircling the two who rode the magic table. "But I can sense lightning."

Merlin held the Caduceus skyward. As if responding to an unseen magic, the crystal ball at the tip of the Serpent Staff flashed and the winged table halted. Just above the tree line, they hovered over Parliament Hill, then the beam abruptly shifted, finally halting in the meadow near Boudicca's Mount. The Round Table and its passengers descended onto Hampstead Heath.

Once on the planet, the gravitational pull exhausted Lady Gaea, who became sleepy. Lying on the table, she dozed lightly. She dreamt of the battles between the Titans, the Olympians and the Celtic tribes. In the country of Erin, she saw battles between the Fir Bolg, Fomorians, Tuatha Dé Danann and the Milesians. The victors decided who would rule the land and who would be forced underground. Other deities lifted off to reside in realms between sky, land and sea.

"Wake up, Gaea!" Delphyne shouted to her.

In her dream, Lady Gaea felt as though her clothes and body were becoming light.

"Wake up, Gaea!" Merlin yelled.

"I am awake!" Lady Gaea declared, but her eyes were still shut. "I have been here since the beginning, when the planet was considered a garden. The realms of the elves and faeries are so vibrant, stunningly magical. I quite like the gnomes who tend seeds too...."

Lady Gaea yawned and attempted to sit up. Merlin stood beside her, still observing his staff. On the Round Table, the stars in the constellation of Aquarius glimmered.

"In the Foretime, humankind split apart from Source," Merlin noted. "Like apples falling from a tree. It's time to unite with Source again... with Wisdom."

The serpents on his staff awoke and began to hiss and snap. He did not have fruit to calm them. The Star Spirit glowed and images of lightning flashed inside the crystal ball.

"It's happening," Delphine called out as she circled above them.

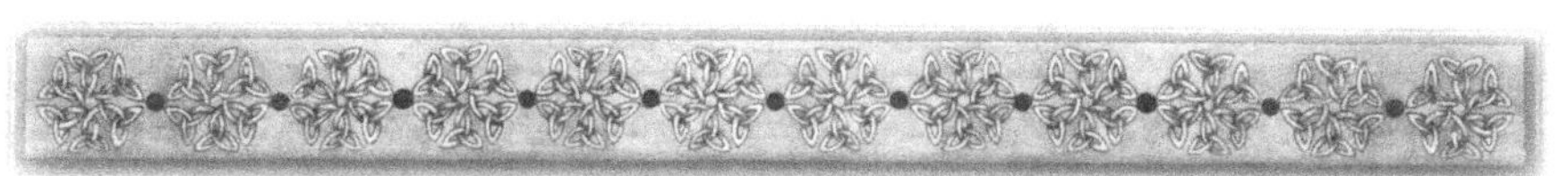

Chapter 56

Uranus Returns

Hampstead Heath, London, 21ˢᵗ Century

Lady Gaea stood on the ground beside the winged table. She swayed slightly, being unused to gravity. A giant of a man had taken a tentative stance near her. His long, luminous, white hair and pale blue eyes made him seem celestial, yet his muscular body suggested that he had been a warrior. An aura of weariness surrounded him. There was a notable tension in the air as the two met again. His robe was filled with stars and the faces of mythical beings. God of the sky and starry heavens, Gaea's husband smiled at her.

"I thought you might need help settling your ship," Uranus remarked. "Boreas, the north wind, helped with your landing."

Uranus blinked, remembering the beauty of Gaea. He extended a large muscular arm and touched her cheek, then pulled her into a warm embrace. She melted into his form, the Earth and Sky merging into one.

"I've missed you."

"We arose out of Chaos," Gaea reminded him. "And we had many children."

"Indeed, we did," he murmured, still holding her close.

323

Delphyne and Merlin observed them—ready to respond to Gaea's needs but giving them a special moment for their reunion.

"The last encounter with our son Chronos was unpleasant," Uranus recalled, withdrawing his arms and stepping back. Lightning flashed in the sky and thunder rumbled. His eyes flashed with fury.

"Yet all things heal with time," Lady Gaea soothed. "Merlin assures me that Chronos, who became Saturn, has been obstructed. His dark reign has ended."

Lady Gaea stepped back, and they stared at each other for an instant as if not sure what to say next.

"You are still magnificent!" Uranus declared.

"I am about to change," Gaea said. "I wanted to see you one last time just to say I love you, and it was all worth it."

Uranus was silent. Her tender words had an impact on him, and he softened. "Jupiter said something about the Aquarian Age?"

"The New Epoch has arrived, and you are the ruler," she told him.

Uranus pondered her words and then laughed in a good-natured way. "So, power and rebellion return to the planet?"

"Perhaps for a while," Lady Gaea admitted. "But the New Time is an invitation for something fresh and innovative. It's a time for Earth and Sky to harmonize."

"I really never thought I'd make it back to planet Earth, or even Olympus," he said. Uranus turned his focus toward the sky. "I belong in the Cosmos now."

"It is time to align the Planetary Earth Star with the Milky Way and your Cosmic Light," Lady Gaea revealed. "I am feeling birth pangs, but they are odd. I don't sense any more children will come from my womb."

Delphyne, although still invisible to most, had come out of hiding. Uranus petted her head like she was a good dog, and the dragon bared her teeth at him.

"There's my pet." With a last pat and a laugh, Uranus withdrew his hand and looked over at Lady Gaea. "Things always change beneath Earth and Sky."

"It's time for Sky Heaven on Earth," Gaea said. "That is if we can get along."

"Should we marry again?" asked Uranus.

"I'd like that." Gaea smiled at him. "But we might need to start over again."

"How would we begin?" asked Uranus. "We've been apart so long, and, well, we're old."

Lady Gaea straightened herself up. "It starts within."

The Lady started to sing a melody that was as ancient as the mountains and meadow streams. The seeds sleeping in the Round Table heard her and pushed up shoots, which burst forth flowers.

"You are so abundant," Uranus said. "And I'm just old, cold and rather blue."

"Sing to the stars," said Delphyne.

"I don't know how." Uranus frowned.

"Listen to my heart," the Lady told him.

Uranus bent his head down by Lady Gaea's heart.

"I'm starting to give birth to something new… can you hear it?" she asked.

At first, Uranus didn't hear anything, and then he thought he could hear a tune trickling like the sound of babbling brooks and bird song. He hummed along with it, and a strong breeze began to blow through Hampstead Heath.

When he lifted his head, Lady Gaea recognized him as a celestial king—tall, strong and full of radiance.

"I've missed you," she admitted.

Uranus looked at Mother Gaea and saw all life in her. The ancient god thought of their many children, and all the experiences they had been through together, and he wondered how many more good times might be coming.

Uranus leaned forward and kissed the Lady on the lips. She relaxed into his arms but then she fainted. He held her, and then he lifted Lady Gaea back onto the Round Table.

"Sweet Gaea," said Delphyne, encircling the meteorite table.

"What's wrong with her?" asked Uranus with concern.

"I am just changing." Lady Gaea opened her eyes. Her eyelids fluttered, and she fainted again.

Merlin joined the cosmic gathering. His staff was gleaming, but Uranus hardly noticed.

"The new energy is overwhelming her," Uranus said, adjusting Gaea's cloak as she lay in the center of the Round Table.

"Earth and Sky must be harmonized," said Merlin.

"Earth, Sky and Sea," Delphyne corrected. "The gods and goddesses, plus all the folks of the Earth, must unite in love. Many tribes share love for Gaea."

"I hope people still love the sky gods too!" Uranus declared.

"We must call upon the goddess of the sea, the Morgen," Merlin stated. "And those who dare to love. I can sense she and Accolon are close."

"Perhaps the Elysium fields will blossom once again," Delphyne added, lying down beside the Round Table, guarding Gaea.

Chapter 57

Boudicca's Mount

Hampstead Heath, London, 21st Century

Black and sleek, a stretch limousine emerged from the fog. Merlin watched as the vehicle stopped and several faces peered out. Accolon and Morgen were the first to step out and join the gathering tribe. Then Nimue exited the limo. Without thinking, he went to her, surprised by the wave of overwhelming passion that flooded his heart.

"My love," Merlin said in greeting.

Nimue responded to Merlin's affection by taking his hand. He scrutinized her quiver that contained Diana's arrows and Jupiter's lightning bolt, which seemed magically contained, at least in the present moment.

"So now you know you are a demi-god," he stated.

Nimue smiled and gave a small nod. Together they approached the winged table with respect. They observed Lady Gaea, who appeared to be sleeping on the table, then glanced at the giant Uranus who stood beside her, and at the protective dragon. Morgen and Accolon also gazed at the resting goddess. Uranus glanced at the new arrivals but was more focused on Lady Gaea. He was concerned that Mother Earth might be dying.

"Is she ill?" Uranus asked Morgen.

"Just transforming," Morgen told him.

Pulling back her emerald cloak, she revealed a meteorite pendant that she removed and handed to Uranus.

"This tiny yet powerful meteorite comes from the Foretime," Morgen explained. "I have kept it safe in the sea. Uranus, you must take this to your Sky realm. The Sky, Earth and Sea must be bonded. We will do everything we can to weave the worlds together."

Uranus observed the tiny meteorite fragment in his large hands.

"It is a piece of a dying star."

"It needs to come alive again," said Merlin, igniting a flame in his palm and then blowing the golden ray into the meteorite stone.

It began to glow like a small star or sun, yet the sky god Uranus was unharmed.

Uranus' eyes widened. "Are you certain?"

Merlin locked eyes with Uranus. "Yes."

Uranus nodded, then as quickly as a flash of lightning, he rose up through the haze, and disappeared. The mist lifted with him, and the sun began to shine on the Heath.

Delphyne looked with worry at Lady Gaea, who was still sleeping.

"Inner Earth, Middle Earth and the Celestial Template must align," Merlin declared.

He walked to the northern point of the Round Table. Then, sensing the correct location, he planted his Serpent Staff into the ground with force.

In response, they could hear a knock from inside Boudicca's Mount. The soil and rocks gave way, and the mound became a cave that buzzed with blue swirling lights. A dozen white hounds with pink ears emerged and leapt over the iron fence. They walked cautiously forward to the Round Table, then began to howl. Through the blue stargate, Lady Gwenabwy and Gwyn Ap Nudd emerged. The white goddess was pale, almost translucent in the sunlight. Gwyn was darker and more robust. The iron fence stopped their progression.

"Ganieda has activated the star of Inner Earth," Lady Gwenabwy confirmed. "The folk of Inner Earth stand united with Gaea, Uranus and all of life."

Lady Gwenabwy and Gwyn Ap Nudd stood inside the fenced-in area as if awaiting guidance.

"Delphyne, you have an important task," Merlin commanded. "You must take the Star Spirit to Ganieda so the realms are permanently linked."

Merlin started to separate the crystal ball from the Serpent Staff, but Delphyne grabbed it with her teeth. Stunned, the two smaller serpents became quiet. Then, with full and mighty focus, the dragon moved with the Star Spirit toward Boudicca's Mount and the buzzing blue portal. Tearing off the metal gate with one easy swipe of her mighty claws, she walked to the center of the Nemeton and then disappeared through a stargate that led to the Underworld.

Lady Gwenabwy and Gwyn Ap Nudd were able to walk through the gap in the fence, pleased that without the iron fencing blocking them they were now free to move as they chose. Gwyn whistled, and his hounds disappeared within the mound, but soon returned baying. Adhan and Morfryn stepped through the portal and joined the gathering. Merlin stood still, still grasping his staff with the confused snakes and the missing crystal.

Morgen and Accolon had observed the entrances and exits with interest. Giving a nod to Lady Gwenabwy and Gwyn Ap Nudd, they began to march sunwise around the winged table. As they walked, Morgen touched the astrological glyphs on the table, but Gaea did not stir. Nimue joined Merlin and took his hand.

The Lady's eyelids fluttered, as her awareness floated back up. In a low voice, she said, "Let's bring in New Earth, so I can rise again."

"What is the next step?" asked Adhan.

"You must take each other's hands," said Gaea. "The planet needs love."

Nimue took Merlin's hand, and he took his mother's hand. Adhan grasped Madog Morfryn's large palm, and he reached out to Morgen, who begrudgingly accepted. Accolon kissed Morgen's hand, after she held his, and they all laughed.

"Keep gathering my family, so all things align," Gaea whispered. Her head then softly rolled to the side, as she lost consciousness again.

"Rest, sweet Mother," Morgen said with gentleness. "Your soul has not been fully on this planet in a very long time. Too much war and ignorance have divided you from your true realm. For that, we all suffer."

In her semi-sleep, Gaea began to hum a melody only known to the Sun, Moon, Stars and all the planets. Far up in the sky, Uranus heard her, and he hummed in return.

"Follow the pattern on the Round Table and the Planetary Earth Star will open," communicated Lady Gaea in her semi-conscious state. "Merlin, you know how. I leave the task to you.

"I will assist you to the best of my ability, Lady Gaea," Merlin responded.

"The right people will arrive at precisely the right time," the Lady added.

Looking across the Heath, Merlin saw that Diana and Lance were striding their way.

"The tribe is already gathering," said Merlin. "The Planetary Earth Star is activating."

The white hounds bayed, and another figure stepped through the blue portal.

"I made it!" Taliesin yelled to Merlin.

Chapter 58

London's Zodiac

Hampstead Heath, London, 21st Century

Abigail had been having tea in her healing garden when she felt the sudden urge to walk to Hampstead Heath, and specifically to Boudicca's Mount. As she hiked through the uncultivated park, she thought of rebellious Boudicca and how people were still drawn to her. According to popular culture, the famous queen of the Iceni tribe was entombed there, although local experts said it was a Bronze Age barrow. Abae had learned to trust her intuition, and she knew each sacred site had multiple layers. Whether or not Boudicca's body was interred there, she could intuitively sense the pulsating energy of a landscape stargate. As she reached the barrow hill, Abigail noticed that a strange blue light was emerging from the mound. Puzzled, she noticed the gates and spiked iron fence had been twisted beyond repair. A group of people was gathering, and she strode over to join them.

With some surprise, she could see the winged table which was emitting rainbow-colored lights. While approaching, she realized that many of her magical friends were looking at something. Abae's heart gave a little flutter when she noticed Taliesin was just in front

333

of her, walking from the mound toward the circle. His back was to her, so she called out to him.

"Taliesin!"

The wild romantic poet stopped, turned and smiled at Abae. She quickened her pace and soon they enjoyed a warm embrace.

"Lovely Abae!" the poet declared.

"I wasn't sure I'd ever see you again!" Abae told him.

"I show up for each age," Taliesin revealed. "Especially when there is a mission to accomplish."

Holding hands, they joined the group. That is when they saw Lady Gaea, who was sleeping on a table.

Taliesin glanced around, taking in the scene of the winged table with the now-giant Mother Goddess sprawled across its surface, the Zodiac around her with shimmering colors. Although the Lady was in the middle, the astrological glyphs were still visible.

Adhan was now carrying the Moon Dish, as promised, with Morfryn at her side. The platter was filled with delicacies, enough to nourish the entire family. She refrained from placing it on the table. She was awaiting a synchronicity, or some sort of sign so she would know how to proceed. Since the Moon Dish kept filling with warm tea and pastries, she walked around the gathering community offering nourishment to everyone.

Diana and Lance, observing the scene from afar, had arrived somewhat breathless but were now part of the tribe. Merlin noticed the flash of Diana's engagement ring, and Abae let out a squeal of delight.

"Are congratulations in order?" Merlin asked.

Diana blushed and showed off her ring. "Yes, a new time has come for us too."

"Mother! How wonderful!" Nina, known to some as Nimue, exclaimed with joy.

Then Diana looked at Lance Pelleas and smiled. He smiled in return, and Merlin cleared his throat. The couple turned their focus back to the winged table.

"It is time to take your place around Lady Gaea," Madog Morfryn declared, standing by the constellation of Aries, the Ram. "Each of you intuitively knows where you must stand. The ancient template of Logres is encoded in the table, and when it activates, a new Camelot will arise."

Morfryn held his hand out to Adhan, who set the Moon Dish in the grass, and then she placed her hand on the constellation of Taurus, the Bull.

Lance Pelleas stood beside Adhan, taking the position of Gemini. When Diana laid her harp necklace on the constellation of Cancer the Crab, the wind began to move through the trees, and an enchanting music could be heard. This was accompanied by the roar of an engine. After bumping up Parliament Hill, a blue Mini Cooper pulled over and parked, and Blaise got out. Daphne was right behind him.

"What the devil is going on here?" Blaise asked. "I've been looking everywhere for my sister! She sent me some crazy text about Lance Pelleas and meeting at Boudicca's Mount!"

"We are creating a landscape zodiac right here in London," Diana said, reaching her hand out to Blaise. "Stand here beside me as Leo the Lion."

Daphne situated herself by the image of the Maiden in the position of Virgo, then took Blaise's hand. Lady Gwenabwy stood beside Libra and the scales of Justice. Blaise glanced with approval at Gwenabwy, the White Goddess, and took her hand. Gwyn Ap Nudd walked to the constellation of Scorpio. Gwyn Ap Nudd smiled at Nimue, who stood beside Sagittarius. As the white hounds trotted around the table baying, Gwyn offered Nimue his hand. She took it reluctantly.

Merlin continued to stand beside Capricorn. Abae intuitively picked up Adhan's Moon Dish then walked toward the constellation of Aquarius. Taliesin, standing beside Pisces, took Abae's hand. At that moment there was a sharp crack, the sky rumbled, and lightning flashed. Surrounded by a blue glow, the table began to rotate.

"My children…" Lady Gaea whispered. "My loves."

Blaise gazed wide-eyed at the Goddess strewn across the zodiac. Observing the the flickering constellation of Leo, he realized that the Logres template had activated. Then noticing Diana's hand resting on the Crab, he did a double take at the sparkling engagement ring.

"It's the birth of the New Time!" he exclaimed with glee. "Logres is imminent!"

Diana offered a dazzling smile.

As the landscape zodiac formed, Lady Gaea let out a muffled groan.

"Abae," Lady Gaea uttered. "What is your prophecy?"

"A bright future," Abae answered without hesitation.

Lady Gaea smiled, then fell back into a deep sleep.

"Should we let her rest?" Adhan asked, grasping the hand of Lance Pelleas.

Suddenly, numerous sirens could be heard. Police cars were seen rolling across the Heath. Like ants swarming a plate of sweets, vehicles traveled across the Heath in the hundreds. They stopped near the table. Unable to see the light, it looked like an ordinary object to them. A British bobby wearing black stepped out of a car and walked over to them

"Where is your permit for gathering on the Heath?"

"Here it is," said Taliesin, producing a piece of paper, which the bobby eyed with suspicion.

"You must have permission from the City of London Corporation," the bobby stated. "And that table requires a hire fee."

Other officers began to emerge from their vehicles, looking menacing. The largest of them wearing a black suit walked in their direction. Observing the scene, he stated with great authority.

"Step back!"

The police obeyed his command.

Having been awakened by the sirens, the Lady opened her eyes and sat up. Looking at the giant of a man, she offered him a radiant smile. "It's Hades!" Gaea exclaimed. "My grandson."

Hades and others dressed in black walked over to the table. Gwyn Ap Nudd turned and looked at Hades.

"You must be cousins," Morgen said, stepping between them.

Hades looked at his grandmother and at those gathering around her. Then he snapped his fingers and the men in black stood, unblinking and frozen in time.

"So, this is the beginning of the New Era," Hades stated. He looked at Nimue and gave her a wink. "I could use a new Persephone."

Nimue menacingly produced one of Diana's arrows, and Hades raised his arms and backed away, then gave an acquiescing shrug. Defiantly, Nimue strode back to the Sagittarian image of the Archer. She smirked at Hades.

"I'm here to help," Hades proclaimed. "Death has to be present before birth."

Gwyn Ap Nudd gave Hades an approving nod.

"In this moment, I grant all of you a boon of invisibility to the Niente," Hades told the group. "Hopefully, someone will find some real criminals in London and bring them to me," Hades added with a laugh. "I have a perfect place where I can hold them indefinitely."

Hades threw a black shawl over his left shoulder and disappeared in a cloud of smoke.

Morgen and Accolon stood outside the circle, observing and protecting the tribe.

"I hope the next pantheon will be a good one," Morgen declared. "Preferably with better family dynamics."

Accolon raised his sunglasses and peered at her with a questioning look.

"I suppose it begins here." He pulled Morgen close and kissed her on the lips.

"Definitely," she added.

There was a sudden commotion. The group turned to see that the men in black had unfrozen, and chaos was ensuing. Perplexed, the bobbies stood around the bent iron fence, and then they shrugged. Unable to see the portal or those who gathered, the officers sensed something was awry but didn't know what. Speaking to each other in anxious, high-pitched voices, they decided to depart. They returned to their vehicles and sped off across the Heath.

"The Lords of the Underworlds like you," Merlin whispered to Nimue, who stood by the constellation of Sagittarius holding the hand of Gwyn Ap Nudd. Lightning streaked across the sky.

"Let's get on with it," Morgen snapped. "Hand me the Moon Dish!"

Abae obliged.

Lady Gaea fainted again and lay prone across the table.

"We finally made it through this portal. Let's birth this next epoch!" Morgen declared. Accolon stood protectively behind her, but Morgen pulled his hand onto Moon Dish with her own.

"We are going into the next epoch together," she said. The scent of roses and apple blossoms perfumed the air.

339

Chapter 59

The 13th Secret

Hampstead Heath, London, 21st Century

A tremor in the earth unsettled the group gathered around Lady Gaea. A white horse emerged from Boudicca's Mount. The rider held a blazing sword, and he rode swiftly toward the gathering. The tribe scattered as he aimed for the table.

"May the template of Logres activate now!" shouted Morfessa, thrusting the sword into the Pisces symbol of the two fish. Water poured from the table making the group scatter.

Blaise offered a supporting roar. The winged table suddenly turned white, and then translucent.

The movement of the table shook Gaea. She groaned but was now deeply sleeping. Many of her tribe had gathered around her, as she lay on the winged table, which was starting to shake as if it were trying to move. The gods and demi-gods stared at one another.

"There is a thirteenth secret," Morfessa said. "He knows his role!"

Off in the distance, they could see a young man running toward them.

"Have I missed it all?" Owen asked, coming to stand beside Lance Pelleas.

"It's so good to see you, Son," said Lance. "Where have you been?"

"It's a long story," he replied, looking at Morgen. "It's a tale for another time."

Then he glanced over at Nimue, who was standing beside Merlin who held the Serpent Staff.

"The Caduceus must work with you now!" Merlin told Owen, handing him the Serpent Staff, and the young man looked at the writhing serpents with dismay.

"*Siochain*," said Merlin. "*Siochain!*"

Everyone stopped speaking, and then the birds paused their singing. Looking up, they could all see a comet coming from the sky.

"You must embody the healer Asclepius," Merlin shouted to Owen. "I have a comet to focus on!"

"Feed the snakes some apples, Owen," Nimue said, tossing a few in his direction.

Owen fed the two snakes, and they quieted, turning their gaze upward.

Stepping between Nimue and Merlin, Owen placed his hand on the thirteenth constellation of Ophiuchus.

"I have some explaining to do," Owen whispered to Nimue, who ignored him.

"Lady Gaea, I offer you the healing Caduceus," Owen declared, holding the staff.

Accolon still holding Delphyne went to stand beside Owen. The dragon was increasing in size and beginning to squirm. Accolon let her go and she slithered away into the shadows.

"Whatever comes of this," Merlin declared, "know that throughout all time I have loved all of you and I always will! May Lady Gaea and all sentient beings experience the Golden Age."

At first, nothing happened.

Nimue turned to look at Owen and glared.

"Different timeline," he mouthed to her, then glanced at Merlin.

"Serpent Bearer," Merlin shouted. "The time is now."

Owen took the Serpent Staff and gently laid it on Gaea's sleeping form.

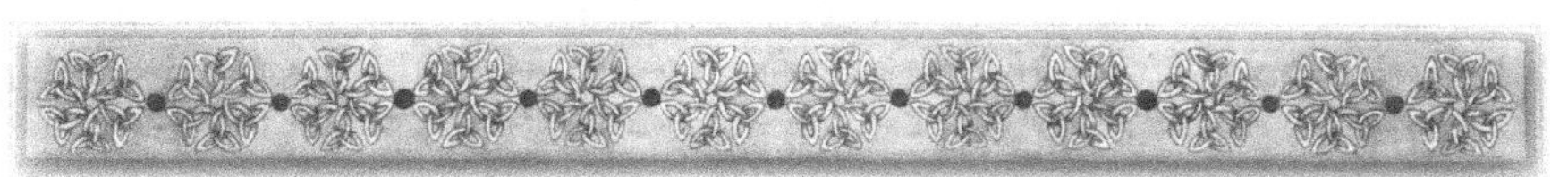

Chapter 60
Gaea & the Rose
Hampstead Heath, London, 21st Century

As Owen set the Caduceus on Lady Gaea, Merlin told everyone to step back. The winged table groaned and then started to slowly rotate clockwise. Sitting up, Lady Gaea blinked at those now standing around her. A silver butterfly flew onto Gaea's bosom, and she giggled. They all began to laugh, feeling a sudden lightness of being. Then the winged table began to rise.

"Grab the Caduceus!" Merlin shouted.

Owen whisked the staff off the winged table, and everyone stepped back again. The Earth started to shake, and a symmetrical thirteen-pointed Earth Star formed beneath their feet. Golden light encircled them. They each looked amazed, feeling the power of the moment.

"What's that?" Owen asked.

Looking skyward, they could see a meteorite hurtling toward them. Abigail let out a muffled scream.

Then it struck, right in the middle of the winged table. Everyone felt the shock of the impact. When the smoke cleared, Gaea was gone.

"What happened?" asked Daphne.

I am you now, they could hear Gaea say. *I am all of you.*

Nimue choked back tears. "I didn't know this would be her death."

The council broke apart and looked at the black hole where the winged table had been. Miraculously, none of them were injured when the meteorite hit the ground.

"It was a flash of cosmic light," Blaise exclaimed. "Our god and demi-god status protected us."

"But Gaea is gone. This is terrible," said Daphne, turning toward Abae and letting out a sob. The white hounds also peered down into the hole and whined.

"Where is the promise of Logres?" asked Blaise. "The rebirth of the age?"

The crater seemed empty, void of all life.

Morgen handed the scorched platter back to Adhan, who realized it was not hot. As she held the platter, it began to change shape. They all watched as it became a pitcher.

"It's for the water bearer," Adhan exclaimed. She lifted the small golden pitcher up and sniffed it. "It does have liquid inside."

"Empty the liquid into the crater and see what happens," Merlin said.

Adhan looked to Morgen, who took the golden pitcher and, with Accolon, very gently poured the fragrant ambrosial water into the hole. A little puff of smoke arose from the darkness.

"In the New Time, Lady Gaea, may you persevere through these changes and reimagine yourself!" said Morgen, with firm conviction in her voice.

The incantation had an impact. As they all watched, a giant rose stem with sharp thorns emerged from the place where the Round Table had once stood. They stepped farther back, not wanting to be ensnared in the enchanted bush. Large pink rose buds began to appear on the exterior branches, and a lovely fragrance filled the air.

"What a lovely gift from the goddess!" Diana remarked.

"A reminder of the importance of love," Lance Pelleas added, kissing Diana's hand.

Morgen began pacing. Her emerald-colored dress shimmered with the same hues and tints as the new unfurling leaves.

"We haven't finished the work we have gathered here to do," Morgen said.

"We must send Gaea love to sustain her!" Accolon exclaimed.

The otherworldly rose bush was continuing to grow, and more tight green buds were forming. Gaea's tribe of friends formed a circle around the crater.

Morgen declared, "Gaea, I love you with all my soul, may you flourish in your new life!"

The transformation was extraordinary to witness. What had been an empty crater was filling with a rapidly expanding plant. Morgen glanced at Accolon, who took his sunglasses off.

Closing his eyes, Accolon said in a loud and commanding voice, "I send Gaea love—also vitality. I am here to protect you and all your children!"

The unfurling leaves rapidly expanded out of the top of the crater. A golden butterfly flew sunwise around the enchanted rose bush and then departed.

Lance cleared his voice and then stated: "I adore the way you continue to evolve! May you always continue to grow and thrive."

His words had an immediate effect. It was now clear that the leaves were that of an enormous rose bush. Emerging out of the crater, the bush formed a large green circle, which continued to grow upwards.

"I speak as Goddess of the Moon," contributed Diana. "May the Moon bless you with comfort, safety and deep happiness."

The enchanted rose bush had filled in the entire crater and was now moving upwards at a rapid pace.

"May the living being that is the Sun grant you vitality, creativity, even genius. And may your prophetic gifts be strong," offered Blaise with a playful lion's roar.

With those words, a very thick and thorny stalk grew up through the center of the crater. Above them, the clouds parted, and sunlight fell onto the burgeoning bush. Leaves waved in the breeze, for a moment forming the face of a Green Lady.

Daphne bent down and gently touched the leaves that were growing into the scorched meadow. "I respect you, Mother Gaea. I honor the verdant fields, fertility and motherly devotion you bring us. And I share all of this love with you too."

The group observed a very large bud form on top of the uppermost stem.

"The magic is working," Merlin declared. "Keep going!"

"I am the Oracle Abae," said Abigail. "My prophecy is that we will birth a New Time in which harmony and balance will be natural. I love you, Gaea."

As if in response, a symmetrical pair of leaves unfurled beside the largest bud.

Taliesin pulled a small harp from his cloak. He played a passionate melody that the rose bush responded to favorably by leaning slightly his way. "May you have the courage to face all battles, including your own transformation. May the powers of the Inner Earth help your roots grow strong, and may you, Mother Gaea, rise like the phoenix from the ashes."

A brown wren landed on Taliesin's harp, then fluttered to the widening rose bush. The bird pecked the large bud, and the pink petals responded by opening ever so slightly.

"Mother Gaea, I cherish you," Nimue said. "By the light of Jupiter, may you always have good fortune and a broad vision."

The wren began to sing a series of high-pitched whistles and chirrs. Some green nubs turned pink, and a few buds began to open and unfurl.

"I speak as the Oracle of Asclepius, god of medicine and healing," added Owen. "By the healing gifts of Chiron, I demand that the gods make you whole again."

In response to his words, the charmed rose bush began to emit a hum that sounded like an OM. A little green serpent slithered up out of the crater and lay exhausted in the sunlight.

"Delphyne?" Morgen asked.

The little dragon, only a few inches long, looked up, then closed her eyes with exhaustion. Owen, as the serpent bearer, picked the creature up and handed her to Accolon, who cradled her.

Merlin waited for the correct moment to speak. A wren flew to Merlin, landing on his left shoulder and whistling.

"My dearest Gaea," said Merlin, "I declare that this is the time of your renewal."

A large bud extended just above the mouth of the crater. The flower petals opened a little more, and the perfume of a thousand roses filled the air.

Adhan began to speak, but a lightning bolt streaked across the sky, and standing there was a cosmic boy made of starlight, not fully manifest.

"I love you," the glimmering boy announced. "It is the Age of Aquarius and the time for you to awaken, Mother Gaea."

At the very top of the stem, the petals of the enormous rose bud began to open.

Then Adhan placed the golden pitcher on the ground in front of the rose bush. Her tribe waited, and then suddenly, the petals of the large rose unfurled. And then the flower opened fully.

Adhan gasped.

Inside the full blossom, they could see a baby girl.

Ever so gently, Merlin picked her up. "Welcome, little Gaea, welcome to New Earth."

Greco-Roman Oracles & the Celtic Druids

In the Greek poet Hesiod's *Theogony*, Gaea (Earth) emerged from Chaos or Khaos, the endless void. As a *protogenoi*, Gaea did not need a partner to create other beings. Mother Earth gave birth to all elements, including the mountains, oceans and the entirety of the living landscape. Overseeing the creation of the world from Mount Olympus, she then brought forth the Titans, the Gigantes and the Cyclopes.

According to the poet Sappho, Gaea, desiring a mate, brought forth the sky god, Uranus. One of their children was Eros, the god of love. As more beings were born, questions were asked of Gaea regarding war and peace, and she provided motherly counsel. Around 8th century BC, in ancient Greece, temples were constructed in Gaea's honor. The origins of the oracle, or divine intermediaries, began at this time.

According to legend, Gaea eventually chose to remove herself, reconsecrated the temple and handed the position to the nymph Daphnis who became the oracle and prophetess of Gaea for a while.

The oracle had been protected by a dragon, named Delphyne (or Python), but times changed. The dragon who was devoted to Gaea was killed by the god Apollo, who wanted to establish another oracle at Delphi.

The oracle Apollo established was named Pythia, after the murdered dragon Python, and she became the mouthpiece of this god of prophecy, poetry, music, healing and the sun. Apollo's voice was the dominant one that Pythia channeled. Working in alignment with Apollo, Pythia earned worldwide fame. Although she spoke in riddles, the Pythia was never wrong. There was such demand that eventually three women took on the role of Pythia.

The Oracle of Delphi came to an end in the 4th century AD, when Emperor Theodosius called a church council and enforced Christianity on the Roman Empire. He then placed the position of Emperor beneath that of the church, closed the temples, and forbade all pagan worship. Emperor Theodosius made Christianity the official faith of the Roman Empire. The temples of Apollo, god of the Sun, were torn down, and churches to the new Son of God were built in their place. Because of his earlier influence, when Theodosius died in 395 AD, his passing was significant to the church community.

In the 2nd century BC, Greek philosophers became interested in the mysterious Druids who were believed to have had religious rites like their own. The Druids were said to act as mediums between the gods and the people. The Greek philosopher Posidonius, who died around 50 AD, visited the Celts of Gaul (present-day Northern France) who were said to paint their bodies and decapitate their foes. During his journey, Posidonius discovered the Celts were not barbarians, but sophisticated warrior-poets and astronomers. They called their priestly class the "Druids." He was impressed by the women, who enjoyed more freedom than females in Rome. Posidonius recorded a way of life that was soon to disappear.

The mysterious Druids thrived from the 4th century BC to the 2nd century AD. They were considered the top branch of the three-tiered Celtic society, which also included warriors and serfs. Knowledgeable in mathematics, physics and astronomy, the Druids were not patriarchal. Druids could be male or female, and women were regarded as equals. The Druids were the judges, doctors, scholars and priests who lived in Britain, Ireland and Gaul (now France). They shared their wisdom through oral storytelling and tended sacred groves, stone circles, and landscape zodiacs around the British Isles.

The Druidic law forbade the written word, so their teachings are largely lost. Some scholars trace their traditions back as far as 3000 BC. Their name comes from the Celtic word *Duir,* which means Oak, their most sacred tree. The Druids believed that all of life has intelligence. Over approximately twenty years, they first trained as poets, then as ovates (or oracles), before becoming Druidic leaders of the community. They revered nature and developed a relationship with the living light in the land. Druids worked with a spiritual lifeforce they called *Nwyfre.*

The Druids were a rebellious group and a spiritual threat to Rome. Although there is no evidence to prove it, the Romans claimed that the Druids committed human sacrifice. Modern-day evidence supports the understanding that Druids may have presided at executions as a spiritual presence, just as a priest does today. Useful sources on Druidic culture can be found in the Welsh prose stories known as the *Mabinogion.*

Since there is no evidence to support that Druids sacrificed humans, it was likely propaganda. Yet the Romans needed a reason to destroy the highly organized and refined educational, legal and spiritual systems of the Druids. In 54 AD, Roman Emperor Claudius declared that the practices of Druidry were illegal. Afterward, the Roman legion planned an attack on the last stronghold of Druidic culture, Ynys Môn, now known as Anglesey or *Môn* in modern Welsh. *Môn* is an island off the coast of North Wales in the Irish Sea.

The Roman conquest of *Môn* took place during the 1st century AD. The initial invasion was led by Gaius Suetonius Paulinus in 60 or 61 AD. His focus was on the massacre of the Druid priests and the destruction of the Sacred Groves. However, Suetonius had to withdraw his forces because of a rebellion led by Boudicca, the Warrior Queen, in other parts of Britain. Suetonius mysteriously died after her defeat. The story of his death remains unknown.

In 77-78 AD, Roman general Gnaeus Julius Agricola invaded Ynys Môn, and he was able to subjugate the last of the Druids. Afterwards, Agricola pushed north into Caledonia (now Scotland) forcing the Celtic tribes there to serve Rome. In Caledonia, he led the slaughter of ten thousand men. Agricola returned to Rome, where he was decorated, but died at the age of fifty-three. There are rumors that he was poisoned, possibly by the Roman Emperor, Domitian, who was jealous of Agricola's accomplishments.

Glossary
Names & Magical Places

Accolon: a knight in Arthurian legend. Author Thomas Malory refers to Sir Accolon of Gaul, **Morgan le Fey**'s object of desire.

Adhan: Merlin's mother from Arthurian legend.

Albion: the oldest known name for the island of Britain, and it is still used poetically when referring to the soul of Britain. The Celtic name for Scotland was Alba. In a broader sense, Albion can also be defined as the soul of the living Earth.

Anglesey: once known as **Môn** (or Mona), this is an island off the northwest coast of Wales; it has been linked to the **Druids** for centuries.

Anna: linked to the Goddess Anu, she is a High Priestess of Avalon.

Annwn (Welsh pronunciation "Ah-noon"): the Celtic Underworld of eternal youth and delights ruled by **Arawn**, also known as **Gwyn ap Nudd**. In Christianity, it is the equivalent of Heaven. The Druids spoke of Annwn as the Abyss, a place where the soul-force abides.

Apollo (Greco-Roman): one of the Olympian deities; god of sun and light. (See: **Blaise** & **Latona**.)

Arawn: the Lord of the Underworld (a place referred to as **Annwn**). He is also known as **Gwyn ap Nudd.**

Artemis (Greek): a goddess of wild animals, she became Diana in Roman mythology.

Arthur (See: **King Arthur.**): a Hero of Britain who rode into **Annwn** and seized a cauldron or **Grail**. This quest becomes a journey of secrets and magic, a quest for the grail. Some scholars claim that Arthur is a title that a person earns after establishing unity consciousness and that there is an Arthur for each age.

Asclepius (Greek): the god of healing and medicine had incredible skills and was even capable of raising the dead. He is associated with the snake because of its ability to shed its skin.

Astrology: A system of divination, astrology can reveal the personal and planetary impressions of the movements of the celestial bodies. A horoscope, or an astrological birth chart, determines personality traits, also the timing of major life events. Western astrology is largely based on Hellenistic and Babylonian systems, which track the path of the Sun, Moon, Mercury, Venus, Mars, Jupiter, Uranus, Neptune, Pluto as well as asteroids. Astrologers were popular in ancient Rome and, for this reason, the planets align with their pantheon of gods and goddesses. The Greeks had an older pantheon that mythologically interweaves with Zeus as the more ancient form of Jupiter. Yet some gods stay the same; for example, Uranus is a Greek, not a Roman god. Western astrology uses the tropical zodiac, which is no longer related to the positions of the planets. Those with true genius, such as Carl Jung, understood astrology as a symbolic archetypal (yet often unconscious) language that powerfully influences a person's life.

Atlantis: a fabled city described by the Greek philosopher Plato that suddenly sank into the ocean. Atlantis was depicted as a highly advanced civilization, visually splendid and utopian.

Avalon: the Otherworldly dimension with portals in Glastonbury. Avalon is similar to *Tir Na Ban*, the Land of Women in Irish mythology.

Bacchus (Roman): god of wine, agriculture and fertility, equivalent to Dionysus (Ancient Greek), God of the Grape Harvest. Bacchus is associated with his festivals, the Bacchanalia, which were known for wild celebrations.

Banduri: female druids with mystical powers who fought in the last battle of Môn or Mona.

Blaise: appears in Robert de Boron's epic poem "Merlin" as a teacher to young **Merlin**. He is presented in *Riddles of the Ancestors* as a modern scholar, perhaps a reincarnation of the original Blaise. Archetypally, he is related to the ancient Sun gods such as Apollo.

Bors de Ganis: from Arthurian legend, he was one of three knights of the **Round Table** to achieve the **Grail** and the only one of the three to survive and return to **King Arthur**'s court.

Boudicca's Mount (London): a tree-crowned barrow in Hampstead Heath, and the mythical grave of Queen Boudicca, leader of a British Iceni tribe, who led a rebellion against the Romans. Mystics say the mound is the northern tip of a planetary earth star.

Brocéliande (Arthurian myth): a legendary enchanted forest in Brittany, France. *Forêt de Paimpont* is another name for this forest from Arthurian legend.

Bryn Celli Ddu (site in Wales): also known as the Mound of the Dark Grove, this prehistoric earthen burial chamber or passage tomb is located in Anglesey.

Caduceus: (Greek myth): a staff with one or two serpents used for healing by the god Asclepius. It is also known as the staff of Hermes.

Cairn: Neolithic (Stone Age) monuments used for rituals, social gatherings, and as burial chambers. Many cairns are astrologically aligned for events like solstices and equinoxes.

Camelot: the legendary court of **King Arthur**, linked in legend to Cadbury Camp in Somerset. Camelot was an ideal kingdom where honorable knights gathered around the **Round Table**, a symbol of unity.

Cauldrons: in Celtic mythology, there are many, including the **Undry** (that provides endless nourishment), the **Pair Dadeni** (Cauldron of Rebirth), as well as the Cauldron of **Ceridwen** that offers wisdom and inspiration. (See: **Faery Grail** & **Grail**.)

Celtic Reconstructionism: a mixture of Celtic studies with pre-Christian spiritual practice.

Ceridwen: a Welsh goddess, shapeshifter and wise woman; also the reluctant supernatural mother of the poet, **Taliesin**, who gave him the gift of inspiration.

Cernunnos (pronounced "ker-nun-nous"): the most ancient and perhaps the greatest of Celtic Gods. He is usually depicted with antlers and called the horned one. The Celts believed horns were related to male potency, but the symbolism was misunderstood and demonized by the Christian church. (See: **Gwyn Ap Nudd**.)

Chalice Well: one of Britain's most ancient wells, located in the valley of **Avalon** in Somerset at the base of a sacred hill known as the **Glastonbury Tor**. In folklore, it is said that the well opened in the earth when the **Holy Grail** (the Cup or Chalice used at the Last Supper) was placed there by **Joseph of Arimathea**. It is more likely that it was built by the old **Druids**. The well is said to have magical powers, perhaps even to provide a bridge to the Afterlife.

Coracle (Welsh *cwrwgl*)**:** a small light-weight boat. The vessel is usually made of willow rods and animal hides. (See: **Currach**)

Currach (Irish): a type of river boat or sea vessel.

Cygnus: a northern constellation in the Milky Way; it means "swan" in Latin.

Cymru (Welsh; pronounced "kum-ree"): means "the people" and refers to the Welsh or Old Wales.

Delphi (Greece): in the 8th century BC, the Greeks considered Delphi to be the center of the world. The sanctuary was home to the Oracle of Delphi, who divined the future.

Deva: a nature spirit or spiritual force within nature.

Diana: Roman Goddess of the Hunt, and the mythological secret mother of **Nimue**. (See: **Latona**.)

Dinas Affaraon or Dinas Affaron (Welsh): a place of illusion where the Pheryllt dwell. These magical druids, wizards and healers reside in this city of higher powers. **Ceridwen** visited this place to make her magical wisdom potion, accidentally received by **Taliesin**. It may be **Merlin**'s home.

Dragon: a mythological beast and a symbol of the Goddess; usually linked in mythology with the Grail codes.

Druids: the name is derived from the Celtic words "dru" meaning tree and "wid" meaning to know. Trees have always been respected by the Druids, learned people of the Celts. Some mystics say the druids came from the stars. The Druids were the respected wise men and women who lived amongst the ancient Celts in the landscape of Ireland, Britain and Gaul (now Northern France). It is thought that Druids believed in reincarnation and practiced spiritual rebirth in caves to awaken creative powers. Although accused of human sacrifice (which the warring Celts practiced), it is now widely believed that the Druids were not generally violent, but focused on astrology, poetry, philosophy and spirituality, training up to twenty years. There is currently a strong **Neo-Druid** revival.

Dryads (Greek): nature spirits or nymphs who live in trees but can shape-shift into beautiful young women.

Ephesus: An important city in ancient Greece that is now in modern Turkey. Diana's Temple there was considered one of the seven wonders of the world. It was destroyed by the Goths in 262 AD.

Faerie/Fairy: comes from the French word "faerie." Faeries are generally connected with the elemental forces of nature, and they are considered to have magical powers. Those of the Faerie Faith (the Gaelic term) are described as beautiful and immortal, and sometimes dangerous. In Wales, the Faerie-folk are known as the **Tylwyth Teg.** They are also sometimes referred to as the Fey.

Faery Grail: a pre-Christian vessel or cup guarded by Faerie women who offered hospitality to respectful travelers; a sip from their sacred healing cup was said to unify life and the elements. The ancient Faery Grail appears as the Dagda's Cauldron of Abundance, Ceridwen's Cauldron of Wisdom, King Bran's Cauldron of Rebirth, and the **Pair Dadeni,** amongst others. (See: **Cauldrons** & **Grail.**)

Fey: (See: **Faerie.**)

Foretime: the past; former time.

Gaea (Greek): personification of the Earth; both creator and partner of Uranus.

Galahad: a Grail winner in Arthurian legend. Son of **Lancelot** and Elaine, Galahad was born at Castle Corbenic, home of the Fisher King.

Ganieda (Welsh): in the *Red Book of Hergest*, Ganieda is **Merlin**'s twin sister and possesses the same magical abilities. Ganieda is also known as **Gwenddydd**. In some tales, her true love was the romantic knight **Guiomar**, Lord of Avalon. In *Vita Merlini*, Ganieda is the beautiful and powerful wife of King Rhydderch Hael of Cumbria, and eventually lives with Merlin in the forest and develops prophetic abilities.

Glastonbury: a town in southwestern England recognized as a spiritual center since the megalithic era. A five-thousand-year-old astrological wheel is carved into the landscape. It has long been recognized as the heart chakra of Earth. Legend has it that after the resurrection of Christ, **Joseph of Arimathea** brought the **Holy Grail** with him and shifted the energy of Jerusalem to Glastonbury. Lady Chapel was built in the center of the spiritual vortex. Glastonbury is the **Avalon** of Arthurian legend and the site of the first Christian church in England.

Glastonbury Abbey: a monastery in Glastonbury, Somerset, England, founded in the 7th century. In local folklore, a wattle hut was built on the site by boy Jesus who traveled with his tin trader uncle, **Joseph of Arimathea.** Mystics say the risen Jesus and/or the Magdalene and their daughters returned in the 1st century. Since the 12th century, it has been associated with the legends of **King Arthur.**

Glastonbury Tor: the Celtic name for the Tor is "Ynys Gutrin," which means Isle of Glass. Thousands of years ago, it was an island. Various mystics have used the Tor from 2500 BC and perhaps before. Many still consider it to be their spiritual center. The roofless St. Michael's Tower stands at the top of the hill, and people from all around the world make pilgrimages to the sacred site. The Tor is associated with **Avalon, Annwn** and the myths of **King Arthur**.

Goddess: female Deities that appear in polytheistic religions, including that of the ancient Egyptians, Romans, Greeks and Celts. In some traditions, there is also a monotheistic Great Goddess or Earth Mother. Feminists have turned to the Goddess in an attempt to discover the feminine face of God/Goddess, which is missing in Judeo-Christian theology.

Grail or **Holy Grail:** in Arthurian legend, the Grail is the cup or platter that Jesus used at the Last Supper, or the cup in which the blood of Christ was collected at the crucifixion. After the resurrection, **Joseph of Arimathea** took the cup through France to Britain. Some say the Grail was Mary Magdalene and her daughters.

Guendolonea: Merlin's beautiful Nature Goddess wife.

Guinevere: Old French form of the Welsh name **Gwenhwyfar**. Gwen means "fair or white"; hwyfar means "smooth." In Arthurian legend, she is the beautiful **May Queen** and wife of **King Arthur**. Her dowry was the **Round Table**, the focus of **Camelot**. After the 12th century, she becomes ensnared in a love triangle with **Lancelot**. Guinevere may have been based on historical Eleanor of Aquitaine, the powerful 12th-century Queen of France and then England, who loved Arthurian legends and helped spread their popularity. (See: **Gwenhwyfar**.)

Guiomar or Guigomar: a name that means "horse" in Breton, Guiomar appears in Arthurian legend as a romantic figure. He is linked to Faery women and the Celtic Otherworld, especially Avalon.

Gundestrup Cauldron: a silver religious vessel created about 200 BC and found in a peat bog in Himmerland, Denmark in 1891; it is decorated with mythical symbols including the horned god Cernunnos, the Lord of Animals.

Gwenabwy (Welsh): known as the White Goddess, she is the twin sister of **Gwyn Ap Nudd**, Lord of the Underworld.

Gwenddydd: (See: **Ganieda**.)

Gwenhwyfar: Heroine or goddess in Arthurian legend. (See: **Guinevere**.)

Gwenllian (Welsh): daughter of Llywelyn ap Gruffudd and Eleanor de Montfort. Gwenllian was a baby when her father was killed. She spent her life imprisoned in a convent in England, dying at age fifty-four. A memorial near Sempringham Abbey has been erected in honor of the lost princess of Wales.

Gwyn Ap Nudd (Welsh pronunciation "gwin ap nead"): Son of Nudd, he originally comes from Welsh folklore, where he is known as the king of the **Tylwyth Teg** or Faerie realm and ruler of the Welsh Otherworld, known as **Annwn**. He is often depicted as a warrior with a blackened face and the leader of the Wild Hunt, who rides through the skies on rainy autumn nights. Mystics say he lives in the hollow hill of Glastonbury Tor. His name means white or holy. He is sometimes connected to the more frightening antlered Herne the Hunter. He is also known as **Arawn**, King of the Underworld.

henge: a prehistoric circular earthwork, usually with standing stones.

Hermes (Greek myth): the messenger of the gods who carried a healing staff known as the **Caduceus**. His Roman counterpart is Mercury.

Historia Regum Britanniae (Latin): *History of the Kings of Britain;* this historical collection was written around 1135-1139 AD by Geoffrey of Monmouth. The book chronicles two thousand years of British kings and was acclaimed as a true history until the 16th century, but it is now considered fictitious.

Holy Grail: (See: **Grail.**)

Imworth: during the Middle Ages, there was a manor called Imworth, and in the 6th century, a moat was built around the building. The Saxon manor has been rebuilt many times and is now known as Great Fosters Hotel in Egham, Surrey. Queen Elizabeth I spent time there, and it was used as a hunting lodge by King Henry VIII. It later became an asylum and may have housed King George III during his treatments for insanity.

Isle of Avalon: (See: **Avalon.**)

Joseph of Arimathea: a biblical and Arthurian hero who buried Jesus after the crucifixion on Mount Golgotha, the mountain of the skull. In early Christian lore, it is said that he took the cup or **Holy Grail** that had held the blood of Jesus around the Mediterranean, converting people to Christianity. He eventually settled in **Glastonbury.** When he thrust his staff into the ground on Wearyall Hill, it blossomed into a tree known as the Holy Thorn. A piece of the tree is still growing in the Chalice Well gardens. It was supposedly Joseph who built the first church in England.

Jupiter (Roman): the equivalent of the Greek Zeus, the God of Sky and Thunder, Jupiter is associated with eagles and lightning. (See: **Zeus.**)

Kali Yuga (Hinduism): the era of darkness, which according to Vedic scriptures began at midnight on February 18, 3102 BC (other sources say on February 7, 3104 BC); it is a time when culture degenerates. The end of the Kali Yuga may have been in 2014, others say it will be 2025 AD, or another date in the future.

King Arthur: a historic early Celtic king or warrior named Arthur existed in the 5th to 6th centuries. The tales of King Arthur are largely mythological. The first legend was originally recorded in 6th-century Wales, and the stories were made popular in the 12th century by British writer Geoffrey of Monmouth and the French poet Chretien de Troyes. In short, **Arthur**, son of Uther Pendragon and the deceived Queen Igraine, was snatched away at birth by **Merlin** and raised to be King of **Camelot**. Sir Thomas Malory, Alfred Tennyson, T. H. White and other writers have added to the tales, which continue to inspire writers and spiritual seekers today. It is said that Arthur never died but was taken to **Avalon** where he is becoming the once and future king.

Lady of the Lake or the Ladies of the Lake: an Otherworldly Goddess (or several Goddesses) who sometimes empowers humans so they can work for the greater good. In Arthurian legend, the Lady of the Lake has at least ten names and faces, returning always in new forms. The Lady of the Lake is an eternal Goddess of Sovereignty, whose work is to heal the land. Perhaps when the time is right, she will awaken **Merlin** and usher in a new Renaissance of Light.

Lancelot: a knight in Arthurian legend, lover of Queen **Guinevere** and Elaine, and father of **Galahad**.

Latona or Letona (Roman): mother of **Apollo** and **Diana**. She was Leto in Greek mythology.

Ley Lines: subtle lines of energy that run across Earth, forming a grid or matrix. Ley lines cross in certain areas, creating power spots, and sacred sites, such as the Avebury and **Stonehenge** stone circles, are built on them.

Llywelyn Ap Gruffudd (Wales): Historical Prince of Gwynedd in northern Wales (1223-1282). He tried to drive out the English but was killed on December 11, 1282.

Logres or Lloegr (English/Welsh): Lloegr is the early Welsh name for England. Logres is **King Arthur**'s realm in the matter of Britain; it roughly corresponds to the area now called England. Also, logres refers to a civilized Arthurian template from which Camelot can be rebirthed as a symbol of humanity's goodness.

Mabinogion (Welsh; pronounced "mab-uh-noh-gee-uh-n"): an influential literary collection of prose which gave rise to the stories of **King Arthur** and **Merlin**. In the mid-19th century, Lady Charlotte Guest published eleven medieval folk tales as the *Mabinogion.* This collection arises out of an older tradition of oral story-telling. The character Pryderi links the tales, which are all set in the magical landscape of North Wales. A story of **Taliesin** is included in some collections.

Mage (late Middle English): from the Latin, "Magus." A person who has magical powers; a learned person.

Mag Mell (Irish): Mag Mell means "delightful plain" and is a name for the Celtic Otherworld.

Mandorla: an almond-shaped frame, often found in sacred art around a holy figure, such as Christ.

May Queen: the fertile Maiden of Earth selected to represent the continuation of life. When she is happy, the landscape flourishes. Her holiday is Beltane. **Guinevere** is celebrated as a May Queen.

Merlin or Merlyn and Myrddin: ancient wizard, **Druid** and wise magician featured in Arthurian legend as **King Arthur's** guide and mentor. Some mythologists say Merlin, the Elohim and angels are star beings that co-created the template of **Albion**, the soul of the living Earth. (See: **Myrddin Emrys**.)

Môn or Mona (Wales): now known as **Anglesey,** this island was once the home and international training center of the Druids. (See: **Ynys Môn**.)

Mona (Latin): the Roman name of ancient Anglesey, Island of the Druids. It is located off the northwest coast of Wales. (See **Môn**.)

Morfessa / Mórfís (Irish) the wizard from Fálias; also known as **Mórfís,** he is a druid, seer and poet.

Morfryn/ Madog Morfryn (Welsh): Madog Morfryn was the father of **Myrddin / Merlin**. A sea spirit, Morfryn is linked to the ocean divinity Manannan and the original druids.

Morgan le Fey or Morgena (Arthurian): Sometimes Queen of Avalon in Arthurian tales, she is paradoxically a Priestess, healer and a dark magician in the stories.

Morgen (Welsh and Breton/Arthurian): An Arthurian heroine who has tremendous powers of enchantment. In Breton version, a sea Deity, sometimes thought of as a beautiful but dangerous water spirit.

Morrigan or Morigú (Irish/Arthurian): Irish triple Goddess of War, combining Macha, Badb and Nemain (or Anand). She is mentioned in the *Lebor Gabala Erenn* as one of the Tuatha Dé Danann, daughter of the Creator Goddess Ernmas. She may be linked in Arthurian legend to **Morgen le Fey**, sister of **King Arthur.**

Myrddin Emrys (Welsh; pronounced "Mervin Im-rys"): the Welsh legendary prophet known as **Merlin**. Author Geoffrey of Monmouth transforms him into **King Arthur**'s wizard.

Naradek: an ancient **Lady of the Lake** with Atlantean lineage, one of **Nimue**'s teachers.

Nemeton: a sacred site used for rituals, especially a grove of trees.

Nemetona: an ancient Goddess of the Celts. Nemetona is the guardian of open-air places of worship. Her name means sacred grove.

Neo-Druids: modern **Druids**; specifically the Order of Bards, Ovates & Druids, an earth-based spiritual path free of dogma and focused on being. Some Druids identify as Christian and others as Pagan, some as Christo-Druid, or Zen Druids.

Neopaganism: a movement based on Paganism from many sources, including Celtic, Norse, Slavic, Greek, Roman and Egyptian influences.

Niente (Italian): literally means "nothing." In this book, the term refers to sinister and dark entities out to destroy the spiritual beings and feminine consciousness.

Nimue or Nymue (Cornish pronunciation "nim-we"): one of the nine **Ladies of the Lake.** The lover, student and sometimes nemesis of **Merlin.**

Nymph (Greek): a nature spirit or supernatural being associated with the elements.

Olympus (Greco-Roman): the home of twelve deities of the Greek pantheon; the Roman pantheon was on Mount Olympus.

Ophiuchus: the constellation, also known as the "Serpent Bearer," is located between Scorpio and Sagittarius. It is depicted as an old man holding a snake and is associated with **Asclepius.** It is potentially the 13th astrological sign.

Oracle (Greek): a priestess through whom a god or deity speaks; one who offers divine messages and prophecy.

Otherworld (Celtic): Celtic Deities and **Faeries** live in an Otherworld, a domain generally hidden from mortals; in Welsh myth, it is often called **Annwn.**

Ovate (Druidic): one who practices herbalism, healing and divination; an interpreter of nature. Like Oracles, Ovates have a strong connection with the Otherworld.

Pagan: is derived from the Latin word *Paganus*, which means "country-dweller"; the term was originally meant to be an insult, rather like "hick" or "hillbilly." Some Neo-pagans say Paganism is a way of dwelling with the elements, a way of worshipping amongst the living landscape. (See: **Pantheism**, **Panentheism**, **Neopaganism** & **Celtic Reconstructionism**.)

Pair Dadeni (Welsh; pronounced "pear da-denny"): from the second branch of the *Mabinogi*, the Pair Dadeni is a magical Cauldron of Rebirth. One sip is said to bring a person back from the dead. (See: **Grail** & **Undry**.)

Pan (Greek): a god of the wild who oversaw shepherds and hunters, Pan could also arouse panic. He loved to play panpipes and chase nymphs. Pan is generally depicted with a beard and has horns on his head. His upper body is that of a man, and his lower body is that of a goat. In Greek, Pan means "all." He was portrayed as the goat-fish of Capricorn in ancient astrology.

Panentheism (Greek/German): a universal spirit permeates everything. The German philosopher, Krause, coined the term Panentheism to reconcile pantheism and theism. It arises out of a Greek expression, "all is in God."

Pantheism (doctrine): Pantheists believe that God is in everything; Nature is conscious; Divinity is not separate from the natural world. Goethe, Einstein and Carl Jung were pantheists.

Pelleas or Sir Pelleas (Arthurian): one of **King Arthur**'s Knights of the **Round Table**; he falls in love and marries **Nimue.** His story first appears in the Post-Vulgate Cycle and is then reworked in Thomas Malory's *Le Morte d'Arthur.*

Percival, Parsifal or Parzifal (Arthurian): Percival is a Grail Champion in Arthurian legend, and brother of Dindraine.

Pythia (Greek): the high priestess of the Oracle of Delphi would enter a trance and channel prophecies from Apollo, often in the form of riddles. The Pythia was consulted by rulers and other individuals before making important life decisions. With the emergence of Christianity, the Oracle of Delphi declined.

Python (Greek): considered a child of Gaea, Python originally guarded the oracle of Delphi. He was slain by Apollo. The **Oracle** of Delphi became known as the **Pythia.** Python is often portrayed as a large serpent or dragon.

Round Table: a table built in the Otherworld, which symbolized unity and spiritual brotherhood.

Scrying stone (magic): usually a black stone that can be used for scrying, a method utilized by mystics to peer between worlds. Scrying is usually practiced with a reflective surface, such as a dark polished stone or a dark bowl of water.

Sidhe (Irish pronunciation "Shee"): the tall, beautiful people of myth and legend.

Siocháin (pronounced "shee-akh-awn"): an Irish Gaelic word for peace. *Si* means peace and *chain* means gentle or fair.

Stargate: a portal or wormhole that allows travel between dimensions.

Stonehenge: a henge built 5,000 years ago; prehistoric stone circle monument located on the Salisbury Plain in Wiltshire, England.

Suetonius / Gaius Suetonius Paulinus: Roman general who subdued Mona (60 or 61 AD) and defeated the rebellion of Boudicca.

His fate is unknown. Agricola finished the destruction of Mona in 78 AD.

Sunwise (Druid): A reference to moving in the direction of the sun, or clockwise. It was also called *deiseal* (pronounced jay-shall). Druids and early Christians of ancient Ireland believed that walking sunwise invited the luck and good fortune of the sun.

Sylph (Latin)**: an** elemental being connected with air, often called a **Faerie.** The term Sylph was created by Paracelsus in the 16th century in reference to air spirits.

Taliesin: Celtic bard, poet and historian. Child of **Ceridwen**, a Welsh goddess and reluctant supernatural mother.

Tarbh: the hide of a bull that mystics slept in for prophecy.

Theodosius I / Flavius Theodosius I: a Roman Emperor (347-395 AD) who enforced orthodox Christianity on the people. In 391, he closed the Pagan temples and worship of the Goddess was forbidden.

Tír na nÓg (Irish): a realm of the Otherworld, just outside the dimension of humankind, where there is only happiness and beauty; a land of eternal youth.

Tuatha Dé Danann or simply Tuatha Dé or the Dananns (Irish pronunciation "Too-a-ha-dae Donnan"): Tribe of the Goddess Danu or Anu, a supernatural race in Irish mythology.

Tylwyth Teg: in Welsh lore, they are small child-like beings or Faerie-folk who live in lakes or underground. Their king was known as **Gwyn Ap Nudd.** Also known as the fair-folk, they generally wore homespun, blue clothes. They are attracted to toadstools and have a mixed reputation.

Una (British): Queen of the **Sidhe**, also known as the Queen of Elphame or "Elf-hame" (or Elf-Home).

Undines (Latin): elemental beings associated with water. The term Undine was created by Paracelsus in the 16th century in reference to water spirits. There are tales of beautiful water nymphs, merrows or mermaids falling in love with mortal men and becoming human.

Undry (Irish): the Dagda's cauldron that never ran dry. (See: **Cauldrons** & **Pair Dadeni**.)

Uranus (Greek): primordial god of the sky. His consort, **Gaea**, was the Earth.

Vesica Piscis (Latin; means "bladder of a fish"): a symbol showing two merging circles that form an almond shape in the center. There are many descriptions of Vesica Piscis. In Christianity, it is the symbol of Jesus. In Tantric circles, the almond between the circles represents the Yoni. A more modern perspective is that it is symbolic of the dance between the masculine and feminine, creating balanced consciousness.

Ynys Môn (Welsh) or Mona (Latin): is now called **Anglesey**, an island off the west coast of Wales. (See **Môn.**)

Zeus (Greek): the god of sky and thunder is King of the Olympian gods. His primary symbols are the thunderbolt and eagle. He is known as the upholder of world justice. The Roman equivalent of Zeus is Jupiter. (See: **Jupiter.**)

Zodiac (Greek): The 2nd-century Greek astronomer Ptolemy described a celestial belt that followed the path of the Sun, a concept he obtained from Babylonian texts. The zodiac is composed of twelve (or thirteen including **Ophiuchus**, the Serpent Bearer) constellations that are linked to the way the Earth moves through the sky. (See: **Astrology.**)